HAWK'S VALLEY

a good place to die

MINNESOTA RIVER VALLEY
AT FORT RIDGELY

HAWK'S VALLEY

a good place to die

ARVID LLOYD WILLIAMS

EVERGREEN PUBLISHING
MINNEAPOLIS

HAWK'S VALLEY

a good place to die

First in a Series

Evergreen Publishing
15539 Shadow Creek Road
Minneapolis, MN 55311
www.evergreenpublish.com

ISBN 0-9633480-7-8

Printed in the United States of America.

COVER: REDWOOD FERRY CROSSING
ON THE MINNESOTA RIVER

DEDICATION

TO MY KIDS AND GRANDKIDS

Thank you to...

*My daughter Sue and her husband Chris,
whose experience in publishing and design
helped make this project a reality for me.*

*And a special thank you to
my dear friend and writing partner,
Bonnie Shallbetter
for her help and support in the production of this book.*

*Thank you to my hunting partner
Jim (Sunkist) Whistler
for lending his name to the story.*

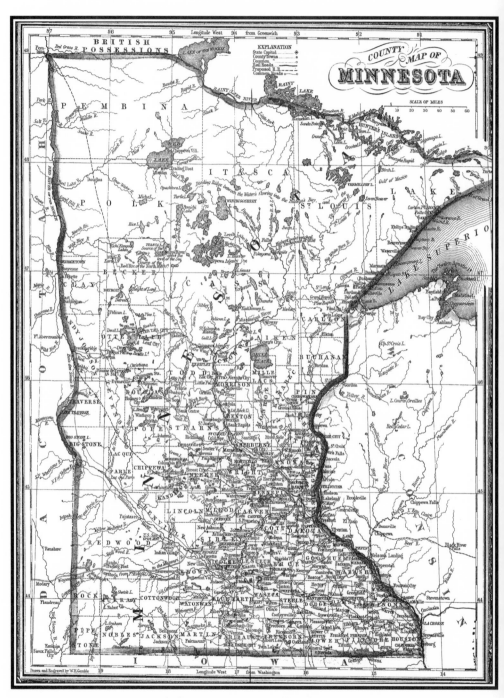

MINNESOTA IN 1862 *(Minnesota Historical Society)*

TABLE OF CONTENTS

SEVENTY THOUSAND YEARS AGO snow was falling in the north-
ern parts of Canada. The snow accumulated over time until its weight turned the
lower layers to ice and squeezed them out and away from the center. As the ice
was pushed along it picked up earth, rocks, and boulders and carried them along
within its mass. The front edge of the glacier worked like a huge bulldozer pushing piles of earth before it forming moraines to its front and along the sides. The
ice, as much as a mile deep, moved slowly southward until it reached warmer air
in the lower latitudes where the forward movement equaled the rate of melting.
The ice dropped its load off its front, much like a conveyor belt, and formed the
lines of tall, rugged rock-filled moraines found throughout Minnesota.

When the earth's climate began to warm, the ice stopped its forward movement and began to melt. The slow melt caused the front of the glaciers to retreat
northward. The water running along the front of the ice flowed into a channel
that ran southward and carved out the shallow beginnings of the Minnesota Valley.

Blocks of ice were buried beneath overlying layers of earth carried in the
body of the glacier. When these buried blocks of ice melted, the earth that covered them settled into the voids and depressions were left in the surface. These
depressions filled with water and formed some of Minnesota's lakes.

Today, in east Ottertail County, the landscape displays sparsely vegetated
flat sand plains left by water running from the glaciers. A few miles west, the
rugged, heavily forested hills are the remains of a stagnant glacier as it melted
and dropped its load where it stood. As the ice continued to melt, rivers of water
flowed from the forward edge of the glacier and ponded behind the moraines.
With the hills of glacial drift to its front and the ice blocking the drainage to the
north, the water had nowhere to go. It formed what was once the great glacial
Lake Agassiz, larger than the combined area of all of the Great Lakes. The flat

plains in northwestern Minnesota and northeastern North Dakota are the dry floor of Lake Agassiz.

As the water rose it finally found a low place near what is now Brown's Valley and started to trickle over the ridge. It probably started with a small trickle that could have been stopped by your finger, but there was no finger there to stop it and it trickled through the opening washing dirt and sand away until the break became bigger. The water ran faster, washing more sand and now gravel away with ever-increasing force. Eventually, the water became so forceful that it completely washed the earth dam away at that point. A torrent of water rushed southeast through the channel that was made during the melt, carrying everything in its path along with it. The water scoured the channel with a volume and force unimaginable today. It carved a ditch from Brown's Valley to the Mississippi. The gorge it cut is one to four miles wide and as deep as two hundred-fifty feet. The water rushed so swiftly that the valley was cut in nearly a straight line the length of its two hundred-mile course. Nothing could change its course until it reached the place where Mankato now stands. The water then flowed northeast to what is now Fort Snelling where it joins the Mississippi to flow to the Gulf of Mexico. The waters ran for twenty-seven hundred years before the drainage was opened to the north to Hudson Bay.

Today small rivers and springs from above and beneath the layers of glacial deposits feed the small wandering stream at the bottom of the gorge called the Minnesota River. The stream is all that remains of the once great River Warren. Streams with names like Lac qui Parle, Chippewa, Pomme de Terre, Redwood River, Cottonwood River, Birch Coulee Creek, and Hawk Creek supply water to maintain the river as it is today.

*If not for the beautiful countryside the trip would
have been a long one, but I like seeing the hills
and wondering how they got that way...*

CHAPTER ONE

A HALF-DAY'S RIDE UPSTREAM from the Minnesota River on Hawk Creek stands a well-built log cabin surrounded by the beautifully colored autumn forest. The back of the cabin overlooks the shallow valley of the creek. At the bottom of the valley is a stream twenty yards wide that flows quietly past the cabin. The bottom is covered with stones and gravel carried by the glaciers from some unknown place in Canada.

An old man sits on a rocking chair staring at a jar of blue glass marbles. His hair is white and his beard is whiter, his mind is not as quick and his body not as strong. But his eyes still have the sparkle they had many years ago. A young couple walks up to the front door and knocks. A middle-aged woman opens it and asks them in.

"Hello. I'm Lorraine—Mister Owen's daughter," the woman said softly, extending her hand.

The man in the gray wool suit replied, "I'm Mister Holcombe from the *Saint Paul Press*," shaking her hand. "We'll be interviewing Mister Owen."

"Yes, come in. He's been expecting you. He's on the porch in back. I'll tell him you're here." Lorraine walked to the back of the cabin and said, "Dad, the reporters are here."

"Bring them out here. I don't want to be inside today."

Lorraine showed them chairs on the porch and they sat down. "Mister Owen, I'm..."

"No need to introduce yourselves, I know who you are. It's about time you got to me. I get damn tired of these storytellers who don't want to tell it like it was."

"Mister Owen, we would like to hear your story as you remember it."

"That's the only way I can tell it."

"May we begin?"

He turned to his secretary and said, "Put this down exactly as he says it—no grammar corrections this time."

She shot him an angry look.

He turned back to the old man and said, "Please tell us your story, Mister Owen."

"Yes. Well, I suppose I should start from the first day I was on my own..."

. . .

My brother Jake and I were helping Pa bring in firewood for the winter. I was walking next to the wagon trying to get the mules to pull harder. Pa was yelling at me to whip them and get them moving, but I didn't like whipping the mules. Pa had been to the tavern the night before and was kind of sick. He had a mean streak in him a mile wide when he was sick from drinking. As it turned out, that was a short workday for me. The last thing I remember of that day was turning around and seeing Pa standing behind me with a broken axe handle over his right shoulder and a crazy look in his eye. I tried to duck his swing but I was just a bit slow and it caved in the side of my head like an egg, as Ma put it.

The sunlight coming through the window set my head on fire and made my eyes feel like they'd pop right out of my head.

"How ye feelin', son?"

I opened my eyes and saw Ma looking into them like she was trying to see something that wasn't there. Her hair was wet with perspiration and what wasn't tied in a bun behind her head was hanging in strings on either side of her face. I tried to keep my eyes open and talk to her but it was too painful to let the light in. Through the haze of delirium I could feel Ma putting cool cloths on my forehead and trying to get me to wake up and talk to her but I couldn't seem to raise the strength. My mind was total confusion and so many thoughts were going on in my head that I couldn't pick out a particular one to focus on.

Out of my right eye I could see Pa sitting at the rough board table pushing food in his mouth and swallowing it unchewed. I could see the wickedness in his eyes and his lack of concern for what was happening around him. I felt a deep hatred for this man—he seemed to have a need to dominate and control everyone around him. Ma was his housekeeper, and my brother Jake and I were his farm hands. His part was to sit back and make sure we all did as we were told.

After having Jake, Ma couldn't have anymore kids. Pa said it was just because she didn't want anymore kids in the house, but I know it was because he treated her so bad when she was making Jake that he'd hurt her woman parts on the inside. She just couldn't make anymore babies.

Ma put cool packs on my head until I started to wake up and was able to see her and talk to her. "How do you feel, son?"

"I hurt." I tried to turn my head to look at her but it hurt too much.

"You just lay still for a while. I'll get you some water." My throat was parched, but I didn't know it until Ma mentioned water. She brought the water in a tin cup and said, "Just a sip at a time, Hawk, or it'll make you sick."

"Ma, why did Pa have to hit me?"

"I don't know why. He just said you were too slow with your work, and you know how he needs to have things done on time."

"Ma, you can only work them ole mules just so fast."

"Yes, I know that Hawk, but yer Pa ain't got no patience."

"S'pose I better git up and get back to that woodpile."

"Wood's all cut and split. Your brother Jake took care of it while you were out."

"He got it all done?"

"You've been out for three days, Hawk."

My name is Harlan, but Pa started calling me Hawk when I was just a kid. He used to say, "You ain't no good fer nothin' but huntin' and flyin' around the county goin' nowhere, just like a good-fer-nothin' hawk." I wasn't good at farm work, and no one in the county had a job for a kid who can't read or write, so I took up what I do best—my old hunting rifle my Uncle Robert gave me before he died. I'd head for the woods around the county every chance I got, hunting squirrels or birds or anything else I could find, and brought home most of the vittles. Pa got after me more than once for bringing home such small game that it took ten of them to feed the family. But I figured that if I shot a deer or a boar most of it would go to waste before it got ate. There was just the four of us— Ma, Pa, Jake, and me, and there's a lot of meat on a deer. Ma knew how to dry the meat and smoke it so it would keep, but she needed salt to do that and salt was hard to come by out in the middle of nowhere like we were. Besides, she had plenty of other work to do. It was fine with everyone else to eat rabbit, partridge, and turkey during the summer months. Shooting a big animal like a deer is no fun anyway—it's more fun to try to hit a squirrel at fifty yards with my forty-five caliber Tennessee rifle. Sometimes a hog would get loose and turn wild, and then it was fair game for anyone who saw it. Ma would smoke the hams and boil the rest and put it up in jars. It made good meat. In the winter I could bring home deer and elk because we could keep it froze in the woodshed so it wouldn't spoil.

I slept through the night and woke up feeling better, but my head was still pounding with each heartbeat. Ma had put a cloth around my head to keep the split scalp from festering and sewed the split with hair from a mule's tail. She put a plaster of mustard over it to help it heal faster, then gave me some tea she'd made from boiling willow bark to ease the pain.

"Hawk, git otta that bed. We got work needs doin'."

I looked over at Pa sitting at the table as usual, yelling out orders to the rest of the family with that high-pitched voice he had. I slipped my feet over the side of the bed and stood up, but my legs wouldn't hold me. I dropped back to sit on the bed.

"Come on, boy, you ain't hurt that bad. Git up and git goin'."

"I'll be there, Pa—just give me a minute."

Ma gave me a big pitcher of water and said, "Drink as much as you can, it'll help you get your strength back."

"Well hurry up, we got work to do!" Pa yelled. I stood up again and this time I stayed up. I walked to the table and sat down to a bowl of cooked rolled oats and cream Ma had set out for me. It was cold but I ate it anyway.

It was early in the morning and the sun was shining over the trees, lighting the barn through the open doors. It looked like it was going to be another one of those hot August afternoons that makes working so unpleasant. Jake was in the barn harnessing the mules. Pa was getting the wagon loaded with axes, chains, and saws to make another trip to the woods for firewood. The morning was still cool with a few white clouds drifting across the deep blue Minnesota sky. The mules plodded along at their usual slow pace, ignoring the heeyas Pa was making at them. Those mules would only work as hard as they wanted and nothing we could do would speed them up. Finally, we got to the woods where Pa had seen some dying poplars and oaks he thought would be good for the winter fire. Me and Jake ran the two-man saw, dropping the trees while Pa cut the limbs off with his double-bit axe. The mules dragged the logs to the wagon and with Jake on one end and me on the other, we'd toss them up onto the wagon, then go for the next one. After half a dozen drags the mules knew what to do and did it without anyone leading them. By the end of the day we had a pile of logs in the yard

HAWK'S VALLEY

that would keep us busy for a week sawing and splitting stove wood. Jake and I took turns sawing and splitting wood and stacking it in the barn while Pa sat and complained about how slow we worked.

My head was still pounding and each swing of the axe made it hurt worse. My disposition got worse right along with it. It was my turn with the saw so I took the bucksaw and started to cut the logs off into stove lengths. I'd made only a few cuts when suddenly the saw caught in the log, pushed the sawhorse over, and broke the blade. Pa jumped up and came running over to me screaming, "Dammit Hawk! What da hell's wrong wit chew? That makes three blades you broke now yer brother here ain't broke one yet! What da hell I'm gonna do wit chew boy?"

Jake and I had been working hard since we were old enough to hold an axe. Jake was seventeen and about five feet-seven inches tall and weighed two hundred pounds. I was eighteen and just under six feet tall and weighed two hundred-twenty pounds. Pa was smaller than either of us and should have taken that into consideration before he came at me again with that axe handle. Instead of trying to duck his swing I charged at him, wrapped my arms around his belly, and threw him to the ground. With one knee on each side of his chest I took the axe handle out of his hand and was ready to give him a taste of what he seemed to like giving me and Jake. But Jake stopped me.

"Don't Hawk, yer mad and ye might kill 'im," he said in a soft voice.

"So what?" I shouted. "He don't care if he kills one of us."

"Think of Ma, Hawk. What's she gonna do if she don't have him?"

"She's got us, Jake, and she's better off with this old bastard out of her life."

"Don't kill 'im, Hawk."

I threw the stick off to the side and turned loose of the old man's throat. I waved my work-hardened fist in front of his face and said, "If you ever touch me or Jake or Ma again I'll kill you deadr'n hell."

"Yer a worthless saddle tramp, Hawk. I'll see you leave this farm and don't you never come back!"

I looked at him for a few seconds and then at Jake. "You comin' with me?"

"Naw, Hawk. Think I'll stay with Ma. She'll be needin' me. Pa won't be no trouble from now on."

I went in the cabin and started pulling some of my things together that I'd need to get me to wherever I ended up. There were things I'd heard of west of Minnesota Territory that I wanted to see and there would never be a better time to go than that minute. Pa sat at the table in the middle of the room and watched me put my winter coat, hunting bag, rifle, shot, and powder in a pair of sacks. He came at me when I reached for the second can of rifle powder.

"You got enough of my stuff. You leave that here."

"Pa, this is my powder. I got it from Mister Belleair for some deer hides. Git out of my way." I pushed him aside and continued to pack.

"Jist take it then, and git," he grumbled. I could see in his face that, though he was angry, he was having trouble about my leaving but he was too blamed stubborn to ask me to stay. And it was just as hard for me to leave, but I couldn't change my mind now or I never would be out from under his thumb.

"Where'll ye go, Hawk?"

"Don't know for sure, Ma. Guess I'll head on down to Saint Paul and west from there. Hear there's lots of country to see out there."

"You ain't takin' no mule with you!"

"Pa, I don't want none of yer broken-down mules," I snapped at him. "You beat the good out of them just like you do everything you touch. Them mules wouldn't make it fifty miles anyway."

"Jist pack yer stuff and git, Hawk."

I walked over to Ma and said to her, "Don't worry about me, Ma. I'll be just fine. There's freighters goin' up the rivers and I hear they're lookin' for men. I'll git on one of them and make my way."

"Be careful, Hawk, and come back when you can." Ma knew I had to go.

"I will Ma," I said and picked up my packs.

"Hawk?"

"Yeah Ma?"

"Take yer Grandma's Bible with you."

"Ma, you know I can't read. What good would it be to me?"

"Just take it, Hawk, please?" I took the Bible and pushed it down into my pack, gave Ma a hug, kissed a tear from her cheek and walked out the door. I passed Jake in the yard and stopped to say goodbye.

"Don't s'pose it would do any good to ask you to change yer mind, huh Hawk?"

"Jake, if I stay now Pa will own me just like he owns those two broken-down mules and that dry-rotted wagon—no, I gotta go."

On the ground in the dirt I saw that busted axe handle Pa seemed to like so much. I picked it up and shoved it down into my pack next to Grandma's Bible. Jake and I shook hands and hugged. I started down the road and didn't look back.

It was getting toward evening by now and I had no idea which way I should go. I knew south was the direction to go—but how far? On the prairie where I stood, the southern horizon was a line of hills that I knew from my wanderings led to more hills and heavy forest. East of there was a break in the hills where the river flowed. Someone had built a wooden bridge over the river, so that's the way I went.

It was dark when I reached the bridge and I crawled under it, rolled out my blanket and laid down for the night. During the night I could see lightning flashing in the west and hear thunder rolling across the prairie. I was glad to be under the bridge where the rain wouldn't get to me, but the bridge served as a poor roof. I woke up shivering under a wet blanket. I thought of building a fire but I had neglected to bring in wood and everything outside the bridge shelter was wet. I had learned something already. I've spent nights shivering before so this was not a new thing for me. I rolled over and dropped off to sleep. My body heat warmed the wetness next to my skin and as long as I laid still I would stay warm enough to make it through the night. I decided to myself, *the first chance I get I'm going to have to get me more blankets or some elk robes to sleep under.*

Morning came all too soon and I woke up wet and cold. The weather was cool and the sky was covered with gray clouds that promised more rain—and rain it did—a light drizzle that lasted all morning. On the bank of the river a foot below the sod, I saw a patch of black dirt about a foot thick and three feet wide. The bank was about twenty feet above the river. My curious nature taking over, I crawled out from under the bridge and made my way to the patch of black. A flow of dark wash streamed from the patch down a few feet toward the river. I found an arrowhead, but it was different than the ones we'd found in the field when we were plowing or tilling. I picked it up and examined it. It was like new, sharp and perfectly shaped for killing. I found several more and put them in my pack for safekeeping. I told myself, *you can't be saving everything you find Hawk, or you'll need a wagon to haul it in.* So I contented myself with about a dozen of them. As I climbed up the bank my foot slipped on a shiny, slippery stone. I dug it out of the mud and I had in my hand a perfectly shaped, very sharp stone axe head about six inches long, three wide, and a full inch thick, made from a hard, yellow-ish stone. I stuffed it in my pack.

I started back up the bank and had just gotten to the top when I heard sounds coming from the road. I slipped into some bushes thinking it might be Pa coming to look for me but it was just a farmer driving his team down the road with a load of feed sacks covered with a canvas tarp. He rumbled across the bridge without seeing me and went on his way. It wasn't until he was gone that I thought of asking for a ride. But then, I wanted to stay away from people all together until I got to new country, so it was all right.

I followed the road through the day staying to the brush when I could. It was plain to me that these shoes Ma had made for me weren't going to last long and I would be making myself some moccasins as soon as I could get the skins to do it. Ma had made them by sewing the neck hide from an elk to soles made of buffalo neck hide. They were fine for the work we did around the farm but this all-day walking was tearing them up fast—being wet wasn't helping any either. The deer sinew Ma used for stitching was wet and had gotten too soft to hold things together. We'd spent most of the time on the farm barefoot so I took off the shoes and put them in my sidepack. Shoes get wet and fall apart. Feet get wet, but they stay together. I walked all that day and into the next week, crossing several streams and some open country, feeding myself on squirrels, rabbits, an occasional partridge, and sometimes fish. I slept under fallen trees or in a hollow I'd find next to a river. Sometimes I just had to curl up under a tree for the night 'cause there just was no shelter to be found.

I found some settlements on the way but skirted around them so's not to be seen by anyone who might report seeing me to Pa. Though, I was far enough from the farm that no one would know me if they saw me. I was leaning over a stream trying to catch a fish for my supper when I saw an unfamiliar sight. The reflection in the water didn't show that boy who walked away from his home a month ago. I saw a brown-faced man with a growth of dark red beard starting to cover my face and a head of red hair that reached nearly to my shoulders. *Ain't no worry about anyone recognizing me now*, I thought to myself and chuckled. I walked through the towns and settlements from then on.

A cloud of dust rose in the west. *What in the world can this be?* I wondered. I settled into a thicket and waited to see what it was. It moved slowly and got closer until I could hear a strange sound coming from the cloud. It was a kind of squealing, moaning sound that cut across the hills and up the valley where the road went. I could see carts pulled by oxen with strange-looking men driving them. There were people walking alongside and some riding on top of the carts, a quarter-mile of two-wheeled carts loaded to heaping and covered with canvas tarps. The noise got louder as they came closer. Thinking that these people were no threat, I stepped out of the brush and stood in the open as they passed. One of the men raised his staff and waved at me and then went back to his ox. They were dressed in the strangest clothes I had ever seen. Bright reds and yellows, belts of woven wool tied fancy-like around their waists. Caps of knit wool on their heads, mostly the same color as their belts with the point flopped to one side and a tassel waving with the breeze. Some wore brimmed hats and some had bandannas tied around their heads. Some wore pants that came to their knees with colored stockings over their lower legs and some had bare legs with plain moccasins on their feet. Many were barefoot like I was. Some had leather pants with fringing on the sides. All wore shirts of bright colors and kerchiefs around their necks. Their skin was brown like the Indians that would come around the farm begging, but they didn't look like Indians. They were bigger and more solidly built, although few were taller than about five-foot-five. Some of them made me uneasy when they looked at me and laughed, but I figured they thought I was dressed as funny as I thought they were. My clothes were down to rags by this time and I must have been a curious sight to behold. I wanted a pair of those leather pants some of them wore. My corduroy pants were becoming more like rags everyday.

I stepped out and walked up to a fellow who was driving a yoke and motioned that I'd walk along if it was all right with him. He smiled and waved his staff as a gesture for me to "come on along." No one talked. The only sound was the dreadful noise coming from the wheels of the carts. The road was no more than two ruts worn into the sod by the cart wheels. My bare feet were getting cut up from the broken stones so I sat down and pulled my shoes out of my sidepack and put them on. They were almost too stiff to put on from drying in a crumpled position. One of the drivers who walked by looked at me and laughed and said something I didn't understand. He spoke in a language that I had never heard before so I gestured that I didn't understand. He pointed at my ragged shoes and smiled in a friendly way, then motioned for me to take them off and throw them away. No, I couldn't do that—my feet were in too bad of shape. He walked to his cart and pulled out a pair of new moccasins and handed them to me.

"I got no money to pay for these." He must have understood 'cause he put up one hand to indicate he wanted no money.

"Don't you speak English?" I asked.

"Ah, d'Anglase, oui," and pointed to a tall man in a heavy blue coat with large, bright, polished brass buttons and said, *"La, sa parle D'Anglase."*

"Thank you for the moccasins."

He held out a hand, palm forward, and said, *"Sen fay rien."* I had no idea what those words meant but I figured he meant "You're welcome."

I let the train pass until the man he pointed to came near and said, "Howdy."

"You English?"

"No, I am *not* English," he said with a distinct growl to his voice like I'd said something wrong. "We are Métis."

"Where are you going with all these carts?"

"Trade station at Saint Paul."

"My name is Hawk," I said and stuck out my hand.

He said nothing and ignored my hand, but kept walking alongside his ox. We didn't say anything more for the rest of the day and I started to wonder if it was a mistake taking up with this train. But when the day was over and they found a campsite that they must have used before, things changed. They circled their carts and put the backs to the inside of the circle with the tongues pointing to the outside. They brought out canvas tents and set them up inside the circle and built a fire in the middle of that. The cattle were put out to a grassy field and men were stationed around them to keep them from wandering off.

The community got lively then. Everyone was talking at the same time but I couldn't understand any of it. They were all talking in different languages. It seemed like each man had his own way of talking but they all seemed to be able to communicate with each other. Some sat in small groups singing songs in their own language. The man who spoke English came over and sat down on the ground next to me.

"Where you going, boy?"

"Don't know for sure, down to Saint Paul and then from there I mean to go west, maybe to the mountains."

"Ever been to the Rockies, lad?"

"No, but I've heard they're the biggest mountains in the world and I want to see them."

"I been there," he said quietly, looking at the western horizon. "Spent ten year trappin' fer the big fur traders. It's a big country lad—and dangerous. Injuns, griz, cold, heat, everything you can think of that'll kill a man is out there, and they's all at work to do their job day and night. You sleep, they don't."

I saw someone in wool pants and a blanket capote coming toward us carrying two bowls. I nearly fell over when the person got close. It was a girl—the most beautiful girl I had ever seen. Her face was dark brown and her eyes were almost black with black lashes and eyebrows shaped like crows wings. Her skin looked like the softest fawn skin I'd ever felt—smooth and flawless. Her lips were full and deep red and her hair was dark brown and came to her shoulders. My heart stopped for a second when she looked at me, smiled, and said, "*Monzhay*".

HAWK'S VALLEY

My God, no woman that beautiful had ever smiled at me before, much less spoke to me. She turned her body to walk away but her eyes held mine for a bit before she looked away and left.

"Wha'd she say?"

"She said 'eat'." His black eyes burned into mine and he said, "Forget her."

"I'll tell ye something, son. The most dangerous critter out there ain't the griz, nor the Injun, or the cold. It's the fella just like you what goes out there not knowin' nothin' and ending up having to kill and steal from other men to live. There ain't no law out there to hide behind when you get in trouble, and ye cain't go runnin' to yer ma's apron when things get tough. Ye gotta know how to take care of yer self 'cause ain't no one gonna do it for ye."

"You make it sound like you don't think I should go out there—like it's a bad place to be."

"It was a good place to be back in the trappin' days but the trappin's all done now. No one wants the furs even if you can find 'em. Men used to work together and help each other in times of need, but not no more. Yer more likely to git yer friend's knife in your back than a stranger's."

"Maybe I should think again about where to go."

"Yer a farmer, ain't cha, boy?" he said, more telling me than asking.

"Yeah, growed up on my pa's farm up in Otter Tail County."

"Y'ain't growed up yet, son, not till ye go where yer headed and git back to yer pa's farm. You have a lot of things to learn before you can be growed up. Want some advice?"

"Always willing to listen to someone knows more than me."

"Now that shows smarts, son. You'll do fine with a mind like that."

"Your advice, Mr....ummmmm?"

"Charbonneau. Name's Charbonneau."

"You ain't the one..."

"No, I ain't that one," he said with a clear loathing in his voice. "He warn't no relation to me. He was a squaw-man and lazy as they git. There's more Charbonneaus out here than leaves on the trees. Most of 'em ain't really Charbonneaus. They take the name 'cause it's the one they hear the most and they don't want people knowin' their real name for one reason or the other— which is their own business, by the way," he said, focusing directly on my eyes, "not no one else's."

"What do you advise for me, Mister Charbonneau?"

"First off, call me Jean."

"Okay, John…"

"Not John, dammit. Zhawn!"

"Sorry…Zhaaaaawn," I said sarcastically.

"So you want to be a farmer, right?"

"No, I don't want to be a farmer. I was one and didn't like it. I'm not sure what I want—I just know I don't want to farm no more."

"My advice to you is to go back home."

"Can't do that."

"Got trouble back there?"

"Not that, it's just I can't work that worthless farm no more. Nothin' but rocks and sand."

"Then go to the valley of Saint Peter. They're callin' it the Minnesota River Valley now. It's all new country and people are moving in and settling on farms and setting up trades. The riverboats need men to work for them. They might need hunters too—that's what you want, right?"

"Right."

"Everyone wants to be a hunter. You can find work there, son—all you need. Small problem with the Sioux, but they ain't nothin' to worry about. Jist a lot of beggars botherin' folks."

"Why ain't you there then, Zhaaawn?"

"Me? Hell, I cain't work for those stuffy businessmen. They work you like a mule and don't want to pay you for it."

"Then why do you say I should go out there?"

"To git you some learnin', son. Ain't no better teacher than making mistakes and having people steppin' on yer toes."

"Sounds like good advice, Mister Charbonneau."

"Jean."

"Right. Zha-a-a-awn."

He looked at me from the corner of his eye and shook his head.

"If yer looking to go south yer welcome to tag along with us—we can use an extra hand. You can work, cain't ye?"

"Strong as one of those oxen," I said.

"You'll get yer chance to prove that. Better git out yer robes and git comfortable—gonna git cold tonight."

"Ain't got no robes—just a blanket and my winter coat. I'll be fine."

"Here, roll up in this." He threw me a heavy buffalo robe that nearly knocked me over. It must have weighed eighty pounds but it turned out to be the warmest night I'd spent in a month.

The sounds of people moving around woke me just as the sky was beginning to get light in the east. The cook had a fire going and a big cookpot boiling over it. The tents were being taken down and loaded onto the carts. I felt like I was more in the way than any help so I just sat back and watched the activity. When the carts were loaded and the oxen hitched up the people gathered around the pot, dipped their cups and bowls in, and started to eat.

"Hawk, git over here and eat. We got a long way to go today," Jean said to me.

Breakfast was pea soup with bits of meat mixed in. The meat tasted like it had spoiled, but everyone ate it and went back for more until it was gone. The cook wiped out the pot and tied it to the back of one of the carts. The men took their places next to their oxen and we were off. Each man had four carts with one ox pulling each.

I didn't get to see that girl again and wondered where she might be. All day we walked. We stopped once for a rest for the animals but soon got up and walked some more. I ran to the brush to do some necessary chores and coming out I hooked my corduroys on a stick, ripping the leg almost off. I sat down and pulled a strip of cloth out of my sack, wrapped it around the tear, and got back to the train.

If not for the beautiful countryside the trip would have been a long one, but I like seeing the hills and wondering how they got that way. We passed some small ponds by the road that reflected the trees around them. I wished that I could paint pictures like some folks can—I would paint pictures of those ponds. We climbed tall hills from where we could see forever, and we went through valleys where we could see only the trees next to the road. We crossed what must have been a hundred streams and rivers, some so deep and wide that we had to raft the goods across and swim the animals. Some were small creeks that we could just slosh across.

About the time the sky was starting to get dim we circled the carts and set up camp and made ready for another night. I walked to the cookpot and dipped my cup in like the rest and went to my place next to the cart I'd walked with all day. Of course the girl was still on my mind but I had not seen her at all today. I finished my cup and walked over to see if there was anything left in the pot. I got about half a cup and went back to my place next to the cart.

There she is! My heart started to leap and jump in my chest. She was walking right toward me. *Oh my God*, I was terrified. She didn't look like she was walking—she was floating over the ground. The only movement was her feet. She stood as straight as a fence post and held her head right above her shoulders. She looked straight ahead as she walked. She came to me and pointed at my torn corduroys. I shrugged and smiled sheepishly. She made a gesture like she wanted me to give her my pants. I didn't know what to do—how can I give this girl my pants? She looked at me with a pondering look and said, "Give me your ponts."

"You speak English?" I asked.

"You speak English?" she replied.

"Yes, I speak English."

"Well, why didn't you say so?" she asked.

"'Cause you didn't ask." Then she laughed, and I did too. Even her teeth were perfectly straight rows of the whitest teeth in the world. My heart melted.

"Well give me those ponts and I will mend th'm for you." She talked with a beautiful accent that I figured was French—but not quite.

"But..."

"Well wrop yourself in thut blanket and give th'm to me." I went into the brush and did as she said. When I came back with the blanket wrapped around me she laughed and said, "Shy?" I grinned sheepishly again and shrugged one shoulder.

In about an hour she came back with the pants. "These will not last long but they'll do for now."

"What's your name?" I asked.

"Lorraine. My father named me after the county in France where he was born."

"I'm called Hawk," I said and stretched out my hand.

"I have to get back to my camp. *Bon soir, monsieur* Hawk."

She walked away without taking my hand, but that was probably all right because I might have fallen down had I touched her.

'Monsieur Hawk', hmmm...had a nice ring to it, I thought. I rolled up in my robe and went to sleep with black eyes, brown skin and pure white teeth painted on the inside of my eyelids. I slept well that night, waking up a couple of times to see the clear sky filled with millions of stars that seemed so close I could have reached out and touched them. The last time I woke up the sky was beginning to lighten in the east but I rolled over for a few more winks of sleep before starting the new day.

Suddenly there was a commotion in the camp. No talking, just a lot of movement. I sat up to see several men digging their guns from the carts and from under their blankets. Then they all moved to one end of the camp. Thinking there might be trouble coming, I reached for my rifle and pouch and followed them. I was about halfway to where they all stood in a line, aiming their rifles in the same direction, when all of the guns went off at the same time. I looked in the direction they were aiming and saw three deer standing about one hundred-fifty yards away. When the guns went off, one of the deer stumbled and dropped to its knees, then got up and ran with the rest into the woods out of sight with one front leg dangling uselessly from the shoulder. All the men stood for a minute and then walked silently back to their camps to reload their rifles. I stopped one man who had a fine looking rifle and asked why they all shot at the same time. He looked at me and shrugged his shoulders and walked away. I had forgotten that none of these men spoke English. I looked around hoping to find Lorraine but she was not to be seen. In fact, there were no women to be seen, so I looked for Jean. I spotted him on the other side of the camp and went over to him. He was busy organizing the camp and getting them up and ready for moving out.

"What happened there with that shooting?"

"Can you shoot, boy?"

"Yes, in fact I'm pretty good with this rifle."

"Can you get us some meat?"

"Yes."

"None of these fellers here are hunters. Most of them are engages from the canoe brigades who have outlived their usefulness to the traders. All them traders want for workers is young boys with strong backs and weak minds. Most of these men are way past their hardworking days and have been dismissed from the canoe brigades or they ran off on account they just didn't want to do it anymore. They can't make money for the traders so they ain't no good to them. They don't hunt good and they don't shoot good. They haven't had meat for a long time and they need it. Pemmican is our only meat and it's gettin' rancid. We take it from the goods we're carrying, but the traders don't like it if we take too much and take the price they say it's worth out of our pay. Mostly we don't get enough pay in the end anyway but we can't do anything about it. That's just the way it is."

"Mister Charbonneau…"

"Jean."

"Right, Zhaaaaawn. Can I go get some meat for the camp?"

"Boy, if you can get us some meat you'll be earning your keep and you'll have all the friends you can handle in this camp."

I walked back to my gear, swung my shootin' bag over my shoulder, and my powder can over the other shoulder. I tossed my packs on the top of Jean's cart and walked toward where the deer went into the woods. I checked the flint on my rifle to make sure it was freshly knapped and sharp. I picked the touchhole, primed the pan, and flipped the frizzen down over it making sure it didn't knock any of the priming powder out. Uncle Robert always told me when he left the farm, "Keep yer powder dry and yer flint sharp, Hawk." I never forgot that.

I wasn't in the woods long before I saw the tracks of the deer in the early morning frost and started a slow walk into the brush. I didn't try to be quiet because a deer can hear you no matter how quiet you think you're being. So I walked softly, stopping every few steps trying to sound like a deer browsing in the brush. It didn't take long to get to the deer. They were in a small group in a clearing about thirty yards ahead of me. The deer spotted me at the same instant I saw them and they took off into the brush, but it was too slow for one of them and she went down like she'd tripped over a log. I paid no mind to the deer on the ground 'cause I knew I'd made a good shot and went right to work reloading my rifle. In short order I was reloaded and stood for a few seconds before moving ahead. The deer had gone only a few yards and stopped. My rifle came to my shoulder, the flint hit the frizzen, and another deer was down. Both were young does, the best kind for good meat. I stood still for a few minutes making sure the deer were down before I walked over and knelt down to start the field dressing. I heard sounds coming from behind me. I turned around and saw Jean coming through the brush.

"D'ja git 'em, boy?" he shouted.

"Yeah, got two."

"Iz zat all?"

"Well that's a hell of a lot more than yer army got."

Jean laughed, slapped me on the back with a wide grin, and said, "Boy, yer gonna enjoy earnin' yer keep with these people." I knelt down again to start opening the deer. "What you doin' now? Men don't do that, that's women's work."

"I only saw one woman in this whole camp—who's gonna do it?"

"Yeah, I know you only saw one, boy, and she ain't left yer mind since you saw her has she? You jist let that deer be and I'll get you some help."

He walked to the edge of the woods and hollered something to the camp. Out from the line of carts came about six men all dressed in wool pants with bright-colored blanket coats wrapped around them and hoods pulled up over their heads. When they got close I nearly fell over—they were all women. No wonder I didn't see any women in camp, they all dressed like the men and were totally covered up so as to hide the fact that they were women. All were pretty, what I could see of them. Well, to me all women were pretty. Most of these were a lot older than me. Shining out from the group of faces was Lorraine. I almost stopped her from getting down to cut open the deer when Jean stopped me.

He grabbed my arm and said, "Hawk, this is their work. If you try to stop them it will be an insult. They figure any woman who can't butcher a deer ain't worthy to be a called woman. You try to do their work and they'll fight you then they'll laugh at you and call you 'squawman'. Let 'em be. C'mon back to camp—we got things to do." He said it like Pa used to but with a much softer tone in his voice.

When I came into camp the men gathered around and all reached out their hands to thank me. All were smiles and slaps on the back. These men were most-ly shorter than me but they were all heavy-built and their faces showed the years of hard work and fighting the weather and flies and mosquitoes. Their hands were as hard as stone and rough as oak bark. When they shook hands they didn't try to impress me with a tight grip—it was firm but not rough. One of them was a short fellow with a comical looking face because all his features were pushed off to one side. I noticed him when he came up to me and said with much difficulty, because of a strong French accent, "You teach Renard shoot?"

"Ah, you speak English."

"No, not speak *d'Anglase*—just little," holding up his thumb and forefin-ger indicating small.

"Yes, if you want to shoot I will teach you." He grinned showing that he had teeth only on the left side of his mouth, the same side as where the rest of his face was. I tried to keep a sober look but it wasn't easy. As comical as he appeared I couldn't help feeling sorrow for this man because of the way he looked and the fact that it had an obvious effect on his self-esteem. I saw, as time went on, that he stayed by himself most of the time and avoided the others.

I walked up to Jean and said, "Zhawn, can I ask you something?"

"About the girl, right?"

"No, about Renard."

"Guess you should know about the Renard since you seem to have taken favor with him. Renard was our hunter. He could shoot anything he could see, no matter how far. He's got a fine Hawken rifle he got in a trade when he was paddling for the Hudson's Bay people. Seems it came from out West when some

Injun took the rifle and scalp off a lost trapper. Somehow the rifle got traded from one Injun to the next and ended up with one of the Injuns around Pembina. Well, the rifle was no good to the Injun 'cause he ain't got no powder or ball for it so he traded it to Renard for an axe. Ain't never heard of such a trade, but that's the story. It shoots a fifty-four caliber ball that'll knock a small deer into next week. Anywise, Renard was out hunting one day and took after a baby fox, thinking it would make a good pet. That's how he got his name—Renard is 'fox' in French. He didn't know there was a she-bear in the brush when he went in but he knew it when he came out. He ran smack into the bear. It turned and took a swipe at Renard and hit him so hard on the side of the head that it broke all the bones in his face and pushed everything to the side. Broke something in his head too, 'cause he ain't been the same since. He should'a died but the women took care of him for weeks before he came around and started healing up. Well, he's been kinda simple-minded since then and he can't shoot his Hawken on account his right eye ain't no good no more. If you got a mind to teach him to shoot again I think you should forget it—he ain't never gonna be that good no more."

"Well, I think I'll give it a go just to see what happens. I think he needs a friend anyway. We got powder and shot?"

"Got all the powder you can use and Renard's got a mold for balls. Good luck, son."

We walked all day—made maybe ten miles. The countryside was one hill after the other, tall hills and deep valleys between. If we could have gone in a straight line we might have made better time, but there were so many potholes and swamps. We must have zigzagged five miles for every mile as the hawk flies. The oxen kept up a steady pace, never seeming to tire. The wide, five-foot tall wheels on the carts rolled easily over the wet places and the oxen didn't seem to work any harder in the wet ground than they did on the dry hard ground. They just plugged along not paying any attention to the difficulties.

"How come you use oxen to pull your wagons and not horses?"

"An ox is better to work with. They're stronger than a horse and they never tire. Horses like grain—we got none. Horses run off at night or whenever they can but an ox will stay right where you put him and never roam like a horse or a mule. And an ox don't have no trouble walking through some of the swamps and muddy ground we go through. Any more dumb questions?"

"Just one."

"'Bout the girl?"

"No, not about the girl."

"Well, what then?"

"Why the hell don't they grease the wheels on these wagons?"

"Finally got around to that, did ya? You get us some grease and we'll grease our wheels."

"Won't bear grease work?"

"Nope, too sticky. The dust and dirt gets in the bear grease and works just like a file cutting up the hubs of the wheels. Besides, it just gets warm and runs out anyway and we're back to wood on wood and the noise. When wood rubs on wood it wears one piece into the other, then it'll turn forever without wearing out. These carts will go from Pembina to Saint Paul three times before wearing out. You talk too much—go find supper."

When I got back to the camp they were all set up for the night and the cookpot was boiling. The women went to work on the two deer I had brought in and the meat went into the pot with the peas and flour. Everyone sat down to a good meal and filled their bellies with fresh venison. So it went for days. Walk and eat. There was plenty of meat in the country—bear, deer, turkey, even an occasional buffalo, but that was rare.

One night I was sitting on my usual spot when Lorraine came up to me and handed me a pair of leather pants.

"What's this?" I asked.

"Those corduroys of yours are rotting right off you. I made these from the skins of the first two deer you got. Take them and put them on. They're yours." Then she threw some moccasins at me and said, "You'll be needing these too when it gets cold." Hell, it was already cold. She'd made the moccasins with two layers. The outside layer was buffalo that had the hair in, and the inside layer was deer with the hair on the side away from my feet. I had two layers of hair between my feet and the cold. The stitching was so fine as to be invisible. They looked like they'd be heavy on my feet but they were not. They looked big but were very warm and comfortable.

The next day, after the morning duties, we were off again. About midday the countryside leveled off and we were once again on level ground.

"We can make better time now that we're out of those hills," Jean said.

Suddenly the train stopped. Jean walked to the back to see what was going on and I followed. One of the carts had broken a wheel.

"Well, might as well sit down and wait it out," he said.

"Guess I'll go find Renard and do some shootin'."

"If that's what you want, then go ahead. See if you can find some meat while yer out there."

Renard wasn't hard to find. He was crouched down in his usual spot rubbing his rifle with a piece of oiled deerskin.

"Wanna go shoot, Renard?"

"Huh?"

"Shoot. You know…" I mimicked a rifle to my shoulder pulling the trigger.

"Oui! Bon, we shoot now?" He gave me a big half-tooth grin. He jumped up and went into his small tent and came out with a pouch that was beautifully decorated with Indian quillwork and fringing a foot long hanging from the bottom. The quillwork was an image of a fox hunting. He took up his rifle and ran his fingers over the fine-grained walnut stock. I could see that he thought his rifle his lover and friend. A close bond between rifle and shooter makes for good shooting.

We walked out to an open prairie and picked a spot to shoot from. I went out about fifty yards and carved an *X* on a tree and walked back to Renard. I pointed at the *X* and indicated for him to hit it. He took his time loading the rifle, first measuring out the exact amount of powder by pouring it from his buffalo horn flask into his hand until it covered just the right amount of hand, then poured it down the barrel. From his pouch he took a strip of cloth that had been soaked in oil, laid the end of the cloth over the muzzle, laid a ball on the cloth, and cut it off with a small knife he had hanging from his neck on a leather thong. Then he pushed the load down the barrel and bounced the ramrod on the ball a couple of times to seat it. He reached into his pouch again and came out with a small priming cap. I'd heard of these caps but this was the first time I'd seen one used. Then the rifle came to his shoulder. By his posture I could see that this man knew how to shoot, but when I saw him lean his face too far over the stock I knew he wasn't going to hit anything. He was trying to sight with his left eye in a right-handed position. *Of course*, I thought, *he can't see out of his right eye. No wonder he can't hit anything.*

I put my hand on his shoulder to stop him. He lowered the rifle and looked at me with a questioning look. I took the rifle from his hand and put it up to his left shoulder and said, "Try it this way."

"No, Renard shoot like this," looking at me quizzically.

"Not no more," I said and put the stock back into his left shoulder. He looked at me not knowing what I was doing, so I pointed at his right eye and waved my finger over it to say "this don't work." I pointed at his left eye and said, "This eye is good. Use it."

He pondered that for a few seconds and then smiled and nodded his head in approval.

"Ahhh, *oui, Je comprend.*"

He sighted over the barrel and squeezed off his shot. The bullet dug a crater in the tree about two inches to the left of the center of the *X*. He looked hard and when he saw where the bullet hole was he jumped up and down laughing and saying, "*Merci, merci.* Tank you, tank you." Then he quickly loaded up and shot again. This time the bullet hit on the other side of the mark. Disappointment showed in his face. He thought that shot should have hit the center of the *X*.

"No, Renard, that is a good shot. You just need to practice. You will be a good shooter again, I promise." I indicated for him to stop shooting and walked out and carved an *X* on another tree. I told Renard, "That's my *X*."

Renard nodded up and down quickly.

I took a shot and centered the *X* then mimicked how proud I was by throwing my chest out and pounding it with my fist. I pointed at him and said, "You do that now." He got the message. We were going to compete and that was fine with him. He did his best to beat me and after a dozen shots, he did. The man laughed and stomped his feet, pointing at me and laughing like a kid. I figured he was a little touched in the head. We burned a lot of powder the rest of the day and when he was done he was putting all of his shots in the center of the *X*. I didn't know who was more proud—me, or the Renard.

When I saw Jean again I told him about the day's shooting and he said, "I'll believe it when I see it."

"You'll see."

The Renard did a lot of shooting the next few days and with each day he got better. He was hitting targets at one hundred yards with amazing accuracy.

"You got anything else to put on besides that old coat?" Jean said to me.

"No, but this is a warm coat and these moccasins Lorraine made me are plenty warm. Why?"

Jean nodded his head to the west and said, "Storm coming."

Being midday, the wagons didn't want to stop, so we kept up our slow pace as the storm moved in. First the wind picked up and ice-cold air rolled over us. Then the snow started. It blew hard across the flat plain leaving drifts behind every tree and rock and bump on the ground. The oxen didn't seem to notice the cold air or the wind and snow, but the men were walking on the sheltered side of the carts bundled in their capotes and holding their collars tight around their necks. Snow blew like a white sheet across the ground. One man had to scramble to catch the tarp that had blown loose from the top of his cart. The storm stopped as quickly as it started, but the cold stayed. The gray clouds moved off to the east and the sun came out but did nothing to warm us. The air was winter air. It would be cold from now until spring.

We needed meat for the pot. When Jean told me to go find some, I went to get Renard and took him with me. We were not in the forests like we had been for the past couple of weeks so deer were not as easy to find. After some long hours and hard walking we did find one browsing in a thicket. I told Renard to shoot and he did. The deer went down and didn't move. Renard had taken it through the neck and broke its spine. Best shot you can make, I figure.

"Now we have two hunters in the camp," I said slapping him on the back. Renard looked at me and grinned so hard I thought his funny-looking face would break. We brought the deer back to camp and dropped it in front of the women who took over the job of dressing it. Some of them started to thank me but I indicated that it was the Renard who shot the deer. They looked surprised and looked at me, then at Renard, then at me and finally got the reality of Renard being the hunter he once was—and all cheered for him. I thought he was going to bust open with pride. He laughed and stomped his feet and clapped his hands like a kid who just won his first marble.

Lorraine came to me and said, "Thank you, Hawk," and walked away.

From that day on Renard was always with me. I couldn't go anywhere without him. He got my meals for me, built my fire for me, and carried my packs when I needed them carried. It got a little annoying at times but he was having such a good time having a friend, I just went along with it. Lorraine was around more too, but not for me. She seemed to be watching out for Renard, making sure he wasn't being a bother and watching to be sure he fed himself as well as he kept me fed. But he didn't seem to notice her. I sure didn't understand that. We shot a lot of deer and elk for the camps from then on and no one went hungry.

Jean said to me, "Tomorrow we'll be at a trade camp on the Elk River. We're gonna pick up some cargo and from there we'll be in Saint Paul in two days. You and your pal there be damn careful hunting. Word is there's trouble south of here with a band of outlaw Injuns who's raisin' hell with the settlers—some guy calls himself Ink pa duta. So stay close to camp and don't go runnin' off where ye can't git back quick. And keep the Renard by yer side. He ain't right ya know, and he'll get himself killed."

About noon the next day we came into a camp with two log buildings with sod roofs set on a low hill above the Elk River. The river was about twenty feet below the camp and about fifty yards wide. On the other side was river grass and heavy forest that laid on a flat plain that stretched away from the river. A long island lay between the two banks of the river. Jean went into the cabin to do the business he needed done. Our people set their camps in the open grass in front of the cabin. They didn't circle the carts like they always did when we were traveling. I guessed that was because it was so much safer here from Indians. There was no need to go hunting because the trader fixed us up with the best meal we'd had for months—deer meat, elk, bear, wild oats, and wine—plenty of wine. I'd tasted Pa's wine once and decided I didn't like the way it burned my mouth and throat so I turned down what was offered me.

"This ain't whiskey, Hawk. It's smooth rum and it don't burn ya," Jean said.

"That's all right," I said. "I don't need any."

About an hour after dark everyone was sitting around the fire singing and laughing and getting very happy. I found out that most of these people did speak English but preferred their own language, so they stayed away from the English tongue.

"How come no one talked to me if they speak English, Zhawn?"

"Guess they just didn't have nothin' to say."

"Well they could have come over and talked."

"About what? They don't care where you come from and they don't care where yer goin'. People who just come around to talk always got to ask you about your personal business. These people walked away from their lives back there and figure you did, too. The past ain't nothin' but learning and when you've learned something there ain't no point to hashin' it out again. If you ask for advice or help they'll be glad to talk to you, but to just make small talk—they ain't interested. Most of them don't talk English that good anyway. Don't worry about it."

The fun and drinking went on far into the night. I went to my robes and laid down to get some sleep. Next morning I was up before the rest of the camp. The snoring was almost as loud as the wheels of the carts. One poor guy was in the woods pushing up as much of last night's rum as his straining stomach muscles could push. His sounds of agony could be heard all around the camp.

Slowly the camp came alive. People walked around with their heads down looking at the ground. They were wrapped up tight in their blanket coats and headed toward the fire the cook had going in the middle of the camp. Figuring it would be a while before there was food to eat, I took my shirts down to the river for a badly-needed washing. I was about knee deep in the water when I saw the grass move on the other side of the river. Thinking there was a deer or elk over there I turned and climbed the hill to get my rifle. One of the men was walking toward me with his coat pulled tight around his neck to keep the cold out.

Suddenly I heard a sharp, loud snap next to my ear and a bang from behind me. I searched my memory trying to find where I'd heard that sound before. It was one day when Pa took a shot at a deer right past my head. I heard the ball snap by my head. He missed the deer and me both. I wondered which one he really missed—me or the deer. Then I saw the man in front of me collapse to the ground. His knees went limp and he dropped straight down. I was straining my mind to figure out what was happening when another crack came to my ears, then another and another. Then I realized we were being shot at. Men started running in all directions. One man fell to the ground and lay there curled up with blood pouring out of a hole in his belly. Then arrows came whizzing in so thick it was like mosquitoes. People ran in circles. I panicked and ran for the woods. I got halfway there before I got control of my fear and turned toward my rifle. I picked it up and ducked behind a log to look for whoever it was shooting at us, but I couldn't see anyone.

In an instant Jean was next to me with a Hawken just like Renard's. From our side of the river I heard a familiar "boom" and knew it was Renard's fifty-four. I looked around and saw him standing behind a big maple tree loading up. He looked at me shaking his head up and down and grinning like a skunk eatin' crickets. I pulled a bead on an Indian across the river, put my front sight on the middle of his chest, and squeezed off the shot. He jumped up and fell face first into the water. This was the first time I had ever shot at a human being, and I'd killed him. I stared at the dead man in the water shocked at the idea of killing men. Then a bullet smacked into the log I was behind and it woke me out of my thoughts. I loaded up and looked for another target. The booms from Renard's rifle were coming fast. I wondered how that man could load and shoot as fast as he did but dared not look to see. If that bear messed up his head, it sure didn't hurt his shooting instincts. I fired again and another man fell into the water. Jean fired and dropped one. Every time a red man stepped out into the open he died. Jean was as good as either Renard or me and each shot he took killed another Indian. My hands were shaking and my heart pounded. I was terrified by the sound of the bullets and arrows coming from the other side of the river. There is a big difference between the sound from in front of a gun and the sound from behind—loud and sharp and terrifying. The sound of the bullets ripping through the trees and smacking into the wood of the log building was frightening enough, but the thump of a big slug tearing into a man's belly made me sick. And the whistle of the arrows as they flew overhead and slammed into the ground or a tree made me want to crawl into a gopher hole. My shots were not going where I wanted them to but I was too scared to wonder why. I wanted to settle down and take my time but the fear had me and I was close to panic.

"Patch yer damn balls, Hawk. It ain't the trees shootin' at us!" Jean yelled at me.

I should'a known it's better to get off one good shot than a lot of bad ones. I got hold of myself and took more time loading and aiming. Then the battle started to take a turn for the better. The bow-and-arrow shooters were the best targets because they had to show themselves to shoot and when they stood up, they died. Other men in the camp had taken up the shooting with old rifles and shotguns they finally got dug out of their packs. We filled the grass with lead and smoke. Water sprayed up from the river from the bullets hitting. Now and then a pattern from a shotgun would churn up the river. Our fire cut down small trees. The Indians didn't have a chance. They might have taken our position if they'd had the nerve to come over and make a determined assault, but I guess they were no more interested in dying than we were. Soon the women came over and tore off patches of cloth and soaked them with spit so we didn't have to. The fire from our rifles and shotguns drove the attackers back into the woods.

Jean saw, at the same time as I did, three Indians wading across the river just out of range.

"You and Renard stay here and keep shooting. I'm going to stop those three," and he grabbed up his pouch and horn and took off to the right of the camp.

The Indians weren't giving us much to shoot at while they waited for the ambushers to get behind us. When we had a shot we took our time aiming and cut him down. Then a shot came from the right. *One Indian dead,* I said to myself. Then silence. Renard and I held our positions watching the river. A head poked up from the weeds.

"Take him, Fox," I said. "I ain't loaded."

Renard looked at me, "Huh?"

I pointed at the head and yelled, "Shoot!" He looked at the river, pulled up quickly, and removed the top of the Indian's head. Another Indian was wading across the river to the left of us. I pulled up but didn't get a chance to pull the trigger before I heard Renard shoot and the Indian fell into the water. I looked around to see Renard looking at me and laughing. How the hell he got loaded so fast was a mystery to me, but he'd gotten off a shot while I was sighting. A scream came from the place where Jean had gone. I knew it wasn't Jean—he wouldn't be able to make that sound. Then I saw an Indian splash through the water back to the other side at a dead run. Jean came back holding the scalp of the dead Indian in his left hand.

"Aww Jean, did you have to do that?" I said, trying to hold my stomach from tossing its contents on the ground. I failed.

"Puts the fear into an Injun," he said.

The camp was silent. Birds were singing their praises to the morning sun. The wind picked up and made a whispering sound in the tall pines overhead. A squirrel barked at something, then went quiet. I heard a chipmunk making his chuck-chuck sound somewhere in the deep forest. A grouse drummed his mating call, who knows how far off, and the crows were calling the morning sun. Everything was as peaceful as before the shooting started. It made me think of the quiet after a thunderstorm.

A man moaned. I looked around and saw Lorraine tending to a man who had blood pouring out of a hole in his chest. Women were kneeled next to wounded men trying to keep them from dying. Lorraine stood up, made the sign of the cross, and walked over to where another woman was helping a man. In all, four people lay dead on the ground and three were walking around with holes in various places on their bodies. A woman lay dead on the ground with a busted arrow centered between her shoulder blades. Renard came up from below and stared at the dead men. He knelt down next to the man Lorraine had just left and crossed himself and started to cry. He wept deeply.

"Did he know him, Jean?" I asked with a trembling voice.

"Sure, we all did. Renard cries easy since the bear got 'im."

My hands were trembling and my knees shook. My heart was thumping like I'd just run a mile. The chaos of the fight and the fear I had never experienced before had made a wreck of me. Lorraine walked over to Renard, put her arm around his shoulders, and led him away sobbing.

The camp was quiet the rest of the day. Jean and I and two more men stayed at the edge of the camp and watched for any movement that might signal another attack, but the Indians had moved off to safer parts. Some of the men started digging graves through the roots and rocks. The bodies were wrapped in buffalo robes and buried on the north side of the camp with their heads facing east toward their homelands. Lorraine asked for a Bible and I dug mine out of my pack and handed it to her.

"Hawk, this is in English. Will you read for us?"

"Ummm, I can't read." Ma had taught Jake to read some but I didn't care enough about it to learn.

"Then I will do my best."

After the prayers she said to me, "Your name is Harlan?"

"Uh, yes, Harlan Owen. My father is Welsh. My grandfather came from the old country."

Her eyes, showing absolute indifference, trailed down from my dirty face to my dirty clothes and my dirty hands, black from loading and shooting. She handed me the Bible and said, "At least you are not English," and walked away.

Renard came to me later and said, "Hawk, you call me Fox. Why you say this?"

"Renard is 'fox' in English."

"*Ah, bon*, then I am Fox. You, Hawk, are my friend and where you go the Fox goes."

"But they will be needing you here, Fox. Shouldn't you stay with them?"

"They go to a village tomorrow south of here where the bourgeois will give men to follow train to Saint Paul. They don't need me anymore. Hawk, until you teach me to shoot again they didn't need me before either."

"Is that right, Jean?"

"Finally got done with that 'Zhaaaaawn' nonsense, did ya?"

"Yeah, for now."

"He's right. A little town south of here they're calling Elk River they have men ready to escort us to Saint Paul. You're welcome to come if you like."

"Guess maybe I'll do just that. Can I get to the Minnesota Valley from there?"

"We get to Saint Paul and you're right at the mouth of the valley. Just git on a stern wheeler in the spring and go up the river to the richest land in the country. We'll be following the river most of tomorrow and there ain't much chance of Injuns bothering us, so we can relax."

*The bones in his face cracked and the man
screamed in pain and dropped the knife
to bring his hands to his bloody face...*

2

CHAPTER TWO

"I GUESS I SHOULD TELL YOU NOW about what happened after
I left the farm..."

. . .

My mother, Mary Owen, sat on the edge of the bed holding her apron to
her face to hide the tears she didn't want her husband to see. John Owen stood
leaning on the doorframe looking out silently at his son Jacob. Jake stood in the
yard for long minutes looking at the road that Hawk walked on his way to his
new life.

"Guess we won't have to feed that worthless Hawk anymore," John said.

"John, he's your son. Have you no feelings?"

"The boy's gone and I won't hear no more about it. He was never any good
around here and it's better he's gone."

"John, it's *not* better he's gone. How are you and young Jacob there gonna
work this farm? Hawk did a lot of things around here that you never even seen.
He worked best when he was alone without you yellin' at him all the time. How
do you think things got done? We don't have slaves or servants. Jake and Hawk
did it while you was at Mister Belleair's tavern, or when you was asleep from
drinking too much. Hawk is a good boy—he just don't take to being pushed."

"That Hawk was a no-good woods tramp," John yelled at Mary. "No better'n these renegade Indians that come around beggin' food." John walked to the
wall and pulled down his old single-barreled shotgun he hadn't had to shoot in

years and walked to the door. Jake was walking fast to the cabin.

Mary looked up and realized something was going on outside and said, "What 'er you doing John?"

"Injuns coming up the road."

Jake walked through the door and took the iron poker out of the fireplace and stood next to his pa just outside the door. There were three of them dressed in white man's wool trousers and shirts that were too big for them and wide brimmed hats with feathers stuck in the bands. They all wore plain, nearly worn-out moccasins on their feet. Each had a bow and arrows hung on their backs with leather thongs and a short knife tucked in their belts.

The lead Indian raised his hand and said in broken English, "Good day, my friends."

John nodded, "How can we help you?"

"You have something for us to eat? We have not had food for many days."

John turned to Mary in the cabin and said, "You got some of those biscuits left or did you send them all with Hawk?"

"I have a sack full here. Give them what they want and tell them to go away." She brought the sack of bread and handed it to John.

John walked out to meet the leader of the group and said, "Now be on your way."

One of the Indians started to move to the right but Jake stepped in front of him and looked him in the eyes. The Indian stopped and stepped back to the others.

"Thank you my friends. We will go now." They turned and walked away.

John grumbled, "That's just what we need now—Injuns comin' to our door eating food we need for ourselves."

"Pa?"

"What is it Jake?" John said, still looking out the door.

"Is that shotgun loaded?"

"'Course it is. A gun ain't no good if it ain't loaded."

"When did you load it?"

"I don't know when, I just know it's loaded."

"Hawk says…"

"I don't give a damn what Hawk says," John snapped. "He ain't here no more and got nothin' to say about what goes on around here."

"Maybe you should pull that load and put fresh in the gun, Pa."

"Could be you're right, but you can do that later after we eat. Mary git some food on—we gotta eat."

"John, do you have to be so course? We'll do what needs to be done without being hollered at."

"Is everyone turning against me? Just 'cause that no-good son of yours left don't mean you can start getting uppity with me. I'm still the man of this house and you'll do as you're told, without any sass."

"Pa, settle down," Jake said. "Ain't nobody gettin' uppity with you. We're all a little tight on account of what's happened here today."

John grumbled and sat down at the table to wait for his supper. The meal was eaten in silence. The empty chair stood out like a big tree in the room.

"Pa, did you notice anything strange about those Indians?"

"What are you talkin' about?"

"Well, they all had weapons and they all had white man's clothes on."

"That don't mean nothin'. They just begged the clothes off some poor farmer."

"But Pa, they said they hadn't eaten in days, but they didn't have blankets or coats with them."

"What you gittin' at, boy? Spit it out."

"I think there's a camp of Indians close by 'cause if they've been walking for days they would have their blankets with them and packs to carry things in. I think they spend the nights in a camp where they have all that stuff and are just moving around from there."

John thought about it for a while and said, "You're learning son. I saw that too," he lied.

"Pa, you think we should go to the settlement and see what's going on?"

"Yer afraid the Injuns are lookin' for trouble, ain'tcha son?"

"I don't know Pa, but it sure was curious about those Indians."

"Tell you what Jacob, you go to Belleair's store tomorrow and see if there's any word about it and if there's a reason, we'll all go to town. If anyone knows about Injun trouble it'll be Belleair. I need you to get a new saw blade anyway. That brother of yours..." He trailed off when he saw his wife's eyes come up and look at him ready to jump down his throat.

Jake slept poorly that night, getting up and looking out the door and walking around the cabin making sure all was well. The cow and mules were in the log barn and safe from harm. Lightning flashed in the western sky. Soon the rain started and Jake thought about Hawk somewhere out there, probably soaked to the skin.

Morning came and he was up with the first light. His mother had a fire in the fireplace and was boiling water for their breakfast.

"Morning, Jake."

"Morning, Ma," he said and kissed her on the cheek.

"Did ye sleep well?"

"No, Ma, I didn't sleep at all. Them Injuns got me wondering."

"Well, when you get to town you ask around if there's been any trouble, and if there has we'll skedaddle out of here. Sure wish Hawk was here," she said quietly.

"Me and Pa can handle what comes up, Ma. T'would be comforting to have that rifle of his around though."

John rolled out of his blankets and started his morning coughing routine that lasted only a few minutes before he asked if breakfast was ready.

"Be one minute, John."

They sat and ate boiled wild oats and hot biscuits quietly.

"You still want me to go to town for the saw blade, Pa?"

"Might as well get it over with in the morning so we can get that wood cut and stacked in the barn. We're gonna have to go out and get more before the snow flies. We didn't have enough last winter, remember?"

A light drizzling rain fell as Jake walked to the barn to take out one of the mules. Mules are slow but they are faster than walking. He tied a rope on the mule's head to use as a halter which his Pa hadn't seen need for.

"Can I get anything for you, Ma?"

"Not that I can think of, Jake. You just hurry back and be careful."

"Pa, want me to load the shotgun before I go?"

"I'll take care of the shotgun. You just get that saw blade and get back here."

The twelve-mile ride to the settlement was a long one, through a short patch of hardwoods, and then out onto the prairie where Jake could see for miles in every direction. The road was no more than a rut cut into the sandy earth. Nothing grew on that sand but thin grass and thistles. Out on the edge of the plain where the forest started, the dirt was better after the stumps were pulled and the top-soil turned under. That's where his pa's farm was, back in the woods where there was potential for growing crops. John Owen had inherited the land from his father who came to America from Wales to get away from the poor living conditions there. *He didn't improve his lot much...* Jake thought to himself as he rode along the trail. He arrived at the traders' store and walked in. The room was dark with a little light coming in the door and an open window. An oil lantern burned on the board counter close to where the storekeeper stood. Mister Belleair was a

French-Indian mixed blood from Canada, about forty-five years old. His thirty year-old wife Betsy was also mixed blood. Most of the people in Otter Tail County were a mixture of French, Irish, and Indian.

"Well, look what the cat dragged in. Howdy, Jake. Good to see ye. How's yer pa and ma?"

"They're fine, I guess."

"And Hawk?"

Jake thought a minute and said, "Yeah, Hawk's fine too, I guess."

"What can I do for ye, lad?"

"Pa sent me to get a blade for his bucksaw. Got any?"

"Damn. No Jake, just what's on the new saws I got. Tell you what, I'll give you a new saw at my cost, and when you git the money you can pay me the rest. How's that?"

"We need that saw so I guess it'd be all right."

The man walked to the back of the store and came out with a new saw and handed it to Jake.

"How 'bout I just pay you the whole thing when I git the money?"

"Well..." The storekeep thought for a minute and said, "When can I expect it?"

"Can't really say. Ma's workin' on some stuff to sell and when she gits the money I'll come right in and pay you."

"What's yer ma makin'? Anything I might use in the store?"

"She makes things like Indian moccasins and bags from the skins of the deer Hawk..." he paused, "shoots."

"Well you tell your ma to bring some of that stuff in and maybe we can make a deal. Lots of folks around here are wearing moccasins 'cause shoes are kinda hard to come by these days."

"Thanks, Mister Belleair. Ma'll appreciate that. Mister Belleair, have you heard anything about Indian trouble?"

"Heard there's some renegade Sioux down south in Iowa raisin' hell, but nothing around here. Down by Crow Wing River, the Chippaways is forever chasing the Sioux up and down Minnesota Territory trying to keep them out of their huntin' grounds. Both tribes think the Crow Wing River is their huntin' grounds and they been fightin' over it for hunnerts of years, but that ain't no bother to us around here. 'Course there's that rebel Hole-In-The-Day down by Crow Wing who can't settle down and be peaceable. Other than that everything's quiet. What makes you ask, Jake?"

"Well, we been having a lot of beggars coming around the farm lately and they're acting kinda strange."

"How so?"

"They come in and beg food but they don't carry the things they should be carrying if they're just roaming—no blankets or coats, no pack to carry their plunder in. Things like that, Mister Belleair."

"Well, I think yer worrying over nothing, Jake. We ain't had Injun trouble around here in twenty years."

"Thanks, Mister Belleair. And thanks for the saw. You'll get yer money."

"I know that, Jake."

Jake walked out the door and into the street and found several people staring to the east at a column of smoke rising from the forest on the edge of the prairie. "Looks like that could be coming from yer pa's farm, Jake," someone said.

"Hope Pa didn't set the barn on fire," Jake said, half laughing.

Then he thought about the Indians and fear took over. He walked to where he had tied his mule and climbed aboard. He didn't want anyone to see he was scared so he walked the mule away from the store before he kicked it hard and yelled in its ear to get it running. The mule took up a slow gallop but that didn't satisfy Jake. He kicked it harder and swatted the mule on the rump but it wouldn't run any faster than he was already going. It seemed he'd never get to the farm. The road didn't have an end. On he rode, slapping his mule and yelling at it to run, but it still seemed to be walking all the way.

Finally, he broke into the woods where the farm was and galloped the mule as close to the burning cabin as he dared. He jumped from the mule before it stopped and ran toward the cabin. He was too late. The cabin was a smoldering pile of fallen, charred logs with small fires burning around where the walls used to be. The sod roof had fallen in and buried nearly everything. The stone chimney stood blackened from the fire. He looked around at the rest of the place but saw nothing. *Where's Ma and Pa...?* Suddenly panic struck. He ran around the farm looking for his mother and father. He looked everywhere he could think of but there was no sign of them. *Calm yourself Jake,* he said to himself, *look around, find where they went.*

Then he saw the hoof prints in the mud. They were not mule prints, but horse prints. *Oh my God... Indians.* He looked carefully at the ground for tracks. There were moccasin tracks mixed with the hoof prints and some old tracks that might have been his. Then he saw small tracks that could only be his mother's. He could tell from the spacing that she was running. The rain had stopped and the prints were clear. He pictured her running and screaming from the Indians. Then he saw something that bothered him. His mother's tracks were on top of the boot tracks that could only be his pa's. *My dear God,* he thought, *Pa ran ahead of Ma.* He followed the tracks for a distance making sure he was right about his father running in front of his mother and he cried. Bitter tears ran from his eyes knowing his father had turned tail, and rather than staying to help his wife, he ran to save his own cowardly hide. Jake wanted to shout for his mother but knew that if the Indians were still around they might hear him and come after him, too.

He followed the hoof prints into an opening in the woods and saw his mother lying on her side in the grass. Her knees were pulled up almost like she was asleep. He walked slowly up to her and kneeled down and touched her dress. Two arrows were in her back with just the feathers on the outside. He turned her over and both arrows protruded from the front of her shirt. Jake almost blacked out when he looked at her. She'd been scalped. Suddenly his stomach turned inside out. He lay on the grass and puked for five minutes. He cried loudly.

"Goddammit!" he shouted into the air. "Whoever did this, you sons-a-bitches, I'll find you and rip your goddamned heathen hearts out!" The words echoed through the trees. He yelled again hoping the Indians were around and would come to him. He wanted to kill.

He sat for some time with his mother's body before he stood and looked around to see if he could find his pa. He walked in ever-increasing circles scared stiff of what he might find. He searched until almost dark and gave it up. Then he went to the barn and got out a shovel and dug his mother's grave. When the grave was covered he went to go through the ruins of his pa's farm to see if there was anything worth taking with him when he left. He sifted through the ashes of the cabin and found nothing but the kitchen things his mother used. He wouldn't be needing any of that where he was going. He dug a big iron-bladed butcher knife from the ashes.

"This'll take the scalps off them sons-a-bitches," he said out loud. He was surprised at the words he was using but somehow they seemed all right to say now. He was mad and using the words he'd heard his pa use seemed to put more strength into what he was saying.

He kicked at the ashes and found nothing more he could use so he went back to look around the place. In the yard about ten feet from the house he found his pa's shotgun. He picked it up and looked at it. The stock was broken nearly in half and it had not been fired. The soot in the pan told the story. His pa had tried to fire the old gun but the charge was too old and it wouldn't go off. *Goddammit, that goddamned fool didn't change the load. The stupid, stubborn bastard—he probably could have killed one of them sons-a-bitches if he'd just changed the load. Damn!*

It was near dark now and Jake walked to the barn, ducked under the doorway, and went inside. The other mule and the cow were gone. *Got the animals too.* Then he laid down to sleep. He didn't sleep well that night from the visions going through his head. Tomorrow he'd find the tracks of the Injuns and kill the lot of them.

Morning came and he walked quietly to the door of the barn and looked out, then all around, before going out. He sidestepped around the edge of the barn peeking around the corner to make sure he was alone. All looked safe so he walked out into the yard. The mule he'd ridden into town yesterday had kept on running after Jake jumped off and now Jake was afoot. He took up his pa's gun, straightened the stock as best he could and started to walk toward town. In the distance he saw riders coming. It was clear they were white men so he kept walking until they came up to him.

"Everything all right, Jake?"

"No, everything ain't all right. My ma's dead and I can't find my pa, and the farm is burned to the ground."

"What happened, Jake?"

"Injuns. That pack that was at the house two days ago beggin' food."

"Can't be Injuns, Jake. We ain't had Injun trouble around here…"

"I know, in twenty years," Jake interrupted. "Mister Belleair, you ain't even been here twenty years. How the hell would you know?"

Mister Belleair contemplated that for a second and said, "How can you be so sure it was Injuns?"

"Who else rides horses around here besides you and the Injuns? And who around here would take the scalp of my mother and leave her layin' in the dirt? Injuns that's who, and I'm goin' after 'em and do for them what they did for my family."

"Jake, ye'd better give that some thinkin'. Injuns ain't nothin' to be messin' with 'less you know what yer doin'."

"I know what I'm doin'. I'm goin' hunting Injun scalps."

"Come on into town and we'll talk about it and see what the best thing is to do."

"I was coming to town to get me some powder and buckshot."

"Good, get up on the back of my horse and you can ride in."

Jake swung up to the rump of the horse and they went to town. In twenty minutes there were half a dozen men sitting on empty wooden crates and flour barrels in Mister Belleair's store, all talking at once and all knowing exactly what needed to be done. But the plain truth was, there was nothing to be done but sit and wait to see what would happen next. No one had seen Indians but Jake. No one knew where to look for them or what to do with them if they did find them.

"Vee coot sent somebody to da nearest town ver dey heff da army," Charlie Roch offered.

"And where would that be, Mister Roch?" Jake said, "Fort Ripley? That's a hundred miles from here. They can't do nothin' for us. Besides, them Injuns had their blood—they probably won't be botherin' anyone again. I figure they was watching the house just waiting for the time when me and Hawk were both gone to raid the place. They knew Pa warn't no threat, but Hawk and that rifle of his, and me with Pa's shotgun were, and a Injun has to have things in his favor before he'll try anything. Mister Belleair, can you let me have some powder and shot for this here gun? I'll pay you for it soon as I can."

"I'll give you what you need, Jake, but I don't really expect to get the money. You got a long way to go, son. By the way, where is Hawk?"

"Hawk and Pa got in a fight a couple of days ago and Pa run him off."

"Where the hell'd he go?"

"Don't know. He said he was going to see the mountains."

"Headed west then I s'pect, or maybe south to get on a boat to Saint Louis. I wouldn't look for him to be coming back anytime soon Jake. That Hawk had the wanderlust about him."

"No, he won't be back. Guess it don't matter now."

Jake took up his powder and buckshot and went out to walk the twelve miles back to the farm. He took the shotgun and pulled the worthless, caked load, then cleaned the rust and dirt out of the bore with the cleaning jag Mister Belleair had thrown into his pouch. He knapped the flint until it was as sharp as it needed to be, then snapped it a few times to be sure it made good spark, and loaded the gun with extra powder and buckshot. In the barn he found his Uncle Robert's old bearskin coat hanging on the wall. He took it down and shook it once to dust it. More hair than dust flew from the coat. If it weren't for the plaid wool liner the coat might have come apart from the shaking. It was dirty and smelled bad but Jake figured it would still keep him warm.

The tracks left by the Indians were still clear and Jake had no problem following them. The Indians were driving the mule and cow with them. They led to the north and into the heavy timber where the horse hooves dug up the dirt and leaves, making tracking that much easier. He followed the tracks to an old Indian trail that led around the south side of the lake. Here the Otter Tail River flowed into Little Pine Lake. He pulled off his trousers and shoes and waded across the sand bar to the other side. It was dark now so he crawled under a log to get some sleep. The night was filled with the sounds of crickets and frogs. The rhythmic chirping of the crickets made him sleepy. An owl called from the north and was answered from the south. The night was cold but Jake had the heavy winter coat to wrap up in and was warm enough to sleep.

The sounds of the crickets changed to the morning calls of the crows. He remembered that the crows were Hawk's favorite bird. He liked their playful ways and loved to hear them in the early morning. The world was wet with heavy dew when Jake woke up, and the sweet aroma of wet poplar leaves filled the air. God how he and Hawk loved the smell of poplar leaves in the fall. He hadn't brought food along because there was simply none to bring, but he knew where to find it when the time came. It was near fall and the tender shoots and roots he liked would be tough and not very good to the taste, but still edible and nutritious. He sat still next to a maple tree for some time and waited for his breakfast to show up. A squirrel scampering around digging in the fallen leaves got too close and Jake clubbed it with a stick he'd picked up off the ground. He wasn't much fond of squirrel meat but he was hungry and squirrel meat was nutritious and easy to get—so that was breakfast. He didn't dare have a fire so he skinned the squirrel and chewed the meat off the bones and ate it raw. So was the manner in which he fed himself—sometimes a squirrel, sometimes a partridge. He could not be particular about food at this point. When food was available, he ate.

He tracked the Indians for three days. The tracks of the cow and mule were no longer with the horse tracks and Jake figured the Indians had killed the cow for meat and probably killed the mule too. At this point the animals were not a major factor—finding those murdering Indians was. August was a dry month that year so the tracks stayed clear and he had no trouble following them. Night came once again and he found a fallen oak and made his bed under the turned-up root ball.

Something woke him in the middle of the night and he stood up to look around. Off in the distance he saw the flicker of a campfire in the yellowing leaves of the trees. His heart stopped for a second. Blood rushed to his head and made a pounding sound in his ears. The camp was about a mile away from where he was so he started a slow walk in that direction, keeping an eye on the light. He was in hill country and he could get close by staying in the hollows and following the small streambeds. He walked slower as he came close to the camp of Indians. Now he could hear their low voices. He got to his knees and crawled very slowly, feeling the ground for sticks that could snap and give him away if he put his weight on them. He made his way to where he could make out the figures sitting cross-legged around the small fire. He lay quietly on the dry leaves waiting for the Indians to settle in and fall asleep. Jake's heart was pounding so hard he thought they might hear it. It was a long wait, but they finally rolled up in their blankets and dozed off.

Jake waited until he could hear their breathing change to soft snoring sounds and started his very slow crawl to the side of the first Indian. The sky was beginning to lighten in the east and the crows were calling. The morning birds began their songs. One of the horses blew and whinnied but the Indians paid no attention to it. One rolled over and grumbled in his sleep. Jake slithered to within a few feet of the head of the first Indian and swung the barrel of his pa's shotgun down hard on his forehead. The sound of the man's head cracking woke the other two. The one farthest from Jake got up to one knee and Jake fired the shotgun from his hip catching him in the center of his chest. The shot punched a hole the size of his fist through the Indian and dropped him to the ground. The third man leaped to his feet and crouched like a bobcat ready to pounce, exactly what Jake wanted. Jake was confident of his strength and quickness because of his many days of wrestling with his older brother. He charged the startled Indian and knocked him to the ground with a heavy shoulder in his chest. The man had a knife ready to drive into his attacker but Jake made a fist and pounded him on the bridge of his nose. The bones in his face cracked and the man screamed in pain and dropped the knife to bring his hands to his bloody face. Jake wrapped the man's arms under his knees to trap them and make them useless to the Indian, then he hit him again on the end of his nose with his fist and splattered blood across the Indian's face.

The man was finished, his face crushed like a grape, blood from the broken bones and tissues in his face filled his eyes and blinded him. Jake laid the edge of his knife across the throat of the Indian. The man laid still, glaring at Jake's eyes, waiting for his throat to be cut.

"No, you don't git off that easy," Jake said. He put the point of the knife against the Indian's ribs and pushed it in. The sharp knife slid through the leather shirt easily and made a scraping sound as it slid across the ribs. Blood poured from the wound as the man tried to breathe. Bloody bubbles oozed from the gash. Jake said to him, "And this is for Ma." He didn't know quite what he was doing but he laid the sharp edge of the blade on the man's forehead just below the hairline and made a cut from temple to temple. Then slid the point under the scalp to raise it and slid his fingers under it and pulled. The Indian suddenly threw him off and tried to stand but Jake knocked him down with a blow to the side of his face and the man went to the ground and didn't move. Now Jake took his time peeling the scalp from the dying man's head. The Indian moaned as the scalp came off. Jake went to the other two and took their scalps. To keep a promise he'd made, he cut the bellies open and cut out their still-trembling hearts and threw them into the weeds.

He rummaged through their belongings and picked out three more knives, one stone, two steel-headed tomahawks, and three Indian bows and their arrows. Three pairs of moccasins went into one of the Indians' packs, some dried meat, and three blankets. He stuck his hand into the last pouch and felt hair. He pulled his hand out quickly. "Oh my God," he said. He reached into the pack, and took out the scalp of his mother. Then he cried. He smelled the hair and it brought back vivid pictures of his ma standing by the fireplace stirring the cookpot. He went wild. He started hacking on the dead bodies with the stone hatchet until there was nothing that could be recognized as human, cursing and swearing to kill any 'goddamned' Indian he ever saw.

After he came to his senses he picked up the packs and his mother's scalp, took the reins of the horses and tied the packs to the makeshift Indian saddle. He climbed onto one of the horses and headed back to his farm leading the other two horses. It took only two days' riding to get to the burned-out farm. There, he went to his mother's grave and buried her scalp on top of the mound of dirt. He nailed the scalps of the dead Indians to the side of the barn to let them dry before deciding what to do with them. He stayed at the farm for three days not knowing what his next move should be. He thought of trying to make something of this worthless place but couldn't stay with all the memories coming back each time he looked at something of his mother's. *Wonder where Pa is,* he thought to himself. *Hope he ain't dead. I want that privilege for myself.*

In the morning, he took the old dried up saddle his pa had hung in the barn and put it on the best-looking of the three Indian ponies. He tied his belongings, including the three scalps, behind and started to town. He pulled up in front of Mister Belleair's store and went in.

"Jake!" Mister Belleair said, looking surprised to see him. "We didn't expect to ever see you again."

"I come to pay you for the shot and powder."

"Never mind that, son. Sit down and tell me what you been up to."

"I was huntin'."

Mister Belleair looked at Jake not knowing if he should ask the obvious question. But knowing the answer, he eluded the question and said, "How'd ye do?"

"I found 'em," he said with a meanness in his eye that Mister Belleair had never seen before. "Kilt the bunch of them sons-a-bitches and took their scalps like they did Ma." Then he flipped the three scalps hanging from his belt with his fingertips. Silence filled the room.

"Jake, you sure you got the right men?"

"They had Ma's scalp. Ain't that enough proof?"

"Was they just the three of them?"

"Far as I know, but they were the same ones who was at the farm that day, I know that."

"This could be trouble for the rest of the town—you know that, don't you Jake?"

"Don't think no Injuns will be comin' around here. I left a message for them that'll keep 'em scared for a while."

"What message? Never mind, I don't think I want to know."

"Mister Belleair, I got no money but I brought three good Indian ponies— a stallion and two mares—and you kin take one of the mares for the powder and shot."

"A pony is worth a lot more than what you got from me, Jake."

"Don't matter. I got use for two horses, the other one is just baggage."

"Tell you what, Jake. I know them horses are good ones. The Injuns got the best horseflesh in the territory, so I'll take the mare and you can have that Hawken rifle there on the wall. It's been hanging there for pert'near two years and no one wants to pay money for it. It ain't new but I've shot it and it is a good one. Uses those priming caps that are so popular with hunters these days. I'll fix you up with ball, a bag of caps, and a ball mold. Wha' d'ya say?"

"Mister Belleair, like I said, that horse ain't worth nothin' to me. You don't have to do that."

"Jake, the horse will sell for more than I can git for that rifle and all the fix-ins. I won't lose nothin' on the deal, specially considerin' the demand for Hawken rifles around here. I'll sell the horse or ride her myself but I'll get nothin' for that gun. I'll come out ahead one way or the other."

"Well, if you're sure."

"I'm sure, Jake. Take the deal."

"Done," Jake said.

"Where you goin' from here, Jake?"

"Gotta go find Pa. Me and him got some things to talk about."

"I thought yer pa was dead."

"I hope not, Mister Belleair. I looked all around the place and didn't find no sign of him. I think he got away and is hiding somewhere."

"Why wouldn't he come here, Jake?"

"If yer family was killed and you wasn't, would you come to town?"

"Guess you got a point there, son. Don't know just what I'd do. Where d'ye figure yer pa might have gone?"

"It's just a guess but I figure he might go southwest to the Minnesota River Valley he and Ma talked about. Pa always said he'd like to just pull up stakes and go where the ground was good and he could make a good farm."

"Might be—I've heard there's good ground out there for free. Makes sense, Jake."

"There was a man came through here a couple of days ago headin' for Saint Cloud—calls himself Swede. The bastard stole some of my whiskey. Maybe you could hitch up with him and go south to Saint Paul."

"Nope—goin' to the valley."

"Figger'd ye would."

"Well, Mister Belleair, guess I'll be on my way. No sense standin' here jawin' about it."

Mister Belleair pulled the Hawken rifle from the wall and handed it over the counter to Jake. Then he picked up a bag of caps and showed Jake how they're used. He popped a couple of them under the hammer to show that they did what they were supposed to do and handed Jake a leather sack filled with fifty-four caliber balls.

Mister Belleair walked to the back of his small store, came out and handed Jake a cotton sack. "Here, take these with you. It's some biscuits my missus made yisterdee—ye might be needing them."

"Thanks, Mister Belleair."

They shook hands and Jake walked out the door and climbed onto the saddled pony. He took the reins of one of the mares and walked her out of town leaving the better of the two for Mister Belleair.

Not sure which way he should go, he headed to the south where he knew there was an easy trail through the hills surrounding the prairie he was leaving. After half an hour of riding he started a long climb and topped a hill. He could see nothing but more hills and lakes in his path. To his left was a long slope with few trees on it. He thought it would have been fun for him and Hawk to slide down on sleds in the winter. But those days were passed now and he shook the thought from his head and moved on.

The trail he followed was narrow and lined on both sides with oaks and maples just beginning their fall color changes, and bright red sumac brush. Breaking from the trees Jake saw a huge lake and was disappointed that he would have to spend probably three days going around it. But there was no choice to be made here—the lake told him he must. So he turned his horse to the west where he saw the edge of the lake, turned south, and was closer than the shore to the east. As he turned with the curve of the shore he saw that he had made a bad choice. The lake turned out to be two lakes joined by a narrow slip of water. The lake on the right was no more than a swamp filled with lake weeds and wild rice beds, and a river channel flowing through it. It looked to go on forever away from the big lake to his left and another large lake a half-mile away. He could go no further in this direction and contemplated turning around and trying the other route around the lake. One other option would be to swim the horses through the twenty-five-yard river channel. He'd been traveling all day so he made a camp for the night, thinking the horses would be better able to cross the river after grazing for a night.

Morning came and Jake rolled his blankets, loaded his bags on his pack-horse, saddled the stallion, and climbed aboard. He ate one of Mrs. Belleair's biscuits and heeled the horse toward the water. The horse was reluctant to enter but with a few kicks in the ribs he stepped in and waded out to deep water. The water got deep and the horse started to jump rather than swim as Jake had wanted. Unaccustomed to being on a horse he rolled backwards into the water. He held tight to his gun, knowing that was his only means of survival for the next month. He was able to grab the horse's tail and let it pull him to the other side. The other horse stayed close and Jake took a couple of kicks from the trailing animal's front hooves but it did no damage. Climbing out on the other bank Jake held tight to the horse's tail hoping it wouldn't break and run off leaving him afoot. Surprisingly, the horse climbed the bank and stood still while Jake got back into the saddle. *Must be the Indian training,* he thought to himself.

There was no hard ground for the next mile, just wet, soft bog that the horses didn't seem to notice. For days all Jake saw were hills, rivers, lakes, and trees. Some lakes were wide and long, some small, some no more than wet spots in a depression. Game was everywhere—deer to be seen anywhere the eye focused, elk, bear, buffalo, wolves, coyotes, rabbits by the thousands, and squirrels—oh, those detested squirrels. How many had he had to eat for his supper because Hawk found it more fun to shoot at small squirrel targets than the easier-to-hit deer? He also suspected that Hawk figured it easier to carry home ten squirrels than one deer.

He traveled south through the hills for two weeks fighting the water and thick brush. Then one day he realized he was coming out of the thick timber and was traveling over smoother, more rounded hills and valleys with less trees and brush. He also saw that he was dropping in elevation as he walked because of the greater distances he could see. The view went on for miles on end over perfectly flat ground that went on as far as he could see. The horizon was so far away that it was just a black line formed by the distant trees that separated the ground from the sky.

He started his decent from the top of a rise and crossed sand fields that looked a lot like the beaches of the lakes where he and Hawk would go swimming. He wondered if there had at one time been a lake here, but dismissed the idea thinking it impossible that there be a lake that big if it wasn't an ocean. The decent was gradual and he still had small hills to go around and over but he soon found himself on the plain and marveled at its utter flatness. Now he noticed the wind. It wasn't the gusty winds that blew around home—it was a steady blow from the west that didn't slow or change speed even a little. And it was strong. He had to tie his hat on his head to keep it from blowing away.

He turned south keeping the hills to his left, and in easy reach, in case he needed the cover or food. On this flat plain there was no game—nothing but grass and very little of it. To the west he saw dark clouds moving in his direction. He'd had to walk in the rain before and wasn't worried about it until he felt the ice-cold air suddenly move over him. It was late September and it was not unusual to have snow in this region at that time. He saw a grove of trees on the side of a hill and decided it would be wise to get into them for shelter in case the weather got bad. Light flakes of snow began hitting his back and the wind was picking up so he kicked his horse to get it moving faster. That seemed to be all right with the horse as he settled into the mile-eating gallop toward the trees. The wind was blowing hard now and the snow was blowing across the ground faster than his horse was running. Now the horse opened up and ran full-speed to the hills. Jake didn't feel the familiar wind in his face—instead the wind was coming from his back and was blowing faster than he was moving. The snow blowing across the ground in waves like big white snakes gave the impression that he was standing still and the ground was moving under him. They climbed the hills and were finally in the shelter of the trees when Jake slowed his horse to a walk. He found a fallen tree and made a camp under its turned-up roots. The horses turned their rumps to the wind and started grazing through the snow and fallen leaves.

The wind howled for another two hours and then went still. The ground was covered with an inch of snow and where it found a place to drift, it left long tapered lines. Jake spent the night curled up under the roots of the trees and when he awoke in the morning the sky was clear and as beautiful as only Minnesota skies can get. The air was bitter cold and the wind blew in its favorite way—hard and steady. In his haste to find cover from the weather, he'd forgotten to unpack his animals so he had to do that before he started his travels. He unpacked them and rubbed them down with handfuls of leaves and let them graze for the remainder of the day, deciding that he could use a day's rest too. He had a reasonably comfortable camp out of the wind and after he'd built a small fire, it was plenty warm. He shot a small deer and ate the liver for his evening meal then packed the rest of the meat in the skin of the deer. It was cold enough now to keep the meat from spoiling and he'd have food for a week.

Next morning, he packed up his animals, put the saddle on the mare, and walked them down out of the hills and onto the flat ground where he could make good time traveling. The wind still blew and made him feel dizzy from the steady roll of drifting snow under him. The streamers of blowing snow made Jake think of the silk shawl and headscarf his mother wore when she read the Bible at night. So fine was the weave of that shawl, so light and thin was the material that you could see right through it. It would flutter with the slightest breeze, just like the snow dancing across the ground—a thousand reading shawls dancing over the prairie.

Keeping the hills in his left eye, he walked for a full day watching them change from sand-covered to tree-covered. He walked his mount up a gradual incline until he stood on a milelong strip of sand two hundred yards wide. He got down from his pony and picked up a handful of sand. In it he saw small clamshells and tiny fish bones. *This is a beach,* he thought to himself, and looked at the flat ground stretching away from him the to west. Thoroughly puzzled he threw the sand down and looked more closely at the countryside along the line of hills south of him. Now he noticed that there were sand 'beaches' all along the sides of the hills he'd been traveling. "It's not possible," he said aloud. "How could there be a lake that big out here?" Then he remembered the stories his mother had read from the Bible. *The great flood—could this be from the great flood?* It scared him to think that story he'd considered a tall tale might be true. He wished that the snow hadn't covered the ground on the flat so he could see what the ground looked like from here. It was flat as a tabletop to the north and rough and hilly to the south with curious hills between. All the rest of the day he watched the land wondering about how these things came to be. He crossed a small stream that came out of the hills, then flowed along the front of the hills and turned north... *This stream was flowing to the north.* All of the rivers he'd seen before were flowing south and east—something else to confuse his mind.

Two more days he traveled with nothing happening to make the road less monotonous. He did notice a familiar smell in the air. It reminded him of home and being around the lakes nearby. The wind was from the northwest. The hills he'd been following were now guiding him more northwest, which wasn't where he wanted to be. He turned his mount southwest and back into the hill country. Now he found himself among lakes and streams again and the twisting turning valleys he had to follow to get through. *Was it a mistake to be in the forests again?* The traveling was much slower and a lot less comfortable in the saddle because of the hills he had to climb and descend. He moved on through the day and camped next to a small stream where he would have a fire and cook a warm meal. The horses had plenty of graze although it was much less than the green grass he would have preferred for them. The night was cold but being in the trees and out of that incessant wind made it a bit more comfortable.

In the morning, he was awake with the brightening sky, packed his horses, then resumed his trek. He traveled south for two more days over rolling hills of not much character. He shot deer for his meals—they were plentiful in this wild country. Sometimes he could put his pa's shotgun to use on ducks, geese, or partridge.

He hadn't been walking more than an hour one morning when he came to a bluff overlooking the deepest, widest valley he'd ever seen. It was hundreds of feet deep and seemed five miles wide. It stretched as far as he could see in both directions. "The Minnesota..." he whispered. He stared at the flat bottom of the valley seeing the countless small lakes and streams flowing through it. Geese by the millions flew overhead. The ponds were literally blackened by the ducks and geese on the water. The bottom was covered with trees and brush. He saw how beautiful the trees could be even with the leaves fallen and their bare branches reaching to the sky.

He was riding the stallion again. He favored that horse. He found a game trail that led along the ridge of the valley. He knew that the slope down was far too steep for his mounts to descend but he was content to stay above the scenery and marvel at its beauty. The trail suddenly turned toward the slope and led him over the edge and down. The game that made this trail must know where to go so he let the horse follow it down. The trail paralleled the ridge and descended only slightly but Jake knew he was on his way to the bottom. He came to a shelf that was a full quarter-mile of level ground and thought how this would make good farming land. He walked the horse to the edge of the terrace and looked over the valley. *Maybe I'll come back and set up a place to live,* he thought to himself. He turned the horse back to the trail he was following.

After a mile of walking, the stallion became skittish and blew a couple of times. Jake, thinking there may be trouble ahead, checked his rifle to make sure the primer cap was in place and let the horse walk on. Suddenly, two Indians on ponies rounded the curve and appeared twenty feet in front of him. They were as surprised to see him as he was to see them. Jake wrapped the reins around the saddle horn and put both hands on his rifle that rested across his thighs. The Indians glanced at his movement and knew they shouldn't do anything to upset this young, red-haired boy on the horse. Their weapons were strapped to their backs and tucked into their belts and not very handy. They were dressed in leather trousers and shirts with dirty blankets wrapped around their shoulders. They wore nothing on their heads except a feather tied in their long, greased black hair. The trail was just wide enough for two horses to pass so someone had to give—it wasn't going to be Jake. The horse rumbled and lowered his head to watch the Indians like he too was waiting for trouble to start. Jake felt the muscles on the stallion's withers tremble with anticipation. He touched his heels to the horse's flanks and he moved forward at a slow walk. The Indians parted to let him pass between them. They held Jake's eyes as he passed but said nothing and went on their way. Jake walked the pony a quarter-mile before turning him to climb fifty yards up the bluff, then he turned to watch the trail below.

Five minutes passed before he heard the sound of hooves kicking rocks on the trail. The two did exactly as Jake thought they would.

"Figured you'd be back for my horses," he whispered to himself.

He let them go on for a few minutes before tying his packhorse to a small tree and moving down the slope to get on the trail behind the Indians. Once on the trail he quickened the animals' steps, dearly wanting to catch the two would-be horse thieves. He saw them fifty yards ahead of him. The trail was crooked and he was able to approach without them seeing him. They were busy watching the ground looking for his tracks and didn't notice him until he was twenty-five yards from them. One caught him in the corner of his eye and turned on his mount with a gasp that alerted the other. Jake sat straight up in his saddle and let the horse walk toward the Indians.

He said softly, "You want my horses? Come and get 'em."

They turned on him. One of them reached for his bow but Jake jerked the Hawken to his shoulder and shot the man through the chest and he fell to the ground dead. The instant he pulled the trigger he leaned forward and heeled his horse hard and it charged at the remaining Indian at full-gallop. Jake swung his rifle and the heavy barrel connected with the man's chest and rolled him off the rump of his horse to land on his back, knocking the wind out of him. Jake pulled back on the reins and his horse planted all four feet in the dirt and dropped his rear end nearly to the ground braking to a stop. Jake jumped off as quickly as a lynx and charged the dazed Indian, knife in hand. The Indian jumped to his feet but didn't have time to pull his knife before Jake knocked him back to the ground. He pounded him with his sledgehammer fist on the bridge of the nose, crushing the bones in his face. The man screamed in pain and Jake plunged the big butcher knife into the man's chest. He took both scalps and rolled the bodies down the hill into the heavy brush. The Indians' ponies had run off but he had no use for them anyway. He thought about the horses going home without their riders and alerting more Indians but that was to his preference. Quickly he reloaded his rifle.

"Got me a regular warhorse here, I think," he said to himself.

Jake went back to get the packhorse and was once again on the trail to the bottom of the valley. He crossed two more terraces before he got to the bottom. At the foot of the slope he found a well-used path. He was aware now that he was not alone in this valley and the biggest share of his company would be Red Man. "How many?" he wondered aloud. Keeping a close eye on the trail ahead of him and watching the horse for signs of trouble, he moved slowly down the trail to the south. He could only see for short distances now for the trees and brush he was traveling through. He saw there were caves cut into the sides of the valley and planned on making one of them his shelter for a night and maybe longer. Springs of cold clear water poured from between the layers of limestone and yellow sand only to disappear again from sight as the water dropped into the thick brush to flow unseen to the river.

Now he heard shots from somewhere in the valley but couldn't tell where. The shots were far off so he didn't think they were anything to worry about and went on his way. He was hearing sounds but couldn't see anything but trees and water. Curiosity, more than fear, made him pull up into an open spot along the trail. He tied his horses and moved out on foot to see what the sounds were. He climbed the slope to get a better look around and found a well-used trail that led to the top. He climbed up the steep slope and looked over the top of a huge rock, not expecting to see a cluster of buildings with people walking around and a troop of soldiers drilling in the center of the compound. Slowly he slid backward down the slope to where he'd tied his mounts. Thoroughly confused he sat down and thought about this new development. He thought he was coming into brand new country and here he sits right below a modern, populated town with stores, homes, and soldiers.

Suddenly, he heard voices and hooves on the rocks. He slid down a bit to see what was happening before revealing himself. Two men walked by leading their horses about twenty feet from him. They were white men. He waited until he couldn't hear their voices and walked his horses out onto the trail. He led the animals up the slope to the town above, moving slowly and trying to think about what he was going to do when he came to the top. *Who would he find there?* he wondered. *Would he be welcomed or ran out? Was it all white men? Were there Indians there? Did they know about the two he'd killed a few days ago?*

He passed what he recognized as an icehouse from the water running out from beneath the walls. The horses got skittish as he passed the hayricks behind the icehouse. Another road crossed his path and he saw a building with a sign that read "Sutler". That would be where he could find the things he needed to make it through the coming winter. He had some money packed away in his bags from his trip to the store for Pa that fateful day.

He walked into the compound and looked around. He stood between two buildings, not yet ready to walk out and make himself visible. People walked about doing what they were doing and paid no attention to Jake. The soldiers he'd seen in formation earlier had been dismissed and were filing off to the barracks on the north end of the compound. *Damn,* the officer was walking right toward him. Jake stood his ground as the man walked by and nodded his head in greeting but said nothing. Jake nodded in return and watched the officer walk into the stone building to his right. The smell of fresh baked bread suddenly filled his nose. He followed the smell to the bakehouse at the east side of the grounds and apart from the rest of the buildings. Who could resist the smell of bread baking on a cool day? After tying his horses to the rail he stepped up to the open door of the small stone structure and looked in. Inside was a big man with a wooden baker's peel pulling a pair of golden brown loaves of beautifully baked bread from the oven. Inside the oven were half a dozen more just as tempting as the first two. Meaning to get the baker's attention, Jake cleared his throat, "Ahem."

"I see ya," the baker said with a growl. "Been a long time since ye had fresh baked bread?"

"Um, yes sir—a long time."

"Well, there's some rolls on the table yonder. Have one, but don't get greedy. Men around here might take offense at you eating their bread like that."

With trembling hands Jake took one of the still-warm rolls and passed it under his nose, inhaling the aroma of fresh bread like Ma made in her make-shift oven.

"Well don't play with yer food, boy, eat it. Didn't yer mother teach you nothin'?" the baker said with a playful smile. Jake wolfed the roll down and went to the water barrel to wash it down.

"Have another. Nothin' more pleasing than watching a young man enjoy the fruits of my labors. New to this country, son?"

"Yeah, just found this place. Where am I anyway?"

"Called Fort Ridgely. More like a trading post than a fort but we like it."

"I thought forts had walls around them."

"Most of 'em do, but I guess they never figured they'd need one around this fort since the Injuns ain't no problem. Some chief down in Ioway called Ink pa duta causin' problems for the settlers and farmers but don't expect them to be any trouble to us."

Jake stared at the rolls on the table while he listened to the baker chatter.

"I heard there was some Indian trouble up in Otter Tail River country a few months ago, but that's a hunnert miles from here. Well, have another roll before ye start droolin' all over 'em," the baker barked. "Chippaways up there, we got all Sioux around here. They get into it now and then with the Chippaways but they keep their disagreements to themselves for the most part, and do their fighting away from the white people. Say, I heard some Chippaways done in a couple of Sioux north of here just recently. Found their bodies in the brush."

Jake walked to the water pail again.

"Scalped they was, so folks figured it was Chippaways what done it. One of 'em had his face caved in and they think he musta fell from his horse on a rock or something. Got the Sioux a little fidgety about how that face got crushed like it was. They get spooked by things like that, ye know."

"Tell me what you know about the trouble up in Otter Tail country."

"You know about Otter Tail, son?"

"Yeah, some. Knew some folks lived up there."

"Don't know anything more than the Indians raided a farm and killed the family—but then that's just stories. I heard too, that one of the sons of the family found the culprits and done 'em in. Who's to know what the real story is. People like to make these stories sound more exciting by adding things that ain't quite true, ye know."

"Yeah, s'pose yer right about that," Jake said. "Thank you for the bread, guess I'd better get goin'. Got places I need to be. Say, you ain't seen a short older man around—might be riding a gray mule, dark red hair, mean disposition?"

"That could be any one of a dozen men around here, son. Guess you'll just have to find the one you're lookin' for by lookin' at him."

"Thanks, Mister…ummm."

"Blodget. Bill Blodget. Private, U.S. Army.

"Yer in the Army?"

"Yep, best duty in the fort. They pay me and my helper twenty cents more a day and I don't have to do that soldier stuff out there on the playgrounds."

"Playgrounds?"

"Yeah, that's what I call the parade ground where the officers like to play soldier."

"Thanks again, Mister Blodget. Be seeing ya."

"Son, want some advice?"

"Never hurts to hear advice."

"If I were you I'd hide those scalps you're carrying there. Might be some Injun who don't think kindly of his kin's hair on display like that."

"S'pose yer right. I'll put 'em otta sight."

He walked out of the bakery, took his horses' reins, and led them across the parade field. He felt a little more at ease now that he found a friendly face. He stopped a man and asked him where he might find some lead for making ball.

"Just walk between the commissary and the officers' quarters, past the guard house to the sutler's store. They'll have what you need." Thankfully, the man pointed at the buildings he was talking about or Jake would have had no idea where he should go. He didn't know what a commissary was or an officers' quarters.

"Thanks," he said, and he walked on.

He stepped into the store and was completely ignored by the man behind the counter. He looked around for a bit and seeing that he wasn't going to be asked what he wanted he said, "Got any lead?"

"Just hold yer horses. Cain't ye see I'm busy?"

"Yeah, I can see yer too damned busy to take my money. I'll go somewhere else."

"Ain't nowhere else—ye want lead, ye buy it here."

"That why you got that nasty way of talking, 'cause you think people need you? Well maybe some need you but I don't."

He walked out the door right into an Indian who was walking in. It startled Jake and the Indian both. Jake had never been that close to an Indian before and was ready to defend himself. The Indian sensed it and kept a close eye on Jake as he moved around him. The storekeeper came out and stepped between the two men to make sure nothing unpleasant happened. The Indian had a calm but fearless look about him, like a man who could handle himself in a confrontation. He nodded at Jake and walked by him then went into the store. He was dressed in white man's clothing and had his hair cut just below the ears and combed like a white man.

"New around here, ain't cha?" a voice said from behind him.

"Yeah."

"Give ye some advice…"

"Oh good, more advice," Jake said.

"This is worth hearing, my friend. That there is John Other Day. He's a farmer Injun—got a farm up by the Upper Agency. But he's a farmer only because he's smart enough to know that he gets better treatment from the Agent for going along with what they tell him. He ain't stupid, and he ain't all White. He's just as mean and tough as any Injun you're likely to meet up with around here. And he'll kill just as easy as any other Injun. Fact is, since he took to farmerin' he ain't killed no white men, just a couple of other Injuns. He's what they call a friendly Indian."

"Ain't no such thing as a friendly Indian," Jake said glaring into the store.

"What's yer name, friend?"

"Jacob Owen."

"Well, Jacob Owen, you'd do well to make a friend of Mister Other Day. You'll live to be glad you did."

Just then John Other Day walked out of the store. He walked up to Jake and said, "Have a good day, my friend," tipped his wide-brimmed hat, and strolled away. Jake watched him leave and wondered if there was a possibility that he could have an Indian for a friend.

"You want some lead, boy? Come in here and see what I got," the storekeeper yelled out from inside. Jake turned and walked into the store.

"I need fifty-four caliber balls, or lead to make some."

"Got 'em both. Bar lead is cheaper but balls is a lot more handy in a pinch."

"Gimme the bar lead. I still got plenty balls and can make some when I find a place to hole up. Got powder?"

"Yep, got all the powder you need. Dupont, best there is. Say listen, I got some new bullets that they're using in the war down South, called Minie balls. Ye don't need to patch your shots, just drop the bullet down the bore, seat it tight on the powder and yer ready to shoot."

"Can ye hit anything with 'em?"

"Haven't tried them myself, but they say they're better than a patched ball 'cause the powder spreads the skirt on the back of the ball out into the riflings and makes for a tighter seal for the gasses."

Jake had no idea what the hell the man was talking about so he said, "Well, I'll just stick with what I've been using."

"Suit yourself."

Jake took a bag of one hundred balls, paid the man, and started for the door. But he stopped and turned around, "That Indian just left here—they say he's a friendly Indian. That true?"

"You don't step on his toes and he won't bother you. But you give him half a reason and he'll jump down yer throat and kick your guts out your asshole."

"Guess that tells it straight out." Jake paused, "...What war down South?"

"Where you been, boy? Don't you know about Mister Lincoln fighting the rebels in the South?"

"Um...oh, that war," he said, still not knowing but not wanting to look too ignorant.

Jake walked out the door, grabbed his mounts, and rode down the steep trail to the bottom of the valley. It was getting dark now and he needed to find a place to hole up for the night. The cave in the rocks he'd seen a quarter-mile back would do for the night. He got to the cave after dark and unpacked his horses and hobbled them in a small field of grass just above the cave. His shelter for the night was only big enough for him to lie on the ground stretched out with his packs beside him. He knew that in cold weather a small shelter is better because it heats easier. He built a small fire at the entrance and that gave enough heat for him to get comfortable and lay down to sleep.

He woke up as the sun was turning the eastern sky a dull gray. The air had an uncomfortable bite to it. He rolled out of his blankets and looked out the opening of his cave. A two-inch layer of new snow blanketed the world outside and was still coming down in small light flakes. Jake had always liked the first snowfall and this was no different. All the world was covered in pure white. The air was cold and clear and felt good as he sucked in the freshness. He walked out into the snow and stretched his arms high and wide to let the air into his coat and freshen his body. Then he looked at the ground and saw footprints. They were boot prints so he figured it was a white man. If so, nothing to worry about. The tracks didn't stop at his camp but went right on by. Whoever it was probably didn't know he was in the cave. He looked up and saw his horses were still in the meadow where he'd left them so everything seemed to be all right. The thought of someone being so close to him while he slept made him uncomfortable. It could just as easily have been horse thieves—or worse, scalp hunters—who walked by and he would have been an easy victim.

"Time to find more suitable accommodations," he said to himself.

He fetched his horses and loaded the packs onto one. Then he saddled the other and rode up the hill to Fort Ridgely. His first stop was the store where he ran into the friendly Indian. He walked in and the storekeeper looked up and greeted him, "Good morning, Mister Owen."

"How'd you know my name?"

"Word gets around fast when a new person comes to town."

"I don't remember telling anyone my name."

"You told that fella you were talking to yesterday in front of the store. Everyone in earshot heard and knows your name. A man bucks up against John Other Day and people stop to watch. What can I do for you, Mister Owen?"

"Gonna be needing some good winter boots and some warm wool trousers to wear. Might have to replace these long underwear too, if you got some, and wool stockings."

"Got all that right here, but the boots are a bit costly. The soldiers buy 'em as fast as I can get them. You'd be best off to see about gittin' some of those winter moccasins the Indians wear. If you find the right squaw you can get them for a song. And for what you're doing they're much better than heavy boots."

"And just what do you think it is I'm doing?"

"Don't know partic'lar what you're doing, but I do know you ain't farming or working the riverboats or cutting wood so you ain't doin' nothing that you need working boots. Yer gonna live alone and moccasins are the best thing for you."

"Got it all figured out, don't ye?"

"Nothin' to figure out, son, when a man like you comes here lookin' for something and it ain't work. You couldn't work for wages any more than I can fly. What you're doing and where you're going ain't none of my business, or anyone else's, but some things about a man just don't need to be wondered about."

The storekeeper put Jake's purchases into a sack and Jake paid him what it cost and started for the door. He loaded his bundle onto the packhorse and walked them toward the road to the river.

A rider came up alongside him from behind and said, "Good morning, Mister Owen." Jake turned and saw John Other Day sitting in a black buggy pulled by a black horse. He was dressed in a flat-topped hat and a black woolen coat with a silk scarf around his neck.

"Umm…g'morning, Mister umm…"

"I am John Other Day, Mister Owen. I have my camp north of where you spent last night."

"You know where I spent the night?"

"Yes, Mister Owen. I'm surprised everyone in this valley doesn't know where you spent the night."

"Really, and why is that?"

"You sound like an angry bear when you sleep."

"You telling me I snored?"

"If that is what it is called when you growl through your nose, yes you do. And very loudly, I might add."

"Guess I'll have to find someplace a little more secret to sleep from now on."

"You need to learn how to sleep, Mister Owen. You must sleep as much during the day as you do at night, then you don't sleep as deeply as you did last night and men can't walk by your camp without you knowing it."

"Those were your tracks I saw in the snow this morning?"

"Yes, they were mine. You have little to worry about with bad Indians near the fort but if you get away from here you must be alert at all times or you will, at the very least, lose your horses. Mister Owen, many have seen the scalps you wear on your belt. I will tell you now…hide them or bury them. You have Chippewa scalps and Sioux scalps. It is not my concern how you got them but there are men who will not let it go if they have lost friends or family. Some say you are the one who killed the two men on the trail two weeks ago. If it is true, or not, there will be men who will want to find out and avenge their friends. The two who were killed were from a band of troublemakers. Everyone knows that and it is no surprise to anyone that they are dead. But there will be those who were their friends and they will be dangerous to you."

"Those men would have killed me and taken my horses."

"As I said, those men needed killing. But you will have trouble. You can never let your guard down or you will die."

"Mister Other Day, is there an outhouse close by?"

"Yes, right over there behind those buildings," he pointed, "but they are mostly used by the women."

"Perfect," Jake said. "I'll be right back."

Jake went into the outhouse and came out in just a few seconds. When John Other Day saw him come out without the scalps on his belt he laughed out loud.

"Ye don't need to tell anyone who killed those men but do tell them where their scalps are."

"Mister Owen, you may call me John. I doubt you will have much trouble from anyone." John Other Day laughed and rode away.

For three days Jake rode up the valley looking for the terrace he crossed on his way in. Several times he saw Indians riding trails below him but they were far enough away so they couldn't see him and his horses. He kept a close eye on the trail behind him and paid special attention to his horse for any signs of danger. The trail crossed directly through the terrace. Because of this, Jake decided it was an unsafe place to make his home. He turned his mount up the hill along a game trail to a spot about fifty feet above the flat ground. He tied his horses and went for a walk into the brush and trees looking for his home. He found some small limestone caves, but nothing that would be big enough for him so he remounted and moved further up the valley.

He crossed a small stream rushing down the hill and followed it upstream to where it issued from a cave in the valley wall. The cave was about fifteen feet wide and just high enough for him to stand without ducking his head. There was a level stretch of ground above it for his horses to find feed. The cold, clear stream coming out of the cave would supply plenty of water. He unloaded his gear from the horses and commenced building his house. He gathered wrist-sized branches that he stripped of their smaller limbs and stood them at the entrance to the cave. Then he found brush to lay over the frame to conceal the cave. The trail to his shelter passed a hundred yards below him and circled back to his cave so no one could possibly get to him without being seen. He found stones to make a fire pit inside the cave and there were plenty of dry fallen trees for firewood. Jake had his home for the winter. He settled in and busied himself hauling hay for the horses when the weather turned bad. For now he could put them in the field above his shelter to graze and forage for themselves. He cut small trees and circled the horse pasture about fifty yards square with a fence of saplings.

That evening, a deer strolled by and provided his dinner for the next few weeks. The sound of his rifle echoed through the valley and made Jake aware that if he planned on staying secret for very long he'd have to do his hunting away from his camp. Then he thought about the Indian bows he's been carrying around for some reason. He pulled one out of his pack and examined it, not really knowing what he was looking at, but he had some idea how it was used. He took it out, strung it up, and chose a dark spot on the side of the hill for his target. He put the arrow on the string and laid it across his thumb, pulled the string back, and released it. The arrow fell to the ground. *Hmm,* he thought to himself, *might be more to this than I figured.* He picked up the arrow and tried again with the same results. *Maybe I need to find someone to show me how this is done.* He kept trying until he could get the arrow to fly out from the bow in the general direction he chose, but couldn't make it hit his target. He worked hard to learn the bow and by the end of the day he was hitting reasonably close to the spot on the hill he aimed at, though still not good enough with the new weapon for it to be of any use to him. He put the bow back into his pack and went inside for the night.

It was cold sleeping in that cave and the fire he'd built had long since gone out. His shivering made sleep hard to come by, but according to Mister John Other Day he shouldn't sleep that soundly anyway, so he decided it was all right. Twice he woke himself up with a snore. *Gotta do something about that,* he thought. During the night he heard one of the horses blow and whinny. He got out of the cave to see what it was, but found nothing, so he went back to bed.

The next day he took the stallion, saddled it, and headed toward the trail to Fort Ridgely. When he rode off, the mare whinnied sharp and loud and ran in circles, not wanting to be left alone. Jake pulled the rails away from the corral and walked his mount down the trail with the mare following close behind. He knew now that his horses were his and he wouldn't have to go looking for them if they walked off. It only took a day and a half to get to the fort. He knew the trail now and didn't have to search for the fort.

"Morning, Mister Owen. What can I do for ye?"

"Don't need anything right now, Mister Umm…"

"Ben Randal, sutler here at the fort."

"I was just kinda wanderin' around getting familiar with the place. Might need to know something about it someday."

"Good idea, Jake. Never hurts to know folks when times get tough."

"John Other Day been around?"

"Y'ain't got nothin' to worry about with Mister Other Day. He's a peaceable sort."

"Not worried about him—he's just an interesting character."

"That he is. He was in just yesterday and when he comes to the fort he usually stays for a while and visits the Indians in their camps. Mighty educated man, Mister Other Day. Even got his self a white wife and a half-breed kid runnin' around his place."

"Yer shittin' me right? Ain't no white woman gonna marry a Injun."

"Not kidding at all, it's all true. He married a gal from out East when he went to see the president. Lady of the night, she was back there, but no one around here cares about that. Mister Other Day is well respected in the community."

"I'll be damned, never heard of such a thing. Well where can I find Mister Other Day about now?"

"I think you know where the bakehouse is."

"Oh yeah, I know where that is."

"Well, walk past that and you'll find a bunch of Indians on the bank of the ravine. John will be there."

"Thanks, Ben. Be seein' ye."

"Hang onto that perty red hair, Jake. Make a right fine decoration for some brave's tepee."

"Heard that twice now—don't care to hear it no more." Jake walked out the door. He strolled to the bakehouse and poked his head in and said, "Good morning, Bill the Baker."

"Hey, Jake, good to see you still got that red hair on yer head." Jake shook his head and ignored the comment. Joe reached to the table and tossed Jake a fresh roll, "On the house."

"Thanks Bill—love these fresh rolls," and he bit into it.

"Have a good day, Mister Blodget."

"You too, Jake. And please, drop the 'Mister' bullshit."

He walked to the edge of the ravine and saw about fifteen Indians sitting on the ground wrapped in blankets listening to John Other Day. He was talking in what Jake figured to be Sioux. He caught John's eye. John nodded his greeting and kept on talking. Jake was too uncomfortable being so close to so many Indians so he nodded his head to John and walked off, back to the fort.

"Good day, sir," someone said from the street.

"Umm, yeah. Good day."

"I'm Doctor Muller, the post surgeon. You'll be Jake Owen?"

"Yes."

"Heard about you almost giving me some business a coupl'a weeks ago. I don't mind the money but I'd just as soon patch up skinned knees and the butcher's bloody fingers than try to re-attach a scalp."

"I'll remember that," Jake said and walked away. He was tired of hearing about that little thing with John Other Day and had decided to ignore any more comments about it. The doctor stood embarrassed by his poorly-timed comments.

Jake walked to the outer parts of the fort where he saw a group of Indian boys playing target practice with their bows. He'd seen it before but this time he thought it might be a good opportunity to learn something about it. He stood away from them, not wanting to get in too close, and watched. The boys were hitting their targets with amazing regularity and it made Jake wonder if only Indians could do it that well.

"Good morning, Mister Owen." The voice from behind him made him jump and his heart leaped into his chest. "I'm sorry, Mister Owen. I didn't mean to startle you," John Other Day said.

"Well ye damn sure did. I didn't hear ye comin'."

"You're interested in seeing the boys with their bows?"

"Kinda."

"Well, let's go over and see."

"I need to learn to shoot the bow—the rifle makes too much noise and I will be needing meat this winter."

"Do you have a bow?"

"Yes, on my horse."

"May I see it?"

Jake walked to his horse and pulled the bow from the bag and handed it to John. John laughed.

"This is not a bow—a Chippewa made this. This is a stick. Come over here, you will see a bow."

They walked over to where the boys were playing. John walked up to an adult Indian and asked to see his bow. He handed it to John and John handed it to Jake.

"This is a bow—a Sioux bow. Pull it and you will see the difference."

Jake pulled the string back about halfway and let it down.

"So?"

John said, "Pull it back all the way."

Jake hooked the string with his fingers and pulled it back as far as it would go and held it for a few seconds until his arms started to quiver. It pulled much harder than his Chippewa bow. It was shorter but had wider limbs. It had strings of sinew glued to the back and was decorated with tufts of fur halfway up each limb, and a turkey feather tied to the end.

"I see what you mean."

"You can pull this bow as far as your arms will allow without worrying about it breaking. The sinew on the back is from a horse—it gives it more flex and more power. Take that Chippewa stick and throw it in the river or trade it for something useful—a knife perhaps."

"I have plenty of knives."

"If you have knives to trade you might be able to take this bow home with you."

"I have six knives in my pack that I will trade."

"You have much to learn about trading too, Jake. Offer him one."

Jake walked to his horse and picked out one knife and walked back to the Indian.

"I will give you this knife for this bow."

"He doesn't speak English, Jake."

"Well how the hell do I make a trade if he don't speak English?"

"It is all done with signs. You never speak when making a trade. The Indians trade with people from many different tribes and they have to know how to trade even with people who speak a completely different language. He knows what you're offering."

The Indian made a gesture indicating that he would not make the trade and Jake recognized it as such. He motioned with two fingers, "Two knives."

"No."

Jake walked back to the horse and brought out the stone club he'd taken from the Chippewas back in Otter Tail County and offered it to the Indian. Now the man showed some interest. He pointed to the club and the two knives. Jake motioned "No" and pointed to the club and one knife. The Indian wanted both knives and the club.

John Other Day watched with a slight smile on his face.

Jake signed, "The club and one knife."

"No, club and two knives."

Jake shook his head and picked up the two knives and the club and started toward his horse. The Indian grunted at him. Jake turned around and the man signed, "One knife and the club." Jake handed the items to the man and they each nodded their acceptance of the trade.

The Indian said something to John in Sioux.

"He wants that other knife. What do you want for it?"

"I don't know—what does he have to offer?"

"Deal with him."

By now there was a crowd gathered around watching the trade session. Jake held the knife up and opened one hand to the side to ask what he had to trade. The Indian looked him up and down and held his finger up to indicate "Wait here." He walked off and came back in a few minutes with a pair of moccasins. He pointed at Jake's sorry-looking footwear and smiled. Jake wanted those moccasins but he also knew that he couldn't just accept the trade as offered, so he indicated "No." The Indian looked at him as if he didn't believe what he had just seen. He knew the moccasins were worth more than the knife and Jake refusing them confused him. He motioned "…What?" Jake pointed at the badgerskin hat on the man's head, "No" was the reply. Jake pulled out another knife and offered it to him. The man looked at it for a few seconds and indicated he wanted more. Jake signed "No." Then the Indian handed Jake the moccasins and pulled the hat from his head and handed it to Jake. They each nodded. Jake stuck out his hand and the man looked at it for a second before taking it.

"You did very well trading with him, Jake."

"Did it all the time with Mister Belleair back home."

"You got took, you know."

"I did?"

"Sure. Those things he traded you are easily obtained by a Sioux. He makes the bow when he has nothing else to do, and the women make the moccasins and the hat. You see, the white man puts a monetary value on his time because he thinks he has so little of it. Indians have little more to do than sit and make things with their hands and trade stories. All of their time is theirs to use as they please."

Jake looked up and saw his trading friend walking out of his tepee wearing another badgerskin hat just like the one he'd just traded to Jake. He smiled smugly at Jake as he walked by.

"Mister Owen, two things Indians love—trading and gambling—and any trade that makes both parties happy is a good one. You did very well and you have made friends here today."

"I guess it is possible to have Indian friends," Jake said to himself under his breath.

The boys pulled on Jake's arms wanting him to come over and shoot with them. One of the boys handed Jake an arrow and motioned for him to shoot at the straw pile target. Jake strung the arrow and pulled the bow back and let it go. The arrow went over the target and sailed off onto the prairie under the grass. The boys slapped their knees laughing loudly at the shot. Jake was a little embarrassed but then laughed along with them. Another boy handed him an arrow and Jake loaded the bow and pulled it back. Before he could let it go, one of the boys touched his arm without looking at him and pressed it down lowering Jake's aim. He let it go and the arrow hit the straw pile—another round of laughter.

Jake watched the boys shoot and realized that they didn't aim as you would a rifle, but simply raised their bows and pointed them downrange and more often than not, hit their target. He saw that they never even looked at the bows, not even when stringing an arrow. They looked only at the target. That must be the secret—concentrate on the target. So he did. At once he started hitting his target more often. Now the boys were not laughing, but watching intently as Jake began shooting almost as well as they had.

Jake noticed an Indian woman standing off to one side watching the activities. She was not what he would call pretty but at the same time she had a look that caught his attention. She was tall and muscular-looking. Her face showed a woman who laughed easily but at this time she wasn't laughing. She had a look of concern. She walked over to where John and Jake were standing and talked to John for a few minutes then walked away.

Jake watched her walk away and asked John, "Who's that?"

"She is called Sisoka. She is the daughter of the man who just took advantage of your trading skills. She also wanted to know who you are."

"And you told her?"

"As much as I know. Don't worry she is not looking for a husband. I don't know much about you, Mister Owen, and what I do know, I don't think you want others to hear. I have a place I have to go, Mister Owen. There is a man in the fort that bears watching. You should know who he is too, so come in when you are finished here and you will see him."

"I'll just walk with you."

"That will be fine. I will not be talking to him nor will I introduce you. He knows me and I know him but that is as far as it goes with us. He knows I am here watching him and he will not stay long."

They walked back into the compound and found a bench to sit on. The man that John Other Day was watching was in the commissary when they sat down. Soon he came out and looked their way. He stopped and looked directly at Jake—as if he knew him—then turned to the left and walked down the path toward the road that lead to the river.

"That, Mister Owen, is Tao ya te duta. He is a chief of the Mdewakanton Sioux. He's called Little Crow. He is friends with the Whites, goes to white man's church, lives in a house like a White, but he is Indian all the way through. He talks with his mouth but what comes out does not come from his heart. The Sioux do not think of him as a chief but he became Chief by defeating his brothers in a fight over it. They planned to have him shot so one of the other brothers could be Chief but the plan failed. A bullet fired by one of his attackers went through both wrists and crippled him but he survived. The gloves he wears hide the wounds. He is a powerful warrior and you should avoid him. His followers are the ones you will have to watch out for. They are of the Lower Sioux Agency and are very restless because of the way the Agents there treat the Indians."

"Lower Agency? Where's that?"

"Northwest of here a half day's ride. You will know it well if you stay in this valley."

"Maybe I should go there and see for myself what's there."

"You are a curious man, Mister Owen. It may get you in trouble someday."

"Yeah, well, you can never know too much about where you are, John." John nodded his head in agreement. "But maybe another time. I'm going back to my digs."

He stored his trades in his packsack and mounted the horse. He rode off down the hill to the valley floor, turned right, and started the long ride back to his cave. He rode until dark and reined his horse into an opening where he knew there was a small cave in the wall of the valley. He stayed there until morning.

Not comfortable with the road he was on, Jake turned uphill and found the trail he'd used before and followed it. The ride was quiet for most of the day and he relaxed as he let the horse have the reins to take him home. The mare following him whinnied softly and trotted up close behind Jake and his stallion. Jake wrapped his hands around the Hawken on his lap, thinking there might be a bear or wolf nearby. Then the stallion started to act up. Jake touched him with his heels to quicken the animal's pace and the trailing horse whinnied softly right behind him. He knew now that something was wrong. Maybe they were being followed. Maybe there was a wolf close by. Either way, Jake knew things were about to get exciting.

The mare suddenly took off and trotted past Jake a few feet, then stopped to let them catch up. Jake turned and looked behind him and at that instant he heard the yells of six braves on horseback as they spotted him on the trail. Knowing there was no point in trying to best six Indians, he grabbed the saddle horn and kicked his horse, sending him into a wide-open gallop down the trail. The stallion ran faster than Jake had ever seen him go. His hooves drumming on the hard-packed trail, legs stretching out full to the front and back, running like a wild horse from a pack of wolves. The cold wind blowing in Jake's face made his eyes water and he found himself letting the horse do the guiding. He turned to look behind him and saw that he was gaining distance between himself and his attackers, but not enough for comfort. The Indians had passed his packhorse and were whipping their horses, yelling and yipping as they chased him. Suddenly his horse turned off the trail and leapt over the edge of an eight-foot drop. Jake instinctively grabbed the saddle horn, leaned back to brace against the landing, and hung on tight until the horse hit the ground ten feet from where he left it. *Good God*, Jake thought to himself, *this horse is going to kill us both!* But when the horse hit the ground his hooves didn't miss a beat. He lowered his head, stretched out his neck, and opened up into a full gallop through the brush, grass, and trees. Jake laid his head behind the horse's neck and hung on. The Indians behind him tried to stop their horses, but the riders behind were not ready for what was ahead, and ran into them—pushing the entire pack over the bank. Horses rolled over the men, uprooting small trees. Dirt, sand, and snow flew as they tumbled down the hill. They stopped in a tangle of horses and men. Tree limbs struck Jake on the legs and shoulders nearly ripping his clothes off as the crazy horse plunged through the underbrush. He was running full-gallop downhill and Jake thought for sure the horse would lose his footing and they would both be killed.

Finally, the horse slowed to a canter, eyes wide and his head turning halfway around as if to see if he was safe. Jake sat up in the saddle and surveyed the situation. He'd outrun the Indians and still had his red hair, but he didn't have his packhorse. *That will never do*, he said to himself, *I've got the best horse in the valley and I'll be damned if I'll let some Injun have his mare.* He let the horse find its way to his shelter in the rocks and set himself to planning on getting his horse back.

In the morning, Jake got out the bow he'd gotten in the trade and walked up to a white sand bank that he thought would be soft enough for a practice target. Shooting the bow was the primary activity for the next week until he could hit a two-inch circle at most any range and from any position. His pulling arm got stronger and the bow pulled easier everyday. He could hold it at full draw for several minutes now without the shaking and quivering he'd experienced that first day of shooting. That morning, a small deer walked near his camp. Since he was running short of meat he decided this would be the time to try the bow. He pulled the string back, pointed the arrow at the deer, and let it go. The arrow flew straight and hit the deer in the center of its chest, sending a smacking sound back to Jake. It went all the way through and stopped in the trunk of a birch tree twenty feet beyond the deer. The deer ran for a few feet, then stopped to look around, and promptly fell to its knees and died. Pleased with his success he skinned the deer, cut the meat into small enough pieces to make a decent meal, and stored it in the cache pit he'd dug next to his cave.

Time to start his search for his horse. *Where do I start? Follow their tracks? Too many tracks to follow.* He decided to go to the fort and ask where the Indians were camped. *Might as well take the direct approach,* he thought to himself.

"Well, Mister Owen, good to see you. What can we do for you this fine day?" Ben Randal said when Jake walked into the store.

"Wonderin' where the Indians are camped. Any ideas?"

"Which ones? They're all around here and up around the Lower and Upper Agencies. They got camps all over the place. You lookin' for a particular bunch?"

"Just lookin' for my packhorse. Bunch of Injuns got her last week and I want her back."

"They steal her from your pasture?"

"No. Had a race with six of them and my packhorse lost."

"That all they were after—your horse?"

"I don't think so. I think they wanted this red scalp, too."

"What makes you think that?"

"If they wanted only the horse they would have taken it when they caught it, but they kept on my trail till I lost 'em in the brush."

"Word is out that yer the one who killed those two a while back, and it might be the Injuns want revenge."

"Could be, but they ain't gonna get this scalp for free—it'll cost 'em dearly. If you was lookin' for your horse where would you start, Mister Randal?"

"Talk to yer friend Mister Other Day. He might know where it is."

"Has he been in?"

"Not for a week or so. Been expecting him anytime though. He's pretty reg'lar with his visits with the Injuns."

Jake got quiet and asked Mister Randal, "What day is this, Mister Randal?"

"Been in the hills for a while, huh Jake? It's Tuesday, December twenty-fourth—Christmas tomorrow."

"Christmas. Damn, hadn't given that any thought. Oh well, no one around here to do Christmas with anyway. Thanks Mister Randal, have a nice Christmas."

"Uh, Jake—you could come have Christmas dinner with me and the family if you like. My wife puts on a fine table."

"Thanks, Mister Randal. I appreciate the offer, but guess I'll just wander on back to my digs. Think I'll take the long way home—do some thinking."

The men shook hands and Jake walked out the door. Mister Randal didn't say Merry Christmas. He knew Jake's Christmas was not going to be a merry one.

A deep sense of loneliness came over Jake. He took the road that led south toward Saint Peter. He'd never been there, but on this day he wasn't particular where he ended up. On Christmas Day, he rode through a town called Courtland without stopping. Chances of him finding his horse were slim at best, and if he did find her it would be purely accidental because he had no idea where to start looking. A light snow started to fall. The wind was just a slight breeze and the snow on the ground sparkled like a million diamonds. It was getting toward evening now and he walked his horse slowly along the road. The world turned a beautiful, deep blue. It made him homesick and he fought to keep the tears from running down his cheeks. He wanted to be with Ma and Pa and Hawk to celebrate Christmas.

Christmas was never a big event around the Owen house, or anyone else's house for that matter. No one in Otter Tail County had money enough to have a big Christmas. Mostly they made some little item for each family member's gift. Hawk had made Jake a whistle from a turkey leg bone. Jake whittled Hawk a figure of a horse's head from a stick of firewood. Ma made shoes for everyone, or a shirt or pants. Pa never did get into the Christmas spirit. He said it was kid stuff to be passing out presents. But he took the things they all made for him and was tickled to get them.

Jake had never felt such loneliness. The world was silent as death. It felt as if the whole world had disappeared and he was riding in an empty place with not one thing to make life worthwhile. His chest felt like a big empty box. He smelled wood smoke from somewhere upwind and that too brought memories of his home in Otter Tail County. It reminded him of splitting wood out by the barn while Ma cooked the Christmas dinner over the fire in the stone fireplace. This was a tough night for Jake—all of the memories from home came to him at once. Having the thought of Christmas drop on him suddenly like that made it hard. If he'd kept note of the days he could have been prepared for this season and it wouldn't have been so hard to handle.

"So ungodly silent," he said to his horse. The only sound was his horse's hooves on the snow. He turned his mount toward the smell of wood smoke. The stallion raised his head and tested the air and gave a soft whinny.

As they climbed over a rise, Jake saw a camp of Indians. There were six tepees and a few people walking around bundled in blankets. He was a good hundred yards from the camp and they hadn't yet seen him. He stopped his horse and watched the camp for a few minutes. A herd of horses grazed in the field on the northside of the camp. Jake looked very carefully through the herd hoping to spot his packhorse. "Damn," he said. "They're all the same color, how the hell am I gonna know mine from theirs—if mine is even there?" He leaned over to his horse's head, patted him on the neck, and said, "Would you know her if you saw her?" The horse only looked toward the camp. *It's now or never,* he thought to himself.

He pulled the cap off the nipple on his rifle and replaced it with a fresh one, heeled the stallion, and walked him down the hill toward the Indian camp. He was fifty yards from it when one of the women spotted him. She ran to a tepee and brought out a man wrapped in a red capote striped with black. Jake walked his horse directly into the camp, keeping his hand on his rifle. The Indians came out of their tepees and watched this big, redheaded young man in the badgerskin hat walk quietly through their camp. The women with kids kept them close, and the ones who had babies held them tight to their bosoms. No one seemed the least bit uncomfortable with the intrusion, but watched Jake move through their midst. An older man looked at Jake and nodded a silent greeting. Jake nodded back. Two young girls giggled and whispered to each other. One of them looked at him from under her hooded coat with black eyes that offered more of a challenge than friendliness. It was Sisoka. He walked straight through to the horse herd, hoping his stallion would be able to pick out the mare. He walked past a guard standing close to the horses who watched him as he went by, then through the herd. None of the horses made any indication of knowing Jake or his stallion, so he kept on walking down the road and back to the valley.

"Well horse, let's go home." The stallion walked with an easy, mile-eating stride. Jake tied the reins to the saddle horn and let the horse take the lead. This was the first time Jake had actually fallen asleep in the saddle. The swaying of the horse made it almost impossible to stay awake, except when he'd wake up with a jolt thinking he was falling off. It was getting late and Jake was tired so he decided it was time to pull in somewhere and roll up in his blankets for some real sleep. He reined the horse into a thicket of hazel and willow where he would be somewhat hidden from any passersby. He wrapped a blanket around himself, sat down against a tree, and went to sleep. His horse was tied with a long rope to Jake's blanket. If the horse got too far away he would pull Jake's blanket off and wake him. That worked very well, except Jake got no sleep—so he untied the horse from his blanket and tied him to a tree with a long rope.

During the night, the air turned bitter cold and Jake had to get out of his blankets and ride through the night to his cave. When he got there he built a fire and wrapped himself in blankets again and tried to get warm. The fire took the hardness out of the cold but he'd taken a chill in his bones and couldn't stop shivering. Christmas night was not a good night for Jacob Owen. He slept little and feared freezing to death. But the morning came and he awoke to a bright sun, clear sky, and bitter cold. He went about gathering more wood for his fire and laid it in the cave for the next night. He kept his shelter warm hoping that if he got the walls of the cave warm it would be easier to warm it later. He also brought more stones in and laid them by the fire to get warm. All of this work paid off as the nights were spent in relative comfort from then on.

He stayed in his shelter for a week trying in vain to keep track of the days. One afternoon, he heard a volley of shots coming from the direction of the fort. It made him uneasy until he counted the days back and realized it was New Year's Day, 1862. He was getting restless from being in the cave for so many days so he picked up his rifle and climbed the valley wall to see what was above him. It was a long hard climb and he decided he should have left his heavy rifle at home. When he reached the top he looked around and saw nothing but trees. Behind him he could see all the way across the valley and for miles in both directions. The tree line was narrow and when he came out of it he found a narrow trail that followed the rim of the valley. It hadn't been used since the last snowfall, and probably not for a while before that, as it was barely visible. He thought this trail might be an easier route to the fort, but getting from his camp to the top was a challenge, and his horse would not be able to make that climb. He followed the trail for a short distance. Finding nothing that could be considered a trail to the bottom, he turned back home. Now he had a purpose. He had to see where that road went and came from.

The next day he saddled his horse and rode out of camp toward Fort Ridgely. He packed his rifle and his bow with the arrows. He took frozen deer meat that he kept under his coat to thaw while he rode. His body had become acclimated to the cold and, other than his hands, he had no problems. He tied the reins to the saddle horn and put his hands inside his coat to warm them. His rifle was balanced on his knees and the bow strapped to his back, as he'd seen the Indians do. Not thinking anyone but a fool would be out on such a cold day, he relaxed his watch and let the horse follow the trail.

He came to the trail that led to the fort and climbed to the top. Then, rather than taking the road into the fort, he followed a small trail that lead north along the rim of the valley. He thought it could be possible that there were trails that followed the entire rim. The wind blew stronger now and it made travel a bit more uncomfortable. He pulled his coat tight around his neck and rode on thinking he could tell where he was in relation to his cave by the length of time he'd been riding. He figured he was more than halfway to his camp. He watched for trails leading down into the canyon. The day went by with no sign of a way to the bottom so he found an overturned tree and made a shelter for the night.

By morning, the weather had turned warmer and Jake rolled his blankets and saddled up for more exploring. As he walked his horse along the top of the ridge, he watched for that trail he knew would be there to lead him down to his cave. All at once the horse raised his head and tested the air. He gave out a shrill whinny that made Jake jump. He grabbed his gun and had it ready for whatever it was the horse smelled in the air. Then he heard a whinny from upwind.

"Could it be my mare?" he wondered outloud. The horse was jumpy as they walked along the trail. As he came around a bend he could smell wood smoke. "Injuns," he said. He walked on. When he rounded the bend, he came in sight of a small Indian camp. There were four round-top wigwams set in a circle. The horses were now communicating with soft whinnies and low rumblings and Jake knew he'd found his stolen mare. The Indians hadn't seen him behind the grove of trees and he had time to look the situation over. He saw four braves walking around the camp looking for what was scaring the horses. All of them had bows in their hands. This was as dangerous a situation as he had ever wanted to be in. He could be spotted and attacked, or he could turn around and leave the horse there until a better time. Maybe he could negotiate for the horse.

Suddenly the decision was made. One of the braves spotted Jake. He pointed in his direction and yelled to the other Indians. All of the Indians ran toward the herd. Jake pulled his rifle up and took careful aim on the lone Indian watching the horses. He fired and the man dropped to the ground. He knew he had the best horse in the valley and wondered if the mare was up for another race. He'd grab her and pull her along if need be. He kicked his stallion hard and he jumped into his full-battle run. Jake didn't need to steer him—the horse seemed to know where he was going and headed there on his own. He was a hundred yards from the Indian camp and out of accurate range of their bows. He talked to his horse as he leaned over its neck, "Come on horse, we're gonna git that mare and take her home."

The young brave he'd shot was trying to get his feet under him and load an arrow into his bow when Jake got to him. He kicked the Indian as he passed him and pulled back on the reins. The horse planted four feet and slid to a stop. Jake jumped off and knocked the Indian to the ground and clubbed him with his fist on the bridge of the nose. As quickly as he'd gotten off the horse, he was back in the saddle and riding hell bent for the herd. Some of the Indians were still running toward the herd, but Jake could see that he would be there long before they were. Some had stopped to shoot ineffective arrows his way. He ran into the herd at a gallop, screaming and yelling and whipping the ones he came close enough to. He scattered the herd to the four winds. The Indians were afoot now and he had all the time he needed to find his mare and bring her home.

He sat high in the saddle with the mare following behind. The stallion moved at a comfortable cantor toward Fort Ridgely. He had no idea how far the fort was but he would go directly there and sit this out for a day or two. Suddenly something hit Jake's back like a sledgehammer. Instantly his mind tried to figure out what it was that hit so hard. He looked down and saw, sticking out of his chest, six inches of arrow with an iron head attached—just below his ribs and pushing his big wool coat out away from him.

"My God," he said. "I'm hit."

I'm gonna die. Oh God no—no one lives when he's hit through the chest. No, dammit—I'm not going to die. I'll stay on the horse and make it to the fort. He wrapped the reins around his hands and tied them to the saddle horn. *Slow down, horse. Oh Lord God it hurts. It hurts all the way through my chest. Gotta stay awake, gotta make it to the fort. Damn, the world is going black. I'm dying—I'm gonna be sick. Keep going horse—don't stop. Don't fall off the horse—stay on the horse. The world is going away—everything is turning black. Everything is spinning around me. How can I get to the fort if the whole world is spinning around me? Can't stop— gotta keep going to the . . .* the world went into darkness.

HAWK'S VALLEY

What is this? I'm falling—no, someone is…oh God—don't do that. Oh Lord the pain. Where are you taking me? Where am I…? I'm falling into a black hole…
Mercifully, the darkness closed around Jacob Owen.

"Well, you're back with the living. You're a very lucky young man, Mister Owen."

Flighty sleep came to John Owen but he was awake
and shivering... He couldn't get the sound
of his wife's screams out of his head...

3

CHAPTER THREE

"NOW I HAVE TO TELL YOU WHAT HAPPENED with my father the day of the raid..."

. . .

John Owen sat at the table while his wife washed the breakfast dishes.

"Were you going to cut firewood today, John?"

"Yeah, but I gotta wait for Jacob to get back with that saw blade. Ain't no sense piling up a bunch of wood if we can't cut it."

"John, it could take Jake all day to get to town and back. You can't just sit there and waste the whole day away waiting."

"I ain't gonna waste the day away—I got things to do."

Mary knew there was no point in trying to get John to do things without Jake being there. He was a lazy man and there was no denying it. That's the reason this farm he inherited from his father never turned out to be anything but a potato patch. They wouldn't even have potatoes if she and the boys hadn't planted them in the spring.

"John, can you get me a bucket of water?"

John got up, picked up the pail without saying anything, and walked out the door to the pump in the middle of the yard. He no sooner got out the door when he came back in and took the shotgun down from the wall.

"What is it, John?"

"Them Injuns are back—they're on horses this time. Stay in the house, I'll handle this." John stepped out into the yard and stood in the path of the three Indians.

"What you boys doin' back here? We gave you food yesterday."

"Good day, Mister Owen. How are you today?" the leader said in surprisingly clear English.

"What do you want? We have no more food to give you."

"You lie, Mister Owen. We know you have food in the house. We will go in and see for ourselves."

"You got no business in my house—you stay the hell out of there. Go away and leave us be." The leader of the Indians moved his horse forward and John stepped aside to keep from getting walked on. He pulled the hammer back on the shotgun and said, "Stop or I'll shoot you dead."

The Indian turned and looked over his shoulder at John and said, "You cannot shoot all of us with that gun, Mister Owen. Put it down or you will be the one who is shot." John put the shotgun to his shoulder and aimed it at the Indian. He turned at John and raised his club over his shoulder ready to strike him down. John pulled the trigger. The cock fell and the priming pan blew a puff of white smoke into the air but didn't ignite the charge in the barrel. The Indian swung his war club and knocked the rifle from John's hands. It fell to the ground, breaking the stock nearly in two. The Indians heeled their horses and ran over John on their way to the house. One shot at him with his bow as he lay on the ground, but the arrow missed him by an inch and stuck in the ground beside his chest. Mary stepped out the door.

"Stay in the house, Mary!" John hollered.

The Indians jumped off their mounts, pushed Mary aside, and went into the house.

"Run for the woods, Mary!"

She turned toward the trees fifty yards from the house. John was running ahead of her. Mary stumbled and fell—she cried for John to help her but he was too far away to hear her. She got back to her feet and started to run again. The Indians came out of the house and saw them running for the woods. One of them aimed an arrow at John but the leader stopped him and pointed at Mary. The other Indian aimed for Mary also. They released their arrows simultaneously and both hit Mary in the back. She fell to the ground screaming for John who was almost to the woods. She managed to get to her feet and run as far as the trees before she fell again. She lay on her side clutching at the arrows protruding from her chest—her knees pulled up against the pain. She cried for John, but he couldn't hear her. John had found a thicket and had crouched down thinking he was hidden from the Indians. They saw where he was and one of them aimed an arrow at him.

The leader stopped him and said, "That man will die a thousand deaths remembering this day and leaving his wife." He walked over to where Mary lay on the ground. He made a cut around the top of her head and pulled off her scalp. She screamed a high shrill sound that penetrated the forest to John's ears. He pressed his palms to his ears trying to block out the sound.

John sat in his hideout and cried for what seemed like hours. When he finally came to his senses he sat up and looked toward the farm to see if it was safe to come out. He heard hooves run by him but couldn't see who it was. *Oh God,* he thought, *the Indians are looking for me. Oh God—don't let them find me.* The sound went away and it got quiet. He looked up at the farm and saw his son Jake standing by the pump. John almost stood and ran to his son but he couldn't face him after what he had just done. He had just let Indians kill his wife and had done nothing to stop it. *Would Jake believe me if I said I did all I could for his ma? No, I should be dead like her. He would never believe me. He'd hate me. He already hates me just like his brother.*

John stayed in the woods and watched as Jake searched the farm. He saw him follow his and Mary's tracks. He wondered what it was Jake saw that made him stop and look so closely at the tracks and then stand up and cry. John was one hundred yards from the farm but he could see everything Jake did. He saw Jake follow the trail to the edge of the woods and then run a few feet and walk slowly into the trees and kneel down. *Had he found his mother?* John wondered. He watched as his son fell to his knees and vomited for five full minutes.

Then Jake stood up, raised his arms and shouted, "Goddammit! Whoever did this, you sons-a-bitches, I'll find you and rip your goddamned heathen hearts out!" The words penetrated the forest and came to John Owen as clearly as if he were standing next to Jake. It sent a chill through him. John was now scared of his son. *He can't find me—he'll kill me too.* He watched Jake dig his mother's grave and place her body in it and cover it up. He saw him pick up the old shotgun and look at it and saw that it had not fired. John wondered what Jake said as he looked up and around. His mouth was moving and there was hate in his eyes— John suspected it was for him.

Dammit! If that boy would have reloaded that shotgun when he had it in his hands, instead of always waiting for me to do everything, I could have gotten one of them Injuns. John was too afraid of being seen so he stayed in his hideout all night. It got very cold and he cried for most of the night over the events of the day.

When John peeked from his hideout in the morning he saw that there was no one around. Jake had left and the farm was quiet. He started to walk to the farm but the fear that the Indians might be back made him stop. *Better to go away from here and find a new place to be.* He never liked this farm anyway—nothing but sand and rocks. He started walking toward where the road crossed the river. It was about two miles as the crow flies and he could stay in the trees for cover until he got to the road heading east across the river and south to Saint Paul. Suddenly he saw his mule grazing fifty yards ahead of him. *What luck*, he thought. He caught the mule and got on its back and rode to the river, crossed the bridge and headed south. When the sun started to set John realized that he had nothing to keep himself warm nor did he have food of any kind. He knew of some wild plants he could eat but none of them were edible in the fall. John had always thought it foolish to listen to his brother Robert when he told Hawk and Jake how to survive in the wild—now he wished he'd listened at least to the part about eating. John spent his first night sitting next to a tree shivering and cussing the people who had put him in this predicament. Everyone was to blame but himself. He even got after God for doing this to him. "Why me?" he shouted to the sky. "What did I ever do to deserve this?"

Flighty sleep came to John Owen but he was awake and shivering when the sun started to lighten the eastern sky. He looked around to see where his mule was. He looked in all directions but didn't see it. Thoroughly disgusted with his life he took off down the road on foot. He couldn't get the sound of his wife's screams out of his head.

For three days he wandered down the two-rut road. He hadn't the least idea where the road was taking him—he only knew it was taking him away from that farm and all the trouble there. He was nearly exhausted and all but starved. He remembered Robert showing Hawk and Jake how to catch minnows by scooping up handfuls of water and throwing the minnows onto shore. It took him a few tries before he caught on to how it's done, but he soon had his meal, such as it was. He caught one of the minnows and sucked it into his mouth and bit down. Instantly he spit it out. The taste was not what he had expected. Then he remembered that the boys would drop the minnows in their mouths and swallow them whole. This was not as easy as it seemed. Swallowing a flipping minnow, he learned, can be difficult for someone who is used to having someone cook his meals. But eventually he learned how to feed himself on minnows. A deer ran out of the woods and stood almost close enough to touch, but John could do nothing but watch it bound away. "Hunnert pounds of meat and I can't do anything about it." John was beginning to figure out how to feed himself, but he still froze at night.

About noon of the fourth day out, and after the sun had warmed him, he turned and saw a wagon pulled by two big gray mules coming up the road toward him. The wagon stopped.

"Where ye headed, Mister?" shouted the driver.

"South—gettin' out of this God-forsaken county."

"You been walking like that all day?"

"Like what?"

"Well, where's yer coat? Don't chuh have no coat? Gets mighty chilly out here at night." The man talked louder than he had to and John thought at first he was mad about something.

"Well Mister," he said, "that there's why I'm getting out of here. Injuns held me up two nights back. Took my horse and gun and my coat too. Every damned thing I had—left me high and dry."

"Injuns? If they was the ones what murdered the family north of here yer damned lucky to be alive."

"Might have been. They had murder in their eyes, that's for sure."

"How many was there?"

"Didn't count 'em but there musta been fifteen or twenty," John lied. He couldn't let anyone know who he was. He couldn't bear to have to tell the truth about himself. He would have to come up with a phony name. John Olson... that would be it. It's a fairly common name and no one would ask questions about it. "Name's John Olson. How far ye going?"

"Goin' down to Saint Cloud if I can make it that far. These two mules are about wore out, and I gotta carry a big load to make the trip worthwhile."

"Mister, I ain't et for three days onna conna them Injuns stole everything I had. You got something I can eat?"

"I got something fer ye to eat. But first, let's get something straight. First off, yer name ain't John Olson. I don't give a rat's ass who the hell you are and you don't know who I am. Let's keep it that way. And second, stop with the bull-shit story about Injuns. If you was held up by Injuns you wouldn't be standin' there—you'd be coyote bait in some ditch somewhere. And the coyotes wouldn't have to worry about findin' a hair in their supper—ye wouldn't have none." He laughed so hard he nearly fell off his seat. "Furthermore, I don't give a tinker's damn where you come from neither, and I don't care why you don't have nothin'. You want to ride with me you jest climb on up here on the seat, but don't be tellin' me no gud day-um stories about Injuns. You got a story to tell I'll listen, but if you don't want to tell your story, I ain't askin'. Okay? Like I said, you don't know who I am, so you can call me Smith." John Owen climbed up on the seat and sat quietly. He'd been soundly scolded and he knew the best thing to do at this point was to be quiet.

Smith reached into a sack and pulled out two dirty corn biscuits and a handful of jerked venison. "Here, chew on this. You're welcome to ride as far as you please but it ain't for free. You drive mules, John?"

"Sure, drove lots of mules. Had two of 'em myself."

"Well, yer gonna do some driving while I take a snooze in the wagon."

"Go ahead on, I'll take over."

"Not yet. I don't know you good enough yet. Ain't that I don't trust ye, mind ye—it's just that a man can't be too careful out here."

Smith pulled a brown bottle out of his coat pocket, took a drink and handed it to John. He took a pull and thanked Smith. "Not bad, make it yourself?"

"Nah, swiped it out of the store back there a week ago. Got mu self all drunked up and sit in the woods a couple of days."

"That be Belleair's store?"

"Yeah, you know him?"

"Yeah, I knew the old skin flint. I think he's still got the first dollar he ever made."

"He's the one tole me about the family gettin' murdered up there. Guess the woman got killed and skelped. They don't know about the old man. Belleair says it ain't no loss if he did get killed. Lazy, good fer nothin'...Guess there was two boys who did all the work around the place. The old man ran one of them off a couple of days before the attack and the other was in the store when it happened. Belleair says those Injuns is in a heap of trouble 'cause the younger one—think he said his name was Jake—took out after 'em. Big powerful kid, Belleair said. Hope the boy knows what he's up against."

Guilt and regret filled John Owen's core. He'd run and let his wife be murdered and now his son is going out to do what he should be doing. He sat and stared at the floor of the wagon and said nothing. He wished now that he had been killed too. He wanted to jump off the wagon and go back to the farm and help Jacob. But there was nothing he could do now. It was all out of his control. If his son died he would never know. He fought to hide the tears running from his eyes. Smith sat and held the reins and let John Owen suffer alone.

"Mister Smith, gotta tell ye something."

"Don't gotta tell me nothin', John. I don't need to hear it, and I don't want to hear it. Just keep it to yerself. I knowed who you was the minute I laid eyes on you. Hear me now. What's in the past has got to stay there. All the talkin' and bawlin' in the world ain't gonna change it. What you might have done is your own cross and no one needs to know about it 'cause they ain't gonna help you carry it." He looked John in the eyes and said, "Okay?"

"Thanks, Smith."

"Don't thank me. I done things I ain't too proud of too. Ever one does."

"There's a big wool coat in the back there," Smith said, pointing to a pile of old, dirty coats in the wagon. "Dig it out and put it on afore ye shake muh wagon apart."

Hardly a word was spoken for the next week as they moved south to Saint Cloud. Smith had more than one jug in his wagon and he was willing to share it with his newfound partner. He had a partner he could get along with. All the other people he'd run into on his travels had what they called scruples, but John was not burdened by such annoying qualities. John, he knew, had his conscience firmly under control and was a bit on the cowardly side to boot. John was under Smith's control—the perfect partnership in Smith's eyes.

As the days got shorter and the nights got colder, Smith needed more blood thinner, as he called it, to help him fight the cold. John stayed away from it as much as he could. When Smith fell asleep John would go through the things in the wagon trying to figure out what Smith had that was worth traveling all the way to Saint Cloud for. John was on the seat and Smith was lying on top of the load sleeping off a bellyful of cheap booze. He stopped the wagon to go to the brush to relieve himself. When he came back, Smith was on the seat with the reins in his hands. John climbed up and sat next to him.

"Wanna know what happened to the last man who stole things from me, John?"

"Huh?"

"He fed the coyotes for a couple of days."

"I ain't gonna be stealing nothin' from you, Smith. You got nothin' I want. And where the hell would I put it if I did steal from you?"

"Well, you jest remember that next time you go diggin' through my stuff."

"What the hell you got back there anyway that's worth a trip all the way to Saint Cloud?"

"What I got back there ain't no concern to you. Take my word for it—you're better off not knowing." And he laughed like a man possessed. The comment only thickened John's curiosity. Now he had to know what was in the wagon. He couldn't open the bales or boxes without Smith knowing about it. It couldn't be gold—that would be heavy and nothing there was that heavy. So he tried to put it out of his mind. From then on Smith did his sleeping on top of the load. John slept under the wagon.

Smith was taking his turn at the reins and John was laying on top of the packs when Smith stopped the wagon and got down. "Where ye going?" John said. Suddenly, Smith grabbed John by the collar and threw him off the wagon to the ground.

"You son-of-a-bitch. I tole you if you ever tried to swipe anything from me I'd feed you to the coyotes."

"What the hell you talkin' about? I ain't got nothin' of yours 'cept what you give me."

"You was diggin' around in my stuff agin. Goddammit—there ain't nothin' in there for you. You jist stay the hell out of that stuff. From now on you sit on the seat or walk on the ground. If I catch you in the back of that wagon agin I'll pull yer scalp and leave the rest for the coyotes. You got that?"

"Yeah, Smith. I don't know what the hell you think I'm stealing but you're wrong. I ain't took nothin'."

"Well see that you don't."

John thought to himself how he wished he'd gotten mixed up with an honest man. Honest men aren't so damned suspicious. He was afraid of Smith now and decided the first chance he got he was going to leave this situation and go off on his own. One small problem stood in his way. Smith had all the things he needed for survival. If he told Smith he was leaving he'd take his coat and everything he had given him. Just one thing to do—get rid of Smith.

John's mind was busy working on a plan to affect his departure and conversation was nonexistent as they rumbled along the road to Saint Cloud. At night John would put his bedroll out away from the wagon and Smith slept on top of the load. Smith never let John out of his sight. Living on the edge of disaster like that was very uncomfortable for John.

One afternoon, Smith came to John and said, "Next time we get close to people you get off this wagon and find your own way."

"What's goin' on Smith? I ain't done nothin' to make you be this way."

"Ain't that. We're getting close to Saint Cloud and I can't have you with me when I get there."

"Why not? I thought we was partners."

"Yeah, well, you're a real pain in the ass but I don't mind traveling with you. Thing is, I gotta go alone from here. Mebby we'll hook up agin down the road sometime."

"Where'll ye be going when you git done in Saint Cloud?"

"Back to Pembina, I expect. Traders in Saint Cloud will have goods for me to take back there. Hope to have another load waitin' for me there."

"Well, my grandpa came through that town to get to the Otter Tail country and if there was anything there worthwhile I figure he'da stayed. So guess I'll just make my way to Saint Paul."

"Well hell, the boat I'm unloading onto is going to Saint Paul. Ye might be able to catch a ride with them. You could work your way down—they're always ready to hire on more hands."

"Sounds like a plan. So I can ride with you to Saint Cloud then?"

"No, goddammit. Like I said, you ride till we find you a place to get off, and that ain't far from here. Then you find your own way to Saint Cloud. Maybe we can hook up there and I'll get you on the boat."

"Good enough." And they were on their way.

That night they stopped on the shore of the Mississippi and camped for the night. John slept in his bedroll up from the river and Smith had his usual place on top of the wagon. John rolled out of his blankets and walked down to the river to relieve himself. He had an axe handle in his hand. He'd taken to carrying the axe handle wherever he went. It made him feel more secure out here in the wilderness, especially with Smith turning up around every bend. John heard Smith cough and spit. Then he heard footsteps on the gravel. He crouched down in the brush next to the trail that led to the river. Smith walked by him only three feet away carrying the shotgun he kept next to him on the wagon. John came up from the brush and swung the axe handle at Smith's head. The sound of Smith's scull cracking echoed across the river and the splash of his body hitting the water got John's feet wet. The shotgun flew out into the river. Smith lay in the water face down and not moving. John took hold of his coat and rolled him over. His eyes were open staring at the black sky. Blood was running from his right ear and he had a wide gash on the right side of his head.

"Now who'd you say is gonna feed who to the coyotes?" John said.

John walked back to the wagon and climbed aboard. He sat there for a long while thinking about what his next move would be. He climbed to the top of the heap of bales, boxes and bundles and began opening them. He found blankets, furs, cloth of different colors—nothing that could be worth the trouble Smith had gone through to protect it. John was puzzled. "What the hell could be in here?"

He threw the bundles off the wagon after opening them and inspecting their contents. He threw a large one to the ground and when it hit it split open and another bundle rolled out—a bundle about the size of John's chest. He jumped off the wagon and untied the ropes holding it together. He opened it and a pile of black scalps splayed themselves out on the canvas wrapping. They were stretched on willow hoops and painted with different symbols and colors. The hoops were painted different colors too—some green, some white, red, and black. Some of the scalps were adult but some were small with fine baby hair. John felt a rush in his ears and started to feel faint. He sat down on the sand and looked at what he had found. *Smith was transporting illegal scalps. No damned wonder he was so careful about me getting too close to the wagon. What the hell do I do now? I can't carry these into Saint Cloud. If I get caught I'll end up in prison at the least. There's got to be a fortune in scalps here.* He sat and worried about it for a time, then decided he'd wrap them in a waterproof canvas, put them in a good box, and bury them. He reloaded the wagon, rounded up the mules and hitched them to the wagon.

It took him two more days to get to Saint Cloud. He looked around at the frame buildings and log homes wondering where he should go next. He turned the mules west down what looked like a main street. He walked them slowly, checking each building as he passed. Ahead he saw a riverboat. *That must be the boat Smith was talkin' about.* He started moving toward it but realized he had no idea who would be there and he was driving Smith's wagon. Whoever it was Smith was going to see would surely recognize the wagon and mules. So he turned up the next street to find a place to put the wagon until he could get some idea where he should be.

A man stepped out onto the street in front of him. "Where ye goin'? Ain't nothin' up this street but homes. You lookin' for the riverboat?"

"Nope, just trying to find my way through this town. Headin' for Saint Paul."

"Well, either way yer gonna have to go down to the river and take the road south from there. This road ends just ahead. You can turn around right here. It's probably your best bet."

"Thanks, Mister. I'll do just that." He turned the wagon around and headed back the way he came. When he reached the river he saw the road the man had mentioned and turned his mules to the south.

Another man stepped out into the street. "Hey, ain't this Swede's rig?"

"Nope—don't know anyone named Swede."

"Sure looks like the Swede's wagon and mules. You sure this ain't his?"

"The wagon belonged to a guy named Smith. He got his self killed a couple of days back."

"Dead? The Swede's dead?"

"I told you—this ain't your Swede's wagon. It belonged to a man named Smith."

"Yeah, I heard you, but this is the Big Swede's mules. Everyone hereabouts knows the Swede."

"Well if the man I rode with was the Swede he gave me a phony name, 'cause he said his name was Smith."

The man laughed and said, "How long you been out here old man? No one gives their right name the first time you meet 'em. If he told you his name was Smith he just didn't want you to know who he was. Didn't trust you, that's all."

"Well anyway, he's dead."

"How'd he die—drink himself to death?"

"Ye might say that. He got drunk and fell off the wagon on his head and killed his self."

"No shit. I wondered when that would happen. Where'd it happen?"

"Two days back along the river."

"Well, it's obvious this is his wagon so why don't you just drive it up to that building right over there and we'll unload his cargo for ye and you can git back on the road."

"You the man he was comin' to see?"

"That I am. So if you'd rather, you can just hop down and we'll take care of your mules and wagon."

"How do I know you're the one he came to see?"

"You don't. You just have to take my word for it and get off'n that wagon." Two big dirty men stepped out from the building and started toward John. He looked the situation over and decided that he should get down and do as they said.

"I'll be around the town when you git done. Just send someone lookin' for me." And he walked away, keeping his attention to his rear for fear that one of the brutes would be following him. Not knowing where he could go he walked to the waterfront, sat down in the grass and waited for someone to come looking for him. He dozed off next to a tree.

Suddenly he was awakened by a kick on the leg. "Mister Jonas wants to talk to you." John woke with a jump and looked at one of the dirty men he saw earlier. He got up slowly trying to get awake enough to figure out what was happening. They walked to the warehouse where he had left the wagon.

"The cargo we were waiting for is not on the wagon. Where is it?"

"Don't know what you're talking about. I ain't got no idea what Smith had on that wagon. He tole me it wasn't none of my concern what he had and I shouldn't ask questions and I didn't."

"There's a pack missing. I think you know where it is."

"I don't know nothin' about any packs. Smith watched over his load like a she-bear watching her cubs. Just let me have my wagon and be on my way."

"You ain't got no wagon. That wagon belongs to us. The Swede worked for us and used our wagon. You come up with that pack and you can have the wagon and all that's on it."

"Like I said, I don't know nothin' about any missing packs."

"Oh yeah, I failed to mention, if you don't come up with those packs you won't be needing a wagon or anything else. You'll be pushing up daisies in someone's flower garden. Now think—did Swede stop to see anyone on the way down? Did he unload at anytime for any reason? Could he have stashed a pack along the way? Think..." John saw that he was in trouble with this man and tried to think of a way out. How could he come up with that pack without letting on that he knew all about it? He dearly wanted to sell the scalps and keep the profits for himself. But then, he had no idea where to sell them so they were really of no use to him.

"Well, I seem to remember him unloading one day to dry some of the packs after a rain shower. Could be he stashed some of the stuff then."

"Why the hell would he stash anything? Unless..." he looked at the man standing next to him. "You don't suppose he figured on cashin' in on the stuff himself do ye?"

The big man shrugged his shoulders and said, "Wouldn't surprise me a bit. Swede was the crookedest sum-bitch I ever knew. I wouldn't put nothin' past him."

"You remember where it was he unloaded?"

"Yeah, couple of days back, next to the river."

"Can you take me there?"

"I'm trying to get to Saint Paul, but I can tell you how to get there."

"Saint Paul will be there when you get there—you're coming with us."

John was given a horse to ride and he and Jonas and his two thugs rode north. He thought about Smith's body laying halfway in the water. What will he tell them when they ask why he didn't bury him? How can he get out of this situation alive? He already figured he was a dead man no matter how it turned out. Maybe he could lead them around pretending he couldn't find the stash. That might work but it was too much of a gamble for John. He'd take them to the river and hope for a chance to get away while they dug in the sand for the scalps.

After two days' riding they came to the place where he and Smith had turned off the road and went down to the river. He found the tracks of the wagon and the spot where they had stopped for the night.

"This the place?"

"Yeah, I think so." *God*, he thought, *don't let them find Smith's body.*

"Where's the stash?"

"I don't know. He sent me away when he unloaded the wagon."

Jonas turned to the two men with him. "Start lookin' for a fresh dig. If it's here—we'll find it. If it ain't, we'll be diggin' a fresh hole for this man." Chills went through John. He knew Jonas was not making jokes. He was in serious trouble and needed to try something. He stayed close to the horses while the rest of the group spread out looking for the stash.

"Mister Jonas, come look at this," one of the thugs hollered.

John's heart jumped to his throat. *Damn, I hope they haven't found Smith's body.* He walked to the top of a mound of sand where he could see the river and the men walking. He could see where Smith's body had fallen in the river, but it wasn't there. Relieved, he assumed the current had washed it downstream. The three men were busy digging in the sand and John saw his opportunity to get away. He climbed onto his horse, kicked it in the ribs, and ran it through the other three horses sending them running ahead of him. He'd done it—he was free of those men and he had a horse to ride and three more if he wanted them. He kept the horses ahead of him as he ran away from the trouble knowing that the farther he could get their mounts away the better off he would be. John was pleased with himself at the way he had handled it, and was surprised at how money could make such fools of otherwise sensible men. John caught the three horses and unloaded what they had in their saddlebags and loaded it onto his own horse. He walked away with jerked venison, corn biscuits, a rifle with bullets and powder, and food for three days for three men. The rest of the gear on the horses would have to stay there. He didn't have time to find a place on his horse for it and leading three packhorses was more work than he wanted right now.

Do I go back to Saint Cloud or ride south by myself? I do have a wagon back there but if I go to Saint Cloud I'll surely be recognized. He followed the road along the river for a day and turned east on a barely-used trail. He rode through the night to put as many miles as he could between him and Jonas. He found a grove of trees just as the sun was coming up and stopped for some rest. He ate a mouthful of biscuits and jerky and dozed off. He slept for two hours then woke up, mounted his horse, and was on his way. He rode slowly, eating from the bag of jerky and biscuits when he felt hungry and stopping for water when he was thirsty.

He thought about his life on his father's farm when he was a kid, and how his pa had always favored his brother Robert. He even called him Robert. He called John "Johnny"—God, how he hated that name. When there was work to be done, his pa had always taken Robert with him and told John to stay home and help his mother. John was smaller than Robert and couldn't handle the work-load his pa would give him so he was treated like a hired hand around the farm. He fed chickens, pulled weeds in the garden, milked the cow, and helped his mother do chores around the house. He was never allowed to go to the fields and work the mules.

"Robert is bigger and he can handle it better," his pa would say.

Robert's hands were big and hard. John's hands were small and soft like his mother's. If only his pa would have taken the time with him as he did with Robert he might have turned out differently. His mother, on the other hand, doted over him. She wouldn't let him get dirty or run around the yard for fear he'd fall and hurt himself. If he woke up in the morning not feeling well, she'd wrap him in warm blankets and feed him hot soup. His pa was often scolded for making Johnny work too hard. "He's not like Robert. He can't handle that kind of work," his mother would say. John wished his mother were here right now.

He married a woman named Mary—the daughter of a woman his mother knew. His mother had kidded John about Mary being his wife someday. The marriage was not good from the start. The woman was no good. She knew nothing about taking care of a man. She hounded him for everything. His mother could get her own water from the well and bring in her own firewood. This so-called wife was nearly helpless. She needed everything done for her. John couldn't help thinking it was a blessing when his two boys were born, and grew enough to do some of the work around the farm before he worked himself to death—like his pa and his brother.

His mother and father died at an early age and left the farm to Robert and John. John thought it should have been his alone because, after all, he was the one who was here all the time. Robert was always off somewhere hunting or fishing using the excuse that there was work to be done in the fields. Robert didn't have kids of his own so he made it his job to teach Harlan and Jacob the things he knew about living in the wild. Harlan learned the wood-lore better than Jacob. Robert called Harlan "Hawk" too, but for different reasons. He said, "A hawk can take care of himself, and he don't take no guff from nobody. And a Jake is a young turkey—smartest damn critter in the woods." John could see from the start that he would have a tough time getting Harlan to do his work like he was supposed to. *I had to beat him or he'd 'a turned out just like Robert—a no-good woods tramp. He's too much like him the way it is.*

John hated seeing the way Robert and Mary could talk and laugh at the dinner table. He could never talk with his wife. She wouldn't talk to him about the things he wanted. It was always what she wanted or thought she needed. She and Robert should have been the ones his mother pushed into getting married. John had always thought the two of them spent too much time together. Mary had no time to share with her husband and John was always too tired from working all day to make small talk with his wife. When Robert got sick and died the farm was John's alone. Mary took Robert's death harder than John thought she should have. She gave no thought to how hard it was for him to lose his entire family. She cried for herself more than for him or the boys. After all, it was his brother, not hers. But now the farm was his and he didn't have to share it with anyone. He could work it the way he thought it should be done. If those two boys had listened to him, rather than Robert, they would have been more willing to work and the farm might have paid off.

Night was approaching and John was tired so he turned the horse into a patch of woods, tied it to a tree, and laid down on the ground for the night. He reached into the sack for another biscuit. He found just one. He'd eaten three days' rations for three men in one day. *How did those men think they were going to live on one day's food for three or four days?* Then he remembered he had a rifle and could hunt for his food. *Hawk had done it*, he reasoned, *and since it was me who taught Hawk to shoot, I should be able to handle it.*

The night got cold and John had only one blanket. *Should'a took the blankets from the other horses*, he thought. He was colder than he'd ever been and he shivered until his back and legs hurt. *Gotta build a fire.* He dug through the saddlebags but found no matches and no flint—nothing that would get a fire started. "Dammit, now I'm going to freeze to death! Why does everything happen to me?" John tried to get warm by jumping up and down and running in place but nothing could warm him. He rolled up in the blanket and pulled it over his head. He laid down to sleep—or freeze to death.

He did sleep, but not enough to do him any good the next morning. He was still cold, but now he was hungry too. He walked to his horse and started to mount, but the horse sidestepped and turned away from him each time he got his foot up to reach the stirrup. "What the hell's wrong wit chew now? Stand still!" It took him a few tries but he did get on the horse. He kicked him in the ribs and they started down the road. He hadn't been riding for more than half an hour when a small doe walked out in front of him. He raised the rifle, took careful aim, and pulled the trigger. Nothing happened. The gun didn't fire. He pulled the hammer back and tried again with the same results. "Now what?" he said, trying to control his temper. He raised the hammer and looked where the priming pan usually is and saw a nipple that needed a primer cap. "What the hell's this?" A sense of impending doom rolled over John Owen. He knew he had no primers. Now he knew the gods were all against him. "How can so many things go wrong for one man in such a short time?" he quietly asked to the sky. He calmly lowered the rifle and tied it to the saddle. He had to start thinking things through. If he lost his temper now, which was his normal course of action in times like these, he would surely do something he'd regret. Anger was building in his core and he wanted to cry. He remembered the first time he went a full day without crying about something. He didn't remember how old he was, but he remembered his pa saying, "You're too old to be bawling like a baby every time something doesn't go your way." Things were not going his way today—he was cold and hungry, his horse was acting crazy, his gun was no good to him, and he had no idea where he was. The sky was overcast and he couldn't tell which direction he was going. And now, it was starting to rain. A light drizzle, just enough to make John Owen wet through his clothes. The blanket did no good—it soaked up rainwater and its weight increased to the point that John could hardly carry it. He proved wrong the idea that a wool coat would keep a person warm even when wet.

John suddenly saw two riders ahead of him leading a packhorse. They must have just left their night's camp because they were not more than half a mile from him and he hadn't seen them before. He kept his pace slow so he wouldn't catch them before he knew if they were friend or foe. He still wasn't sure if he'd completely lost Mister Jonas and his friends. The two followed the road around a turn and John lost sight of them. When he reached the place where they had turned he rounded the corner expecting to see them but they weren't in sight. Suddenly a man stepped from the brush alongside the road, pointed a large caliber rifle at John, and yelled, "Who the hell are you and why are you follerin' me?"

The sudden appearance of the man made John jump. He raised his arms to cover his face and screamed, "Gad dang, ye skeered the livin' daylights otta me. Put the damn gun down—I ain't following no body. We're just goin' the same direction. Put the gun down."

"I'll put the gun down when I know who you are and why yer follerin' me."

"I tole you, I ain't follerin' you! I'm freezin' my ass off and I'm hungrier 'an a bear in spring. I'm just hoping to find some food and a warm place to sleep. Now put the damn gun down."

"What's yer name?"

"John Olson. I come from Otter Tail County, and I ain't following you. I got no idea who the hell you are and there ain't no reason for me to follow you."

The big man lowered the rifle and looked at John through red bushy eyebrows. "You been behind me for three days. You ain't noticed?"

"No, I ain't seen a human bein' since I left Saint Cloud."

The big man reached up and waved his hand in front of John's eyes. "You blind? We been seein' you behind us fer three days."

"I'm trying to find my way to Saint Paul, but I ain't having no luck."

"Ha, I'll say ye ain't having no luck. You ain't no where near Saint Paul. You ain't even goin' the right way. Saint Paul's down that-a-way." He pointed over his shoulder with his thumb.

"Ye mean I'm goin' north?"

"Yep, yer headin' tords Chippewa country—don't think you wanna be there. You look like a city slicker, 'cept yer so damned raggedy."

John pulled his blanket tighter around his shoulders trying to stop shivering. The big man stood in the rain with a canvas poncho covering a blue capote that showed below the edge. He wore heavy leather moccasins on his feet and under the hood of the poncho he wore a red foxskin hat the same color as his curly red hair and thick red beard.

"Didn't I see two of you up there?"

"That, ye did."

"Well, where's the other one?"

"She's in the trees yonder with yer ear settin' on the front sight of a fifty-six caliber Springfield rifle."

"She?"

"Mu wife."

"You gonna just leave her in the trees or ye gonna bring her out so I can have a look?" The man turned his head a little, keeping his eyes on John and made a motion toward the trees. A woman came out wrapped in a blue blanket-coat. She held a long-barreled rifle tight to her shoulder pointed straight at John. She had long black hair and walked with her toes pointed inward. Her skin was brown and her eyes were as black as the night sky. She walked gracefully without looking down, stepping over the fallen logs and brush as if they weren't there.

"This here's my wife. Her name's Flower in the Rock. I call her Posey. Full blood Cherokee."

"She's-en-Injun," John said.

"Gonna let that bother you?" The man said turning his head slightly and looking at John with hard threatening eyes.

"Nope, just cain't figure out why a man would want a squaw for a wife."

"I'm gonna fergit you said that onna conna yer igner'nce, er just plain stupidness. Little man, if you wanna see the sun come up tomorrow you won't call my wife a squaw again. That's a Frenchy word that ain't too nice and if you call her that again I'll knock you on yer ass and let her finish you." He looked at John again with those threatening green eyes. "She's as soft as a kitten most times, but she can be mean as a cougar when she needs to be—'member that."

"Um, sorry, I didn't…"

"Never mind, I can see how sorry you are. Name's Whistler, I'm known more by the name uh Sunkist onna conna the sun burns my face so bad in the summer. Red Irish, ye see."

"Can you have your, um, wife…put that gun down, Mister Whistler? It's kinda uncomfortable hearing the echo comin' from down that bore."

"She'll put it down when she trusts you."

"Fer da cripes sake," John said with a high pitched whine, "I ain't gonna hurt no one. Put the damn guns down."

"By the looks of you I doubt if you could hurt a toad if you stepped on it." Sunkist motioned for Posey to lower her rifle. "Don't figger on needin' that rifle? That's a kinda careless way of carryin' it, tied to yer saddle like that. What if I'da took a shot at you and you had'a shoot back? You'd be shit otta luck. Ha! Bet you ain't even got it loaded." John had to think that one over. He had no idea if the rifle was loaded or not.

"Wouldn't make no difference if it was loaded. I ain't got no caps for it enna ways."

"Y'ain't? Why the hell not? Ye lose 'em?"

"Nope, traveled with a thief for a while and he stole 'em from me when I wasn't lookin'."

"What, he run off so's ye couldn't find him and get 'em back?"

"I don't think he knew he stole 'em. He took everything I had 'cept my horse and what I have on."

"Well at least you got the powder and ball for it." Sunkist looked at John again from under his brows, "Say, if you carry the powder and ball how come you don't carry caps too? I mean, how could he get away with just the caps?"

"They was in my saddle pack. That's what he took."

"Mister, I ain't even gonna ask enny more questions. You don't make a lick of sense, and on top of that, I really don't care why you don't have caps. What kinda caps ye need? I got a bag full."

"I don't know, just rag-lar caps," John said, relieved to be out of this question-and-answer session.

"Damn man, does it take big caps or small ones? Gimme that gad-damn gun an lemme see." Sunkist reached out and grabbed the rifle from John's saddle, not bothering to untie it. He pulled the hammer back and grunted. "Ump, pissy little rifle caps." He said something to Posey and she turned and went for the horses. When she came back, Sunkist opened his saddlebag, pulled out a deerskin bag, and took out a tin of caps. "Here, take these. They might make that pop-gun go pop. Don't let it scare ye when it goes off. Kin ye shoot that thing?"

"Guess I can shoot as good as you or that squaw you got." Suddenly John's coat and blanket got very tight around him as Sunkist grabbed him, pulled him from the saddle, and pitched him through the air into a patch of thorn apple brush. Two-inch thorns pierced his coat and skin in a hundred different places. He didn't land on the ground but was held up by sticks covered with needle-sharp thorns. His left foot hurt at the ankle. He saw Sunkist walking toward him taking four-foot steps.

"I told you, you sawed-off little mongrel. If you ever called my wife that name ag'in I'd knock you on yer ass and let her finish you, didn't I?" John just stared at him with eyes ready to cry.

"Well didn't I?" he roared.

John nodded his head up and down. His presumed executioner reached into the thicket and wrapped his huge right hand around John's neck and pulled him out of the thorn patch. John was terrified. He knew this was the end for him. His feet weren't on the ground. The red-headed giant was walking toward Posey, carrying him by the back of his neck with one hand. Posey sat on the ground and looked with emotionless eyes at the two men. Sunkist dropped John to the ground in front of her and spoke in Cherokee. She looked at Sunkist, then at John. Still no emotion showed in the woman's eyes. For an instant John wondered how such dead eyes could be so beautiful. Reality returned as Posey stood up, grabbed John by the coat, and pulled him to his feet with no assistance from him. She pulled off his coat, which felt like she was skinning him alive because of the thorns that pinned it to his skin. She started pulling thorns out of his body. She left the ones on his front side for him to deal with and only pulled the ones in his back that he wouldn't be able to reach. The thorns in his lower back were going to be John's worry too.

Sunkist walked over to where they stood carrying John's left boot. He threw it down at his feet. "Yer boot got stuck in the stirrup. Now, what's that word you ain't never gonna say ag'in around this camp?" John looked up at him and slowly shook his head side to side. He would never say that word again as long as he lived, which at this moment didn't seem likely to be a real long time. "Git yer shirt and coat on if ye wanna ride with us." John pulled two thorns from his chest and pulled his shirt over himself. He winced as he felt another one under the shirt. He got into his coat and tied it loosely around his waist. His horse was standing close and John took the reins and tried to mount. The horse sidestepped as he'd done that morning and wouldn't let John mount.

"What the hell's wrong wit chew now?" Sunkist yelled angrily. "Git on that horse and let's go." But the horse shied away each time John tried to mount. Sunkist walked his horse close and took the reins and told John to get up. Still the horse sidestepped his efforts.

"When's the last time you had the saddle off'n this animal?"

"I don't know—a couple of days ago, I guess."

"Ye mean you ain't had this saddle off for two or three days? What da hell's wrong wit chew? You completely stupid? Ain't no damn wonder he won't let you ride—his back is probably rubbed raw. Get the hell otta the way." He swung down from his horse and shoved John back with a sweep of his arm. He loosened the cinch and lifted the saddle off the horse, then the blanket. "Good God," he said, "You damned fool, you ain't had this saddle off for a week have you?"

"I don't know—could'a been."

"I got half a mind to throw you in the thorn patch again and leave you there, but the coyotes would probably find you and poison themselves. You ain't gonna be ridin' this animal for at least a week and you ain't puttin' that saddle on him either. Smell that." He grabbed John by the back of the neck and shoved his face next to the horse's back. The wet patch where the saddle sat smelled of rotted flesh and almost made John vomit.

"Damn," he said, "I ain't never had saddle horses till a week ago. I didn't know you hadda take the saddle off."

Sunkist's voice got loud and angry. He grabbed John's coat collar and pulled him close to his face and yelled at him. "How gad-damn smart do you have to be to figure that one out? You take your shoes off when you sleep don't ye?" John looked at Sunkist, his eyes wide and filled with fear. "Well you do, don't ye?" he barked.

"Yes," John said, looking at Sunkist. Sunkist looked at John for a long moment, shook his head slowly and walked away.

I've had all of this shit I can take, John said to himself and started dreaming up plans for Sunkist's demise.

Posey went to the woods and came back with herbs to rub into the horse's back.

"See this here stuff?" Sunkist said. "You take this stuff on some wet leaves and rub it on that horse's back ever chanst you git. It'll help him heal and keep the sores from festerin'." John nodded his head, took the leaves, and started rubbing the horse's back.

"You comin'?" He looked up and saw Sunkist and Posey walking their horses away from him.

"Yeah, I guess. Am I riding the packhorse or what?"

"You ain't ridin' nothin'. You walk, and bring that saddle. When yer horse heals you'll be wanting it."

"I'll just throw it up on the packhorse."

"Like hell you will. That horse is loaded the way it is. You carry the saddle."

"What? I can't carry this..." Sunkist stopped, reined his horse around, and started toward John. "A'right, a'right...I carry the saddle. Jeez." He picked up the saddle and threw it onto his back holding it over his right shoulder. Sunkist carried John's rifle and Posey had his pack on her horse behind the saddle.

"How far we goin'?" John asked as he limped along.

"Saint Paul. Zat ar-right wit chew?"

"Saint Paul? I thought you said you was goin' north to Injun country."

"No, you was goin' north to Injun country. You jest didn't know it till I tole you."

"If yer goin' to Saint Paul, how come yer goin' north?"

"The road just turns north right here, but it forks. When we find it, the right fork goes east and then south once we get to the river."

"What river?"

"I don't remember what they call it, but it flows south and meets up with the Mississippi and from there it goes to Saint Paul... Rum River, that's what it's called. The Rum."

"How far is it to this river?"

"If we ain't careful we might fall in it any time now. Indians got a trail that follows it south. That's what we're lookin' for." Sunkist stopped his horse and turned in the saddle. John's eyes got big and he stopped where he was.

"Ye know why a horse can carry a saddle with a man on it all day long without getting tired?"

"'Cause he's bigger?"

Sunkist leaned down toward John, "No! 'Cuz he don't waste his wind TALKIN'!" John jumped back at the sound.

Each time they stopped for food or rest, John rubbed the horse with the pine-smelling paste Posey had made from the herbs, then went to the river and washed his sore feet in the icy water. His woolen socks were all but worn out and he had rubbed blisters on his feet. Sunkist gave him a pair of winter moccasins to wear. He told him, "Posey ain't too pleased about this. She thinks you should have the sense to carry extra stockings if you was gonna wear white men's shoes."

After two days' riding and walking, their road turned slowly to the east, then south. Sunkist was watching for a trail that followed the river but was starting to have doubts about its existence when he realized the one they were on was paralleling a river. "Where'd we miss the fork?"

John was falling behind because of the weight on his back and the sore ankle. He fell far enough back that he couldn't see his traveling companions. He took the opportunity to sit down and rest without having to listen to Sunkist yelling at him to "Get on yer feet and git goin'." He put the saddle down next to a tree, sat on it, and leaned back and fell asleep. He opened his eyes with a start. It was almost dark and he was being hoisted to his feet by two big, powerful hands. When his eyes focused they were staring into two flaming green eyes that were glaring back at his.

"You all right? Y'ain't dead aire ye?"

"Umm, no. I musta fell asleep."

"Looks that a-way—too much walking fer ye I guess, carryin' that saddle and all."

"Yeah, I guess."

"Well, come on, Posey's got a warm fire and some meat goin' for us. You can sit and warm yer self and git some rest. You don't look so good." Sunkist picked up the saddle and they walked for half an hour to the camp. She'd built a fire under the roots of a fallen tree and had stretched a canvas over the roots to make a lean-to. The rain had stopped earlier but everything was wet. John was not shivering like he was that morning. The walking had gotten his blood flowing and he'd become accustomed to the cold air on his face. When he crawled into the shelter the warm fire felt almost too warm and he sat away from it. Posey had a tin pot filled with steaming hot stew hung over the fire. She didn't look at John when he came in but he could feel her watching him. It made him uncomfortable knowing that even though her eyes never looked directly at him he knew she didn't miss a move he made. Sunkist handed John a tin cup and motioned for him to take some stew and eat. He looked around for a ladle to fill his cup. Sunkist grabbed John's cup, nearly stripping the skin from his finger. He dipped it into the pot and handed it back.

"We ain't got much for fancy eating yew-tinsils 'round here—we just make do."

John did nothing until he saw Sunkist raise the cup to his lips and sip the soup into his mouth. "If Ma saw me now she'd have a fit." he said out loud, and raised the soup to his mouth.

"You feelin' okay, little man?" Sunkist asked.

"I'm fine, just a little tired is all." John was feeling awful but didn't dare say anything to Sunkist, fearing he'd be ridiculed for being sick. He should have been warm and comfortable but he began shivering.

"You still cold?" Sunkist looked deep into John's eyes.

"Yeah, a little."

"It's warm as the inside of a buff'ler in here and yer shakin' like a coyote shittin' pine cones. You gonna live?"

"I hope not."

Sunkist put his hand to John's forehead. "Damn man, yer burnin' up. Man, it just don't quit with you, does it?" He said something to Posey. She checked John's forehead and talked to Sunkist.

"You still carryin' some of those thorns Johnny-boy?"

"Don't call me Johnny. I'll have to pitch *you* in a thorn patch." Then he smiled apologetically to let Sunkist know he was kidding.

"That was real cute how you said that."

"Think I got one down here." He rubbed the back of his leg showing them where the thorn was. Sunkist reached over and ripped John's pants open at the top of the leg. Posey leaned over and looked, then pointed at the large, round, red patch on John's leg. She touched it with the tip of her finger and John jumped at the pain. She again said something to Sunkist. He looked at her with angry eyes, then he turned to John. "She says you got poisoned from the thorns. Says it's my fault. Hell, I'da thought she'da thanked me."

"Poisoned? I s'pose I'm gonna die now?"

"No, you ain't gonna die. I ain't been that lucky lately. Yer gonna be sick for a few days and then you'll be better. She's gonna dig that broken thorn otta yer leg." Posey put a finger on each side of the red spot and pinched. John hollered loudly at the pain. She did it again and John shouted again. She reached into her bag and pulled out a small knife with a thin blade. John looked at it and watched it as it moved in slow motion to his leg. With a slight smile on her lips, but not in her eyes, she put her fingers on each side of the sore spot ready to pinch it again. Sunkist reached out and stopped her and she shot him an angry look. She put the point of the blade against the white spot in the center of the red spot.

"You ready, John?" Sunkist said.

"Ready for what?" At that moment Posey shoved the point of the blade into and through the center of the red spot. John screamed in pain. Sunkist grabbed him by the arms and held him tight while Posey dug for the broken thorn. John moaned and yelled from the pain. He could feel warm liquid running down his leg. After a few seconds—that seemed like an hour of torment—she had the thorn out. John rested his head on his arm.

"Why the hell did she have to pinch it like that? It didn't do no good for her or me."

"She didn't have to do that. She jist wanted to see how much it took to make you scream. Didn't take much, did it? She's a Injun, ye know."

"Oh really? I hadn't noticed."

"Them thorns you landed in are awful. A man can catch his death gettin' poked by them things. Next time you feel like flying through the air like a little tweety-bird, look where yer goin'," Sunkist said, and walked away.

John drifted off to sleep. When he awoke it was morning. He heard the sound of a shovel digging in the dirt. Posey was digging in the ground a few feet from John.

"What's she diggin'?" he asked Sunkist.

"A hole."

"I can see that, but what's it for?"

Sunkist put his hand on John's shoulder and, looking into his eyes, said, "John, it's the best thing to do. You'll be all right." He patted him on the shoulder and went back to sharpening his knife.

"Sunkist?"

"Don't worry little man, things are gonna be okay. Perty soon you'll be in a place that's much warmer and you won't be sick no more. It won't hurt—she knows what she's doin'. And don't be so nervous." John watched Posey work.

Sunkist had taken out a leather strap and was stropping his hunting knife to razor sharpness. He looked at John, laid the edge of the knife on the back of his hand, and shaved off some hair, then went back to stropping. Posey stopped digging when the hole was about a foot and a half deep and six feet long. Then she went into the woods and brought back four poles, each about three inches in diameter and the length of the hole. She laid them in the bottom and began piling small dry brush on the poles. Then she added larger pieces until she had a pile of wood to the top of the hole and the full length of it. She scooped embers from the campfire, laid them in the hole, and fanned them until she had a fire blazing.

John looked at Sunkist and said, "What the hell's she doing?"

"She's gonna roast that fever otta yer innards. Jest lay down and let her do what she knows best." Posey fed the fire for more than an hour, never letting it burn hard, nor go out. Then she scooped up the dirt she'd dug from the hole and started filling it, covering the burning coals.

"Now that don't make a damn bit of sense. Why the hell's she burying the fire?"

"Little man, if you don't shut yer trap I'm gonna throw you in that hole before she gets it covered. She's making a hotbed for you. It'll git yer body warm and cook that poison otta ye—what ye got from them thorns. Now stop yer belly-achin' and do like she says." Posey laid a canvas over the dirt covering the ashes and then a thick buffalo robe over that. She reached for John, took him by the collar, and pulled him to his feet and led him to the bed.

John looked over his shoulder at Sunkist and said, "Can't she just tell me to stand up 'stead'a jerkin' me up like that?"

"Posey don't speak no English, and I don't try to tell her what to do enna' ways. Don't think you should either." The Indian girl burned her eyes into John's and pointed to the bed. John laid down and Posey covered him with a robe and a wool blanket. Through the robe below him he could feel the heat coming from the coals. She brought a tin of water for him to drink. He put it to his mouth to take a sip but Posey stopped him. She pointed to the cup and motioned for him to drink. John nodded. Posey mimicked the cup turning all the way up telling him to drink it all. John nodded again, tipped the cup up and swallowed all of the contents. Suddenly his mouth was on fire. He coughed and tried to spit the fire out but nothing did any good. She handed him another cup and he pushed it away but she put it to her own lips and showed him that it was just water. He drank it and handed her the cup wanting more water. She brought over a pan of water, set it next to John and pointed at it, then at him. He dipped another cup from the pan and poured it down his throat and went for more. Sunkist was trying not to laugh as John tried to quench the inferno raging in his throat. Soon the fire in his mouth and throat had cooled to a simmer. He started to get out of the bed but Posey pushed him down and pointed at him telling him to stay. He laid down and began to sweat. He went to sleep in his hotbed. For once he was not shivering from the cold. He slept through the night.

When he awoke in the morning he saw Posey and Sunkist loading the horses. The packhorse had a travois tied to it. Posey came to where John lay and pulled the robe and blanket off his body. Then she started to reach for John but he quickly jumped to his feet, not wanting to be jerked up again by this powerful and beautiful, but completely emotionless woman. He promptly fell to his knees. Posey took him by the coat and pulled him up, laid him on the travois, and wrapped him in blankets.

"What the hell's this? I don't need to be hauled around like baggage. I can walk."

"Ye jist fell on account you can't even stand up—how you figger you can walk?" Sunkist said. "Jist lay there and enjoy the ride."

"Was that fire water she gave me last night some kind of Indian medicine juice?"

"Nope, just a drink made from mustard, horseradish and some other hot plants and roots."

"Well if it wasn't medicine why'd I have to drink it?"

"You needed to sweat and to do that, ye need water. The drink makes you sweat and drink lots of water. Worked, didn't it?"

"I do hope you two are enjoying yourselves." Sunkist looked at Posey and said something in Cherokee. John watched Posey and thought for a second that he saw a smile in her eyes but then decided he was wrong.

"I thought all the Cherokee was in Oklahoma Territory," John said to Sunkist.

"All what's left of 'em are. Most of 'em died on the trail of tears back in thirty-eight and thirty-nine. Posey here was born on that trail."

"How'd she get her name Flower in the Rocks?"

"Her mother got pregnant on the trail and she was born on the side of a hill covered with stones. She didn't want her baby to grow up in a world ran by evil white men so she left her on top of a big rock for the Great Spirit to take to his lodge. Well, the next day the mother thought she heard her baby crying even though they were a day's walk away. So she went back and found the baby girl still alive and crying to the Great Spirit. According to the story there was a flower growing up through the snow right next to her. That was in the spring of thirty-eight. The flower would have been a crocus, so the story 'bout the flower is prob'ly true. Everyday her mother would pull her out of her cradleboard and roll her in the snow to toughen her nerves. She made her eat things that you and me wouldn't think of eatin' and go without water or food for a week at a time just to make the girl tough and able to live without the white man's handouts. Made one hell of a woman out of her."

John rode the travois through the day and slept in buffalo robes at night. After two days of this he was feeling better and was able to walk. They kept the saddle and John's gear on the travois and John walked behind the horses. The third night Posey started setting up the camp in her favorite way—under the roots of a fallen tree. She cleaned a spot on the ground for a fire and motioned for John to go for firewood. He came back with an armload that amounted to half of what Posey would normally carry. Sunkist was laughing quietly when John came into camp.

"I s'pose this ain't enough wood to please you."

"You can go back for more."

"What the hell you laughin' about now?"

"Last time I tried to go for firewood she pert'near clawed my eyes out. Says gettin' firewood is woman's work. It's like an insult to her. She thinks I don't think she can do her work." John dropped the wood on the ground and walked away. Posey almost smiled again.

John was angry now. This red-haired monster had humiliated him for the last time. He became sullen and stayed away from them as much as he could. Posey could see the change in him and took to watching him even closer than she had before. Sunkist knew it was being humiliated and laughed at that made

John change, but figured it was a learning experience for him. If he was going to live in a rough land he'd have to learn to live tough like the rest of the men out here. John couldn't make a move without Posey watching him, though her eyes never set on him. It became a problem for him to get away even for the most private, personal chores.

One morning, he woke up early and didn't see Posey in her usual place by the fire. He took the opportunity to get away by himself and do some thinking. He walked down to the river. He heard splashing in the water and crouched down to see what it was. There in the water was Posey, naked to the waist, bathing. His heart thumped so hard in his chest he thought she might hear him. He laid there for a moment watching the beautiful girl.

"Perty, ain't she?" Sunkist said over John's shoulder. John jumped so hard he came off the ground and scooted forward to get distance between him and Sunkist.

"Damn, Sunkist! I ain't been here long. I just now got here and I was just leaving."

"Hey, don't worry little man. If you didn't look at that I'd think there was somethin' else wrong wit chew. I know how long you been here and so does she. She figgered to be back before you got into anymore trouble. See, Indian women don't think the body is sinful like white people do. They believe Mother Earth made it beautiful, and to hide it like it was something dirty is an insult. They do enjoy using their beauty to control the white men though." He smiled at John, "Now, you seen enough. Git back to camp." John walked back as well as his shaking legs could carry him.

Posey came into camp and started their breakfast. She motioned to John to go for firewood, but John sat on the ground and didn't move. Posey hissed at him like a cat and stabbed her eyes into his but John didn't move.

"Go git some wood, little man."

"Go git yer own gad-damn wood."

"Well, looks like the little pizzer wants another trip to the thorn patch."

John stood up and yelled at Sunkist, "You son-of-a-bitch, you been humiliatin' me for three weeks! You laugh at me, you bully me around, you call me stupid names and I'm tired of it. You can throw me in the thorn patch or in the river or whatever the hell you want, but I ain't goin' for wood."

Sunkist looked at John and smiled. "'Bout time you stood up fer yerself. I wondered how much it would take to make you act like a man and git over that spoiled little girl bullshit." He made a motion to Posey and she went to the woods for firewood.

"I think we got another day's ride before we get to the Mississippi. When we git there you take your stuff and ride away. Keep the caps and whatever else we give ye, but you gotta ride away now."

"Be my pleasure."

Sunkist tied John's rifle to his saddle and laid his pack over the horse's rump along with the buffalo robe he'd slept in while he was sick. For the next day neither John nor Sunkist said anything to the other. Posey stayed behind John on the trail. He felt her eyes burning into his back and knew she stayed behind him because she still didn't trust him. Snow fell for the first time that fall and the air seemed cleaner and fresher. So did John. He'd stood up for himself and it felt good. At the end of two days of silence they came to a fork in the trail they'd been following. One trail went straight south and the other went west to the Mississippi. John followed the southern route while Sunkist and Posey stayed on the westbound road. They didn't acknowledge their parting. They separated without out a word or sign of any sort. After ten minutes of traveling, John turned and looked at the two riders disappearing in the distance. He thought he saw Posey looking his way but dismissed the thought.

John was alone again. He had time to think about the things that had happened in the last six weeks—he had lost his wife and farm and both of his boys, he'd been bullied by a stranger who called himself Smith, he was nearly killed by two scalp hunters, and then the humiliation from Sunkist and his squaw was unbearable. *Squaw*—the word echoed in his mind. He was still afraid to say it out loud but then realized he was alone and could say it all he wanted. He hollered "SQUAW!!! SQUAW!!! SQUAW!!!" at the top of his lungs. It felt good to say it, simply because Sunkist had forbidden it. "SQUAW!!! SQUAW!!! SQUAW!!!" Just then a white-tailed buck jumped from the brush onto the road. John screamed as his heart instantly cramped up and jumped into his throat. He pulled back on the reins and almost rolled off the back of the saddle. The deer made one jump and was out of sight. For an instant, John had visions of himself flying through the air and landing in a field of flaming thorns and being buried alive in a fire pit with his scalp ripped from his head. He got control of himself and, aside from the shaking, he seemed to be all right. "That redheaded son-of-a-bitch's got me so damned jumpy I can't even ride the trail without getting the shit scared otta me."

If Sunkist didn't like me, he thought to himself, *why did he take care of me when I got sick? Why did he take me on at all? He could have left me there and walked away. Why did he give me the rifle caps? Why the buffalo robe? Why the moccasins?*

Wonder what he was up to? Guess he just liked me and didn't know how to show it. He smiled, pleased with himself. Suddenly John felt alone. *Sunkist got mean,* he thought, *but never really hurt me on purpose. He could laugh at things that he thought were funny, and he sure loved that squa—uh, woman of his.* John followed the Rum until it came to a small settlement at the confluence with the Mississippi. He wondered if Jonas and his thugs would show up there.

. . .

Posey brought her horse up to ride beside her man. Sunkist saw her turn to look at John riding away.

"What are you thinking?" he asked in Cherokee.

"We will hear of him again."

"Yes, I suppose so. But I doubt if he will be bothering us."

"He will be a dangerous man wherever he goes," Posey said. "He is a coward and cannot speak the truth. He will not face his enemy. He will crawl up behind him like a snake and kill him while he sleeps."

"Yes, I think you are right, but he is gone now and we should not think of him again."

"Why did you not leave him when we found him?"

"He was a man who lied to me from the start and he is not to be trusted. It is better to keep an enemy where you can see him."

"You could have killed him and then you would not have to be concerned about him."

"Only a coward would kill a man just because he is afraid of him."

"You gave him caps for his gun."

"And I kept the gun with me. I doubt if he took the right balls for that gun when he stole it."

"He might have crawled up behind you when you slept and killed you."

"Would you have let that happen?"

"No."

"I knew you were there and did not worry about him." Posey's eyes filled with passion. She took the reins of Sunkist's horse and led them into a grove of poplars.

. . .

John rode into the town of Anoka and down the main street. It was lined with tall brick and wood frame buildings. His nature was to be timid around people he didn't know and this place was much too crowded for John Owen. *Too many people*, he thought to himself, *I can't stay here.* He continued on the main road until he found the edge of town. He saw a church steeple ahead and remembered that churches were inclined to be generous to hungry people. *A free meal might be in the cards,* he thought. He found the front door open and walked in. A dozen benches faced the front of the church where a board laid across two barrels served as an altar.

"Good evening, my friend." John jumped at the sound and turned around to face a tall, thin man in a black robe smiling at him. "How may I be of service?"

"Well, if you have some work that needs doing I'd gladly do it for a bite to eat."

The priest said, "And Jesus said, 'I was hungry and you gave me to eat.' Come my friend, dine with me." John followed the priest to a small room in the rear of the church and they sat down to bread, cheese and water.

"I wish I could offer more, but the Lord has seen fit to provide this humble meal and we are thankful for it." John looked at the meal and was disappointed. He was hoping for something a little more substantial. The priest saw the look in John's eye and said, "I am truly sorry. I see that you are hungry and would like more to eat but I'm afraid this is all I have. Perhaps we will be better fed tomorrow. The Good Lord will provide."

"I'd have thought he could do better than this."

"Yes, well, I'm quite sure he could if he thought we deserved it." John ate his fill of the bread and cheese and bid the man goodbye.

"May God bless you on your journey."

John mounted his horse and rode down the street out of town. The countryside was teaming with people. It seemed that he no sooner left one town and was in another. He stayed on the road that followed the river south through several small settlements. Ahead he could see the city of Saint Paul. He was reluctant to ride into that town because he knew that if he were to meet up with Jonas and his boys it would be there. He had no idea that in this town there were thousands of people, and the chances of seeing any particular one are almost nonexistent. He rode quietly and stayed in the shadows as much as he could. It was dark now and John was very hungry. He reined up to a restaurant and went inside and sat down. He'd eat and then pretend to have lost his money and he would offer to work for the meal. It had worked at Mister Belleair's tavern so it might work here. A man with an oversized belly covered with a stained white apron came to him, "What'll you have?"

"Whatever is ready."

"Brown beans."

"Then brown beans it is."

Two ragged men walked in behind John and sat at the table next to him. "We'll have beans too," one of the men shouted.

"You'll get yours—just keep yer shirt on!" the cook yelled.

"We ain't gonna sit here all night awaitin'," one said in a high-pitched voice. The other man laughed hard at the comment. John got his beans and began eating.

"We want our supper right now," the loud one said.

The cook came out of the kitchen and went to the table. "I think you two better jist git the hell out of my place."

"Yeah? And who's gonna make us go?" The cook grabbed the man by his dirty wool coat, pulled him from his chair, and threw him toward the door. The second man jumped up and caught a fist in the face and fell to the floor. John saw the opportunity to get out without paying for his meal and quietly walked out the door. He was about halfway to his horse when someone grabbed him from behind.

"Seems you forgot something back there." It made John jump when the man grabbed him. He turned and his eyes leveled on the badge on the man's coat.

"Huh? What did I forget?"

"You forgot to pay for your meal."

"I did? Well I'll be darned. I'll just go back there and pay up."

"Well, I'll just go back there with you and make sure you don't get lost on the way."

"No need for that, I can find it."

"You got no money do you?"

John looked at the ground. "No sir, I don't," he lied.

"We get your kind in our town ever'day. Turn around."

"What fer?"

"Just turn around and put your hands behind your back." John did as he was told and the constable snapped heavy iron handcuffs on him. John was terrified. He had never been in jail before and had no idea what he could expect. The constable hoisted him onto his horse and they rode the two blocks to the city jail. John heard the iron door to his cell close and he wanted to cry. They passed another policeman who was coming out of the jail.

"Well, well, well...look what the cat dragged in. Another bum jis' like us." John turned and looked at the two filthy men who had just been thrown out of the restaurant.

"Oh great," he said. "What the hell did I do to deserve this?" The taller of the two stood up and came to him and got his face right in front of John's. He had one tooth showing in his mouth. Thin shaggy whiskers made up his beard and he had a foul odor about his body. His eyebrows were thick and black and his hair hung in greasy strings around his shoulders.

"Wha'd ye do? Try to skip out wid'out payin'?" he said, as he cocked his head and looked into John's eyes.

"None of your damn business what I did. If you two hadn't been so damned noisy none of this would have happened. I'd have paid for the beans and I'd be clear of this damned place a long time ago. Git the hell away from my face— you stink."

"Well, jeez Mister, we didn't mean no harm. We was just havin' fun."

"Well have your fun at your own expense. Leave me out of it."

The other one looked up from the cot he was sitting on and said, "We're sorry Mister." He looked exactly like the man standing in front of John.

"And quit callin' me Mister. Name's John. Call me John."

"Then we can be friends?"

"I don't know. Maybe." John saw an opportunity to take advantage of these two half-wits. He wasn't sure how it would work yet, but he might as well give it a try. "You boys live around here?"

"We was born here but we live up by New Ulm now. That's a town a hunnert miles from here. We come here in the summer on the riverboats. That's where we work, on the riverboats."

"How do you get back home?"

"We jist walk or hitch rides with wagons goin' up there."

"Where is this New Ulm?"

"It's up the Minnesota Valley a ways. Mostly takes us all winter to..."

"Minnesota Valley? You know how to get there?"

"'Course we do. That's where we live." He laughed and the other man caught on and laughed with him.

"What's your names?"

"I'm Eddy. This here's Arty. Say hi, Arty."

"Hi." He sniffed his nose. Arty had a problem with a runny nose from being punched.

"Arty here, he's kinda simple, so I watch out for him, sorta."

"Good boy, Eddy. You brothers?"

"Yeah, this here's my brother, Arty."

Sniff. "Ye jist told him that, Eddy," Arty said from the cot.

"Shut up Arty, I'm the one talkin'."

"You shut up."

"Don't hafta." Eddy looked at John and said, "Guess I told you that, huh?"

"Yeah, ye did. When we get otta here you two can show me the way to the valley. I'll pay you good for it."

"Sure, we can do that."

"You boys been in jail before?"

"Ha! Hell, we spend more time in jail than out of it. The constable here knows us by our first names. We don't do nothin' bad—just swipe a meal once in a while, or steal something to sell. We ain't never kilt no one. Not yet enna ways. How 'bout you? Ever been in jail before?"

"Hell yeah, been in jail a-plenty," John said. "Mostly for fighting and beating up on men. That there's kinda why I'm here in the first place. Had me a big fight with a bunch of Injuns up north. Kilt two and the other one ran away."

"For real? How'd ye kill 'em? Shoot 'em?"

"Yep—shot one and hadda stab the other one with my knife. The third one got so skeered he ran away before I could get to him."

"How come you hadda fight 'em enna ways?"

"Well, they killed my wife and two boys. What would you do?"

"Did ye scalp 'em?"

"'Course I did. Got their scalps buried next to the river up by Saint Cloud."

"Fer real? You kin git lots of money for Injun scelps if you know where to sell 'em."

"And I suppose you know where that would be?"

"Sure, man up town buys 'em. He sells them to some..." Just then Arty punched Eddy in the arm, sniffed, and said, "Eddy, you ain't s'pose to tell no one about Mister Poke. If he finds out you told he'll kill us both."

"I didn't tell where he is. And you jist told his name, you dumb knob."

"Did not." Sniff.

"Ye did too. You said I ain't s'pose to tell about Mister Poke." The door to the jail opened and the policeman came in.

"John Olson?"

"That's me."

The cell door opened. "Come with me." John followed the policeman out the front door and down the street to the restaurant where he was arrested. "This is where you'll be spending the night—doing what you're told, without any sass, to pay for your dinner. Any questions?"

"What will I have to do?"

"That will be up to Mister Iverson here."

"Come with me," Iverson said. John followed him to the back room to a tub of water sitting on a table. Next to the tub was a stack of dirty dishes—cups, bowls, pots and pans, and silverware. "Yer job for tonight is to wash dishes." John couldn't say anything. He'd never had to wash a dish in his life and now he was facing a stack of them nearly as tall as he was. He looked at Mister Iverson. Iverson grinned and pointed at the stack, "Now." John stared at the dishes a few minutes before picking one up and slipping it into the very hot water. He winced when the water touched his hand.

In the morning, the constable walked into the restaurant and took John back to his cell. John's hands were clean but shriveled up like prunes.

"Where the hell you been, John?" asked Eddy.

"Non of yer damn business. Leave me alone."

"We was over at the stables shoveling shit," Arty said after a good sniff.

"You had it good. I hadda wash dishes all night."

"Ah hell, we do that all the time. You just came and took the job away from us this time."

"I'm goin' to sleep. You two keep quiet." The door came open and the constable walked in.

"You boys are free to go." As tired as John was, he jumped out of the bunk and hit the floor walking. "If I ever see any of you three in here again I'll have you working for a week."

"You ain't gonna see me around here again," John said. "In fact, you can take this town and shove it up..."

"Don't say it Olson. Yer in enough trouble the way it is. Now GIT before I change my mind." The three raggedy men almost ran out the door.

"Let's go find something to eat."

"You got any money?" John asked.

"No, but we can get fed in the jail." Eddy laughed like a maniac.

"Real funny," John responded. "You boys got horses?"

"Nope. We walk ever where we go unless we're on the boats."

"You say you know where to sell scalps?"

"Sure, Mister Poke buys 'em." Arty sniffed and punched Eddy on the arm again. Eddy pulled his arm away and said, "Dammit Arty, quit that. John's our friend. He was in jail with us wasn't he? I figger we can trust him."

"You know where some scalps are John?" Eddy asked, his head cocked to the side and his upper lip curled up to show the single yellow tooth.

"Maybe. Have to get to Saint Cloud to get 'em though."

"Wow, Saint Cloud. That's a long ways from here."

"Just a couple of days' ride."

"Yeah, but we ain't got no horses."

"How 'bout if I ride up and pick them up and meet you here in a week?"

"We can do that, I guess. How 'bout if we find horses and come with you?"

"Where you gonna find horses? Never mind, I don't want to know. If you find horses we'll all go. We'll be needin' supplies, food and such for a week of riding. And don't forget to bring blankets—it's cold."

Eddy looked at Arty. They both broke out laughing. "We kin git food. That's easy."

"Done. Git'cher selves ready and meet me here in the morning."

"How 'bout we meet on the other side of the river at the bridge?" Eddy said.

"All right. But why there, not here?"

"'Cuz our horses are on this side and it's safer over there."

"Sorry I asked."

John spent a restless night rolled up in his blanket in an alley, thinking about the prospect of money in his pocket. He hoped the scalps were still where he had buried them and Jonas and his thugs hadn't found them.

In the morning he threw the saddle on his horse and rode to the bridge across the Mississippi River. On the left of the bridge was a lumber mill with stacks of cut boards and mountains of sawdust. The morning crew had just started the wheels of the mill and a loud, obnoxious whine assaulted his ears. He stopped and looked at the wooden pillars and the cables that supported the bridge and wondered if it was safe to cross. Seeing horses and wagons crossing, he decided it would be all right, if he made the trip quickly. He looked up at the placard displaying fees for crossing the bridge. He passed through and approached the man sitting on the rail of the bridge looking at the ragged, slope-shouldered man sitting on the bone-thin horse.

"Good morning," said the man. "Captain John Trapper here. Fifteen cents to cross."

"I gotta pay to get out of this town?"

"Yep, everyone pays to use this bridge."

"I think it's robbery but I'll pay. There'll be two boys coming across in a little while, I'll pay you for them too."

"What do they look like?"

"They look like they been run over by a wagon train—ye can't miss 'em."

"Walkin' or ridin'?"

"I think riding. I hope they are enna ways."

"That'll be forty-five cents." John dug in his pocket and pulled out the money and handed it to the toll taker. "Stay close to the right," he said.

John heeled his horse and started across. The horse shied and refused to cross.

"Git off'n that horse and walk him over," the toll taker hollered.

"I know that!" John yelled back.

"Well do it then!"

He climbed off the horse and tugged at the reins but the horse refused to move. John was getting angry. He cussed and pulled harder on the reins but the horse wouldn't move. The toll taker came and took the reins, then slipped a blind over the horse's eyes and handed the reins back to John. John looked at him, "I was just about to do that. You didn't have to help."

"I can see that," the toll taker said. "By the way, this is a one way bridge. When you come back find another way to cross."

"Don't worry, I ain't comin' back."

"I'll see about getting the newspaper to print a thank you note to you."

John walked his animal across the bridge and climbed aboard. He walked through the streets until he was out on the prairie between Saint Paul and Minneapolis. He found a small grove of birch trees and sat down to wait for his companions.

He waited there for an hour for his new partners. He was cold and hungry but had given his last money to the toll taker and would have to wait for the boys to come with food.

"What the hell took so long?"

"What, we didn't know there was a time we was supposed to be here."

"I thought sunrise was the usual time to start a trip?"

Arty sniffed and poked Eddy on the arm and said, "I tole you we should get here earlier, Eddy."

"You did not. I told you to get yer ass otta bed but you di'nt. That's why we got here so late. It's his fault, John."

"Is not, it's yer fault."

"Is that all you two do is argue?"

"He started it."

"Did not, you did." Sniff.

"Dammit, shut up, the both of you. Let's git going."

"So where'd you get the horses?"

"Otta the stables. Ain't no one watchin' them in the night so they're plenty easy to grab."

"Gawd damn, yer horse thieves too?"

"We better git goin'. There's gonna be law men on our tails perty soon," Eddy said. They kicked their horses into a cantor and headed north toward Saint Cloud. They passed a camp of ox carts on the prairie between Minneapolis and Saint Paul but didn't stop.

It took them five days to reach the spot on the river where John had buried the pack of scalps. On the way they dined on steak and baked potatoes and cooked corn and peas. The boys had plenty of food in their bags.

"Where the hell did you get this food? It's better than I've had in months."

"We raid the cans out back of the restaurants. Sometimes we gotta fight the dogs and cats for it but we usually win. Show him yer finger, Eddy." Eddy held up his left hand and showed John that half of his middle finger was gone.

"Gad damn dog got it. Eddy got the steak but the dog got Eddy's finger." The boys broke down and laughed hard at the story. Arty almost forgot to sniff, but caught it just in time.

"Ye mean we're eatin' garbage?"

"Garbage to the rich bastards—food to us."

"Smartest thing I seen you boys do yet."

"It was my idea," Eddy said.

"Was not. I thought of it."

"Ye did not. I did."

The trio crossed the river at Saint Cloud and found the spot where John had buried the scalps. They dismounted and walked to the place where the pack was buried. "Gimme a shovel."

"We ain't got no shovel."

"Didn't I tell you two to bring the things we'd need for this trip?"

"Yeah, but we didn't know we was gonna need a shovel." Sniff.

"Well, guess it's just like it's always been. I'm gonna have to do all the thinking again. Git some sticks and start digging right here." He pointed at a snow-covered mound of frozen sand. Eddy and Arty picked their way down through the snow and sand until they hit a wooden box.

"Damn, it's still there. Hot damn. We're rich, boys." John sniffed. "Dammit, now you got me doin' it."

They pulled the box out and opened it. There were the scalps—in perfect shape—just as they were when John had buried them. They spent the night and started back to Saint Paul at sunrise.

Five days later they were camped on the prairie a short distance from the ox cart camp. John Owen could see a group of people gathered around a horse that was trying desperately to throw a rider from its back. He fought the urge to go over and watch, but he had more important things to take care of.

"Where's this man who's gonna buy the scalps from you?"

"We gotta take them to town to his store."

"How do you know he won't just take them and not pay you for them?" The boys looked at each other and shrugged their shoulders.

"Eddy, you take a sample into town and show it to the man. Then if he wants the scalps tell him to come out here and bring the money. He can get the goods then."

"How come you don't go?"

"'Cause he knows you. He ain't gonna buy nothin' illegal from me."

"Oh yeah, never thought of that."

"See, you ain't so smart as you think, Eddy." Sniff.

"Shut up Arty. Yer dummer'n me."

"Am not."

"Boys, boys—you just leave the thinking to me."

Eddy took the best scalp, wrapped it in leather, and rode off to town.

"Good God," he said to Arty. "He's riding a stolen horse to the town he stole it from."

"Naw, Eddy, he's smart. He'll drop the horse before he gets to town then walk in. We done it before—he won't git caught."

Three hours went by before Eddy came back to their camp. He had two men following him. John stayed hidden until he knew he was not meeting with anyone he might know. He came out and walked to the men.

"Where's the goods?"

"Where's the money?"

"You didn't say how much you want for it."

"Five hundred dollars."

"Don't be stupid. That stuff ain't worth half that. How many you got?"

"There's thirty of them in that pack."

"We want to see them." John opened the pack and displayed a dozen scalps on a spread deerskin.

"I'll give you two hundred for the lot."

"Three hundred."

"I'll give you two hundred and that's all. Those ratty scalps ain't worth a nickel more than that."

"Mister," John said, "If these scalps ain't worth that you wouldn't want them at all. Three hundred or you can leave now." He pointed his thumb at the ox carts.

Mister Poke glanced at the carts and said, "Three hundred it is. Pack 'em up." The man handed John the money and John gave him the scalps. John kept his rifle in his hand until the men were out of sight.

"Well, that was easy enough. Guess you boys got some money comin'. We'll split this three ways. Of course since they was my scalps I get the biggest share." He counted out fifty dollars for each of the boys and shoved the rest into his side bag.

"What now? Which way to the Minnesota Valley?"

Eddy pointed to the southwest and said, "Let's go."

"You know those people over there, John?"

"Nope."

"How come you pointed at them when you told Poke to leave if he didn't want the scelps?"

"Figgered Poke would think they was with us. He wasn't gonna start anything with that many people watching."

"Wow, yer perty smart, John."

"Can either of you shoot?"

"Sure, if we had guns we could."

John handed Eddy his rifle and said, "Here shoot this thing." Eddy took the rifle and shouldered it, aimed at a birch tree, and pulled the trigger. Nothing happened. He looked at the priming nipple and saw that there was indeed a cap in place and tried it again. The rifle still didn't fire.

"Gimme a new cap." John dug around in his side bag till he found the tin of caps that Sunkist had given him and handed it to Eddy. A fresh cap was placed on the nipple and the trigger pulled. The primer popped but the gun still didn't fire. Eddy pulled the ramrod out and slid it down the bore till it hit bottom. He looked at John and said, "Yer jist funnin' wit me. Diss ting ain't even loaded."

"That's right—it ain't loaded. I wanted you to know how important it is to keep yer gun loaded. Do me a favor and load 'er up for me, would ye Eddy?"

"Sure John." John handed Eddy his powder can and a bag of balls. Eddy measured the powder out in his palm and poured it down the bore. Then he took a ball and patch and laid them over the bore and tried to start the ball down. It wouldn't go.

"Ye give me the wrong balls, John. These are too big."

"What do you mean? I shot lots of deer with those balls. Unless..." John tried to hide the anger he suddenly felt as he told himself that Sunkist must have switched balls on him. It didn't occur to him that he might have gotten the wrong size balls when he took the gun from Jonas' horses. John was furious. His hands trembled and his eyes narrowed. "That son-of-a-bitch," he said slowly, looking at the rifle.

"Wha'd I do?"

"Not you, that son-of-a-bitch Sunkist switched balls on me so's I couldn't shoot this here gun. I'll get him for this," he said quietly. "I don't know how and I don't know where, but I'll kill that bastard and hang his greasy scalp on my horse's tail."

"Jeez, John. You ain't mad at me are you?"

"No, goddammit, I ain't mad at you. Gimme that gun." He grabbed it from Eddy's hand and threw it into the snow. Then in a fit of temper he kicked it and sent it flying four feet into the snow again.

"You got money so when you get a chance you'd best get some guns. Yer gonna be needin' 'em. Either of you two numb-nuts ever killed a man?"

Arty looked quickly at Eddy and elbowed him on the arm. Eddy pulled his arm back and gave Arty a dirty look. "I ain't gonna say nothin'. I ain't stupid, ye know."

"Nope, neither of us never kilt no one."

"First time for everything," John said quietly. "Git on them horses and let's git goin' before the law shows up."

John walked to his horse with an obvious limp from a broken big toe and climbed aboard. The three partners traveled slowly, stopping to raid garbage cans and spend money in every town they came to. They camped for days at a time in the same spot. Not one of them was in a hurry to get anywhere. Christmas came and went unnoticed. The cold weather didn't seem to bother the two brothers but John had trouble staying warm. The boys knew how to take care of things and seemed to be very knowledgeable about being outdoors. John kept them entertained with his stories about how he whipped the man on the wagon and how he'd out-smarted the big, redheaded Sunkist and how Sunkist's Indian wife wanted him so bad. But he, being an old Indian fighter, wanted nothing to do with her. The boys listened and began to worship John Owen.

Arty sniffed.

"Arty, why don't you blow your nose instead of sniffin' like that all the time?" Arty leaned to the side of his horse, plugged one side of is nose, and blew—then the other side. John said, "That's the most disgusting thing I have ever seen, Arty."

"Our pa does it all the time."

"I might have known."

Along the way they spotted a dogsled and riders heading in the same direction they were. They paid little attention but John seemed to be aware of them whenever they came close. The trio stopped in Shakopee where Eddy and Arty each bought a rifle with the necessary accoutrements. John was surprised at how much these two knew about the weapons they were buying. John also bought fifty caliber balls for his rifle and traded the fifty-fours for a tin of caps.

"How come you two know so much about guns?"

"Hell," Eddy said, "our pa learnt us about shootin' since we was old enough to lift a gun."

"Why is it you don't have a gun of your own then?"

"Hadda sell 'em to get something to eat. Gun ain't no good to a man what's starved to death."

"Can you shoot?"

"Sure. Arty here ain't too smart but he ain't never missed a deer since he was a baby. An' I'm better'n he is."

"Y'ain't neither." Sniff.

"Am too."

"Y'are not!" Arty yelled, obviously angry.

"Am too. I kin shoot better'n you wit my eyes shut."

"Can not."

"HEY!" John shouted, "What the hell ye fightin' about? You'll both get yer chance to see who's better. Now, how far to New Ulm?"

"Couple of days," Eddy said.

"Three days," Arty said.

"It's jist two days, Arty."

"Ain't neither. It's three days. You don't know everything."

"I know more'n you."

"Do not."

"BOYS!" John barked, "Quit cher damned arguing and lets git goin'."

Arty looked at Eddy. "I can shoot better'n you."

"Can not."

"HEY! That's enough. I can out-shoot da both of ye. Now let it go." Arty jabbed Eddy in the arm with his elbow and looked at John to make sure he didn't get caught doing it.

"Ow, stop it."

John said, "Am I gonna have to slap the shit out of both of you to make you stop that fighting?"

They were quiet the rest of the day. The air got extremely cold and John was near freezing to death. "John, maybe you better git off'n that horse and walk for a spell. It'll help warm you." John was so cold he couldn't answer. "We'll be in Mankato perty soon and you can get warm there." The boys worried about their friend. Eddy put his coat around John's shoulders and Arty wrapped his blanket around that. They pulled up in a grove of cottonwoods at the bottom of the valley and built a large fire. John huddled close and slowly the chill went out of his bones. Eddy made a broth of meat and potatoes and John drank his fill.

"Hope you boys don't think I'm soft or nothin' like that. Ever since I guided that string of wagons from the Pembina to Saint Cloud and almost froze to death saving them from freezing, I get cold easy."

"We didn't think that John. We all get cold. And besides, yer a lot older'n we are. Tomorrow we should be in Mankato. We can sit out this cold spell there. Then it's jist a couple of days to New Ulm. I got family there we can spend the winter with."

The next day they were outside Mankato. They rode past the dog train they'd been seeing for the past week camped on the prairie in a grove of trees. They rode into town and tied their mounts to the rail and went into a restaurant. They sat down at a table in the corner of the room. Because he was still careful about being recognized by some of his past acquaintances, John took the chair facing the wall. The boys were laughing about how they had gotten away with the horses and how they'd sold the scalps and came to the valley rich men. John was busy trying to get the attention of one of the waitresses—a good-looking girl of about twenty years. She laughed when he made a joke and John thought she liked him. Three men sat at a table across the room watching the three ragged men make fools of themselves. A man at the table next to them asked them to please be quiet, but they paid no attention to him. The young waitress in the white dress walked by and John reached out and touched her dress.

"Come and sit with us and have a drink."

"Please don't put your hands on me, sir," and she walked on by. John heard the young man on the other side of the room say something about a bathhouse and it made the waitress turn away from him. When she did John reached out and put his hand on her hip. She turned on him and said, "I told you to keep your filthy hands off of me."

He grabbed her and tried to pull her to him, "Aw, come on, give ole John a kiss." She picked up the tin plate he was eating from and slapped him across the face with it. John saw stars flash before his eyes and heard the plate ring when it hit. The man at the next table got up and grabbed John and threw him out the door. Two other men threw Eddy and Arty out right behind John. They landed in a heap in the snow on the street.

"Goddammit! I'll get that bitch for that." John got up, wiped the blood from his lower lip, brushed the snow from his ragged pants, and limped to his horse.

"How far to New Ulm?"

"We kin git there by nightfall if we ride right now."

"Let's go. I'll tend to her another time."

They rode to New Ulm and found the farm of Eddy and Arty's father, where they would stay for the winter. Their pa sat in a hard-backed chair whittling on a stick when they came in.

"Where the hell you two been?"

"We jist came back from Saint Paul," Arty said with a good sniff.

"The gad damn river's been froze for three months. What the hell took you so long getting' home?"

"Well, we had some bad luck there in the city. We got blamed for something we didn't do and spent some time in jail."

"Figgered something like that. Who the hell's this?" he said, pointing his whittling knife at John.

"He's our friend. Can he stay here for the winter?"

"Ain't never put no one out in the winter. Long as he can do his share of the work he can stay as long as he likes." He looked at John, "What's yer name?"

"John."

"Yer last name."

"Olson. John Olson."

"Norsk, huh?"

"Yeah, Norwegian."

"Amos Grenges. This here's my place."

"Figured that."

"Arty, go get the dish towel and blow your damn nose. I hate that nastiness."

Eddy and Arty worked cutting wood and selling it to the farmers around the area. John made frequent trips to town on business. The three went on hunting trips during the winter, when the weather allowed, and brought home deer and elk meat.

The weather turned warm and the snow began to melt and fill the river bottom. One day, John, Eddy and Arty were on the north side of the river hunting deer. They sat in a grove of cottonwoods when John heard hooves on the trail fifty yards from them.

"Shhh, someone's coming." The three watched as a red-haired man rounded the corner ahead of an Indian woman.

"I'll be damned," he said.

"What?" Arty said.

"Sunkist and that squaw."

"You gonna kill him?"

"Damn right I am, and you're gonna git that squaw."

"Me? I ain't never kilt a woman before, John. I don't know…"

"You shoot that damn squaw or I'll put a bullet through your head."

"Don't git mad, John. I'll do it. It's just that I…" John had his rifle up and aimed at the red-haired man. Eddy aimed his rifle at the woman.

"Ready?"

"Yup."

"Fire!" Both guns went off at the same time. The Indian woman toppled from her horse and into the dirt. The red-haired man raised his rifle and put a bullet through Eddy's heart killing him instantly. John and Arty lay in the brush watching the redheaded man as he jumped from his horse and ran to the woman on the ground. He loaded his rifle before he knelt down next to her body. His head came up and looked around peering deeply into the brush. Suddenly Arty panicked, jumped up, and started running. He didn't go far before a bullet crashed through his spine and he went down. The red-haired man loaded his rifle and slowly walked to the dying man. He walked by John who was hidden deep in the brush scared to breathe.

The man kneeled by the wounded man and said, "Who the hell are you, and why did you have to kill the girl?"

"I didn't kill no one—it was John made us do it."

"Who's John?" but the question fell on dead ears. John watched as the man took the scalps from Eddy and Arty. Then with his clenched fist he mashed in their faces. John found himself once again hiding in the brush just like on that day in Otter Tail County when his family was killed. He watched as his victim was buried. The red-haired man took the reins of her horse and rode on. When he thought it was safe, John came out of the brush. He went to the bodies and stripped the money from their pockets and took their guns, powder, and shot bags. He walked the hundred yards to where they had tied their horses and rode back to Eddy and Arty's farm.

"Where's the boys?" the old man asked.

"Got bad news for ye Mister Grenges. Yer boys is dead."

"Dead? How?"

"Man I knew back in Saint Cloud named Sunkist kilt 'em. Kilt 'em for no reason. Got 'em from ambush."

"How come you ain't dead too?"

"Sunkist only had two guns. He took off before I could get a bead on him."

"Damn, I figgered those boys would end up dead sooner or later. But I never thought they'd get it from ambush."

"Where'd ye bury them?"

"Other side of the river where no one will bother the graves."

"Damn. First their ma, now them. I'm alone, John. What does a man do when he's alone?"

"Don't know, Amos. Me, I'm heading up the valley and look for some land and settle down."

"Guess I'll ride with you—that be all right?"

"S'pose it'd be okay. How old were the boys?"

"Eddy was nineteen. Arty was just seventeen."

"Same age as my boys when they died."

It gave me a kind of a thrill to finally be where my
mind had imagined for so long.
My imagination didn't do the valley justice…

CHAPTER FOUR

NEXT MORNING, AFTER THE BATTLE, we loaded our carts and moved off to the south toward Elk River. A dozen more carts attached themselves to our train. Most of the carts were drawn by oxen—some had mules and two were pulled by horses. It was a boring walk that morning with nothing to see but trees and flat ground. We'd been on the road for about three hours when all of a sudden we heard shouting and shooting to our rear. I turned and saw about twenty riders coming at full-gallop in our direction. I ran to the nearest low spot in the ground and took up a shooting position.

Jean came running at me. "Hold your fire!" he hollered. "That's our escort."

"What the hell you talking about—escort?"

"The escort I told you we were getting from Elk River to Saint Paul."

"I thought you said we'd pick them up in Elk River."

"Well, looks like they got here a little early, don't it? These guys are all nuts and every one of them can outshoot you, me, and the Renard on their worst day with us on the ground and them on horseback."

"That we'll have to see."

"You will, boy, you will. They love showing off with their shooting."

The men and horses rode into the camp at full-gallop. They circled the carts hootin' and hollerin' and shooting their guns. Some of them jumped off their horses and hugged friends they hadn't seen in a while. Some went for the ladies. A man walked to Lorraine and spoke to her then hugged her. They talked for a few minutes and he walked back to his horse. I wanted to ask someone—anyone—who he was but I figured I'd find out in due time. At that point I really didn't want to know anyway. When all the noise and shooting stopped and the riders had made their presence known, the train moved on at its slow, steady pace. The riders stayed out from the train and seldom came close enough to talk to the ox cart drivers. I don't think a full ten minutes passed when there wasn't a horse race. Anytime one would come next to another they would kick their horses and race to the front of the train laughing and hollering and whipping their horses to go faster. Some of the men showed their skill by jumping off one side and swinging over the running horse to the other side and then back into the saddle. This went on throughout the day.

Finally that night we camped in an open meadow. The carts and wagons were pulled into a circle and the cattle brought inside with the people. The escort stayed outside the camp in their own little circle. Some stayed in the saddle while the others made the camp.

"How come the cattle are inside the circle tonight, Jean?"

"Rumors of Injun trouble in these parts. We don't need to be losin' our livestock to them now."

"That why we got this escort with us? Injuns?"

"As a rule we have an escort all the way from Pembina, but this time we got started too late and couldn't find men to ride for us. They was all gone back to Canada by the time we left. See, usually the carts leave Pembina while there's good grass for the cattle, but this train got held up waiting for some cargo that needed to get to Saint Paul and got to us late. We have people with us that need to be there too, so we didn't have much choice—we had to make the trip. Injuns ain't much trouble this time of year either so we figured we was safe."

"What people? Who would that be?"

"Ain't none of your concern, Hawk."

"Oh yeah, sorry." I heard shooting coming from the other side of camp and went to investigate. The riders were shooting at targets drawn on the trees. None of the targets were closer than fifty yards, and most of them were over one hundred yards out. All types of rifles were displayed—some long-barreled, some short—but all deadly accurate. One hundred-yard targets were being struck on the black mark almost every time. I stood and watched, not sure if I was good enough to join in.

"Go git yer gun, Hawk. These guys'll show you how to shoot."

"They are good, Jean, no doubt about that."

"Well?"

"You gonna shoot?"

"Yep, ain't nothin' better than bein' whipped by the best."

"Got a point there. Be right back." I went for my rifle.

When I got back I took my place in line and waited for my turn. I loaded my forty-five Tennessee with my favorite load and stepped up to the line. I knew I had to make a good show or be the center of the jokes until the next guy missed. I held my sights tight and squeezed the trigger. My bullet hit just off the black. No one said anything. I was a little disappointed that they didn't make a joke of it but thought maybe they were being kind to the new man in line. The shots from the men seldom strayed more than five inches at one hundred yards. I figured I could do that good, and I did.

I took my shot and went to reload. Jean stopped me. He said, "When the man starts counting, you start loading."

"Counting? How far's he gonna count?"

"Ten. Ye ready?"

"*Un...deux...tois...*" Figuring that was the count I started loading. I got the powder measured and poured down the barrel—BLAM! BLAM! BLAM! These guys were already shooting and I had just poured the powder down. I stood and looked, dumfounded. All the shots had hit their mark. Most incredible thing I'd ever seen.

"Think I'll just sit back and watch."

"Good idea. These guys do this every day of their lives and they just keep getting better. If I ever git in a close fight I want these men on my side." The shooting stopped after a couple of rounds of counting and shooting, then they retired to the camp for a meal and conversation.

Suddenly, I saw Renard laying on the ground and Lorraine kneeling next to him. I walked over and knelt down next to Lorraine.

"What happened?"

"He just does this sometimes. He falls down for no reason. It's from the bear attack."

"Does he stay down for long?"

"No, but it seems to be happening more frequently than it used to." Renard started to move and Lorraine spoke to him in French. He opened his eyes and smiled at her, then spoke. She helped him to his feet and they walked to his tent. I followed along to see if there was anything I could do to help. Lorraine led Renard through the tent opening and laid him on his blankets.

"Is he gonna be all right?"

"Yes, he will rest for a while and then be like he was before." The man I saw hugging Lorraine came to the door and said something to her in French. She replied with French words and a nod of her head.

"I'll go now and leave you alone," I said.

"No, Hawk. Stay a minute. This is my brother Goodhorse."

She looked at Goodhorse and said, "*Je vous presente*, Hawk."

"Goodhorse speaks English but not very well."

"My sister say you good to our father and teach him to shoot again."

"He's a good man. Your father?" I looked at Lorraine. "Renard is your father?"

"Yes, I thought you knew."

"How would I know that?"

"Yes, I suppose it would be too much to expect you to figure it out for yourself. Father doesn't know I'm his daughter since the bear got him. I tried to make him believe it but he won't accept it. The bear hurt something in his head and there are some things he can't figure out." She paused. "So many things have changed for him now."

I looked down at Renard and he was looking at me and smiling. "You gonna be all right Fox?"

He shook his head up and down fast and grinned. "Fox get better," he said.

"He has to rest now. He will be up in the morning."

I walked away from the tent to leave Goodhorse and Lorraine with their father. Goodhorse followed me out.

"My sister says you teach Renard to shoot."

"No, he knows how to shoot. He was just using the wrong eye to aim. You should'a seen him shoot when the Indians attacked us on the Elk River. I don't think he missed once. He knows very well how to shoot."

"And you let him shoot deer for the camp?"

"Why not? He can do it."

"He does not remember it, you know." I looked at Goodhorse, not knowing what to say. He looked back at the tent. "It is very sad to see a man like he was go back to being a child. He was the best. He could paddle a canoe all day, carry three packs, and sing a hundred songs, all day and half the night. He was taught English at the Catholic schools in Montreal and he could read and write. He taught my sister and me how to read too. Lorraine can write English but I cannot."

I had more questions but, being aware of the private nature of these people, I resisted asking.

"My sister says you are a good man. She says you shoot very well."

"I can get meat if that counts."

"I would like to shoot with you."

"Maybe tomorrow or another time. It's getting too dark now."

"Yes, tomorrow. *Au revois mon ami. Bon nuit.*"

"Good night, Hawk. *Bon nuit, Bon Cheval,*" Lorraine said from inside the tent.

Darkness fell and the camp got very quiet. I slept like a dead log all night without waking up once. Morning came all too soon. I woke up to the sounds of people loading carts and riders talking as they saddled their horses. The cook had a steaming pot of stew over the fire. I gathered my meager belongings into my sack and loaded it onto Jean's cart. The cattle and horses were hitched to the carts before we sat down to eat. Lorraine and Renard came and sat next to Goodhorse and me for their breakfast.

"How are you feeling today, Fox?" I said.

"Huh?" He looked at me but I don't think he saw me. His eyes were hollow and didn't show any sign at all that he recognized me. I looked at Lorraine. She looked at me and shook her head side to side to say that she didn't know what to do either. Renard sipped from his cup and said nothing. When he was finished he handed the cup to Lorraine. He stood up and walked to the side of the cart he always walked with, sat down, leaned against the wheel, and stared into the open prairie.

When all had had their breakfast, Jean shouted, "*Reveille, reveille nos gens, alons, alons!*" Everyone went to their carts and horses and we were once again moving.

"Where is your horse?" Goodhorse asked as he rode up beside me.

"Don't have one. I wouldn't know how to ride it if I did."

"You don't ride a horse?" he replied, looking surprised.

"Never had one to ride." Goodhorse looked at me for a long moment and rode away.

He came back in a few minutes leading a saddled horse. "Here is one for you to ride. You cannot walk all the way to Saint Paul."

"Why not? I've already walked from Otter Tail County and I'm doing just fine."

"Now you will ride. She is a gentle horse and will be easy for you to ride."

I took the reins and lifted my foot into the stirrup, swung my leg over the horse's rump, and dropped into the saddle. The horse didn't move. I tapped her ribs with my heels like I had done with Pa's mules and she started walking forward.

"Hold on to the horn and kick her to run. Let's go!" I did as he said and the horse took off at a run but not nearly as fast as Goodhorse. I wasn't too sure I was going to like this riding thing. It was awfully hard on the backside, bouncing in the saddle like I was, but I stayed with it until I got fairly comfortable being on top of a horse. I'd ridden Pa's mules enough to be able to stay aboard when she turned or stopped but this was a lot faster than I'd gone before, and it was a little scary at first. A couple of riders came alongside and offered to race with me and I obliged them as best I could. But they were such better riders than I was—I didn't have a chance. I could blame the horse too, I suppose, but even if I had the fastest animal in the herd I still wouldn't have known how to make it run.

It didn't take us long to arrive in a town called Anoka. There we crossed a bridge over the Rum River. We passed a copper shop, a sawmill, woodworking shops, shoemakers, and lots of other places of business. There were homes and farms with their cattle barns next to the streets of town. We moved through the town slowly while people came out to watch us go by. No one in the train said anything. They walked on, not looking either way or directly at anyone on the street. With the noise from the wheels, we couldn't have said much and be heard anyway so we stayed quiet. We passed a ferry that carried folks across the Mississippi but we stayed on the east side and moved along toward Saint Paul. There were more farms and settlements now and we passed a lot more people on the road, mostly farmers going to town and coming home. A few riders on horseback, but most were driving wagons pulled by mules and oxen. We passed one driver who had the biggest horses I'd ever seen. They were taller at the shoulder than I was and they had huge muscles on their legs and necks. Their feet were as big as dinner plates and covered with long white hair—their manes and tails were white too. They were beautiful to watch. We came to a prairie where we could see the town of Saint Paul to the east. There we camped for the night.

"How was the riding, Hawk?" asked Goodhorse as I tried to get down from the horse gracefully. My legs didn't want to work. The muscles on the inside were so stiff it was hard to move them. And my backside was even more uncomfortable. My back hurt and my neck ached.

"Great. Beats walking don't it?"

I guess Goodhorse could see I was sore and said, "Maybe you walk for a day or two now."

"No, I can learn this riding thing all right. I'm fine."

"If you wish. But you need a better horse. I will find you one." He rode off at a slow canter.

Next morning we had breakfast and sat back down on the grass to wait for the traders to let us know when they would be ready for us to come in and deliver our cargo. Goodhorse came to me and said, "I have a fine horse for you—a stallion that was taken by one of the men from the Indians up north. He is a little wild yet but I think you will be able to ride him." A man walked over leading a black horse that was saddled and ready to ride. "This will be your horse, Hawk."

I looked him over and wondered why anyone would give away such a fine specimen of horseflesh. Truth is, I wouldn't know a good horse from an ugly dog. I said my thanks and stuck my foot in the stirrup, then painfully swung my leg over his back, and once again I was in the saddle. The horse stood still with his head hung low to the ground. I touched his ribs to make him go but nothing happened. I touched a little harder and his head came up. Then when I kicked his ribs, his rear end came off the ground and I went flying over his head. I landed on the ground on the back of my neck, thinking I was dead. Unfortunately, I wasn't. I only hurt more than I did before the flight. Goodhorse and his buddies were laughing so hard they almost fell over. I got up from the ground, brushed the snow from my trousers, and grinned at them for a minute. They had caught the horse and were waiting to see what I would do next.

"I suppose you think I'm getting back on the damn horse."

"We were hoping you would. When you ride this horse it will be yours. It is a wild horse that only needs to be trained, then it will be as good as any of the others we ride. When you get on the horse you have to hang on to the saddle to stay on. Don't let the horse think you are afraid of him or he will never stop bucking. Watch his head—it will tell you where he is going to turn next and try to be ready for it."

I walked over to Goodhorse and, looking in his eyes, grabbed the reins from his hand. I swung into the saddle and promptly got thrown off into the snow.

"Hold tight to the reins when he throws you. Don't let him run away from you."

Back on the animal's back, holding tight to the saddle front and back, I kicked him in the ribs. His front feet came up and he stood on his hind legs. I almost rolled off the back but I had a good grip on the horn and stayed on until he jumped straight up and came completely off the ground. He came down leaving me up there alone with nothing under me but eight feet of air and, below that, snow that came up to meet the back of my neck again. This was looking like it could be a long, hard battle and I was starting to think that Goodhorse and his buddy had set me up for some laughs. Not only were the two perpetrators enjoying the show, but a crowd had gathered in a wide circle to see this dumb animal make a fool of me. *Damn, there's Lorraine. Now I can't quit—what would she think?*

One of the men in the crowd caught the horse and brought it back to me. "You don't need to do this all in one day, you know. You can stop and heal yourself for a day or two if you want."

"Gimme them damn reins." I threw myself up on top of the crazy animal and grabbed two handfuls of saddle, kicked him hard in the ribs, wrapped my dying legs around his chest, and prepared for another sail through the air. The horse jumped forward coming five feet off the ground then hopped like a jackrabbit for a few seconds. He twisted and turned and jumped straight up, dropped down on the ground with all four feet hitting at the same time which nearly drove my head down between my shoulders. He bucked and bawled and squealed and ran full speed for fifty yards, then stopped dead to throw me over his head again. By now I had him figured out. I knew what he was going to do before he did. I knew it, that is, until he stopped and stood still like he'd given up. Truth is, I was just scared to fall off. He stood there for a good two minutes.

"Hang on, Hawk. Don't relax just yet," Goodhorse said. I turned to look at him and the wild horse jumped straight up and when he came down he'd moved five feet forward and left me with nothing to land on but the ground. It seemed as if I was just hung there for a few seconds before screaming down into the snow. The brute turned his head and looked at me as if he were laughing at me. I got up, brushed the snow from myself, and took the reins. I tried to get back up on the horse, but my legs just wouldn't cooperate. Goodhorse took the reins and said, "That is enough for today, Hawk. You can work on him when you get healed a little."

The next day we were up early and moving into town. I walked. I couldn't get on a horse from the sore legs and back...and neck...and pride.

"How ye feeling, son?"

"Jean, the only thing on me that doesn't hurt is my hair."

"Ye know, that horse ain't worth gettin' yer self killed over."

"He ain't gonna kill me. He's gonna raise all kinda hell with my body, but he ain't gonna kill me. Where is that critter anyway?"

"They got him roped to a cart back there. He likes to run when he gets a chance. Hawk, that horse ain't never gonna be a riding horse. Let it be. You can find another one that ain't crazy when we git paid for our trip."

"I got no money to be buyin' horses. Besides, I don't even need a horse. I walked from Otter Tail to here and I'm just fine. I'm goin' back there and see him."

I walked to the back of the train and found the horse tied to the rear-most wagon. He rumbled softly when he saw me and his eyes got big. "I ain't gonna git on yer back, Bud. Just came to see ye." I put out my hand to rub his nose but he pulled back and wouldn't let me touch him. I patted his neck and rubbed his shoulder. I walked beside him the rest of the way to Saint Paul.

"What's that smell, Jean?"

"That, my friend, is the big city."

"It smells awful. What is that?"

"People, Hawk. Too many people crowded in one place makes things smell like that."

"How can they live in this? It stinks."

"They can live in it 'cause they're the ones making the stink. They burn their garbage in tin barrels and dump their chamber pots in the alleys. They got chickens and cows and pigs running around their yards. And the factories burn coal to keep their plants running. Look at the air, Hawk. You can see the smoke and stink. That, my boy, is the big city. People don't mind it 'cause they live in it and they don't even smell it anymore. Kinda like your shirt. You can't smell it but Lorraine can."

"She can?"

"Sure, and you can smell her. Difference is, she smells good, you don't."

"Yeah well, you don't ezzac'ly remind me of my mother's petunia patch either, you know."

"We won't be here long so just hold yer breath till we get otta here."

The streets were lined with half-frozen ruts from the dozens of wagons and horses going and coming through town. Jean lead us to a warehouse in, what I guessed, was the business part of Saint Paul. The carts lined up, each waiting his turn to pull in front of the warehouse to unload. In about an hour it was our turn. I helped carry the packs and bundles into the store where they had men sorting, labeling, and moving them to different piles and stacks to be loaded on the riverboats going to Saint Louis, New Orleans, or out East. It took only a few minutes to get unloaded and John and I stood on the board sidewalk looking up and down the street.

"What now, Jean?"

"Now we go back to camp and wait for someone to call us with a load for Pembina. But they ain't gonna have nothin' till spring so we got us a long winter to do nothing. Find someone to work for to make yer self enough money for your trip up the valley. Or just go—take your chances with whatever you find.

"What about you?"

"I gotta stay with the carts. They'll need someone to run the show."

"Guess I'll stay too. Maybe do some huntin' for the traders."

"Hawk, they don't hunt here no more. They buy their food from stores and they get it from people who raise it, or have it brought in on the riverboats or wagons. Cain't find no hunting jobs around the big city."

"Riverboats? They got jobs?"

"They'll take you on right now if you can figure out a way to get a boat up the river through the ice."

"Oh yeah, never thought of that. Can you read, Jean?"

"'Course I can."

"What's that sign say?" I asked, pointing to the sign above the door.

Without looking up he said, "It says 'Fur Trader'."

"What's that one say?" I pointed to the sign above the door next to the fur trader's store.

Jean looked up and said, "Cain't see it too good, ask Goodhorse." Then he yelled, "Hey Goodhorse, what's that sign say?"

He came over to us, looked at the sign, and said, "It says, 'Private Dance Ah-ca-da-mee…Private Dance Academy'." Then, pointing at the one above the fur trader's door he said, "That one says 'Cheritree and Farwell'." Pointing further down he said, "That one says, 'J.N. Schroeder'."

"All right, all right, so you can read. Lots of guys can read," Jean snarled.

"What's a dance academy, Goodhorse?"

"That's where people pay money to learn how to dance."

"Really? I think we should go in and learn how to dance," I kidded.

"We ain't allowed in that place. Only people who got money can go in there." He glanced at Jean.

"Aw hell, I'm just as good as they are. Let's go in and see what they do." I started for the door to the 'Dance Academy'.

Jean looked at Goodhorse and they both shrugged their shoulders and followed along wearing a sly grin. "Might be interesting to see," Jean said.

I pushed the door open and was hit by an odor that might have knocked me out if the door hadn't been open to let fresh air in. Inside it was sorta dark because the windows were all covered with red curtains and paper. The walls had dark red paper on them—even the floor was covered with dark red rugs. The room smelled like lilacs and vanilla. In one corner there was a chair that was stuffed and covered with a soft-looking cloth. It was red like the rest of the room. On a table next to the chair was an oil lamp that was lit.

"If they'd open the curtains they wouldn't have to burn the lamps," I thought out loud.

There was a long couch against one wall with a small table on each end of it and a lamp on each of those. A small potbelly stove sat along another wall. On the other end of the room was a door with a bead curtain hanging over it. I looked around for a few minutes wondering where the dancing was.

Then the bead curtain opened and a lady came through it. I had never seen a woman that looked like she did. She was wearing a dress that you could see right through if she didn't have so many on, and the top didn't cover everything it should have covered. Uncle Robert had kidded me about a woman's breasts but this was the first look I ever had at them. It was real hard not to look. She saw me looking and glanced down at the valley between them and smiled a little when she looked back at me. Her hair was red except for close to her head where it looked kinda whitish. She had it piled high on her head with a pin a foot long stuck through it. She was painted all around her eyes with black lines. Her cheeks had red paint on them too and her lips were as red as buffalo blood. Around her neck she wore a fur like I had never seen before. It had long fluffy hair, more like feathers. She swung it around her neck as she walked in and said, "What can I do for you boys?" Then she looked at Jean.

"Well Jean Charbonneau, you crusty old Frenchman. Where the hell have you been?"

"You know her Jean?"

"Um ... yeah, well kinda. We go back a few years. Uh, but we're just friends ye understand. Good to see ye, Linda."

"Yeah, me and Jean here are just friends like a bear's just friends with his hide. Give Linda a big hug, Jean." She grabbed him and pulled him against her, wrapped her arms around him, and kissed him right on the mouth. Damnedest thing I ever saw—kissin' on the mouth like that. Must be so they can both kiss at the same time.

"What brings you in so late, Jean? Hi Goodhorse, it's nice to see you. Ramona will be glad to see you."

"You know her too?" I said to Goodhorse. He just grinned.

"We got a late start otta Pembina. Got Rolette with us and he ain't the fastest at gittin' his self moving. Kinda walks at his own speed, ye know."

"He may be slow, Jean, but he beat you getting' here. He's in the back with one of the girls right now."

"Don't let him spend all his money till I get paid for his ride."

"You know he don't pay here. That's how I stay open."

"And who do we have here?" she said, turning to me.

"This here's Hawk. Picked him up on the road a couple of months back. Says he'd like to learn how to dance."

"Hi Hawk, I'm Linda. Welcome to our studio." All I could do is stand and look at her. Not that she was so pretty but that she was all painted up like that.

"Jean, does he know?" She swung her finger like she was pointing all around the room.

"Um, no. I don't think so."

"Well Hawk, we're gonna take good care of you."

She turned, "Your tab, Jean?"

"Put it on Rolette's tab. Hawk here fed him half the way down."

"He ain't gonna like that."

"What's he gonna do, take me to court?"

"Who's this Rolette I keep hearin' about?" I asked.

"Never mind, Hawk. Ye don't need to know."

"Dammit Jean, quit bein' such a mountain man. It ain't gonna hurt Hawk to know who he is." She turned to me and said, "He was the state representative from Pembina. He comes down here a couple of times a year to sit and make laws for everyone to follow but him. That's who he is. At least he was. Now do you know?"

"Nope, don't know what a state repre…whatever you said, is. Ain't never saw one before."

"You sure about this, Jean?" Linda said.

"Yep, the boy's nineteen—time he learned how to dance."

"Eighteen," I said.

"I have a new, um…teacher today—brand new to the profession. She's just what Hawk needs. In fact, this is her first lesson."

"Hawk, you come with me. Jean, I'll be right back." Then she said to me, "Jean's got something we need to get straight between us."

"You two have a problem needs worked out?" I said, "Best thing in the world is to talk it out."

"I ain't got no problems, but I think Jean might." She wrinkled up her nose, shook her head up and down, and said with a smile, "I'll take care of it." She led me through the beaded curtain and down a hall to a room in the back. She opened the door and motioned me inside.

"Your teacher will be right with you," she said, and closed the door. The only thing in this room was a brass frame bed and a stand next to it with a wash-basin and pitcher. Towels were hung on nails on the wall above the washstand. The window was covered with red curtains just like the first room we were in. On the other side of the bed was another small table and another oil lamp. The globe on the lamp was painted red. *Who ever owns this place must really like red,* I thought to myself.

The door opened and a lady about my age came in. She was wearing a dress almost like Linda's but she had a robe over it. She was not painted up as much as Linda around her eyes but she had the red stuff on her cheeks. Her thick auburn hair hung to her shoulders and curled at the bottom.

"So…you're Hawk. I'm Sophie. Glad to meet you."

"Um, Harlan—my name's Harlan. People call me Hawk." I couldn't think of anything else to say. The woman looked like she was about to pull a prank on me, like I was going to be someone's entertainment again, just like with the horse.

"Don't be nervous, Hawk. I'm not going to hurt you. Linda says you have never danced before. That true?"

"Well, I danced with my ma once but it was just for a minute when my Uncle Robert got his fiddle. He couldn't play it too good so Ma said she couldn't dance to it."

She looked at me kinda curious-like and said, "Excuse me, Hawk. I'll be right back."

In a minute she came back in and said, "Well, I guess this is for real."

"Where do we start?"

"I think, Hawk, we should start with a bath." She waved her hand across her face as if fanning herself and said, "Phew, come with me."

"A bath? I don't need a bath to dance."

"You do if you're gonna dance with me."

"I think this wasn't such a good idea. I'm leaving."

She took my arm and said, "You just stay here. I think you're going to enjoy this a lot more than I am."

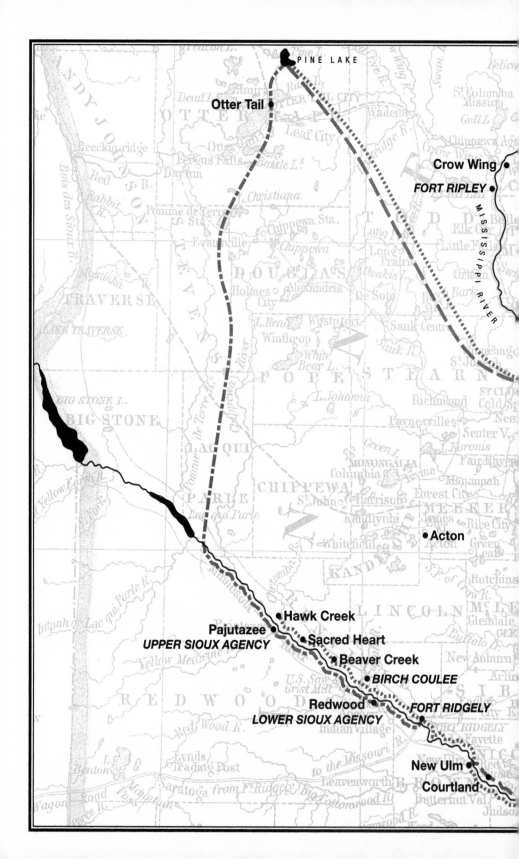

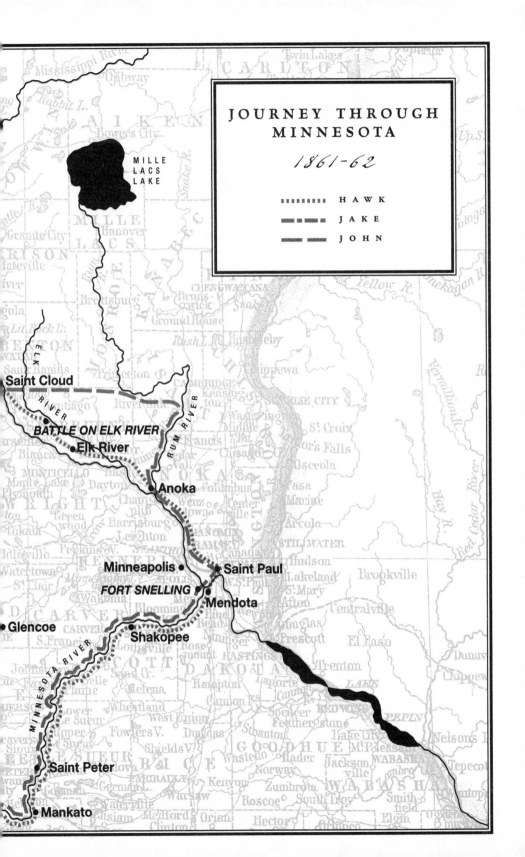

"What's that s'posed to mean?"

"Just come this way." I was taken to another room where there was a copper bathtub filled with hot water and next to it was a table with towels and soap on it. A woodburning stove in the corner had a tub of water sitting on it to stay hot.

"Get out of those filthy clothes and get in the tub. I'll wash your back for you."

"I don't need you to wash my back. I can do it myself."

"Just get in the tub. we'll see what happens then."

I waited for her to leave but she didn't. "You gonna just stand there while I get undressed?"

"Shy?" she said with a grin.

"That's twice someone said that to me. Yes, I'm shy. Turn around or leave."

"I think I'll just step out the door. You call me when you get in the tub."

"I ain't gonna call you. Like I said, I can wash myself."

"Suit yourself," and she walked out.

It wasn't easy getting out of those sticky buckskin pants, and the long underwear was even more difficult to get off without ripping. But I got in the tub and slid down into the water. Damn, it felt good. I didn't know how good hot water could feel until now. I laid back and closed my eyes and let the hot water soothe my aching muscles and joints. Then I thought to myself that I have all winter to train that crazy horse. My thoughts went to the train and the horse and Lorraine and the Minnesota Valley. I might have fallen asleep except the door opened and made me jump.

"Well Hawk, are you ready for me to wash your back?"

"No, I ain't ready for you to wash my back," I said as she took a cloth and started to scrub my back with her sweet-smelling soap. This tough guy act was getting me nowhere with this woman.

"How does that feel?"

"I guess it's ok." I tried to cover myself but it wasn't doing much good.

Sophie poured some stuff in the water and said, "Swish that around and make a lot of bubbles. That'll help you maintain your modesty."

"Huh?" She reached over me and splashed her hand around in the water and made bubbles.

"Like that." She scrubbed my back and up onto my shoulders and started down my chest. "Do you have a girlfriend, Hawk?"

"Nah, never had a girlfriend. Just Lorraine—the girl on the train."

"She your girlfriend?"

"No, just one of the women I know better'n the rest of 'em." Her hands moved down my chest and lower to my stomach. I could feel her body pressing against the back of my shoulders.

"Um, Miss Sophie…maybe I should get out of the tub now. I think I'm clean."

"Not yet, Hawk," I felt her drop something cold on my head and start to scrub my head like Ma used to do when we had cooties.

"Oh no, well would you look at that?" she said and walked around to the front of the tub where I could see her. She showed me where she had splashed water on her dress. The whole front of her was wet and showed things I had never seen before.

"Miss Sophie, I really need to get out of this tub now. I think I am as clean as I need to be."

"Why Hawk, you're embarrassed. You have never seen a woman's body have you?"

"No ma'am, and I don't think this is the time for it neither. I think I need more of those bubbles."

"Well, let me wash that soap from your hair and then you can get out." She pulled the wet robe off her shoulders and put a dry one on over her wet dress.

"Miss Sophie, do you have anymore of that bubble stuff?"

"Need more bubbles, Hawk? How come?"

"Just 'cause, that's how come."

She walked away and came back in less than a minute and poured hot water over my head.

"Ow! Damn. Whad'ya trying to do, scald me?"

"Just rinsing the soap out of your hair. Still need those bubbles, Hawk?"

"Miss Sophie, you leave now or I'm climbing out of this tub whether you're here or not."

"Well you just go ahead and climb out of that tub because I ain't goin' nowhere."

Damn, this was one stubborn woman. "Miss Sophie, I ain't never been this close to a lady before, 'cept my ma, and I don't think it's right we should be doing this. So if you don't mind I would like to just get dressed and go now."

"You're serious, aren't you, Hawk?"

"Yes ma'am."

"You're a decent man, aren't you, Hawk?"

"If you mean I don't do things I'm going to be ashamed of, you're right. I figure if you don't do anything you can't let other people know about, you won't ever have to tell a lie."

The smile left Sophie's face and the devil left her eyes. She said, "Hawk, thank you for that. You have opened my eyes to something very important."

"What's that?"

"Please don't ask. You don't want to know."

"There you go. Everyone says things and then tells me don't ask about it. They tell me I don't want to know. If I don't want to know I wouldn't have asked."

Miss Sophie walked out of the room and left me alone to get dressed in my dirty clothes. I walked out of the bathroom and out through the door we came in, then looked up and down the street wondering where Jean went. I walked back inside to see if anyone was there to show me the way back to the camp but the room was empty. I went to the back where I had met Sophie and found her packing a bag. "Going somewhere?"

"Just out of here."

"Are you all right? I didn't do anything to hurt you, did I?"

"Hawk, if you did anything you saved my life. I have no business being in a place like this. See, I have morals too and they are much more important than money."

"I don't understand."

"Okay, you did ask. About two months ago my husband said he was going hunting. He left and that was the last I saw of him. I had no way to make a living. We didn't own a house, he had no money, I had no money, and I couldn't find a job. So Linda offered me this job. I had no choice, Hawk. It was this or starve."

"What's wrong with being a dancing teacher?"

"Hawk, dear Hawk. I wasn't going to be a dancing teacher. I was going to be a prostitute."

I had to think about that for a minute before I remembered what Uncle Robert had said about prostitutes. He said, "Sooner or later yer gonna meet up with one son, and then yer gonna have the time of your life." Well, maybe it was because a prostitute was something I had never experienced, but I just couldn't imagine anything being better than being out in the woods hunting.

"Where will you go?"

"I can't stay here. No one wants anything to do with someone like me—someone they assume was a prostitute. I'll go to Saint Peter or maybe Shakopee—no one will know who I am there."

"I don't know where those towns are."

"They're up in the Minnesota Valley. Most of the people are new to that country and no one knows anyone. I can start all over."

"That's where I'm going. Maybe we could go together?"

"I wouldn't do that to you. People would know who I am and it wouldn't look too good for you."

"I don't care what other people think of me. If they don't like what I am they can go be with someone else. They prob'ly won't like them either. Besides, who would know you there? Didn't you say it was all new people?"

"Well, I couldn't go till spring anyway so forget it. You go, I'll be okay here."

"Yeah, you can always go back to Miss Linda when things get tough."

"That hurt Hawk. Why'd you have to say that?"

"'Cause things ain't no different now. You couldn't find work before you went there, what makes you think you can now?"

"I'm not going to the valley with you and that's the end of it. I can make it on my own."

"I don't doubt that you can make it on your own and I'm not trying to talk you into anything. I just think it would be easier if you had someone to travel with."

"Well, we can't go anywhere till spring anyway so look me up then and we'll talk about it." She picked up her bag and walked out the door. I went out the door right behind her and ran into Jean and Goodhorse waiting for me on the boardwalk.

"Damn Hawk, you smell like you was rollin' in the flower garden."

"Jean, do you know what this place is?"

"'Course I do. How'd you like it?"

"Well, got me a bath. That felt perty good."

"Yeah?" Jean looked at me as if he were going to hear something good. "What else?"

I thought for a few seconds and said, "Nothing. I got the bath, got dressed and left. Is there more?" Jean and Goodhorse looked at each other for a long moment then broke out laughing.

"You crazy Welshman. Yer jist funnin' with us." They laughed more. "Ye just ain't the kiss-and-tell type. Nothin' wrong with that."

"Huh?"

"Gittin' a whore ain't nothin' to brag about anyway. It ain't like you talked her into it—you paid for it."

"Miss Sophie ain't no whore. She's a nice lady and a good person."

"Ha! The boy's fell in love!"

I didn't see the joke but I guess they did, so I just let them laugh. We started back to the carts to go back to camp.

"Charbonneau!" I heard from behind.

Jean turned and said sharply, "WHAT?"

"That was a perty dirty trick making me pay for what that boy didn't get."

"Whad'ya mean didn't get? He got all that you paid for."

"Linda says the girl he was with packed her junk and pulled out. Said she didn't want to be there anymore."

Jean turned and looked at me, "What'd you do to her, boy?"

"I didn't do nothin'. She just got itchy feet and wanted out while she could."

"Ye mean you didn't even...well, you know..." he said with some non-sense gestures.

"No, I didn't do nothin'. I just had a bath and left."

Jean dropped his eyebrows and looked at me for a second, then turned to the other man and said, "I'll take it out of your fare."

"What the hell's going on here, Jean? That boy ain't never had a woman?"

"Nope, guess not. Don't guess he'd know what to do with one if he did get close enough."

"How old is he?"

"What the hell is this? Ain't it my own business if I've had a woman or not? What the hell happened to the private life thing you preached about, Jean? It ain't none of this old bastard's business what I done or didn't do. Who is this guy anyway?"

"This here's Joe Rolette."

"Ah, so that's *you*. You must be the guy I heard grunting in there like hog rootin' in the manure pile."

"Better you be careful how you talk, boy. You could get yer self in some serious trouble." The man was short and fat, his mouth was a lot louder than it needed to be, and he looked like a little puppy yappin' at my feet.

"Mister Rolette, you don't look like you've worked that hard in a hell of a long time. How 'bout you just mind yer own affairs and leave mine to me and you can skip all that trouble you just talked about."

"Jean," he said, "this boy's got spunk. Does he know who I am?"

"Yeah, he knows who you are, but I don't think he's any more impressed than I am."

"Damn, a man cain't git no respect no more. Come on, I'll buy you both a drink."

"I'm goin' back to the camp, Jean. You two have a good time."

"I'll go with you, Hawk. I'm done here." The three of us, Jean, Goodhorse and I, started down the street headed for the camp outside of town. Goodhorse mounted his horse and rode ahead. I'd never seen a place like Saint Paul. It was dirty and smelly, dogs running all over the place, and horses and wagons going both directions on the mud streets. It was going to be a pleasure to be out of this city.

We turned down one of the streets headed toward the camp. Jean was quieter than usual. He kept looking at me. He'd look for just a second then he'd turn away. He looked again.

"What?" I said.

"Nothin'."

"Well, why you keep lookin' at me like that?"

"Like what?"

"Like I just shit my pants or something."

"Did ye?"

"No, I just had a bath."

"Yeah, I know," he said quietly. "A bath. Just a bath—that's all, nothin' else."

"Oh, that. Ain't none of your business that I ain't never had a woman. I wouldn't know what to do with one. I guess I should have tried something but I was scared of doing it wrong and having her laugh at me. My Uncle Robert told me some things about women, but he was always saying things and pullin' pranks on us boys, so I don't know what to believe and what not to."

"Hawk, there's a first time for everyone. Hell, I never had a woman before my first time neither. Ain't nothing to be ashamed of. Sure, you'll get razzed about it and hear all the funny jokes, but all those people who are doing the joking went through the same thing. They had a first time too, you know."

"Well what about the girl, Sophie? What would she say if I did it wrong?"

"Prostitutes give boys their first time everyday. That ain't nothin' to them. Miss Sophie is different. Linda told me that she probably would have backed out if you hadn't. It was her first day there."

"I know, she told me."

"And Linda knew both of you were first-timers so she put you together 'cause she knew you wouldn't get rough like some of the men would if she backed out."

"Jean?"

"Yeah?"

"Can we walk a little slower? My legs and backside still hurt from that horse."

"Wish ye hadn't told me that. I was pertendin' the girl made ye walk like that." He slowed a little but not near slow enough.

"Like I was sayin', Linda's in a business that the society people don't per-tic'lar like in their town. The women think their men might go find something better. Ye'd think it would make them try to be better wives and lovers but it don't work that way. If they just think their man is thinking about going to the cathouse, they get worse and start nagging till he's had enough and walks out. Then say, 'Oh, why did he leave me?' Miss Linda has a good heart and a good brain. She can read people like a book."

"Jean, I don't know nothin' about women. I ain't been anywhere near them to learn anything about them. I know my ma, she's a good person. She has to be to put up with Pa."

"Yer ma ain't nothin' like the girls yer gonna meet up with from now on. The girls yer gonna meet wanna get married and have kids and a place to live, have a garden, and go to church and take baths. That what you want Hawk?"

"Well, I don't know. It sounds nice but I didn't like bein' stuck on that farm. That's why I'm here, I guess. Might like to have a place of my own someday but not yet. Got things to do yet that I can't have no woman taggin' along for—or anyone else for that matter."

"Guess you'll have to go without."

"Yeah, kinda had my eye on Lorraine anyway."

"'Member what I told you the first time you fell in love with her?"

"Um, no. What?"

"I said forget her. I meant ezzac'ly that. Lorraine ain't the marryin' kind. She's been goin' to schools since she was old enough to walk. She speaks four languages and a bunch of Indian languages too. She reads, writes, and ciphers and knows the Indian sign talk. Renard had her put in one of those Catholic schools for girls in Montreal when she was a baby and she's been there ever since. Now she's going to the Agency in Redwood to teach the Indian kids how to live like the white men. Damn fool thing to try to do but the government wants it that way and she'll be paid good for it."

"Is she one of them there nuns they have in the Catholic schools?"

"No, she ain't no nun but she might as well be for all the interest she has in men. Oh, and one more thing before we get to the camp. Don't ever think you understand women. 'Cause ye CAIN'T!" He barked the last word. "Soon as you learn all the answers, they change all the questions. Most cantankerous critters the Good Lord ever put on Earth.

"Now, yer gonna get picked on when we get to camp but just ignore them..." Jean stopped and looked as if he were sniffing the air. "Something's wrong here—too quiet." He put out a hand in front of me to stop me. He stood still and listened for a minute before walking slowly into camp. People stood quietly in small groups. Some were standing around Renard's tent. I saw a woman cross herself.

"Something's wrong..." We walked fast to Renard's camp. The crowd opened to let us pass and Jean put his head inside the tent flap. His hand reached back for me and, without looking, he caught my coat sleeve and pulled me into the tent. Renard was lying on the blankets with his eyes closed and his hands folded across his chest. A red blanket was pulled over him to his waist and a red knit cap covered his head. The funny-looking face didn't smile when I walked in like it always had.

"What happened?" Jean asked. Lorraine started to answer in French.

"English..." Jean said.

She looked at me and said, "Of course. This morning someone found him on the snow outside of camp. We think he wandered off by himself and died from the cold. He wasn't wearing a coat."

"Has he ever wandered off alone before?"

"No, and I think he may have done it deliberately, Jean. He was just tired of living the way he was. I talked with him yesterday and he was telling me what to do with his things when he died. It sounded then like he knew he was going to die. His mind was poor but I think he was more aware of things than we think." She walked to the back of the tent and picked up Renard's rifle and handed it to me.

"One of the things he wanted is for you to have his rifle, Hawk."

"No, I can't take this. It should go to Goodhorse."

"I have a good rifle, Hawk. Father wanted you to have it. He says the one you shoot is not a good one and you will be needing a good rifle."

"Goodhorse, I..."

"It would not be proper for you to refuse this rifle, Hawk. Father knew that you would take good care of it and now it is yours. Take it."

I took the rifle. Then I looked at Renard and said, "Thank you my friend." I got a lump in my throat and turned to leave the tent so as to not embarrass myself. When I walked past Jean he was in tears and that made it impossible to hide mine. I went outside and cried. Lorraine, Jean, Goodhorse, and I hugged each other and cried.

Soon the people went back to their tents. I went to my little canvas shelter and crawled inside the buffalo robes for the night. In the morning I walked to the breakfast pot hanging in the middle of the camp. Most of the camp was up and had eaten breakfast long before I came out. People were busy laying things out on blankets in front of their tents. Moccasins, fur hats, beaded bags, Indian arrows, tomahawks, and anything they could think of went out on their blankets.

"What's going on here?" I asked a man.

"People come from village to trade." He pointed to the south and there I saw a string of wagons coming down the road.

They came into camp and walked around to each tent looking at the things the people had set out. Some had money to buy with and some had white men's things they thought the Métis could use—needles, cotton thread, thimbles, iron axes, cloth, and other things. The items were not worth as much as the people thought they would be because the Métis had everything the white man had and more.

The Métis were not poor Indians as the tourists seemed to think. They just looked that way. The Métis had ways of dealing with the white people that got them more than they should for some items. Of course the white people thought they were taking advantage of the poor ignorant red men and walked away happy with the worthless piece of beaded junk they'd just traded an axe for. The Métis received what, to him, was a valuable tool. All through the day people came out and traded with the Métis. Some of our people sang songs for the entertainment of the tourists. All day long a man stood guard at the door of Renard's tent.

Jean stayed away from it all. Goodhorse was busy trying to impress the young women folk that came out. The fathers of the girls weren't real happy about that but I don't think Goodhorse was all too concerned about their feelings. I watched as one of the fathers confronted Goodhorse.

"What's he sayin'?"

Jean was smiling when he said, "He told him to stay away from his daughter."

We watched as Goodhorse made some surrendering gestures to the man. He pulled his hat off and swung it under his belly, bowed at the waist, and backed away. He turned and walked past the young girl and bowed slightly at the waist. He tipped his hat when he walked up to face the girl. Then he wrapped his arms around her, bent her backwards, and kissed her hard on the mouth. The girl's father yelled something and ran toward Goodhorse. He tried to grab him around the waist but Goodhorse stepped aside and the man fell to his knees screaming obscenities at him. He stood up and went for Goodhorse again, swinging his small businessman's hands at him, but the tall Métis dodged each swing. Goodhorse laughed at the man who was trying to defend his daughter's virtue. Finally the man stopped, took his daughter, and stormed off. The girl looked back over her shoulder at Goodhorse with a smile on her lips. Goodhorse tipped his hat to her and walked away.

The rest of the day went smoothly and when night came everyone put away the trade stuff and went to sleep. Morning came too soon for me, but for the rest it came just on time. They were all outside their tents putting their goods out for more trading with the town people.

"Yer gonna have to make yer own breakfast today, boy," Jean said when I crawled out of my shelter. "Everyone ate already and is ready for the day to get started." I dug through my packs for any leftover jerky or biscuits I could find. What I found was frozen so I had to thaw it under my coat before I could eat it.

Jean was talking to Mister Rolette at the edge of the camp. His hands were moving as fast as his mouth. Mister Rolette was talking at the same time. I could tell there were angry words being spoken but couldn't tell what they were. Soon they stopped talking and Jean walked to Lorraine's tent and scratched on the door. She came out and stood with her arms folded across her chest talking with Jean. She nodded her head and Jean walked away.

"You wanna go to the valley, Hawk?"

"Figured on going in the spring. Why?"

"I just made a deal with Rolette to take Renard's body back to Pembina. He wants an escort."

"Me? I ain't much of an escort. Why don't he take some of the riders?"

"He's gonna. I just figured it would be a good chance for you to get to the valley. Ye don't have to go all the way to Pembina if you don't want to. You can turn anywhere you want and head down to the bottom, or cross, or whatever you want."

"How many carts will be goin'?"

"No carts. Can't run them in the snow. He's mouchin' up there."

"Mushin'?

"Dog-sleddin'."

"What's that?"

"Sled pulled by dogs."

"Never heard of it."

"You ain't never heard of lots of things."

"Guess not. When's he leaving?"

"Three weeks. He's got some things to do in Saint Paul then he's takin' Lorraine up to Redwood."

"Lorraine's goin'? Guess I'll just tag along for the ride."

"You jest don't quit, do you boy? I told you, Lorraine ain't lookin' for no man. She's a schoolteacher and that's all she wants to be. FERGIT HER!" he barked.

"Can't schoolteachers be friends with people?"

"You just do what the hell you want. Yer gonna anyway. Jest don't go gittin' yerself hurt."

"Now how the hell's a girl gonna hurt me? Tell me that."

"I have a feeling yer gonna find the answer to that one all by yourself. You riding along?"

"Yeah, might get interesting."

"Better git on that crazy horse of yours and teach him to behave."

"Oh yeah, the horse. I still ain't healed from the first time I was on him."

"No time like the present."

"Think I'll just wait for all these people to leave."

"Put a rope on him and take him out in the snow and work him. The deeper the snow, the better. He won't be able to jump and buck if he's buried in the snow."

"Yer just full of answers ain't you, Jean?"

"If I don't know an answer I can make one up right quick."

"That deep snow trick gonna work?"

"Only way to know is to try it. Put a long rope on his neck so you don't lose him when he throws ye."

The horse wasn't going to let me put the rope bridle on him but after a short argument I won. I tied the rope to his front leg so his nose was next to his knee. Putting the saddle on with him tied that way was no problem. He didn't like it much but he stood still. I tied his front feet together so he couldn't run and led him out of camp to the deep snow. He stopped a couple of times, not wanting to walk in the snow, but a few jerks and a pull on the rope around his muzzle brought him along. He couldn't raise his front feet high enough to step over the snow so he was pretty well under my control. I stopped him, talked to him, and rubbed his neck until he looked like he might be in a friendly mood. I rubbed his side and shoulders as I walked around and put a foot in the stirrup. Then I swung my leg over his back and sat there waiting to be tossed off on my head. The brute stood quietly. I kicked his ribs to get him to move but he wouldn't. He made a weak attempt to jump once but the deep snow held him back. This was getting me nowhere, so I climbed down and untied the rope from his front feet but left one leg tied. Now he could run if the snow didn't stop him. I pulled the rope on his front leg and lifted the foot off the ground while I climbed aboard. He stood still until I kicked his ribs. Then he started his attempt to throw me off, but his bucks weren't hard nor high and I had no trouble staying on his back. He tried running so I pulled the front foot out from under him and he fell to his knees. I had a hold of the saddle and stayed on him as he got to his feet. I touched his ribs and he walked forward. He jumped once but I stayed on. I kicked him when he tried to stop walking and soon he was walking along just like he didn't mind me being there. He responded to the reins, which surprised me. I'd pull to one side and he'd go there. We went for a walk through the snow for an hour and I steered him back toward camp. Jean was standing at the edge of camp watching me come in with a big, wide grin on my face.

"Well, looks like you two have made up." I walked the horse into the camp where the snow was packed hard.

"Looks like it. I think I'm gonna like this . . ." Just at that moment the horse's rear end came off the ground and I went sailing head first over his head. I kept a grip on the reins and when I hit the end of them I flipped around and landed hard on my backside. My first instinct told me to get my rifle and shoot a hole in that critter's head. But when I looked at the men and women standing around laughing like fools I decided that I'd just take the horse and tie him to the post where I'd found him.

"Y'ain't giving up now are ye? This is the time to get right back up there and show that critter who's boss. Git back on that horse." I looked at Jean and turned around, grabbed the rope that was tied to the front leg, and climbed aboard. The horse started to make a jump so I pulled the rope and he went to his knees. I let him up and he tried it again with the same results. I pulled the foot off the ground and kicked him hard in the ribs. He couldn't move. I let the foot down. He tried again to jump but thought better of it. I touched his ribs and he walked forward while I kept the rope tight on the front leg to let him know that if he tried bucking, *he* would be the one on the ground. He walked around the camp quietly. All of a sudden he took off running. He ran full speed around a circle and out of camp. I stayed on his back holding tight to the saddle, front and back, and kicked him to keep him running. I was going to run this critter until he was exhausted. He ran into the soft snow, which made running harder for him, but I kicked him and slapped his rump to keep him running. He got into snow that was too deep to run and slowed to a walk. I turned him around and headed toward camp and kicked him in the ribs hard to make him run. His wind was coming hard now but I kept kicking him. By the time we got back to camp he was completely exhausted and walking like an old plow mule. He couldn't buck now if he was on fire. I walked him around the camp and out onto the roads for the rest of the afternoon. When I was finished, I had me a riding horse.

"These boys been workin' that horse all summer. Now you come along and break him. That don't look good for them."

"Goodhorse told me they don't break horses—they get theirs all ready for riding. Besides, I weigh a lot more than most of them do and for that horse to carry my weight they'd have to take a sack of oats up there with them."

"Doing it in the snow didn't hurt anything either," Jean said with a wide grin.

"Okay, you can take credit for that idea."

"Thanks, I do make up a good answer now and then."

From that day on, I rode The Brute as much and as often as I could to get him used to me being on his back. He had been trained to rein by some of the Métis and knew what a kick in the ribs meant before I started with him or, as Jean told me, it might have taken all winter to train him.

Most of the time in camp was spent working on equipment and entertaining tourists. I didn't much care for the people that came around to gawk at us but I learned to ignore them for the most part. I was digging through my packs one day when Lorraine came by to look at what I had. She picked up the stone axe head that I'd found on the riverbank four months ago.

"Where did you get this?" she asked. I told her.

"Hawk, this is very old and could be very valuable to some people."

"Who would that be?"

"Scientists are researching the history of man in this country and finding artifacts like this is important to them because it tells them about the early inhabitants of this area. This axe head may be as old as ten thousand years. Maybe even older."

"Lorraine, the world isn't that old."

"I won't go into that with you, but even though I have been taught by religious scholars, I know that the world is much older than the Bible teaches. So what do you plan on doing with this?"

"I don't know—just hang on to it till I decide, I guess."

"You are not interested in finding out about it?"

"Not really. I thought I might put a handle on it and keep it for the fun of having it."

"May I take it for a while?"

"Sure, but I want it back."

"It is yours and I will bring it back."

"I have arrowheads too that I got from the same place." I dug a handful out and showed them to her. She looked at them and felt the sharp edges on them.

"These came from the same place?"

"Yes."

"Someday will you take me there?"

"Lorraine, it took me four months to get from there to here."

"It doesn't matter how far it is. This is an important find and it needs to be studied."

"Well, maybe someday."

"I just hope that no one finds it before the scientists can get there. I will come back and bring this with me. *Au revoir*, Hawk."

"Huh?"

She looked back at me and said "Goodbye," and walked away. The next weeks were long and boring. Jean and I went hunting but there wasn't much to hunt. We got a couple of deer and some rabbits but the country was empty of game. I rode The Brute everyday and he seemed to like it.

One day Lorraine came to my camp with a rolled up deerskin in her hand. She handed it to me and said, "Merry Christmas, Hawk."

"Christmas? It's Christmas?"

"Yes, Christmas. This is for you," and she handed me the deerskin roll.

"Open it."

I undid the tie, unrolled it, and found my stone axe head with a wooden handle tied tightly to it. It was wrapped with rawhide and red and black beads with an eagle feather attached just below the head.

"Lorraine, I..."

"You needn't say anything, Hawk. I did it for you because you were my father's best friend in his last days."

"Lorraine, I didn't know it was Christmas and I didn't think about gifts and that sort of thing."

"I know, Hawk. You don't need to give gifts. There are no specific days when we are required to show love. Love is shown much better with everyday actions than with gifts." I wanted so badly to take her in my arms and hug her but I didn't know if it was right. Christmas was a time for hugs back home, but this was different. Lorraine wasn't family so I didn't know if I should.

"Lorraine, I'm going to take a ride in the country."

"Yes, I can see you need to be alone. I will see you when you come back."

I saddled The Brute and walked him toward the woods out of camp. The sky was gray and snow started to fall as the sun was going down. Everything turned a deep blue and the wind died. The snow fell softly on the ground and it was so cold and quiet. I heard a dog bark somewhere in the distance. My thoughts went to Otter Tail County and the farm I'd left so long ago. I thought about Christmas with Jake and Ma and Pa. The gifts we'd made for each other and how Ma would cook a bird and sweet potatoes for our Christmas dinner. I remembered how Pa tried to stay out of the Christmas spirit but showed too much delight when I gave him the folding knife I'd traded Mister Belleair a deerskin for. I stayed out of camp until way past dark, trying to hide the emotions that were taking over my mind. Christmas was supposed to be the happy time of year but this year it was just misery.

I went back to camp and took the saddle off The Brute and headed to my tent for the night. I was surprised to see my fire still burning.

"Are you all right, Hawk?" Lorraine asked. She had waited for me to come in.

"Yeah, I'm okay. Just a little tired."

"This is your first time away from home on Christmas, isn't it?"

"Yeah, it's kinda different."

The falling snow made the night as bright as the day and I could see Lorraine's face. She was so beautiful in that light. It made me want to cry.

"Jean told me you will be going north with us when we leave."

"Guess so. Figure on riding to the Minnesota Valley and going there when we get close enough."

"I will be going to the Redwood Agency to teach the Indian children."

"Yeah, I know. Jean told me. How far is that?"

"I don't know. They may even send me to another school farther away. The government wants me to teach the children to live like white men, but I don't believe that can be done. They have a culture entirely different than yours and teaching them to read and write is going to be difficult at best."

"Kinda like training a wild horse."

"Your horse may carry you but he is, and always will be, wild."

"Lorraine, could you teach me to read?"

"I don't see why not. You seem to be fairly intelligent, and you are willing to learn."

"Ma could read and write but Pa thought it would be a waste of time. He didn't figure we needed to read to run a farm. She learned Jake to read some, but I never did learn."

"She taught Jake," she corrected.

"Yeah, she wanted to learn me too, but I didn't take to it."

"I sometimes have trouble understanding what you say when you use that American English."

"What do you mean, American English? Ain't they the same thing?"

"We'll go into that another time, Hawk. Right now I have to go to my tent and get some sleep."

"I'll walk with you."

"I'd like that." We walked and talked until we came to her tent. "*Bon nuit, mon ami.*"

I just looked at her.

"It means, good night my friend."

"Oh, yeah. Good night Lorraine. You can teach me some of that French talk too."

She stepped close and put her arms around me and hugged me. "We'll work on French when you learn to read." I wasn't sure what to do so I just wrapped my arms around her and hugged her back and nearly fell to the ground. She touched my face, turned and went into her tent. I stood there for a minute before walking back to my camp. I sat on the ground and stared into the fire until the sky was starting to lighten in the east. Then I crawled into my robes and slept.

The next few days went by without anything happening except that a few of the men went into town and came back drunk and rowdy. They were quickly hustled into their tents and told to sleep it off—of course they were completely useless the next day.

On New Year's Eve, someone built a big fire in the center of the camp and everyone gathered around for a feast of pork, venison, corn, sweet potatoes, and wine—too much wine. A group of men came out from town and started to give the women a bad time. The men in the camp didn't like it but they stayed away and let them have their fun.

"The women in this camp can take care of themselves when they need to," Jean said.

I saw a couple of the city men get knocked down for their efforts. A big guy with a long bushy beard was being louder than the rest and making himself a fool. He walked up to Lorraine and grabbed her by the arm and tried to pull her into a tent. She slapped him on the face and pushed him away. He came back laughing and grabbed her again. I jumped up and ran to him and put a shoulder into his stomach and he went to the ground. He got up grinning at me.

"You want to hug, boy?" He had an evil grin on his face and a big scar on the side of this head.

"Nope. I just think you should leave the women folk be. Go have your fun somewhere else."

"I think you need a lesson in respect for your elders, boy."

"Respect is something you earn and you haven't earned any." With that he hauled off and hit me on the cheekbone and I went to the ground. Lorraine kneeled down next to me.

"Hawk, don't—it's not worth it."

I pushed her aside and got to my feet and rushed the man. We went to the ground with me on top of him. I hit him on the nose and heard the bones break. He was a powerful man and he threw me off. He kicked me in the ribs, which knocked the wind out of me. He started to kick again but I rolled to the side and he missed. I got to my feet and caught a fist in the face again. Down I went. I thought my nose was broken as blood was running down my chin whiskers and onto my coat. He kicked me in the ribs again and that nearly finished me, but my hand fell on a block of ice on the ground next to me. He came at me ready to boot me again but I rolled and got to my feet and cracked him on the side of the head with the block of ice. He went to the ground and lay there for a few seconds before standing and coming at me once more. Again I pounded the block of ice on his head and he went to the ground. This time he stayed there. He didn't move. I thought at first I had killed him, until he groaned and tried to stand, but one arm didn't move. I turned and looked around the camp to see if any others would be coming after me but they all stood and looked at the man on the ground. The Métis were standing around them ready to get into it. A couple of his friends came to him and picked him up and carried him away.

"Hawk, that was the most barbaric thing I have ever seen!" Lorraine shouted at me. "Why did you have to fight like that? I could have handled that man."

"I ain't gonna let some bonehead treat you or any lady that way. It jest ain't right."

"Fighting has never solved a problem. He will be back and the fight will go on forever until one of you is dead."

"Well it ain't gonna be me."

"Hawk, this is a side of you I never thought I would see."

"Get used to it. Any man ever treats you that way again you'll damn sure see it again." She walked away without looking back.

Jean came over and said, "Good thing you got holt of that block of ice. He'da killed you."

"Yeah, I wouldn't have used it if I didn't know that."

"That's the man they call Swede. Meanest sum-bitch ever come down from Pembina."

"He comin' back, ye s'pose?"

"Wouldn't be surprised, but I think you knocked the wheels out from under his cart. He didn't look too healthy when he left." I walked toward my camp to clean up.

"Hawk," I looked and saw Lorraine standing by her tent.

"You said your piece. I'll leave you be."

"Come over here." I walked to her. She went into her tent and came out with a wet towel and wiped the blood from my face. "That was truly the most disgusting display of animal behavior I have ever witnessed in this camp." Then she kissed me on the cheek and said, "Thank you," and went into her tent.

The Swede had hurt me. My ribs hurt, my cheekbone hurt, my nose was bleeding, my stomach was about to turn inside out, but what Lorraine just did completely disarmed me. I stood like a bag of millet with no legs to hold me up. *I just don't understand her.*

The next week was spent mostly out of camp. If the Swede came in, I wanted to be ready rather than surprised in my tent sleeping. But he never did show up so after awhile I began to relax.

Goodhorse came over. "You want to shoot your new rifle?"

"Yeah," I said, "lets go." I grabbed the rifle and the fancy shooting pouch and powder horn and we walked to the place where they had been shooting.

When I reached into the pouch I found bullets like I had never seen before.

"What's this?" I asked Goodhorse.

"Bullets."

"I figured that but what kind are they?"

"They're called Minie balls. They load faster and shoot as straight as any patched round ball. Try 'em."

I poured the powder down the bore and dug in the pouch for a patch. "No patches," I said.

"You don't use patches with those balls. Just start it down the barrel and seat it on top of the powder and yer ready to go."

"No patch?"

"No patch."

I did as he said and slipped a cap on the nipple of the rifle. I lined up the sights and squeezed off a shot. The rifle kicked me harder than I was ready for.

"Oh yes," said Goodhorse, "I forgot to tell you to use less powder."

The shot went where I wanted it to but that recoil made shooting a little uncomfortable. I soon learned to load lighter and I could hit the mark every time I shot. I also learned why Renard could load so fast when we were shooting at the Indians back on Elk River. No need to patch the ball and no need to prime the pan. Now I wanted to get in one of those counting shoots and try my luck. This rifle was so much better than the one I had been shooting that I made it my main weapon. I kept the Tennessee tied to the back of the saddle, loaded.

I was sitting at my camp poking at the fire when Jean came up to me, "You ready to go?"

"Go where?"

"Yer riding with Rolette ain't ye?"

"Yeah, when's he leaving?"

"In about half an hour."

"Kinda sudden, but I can get this stuff packed up by then, I guess."

"Goodhorse and the boys will be along in a minute. Be ready to ride."

I rolled up my canvas, stuffed my packs, and went for The Brute. I started to load my camp onto his back when Goodhorse rode up and told me to throw it on one of the sleds.

"You cannot ride guard with a horse loaded down with junk."

"Guard?"

"Yes, we will be trail guards for the dog sleds until we get north of the valley. They're saying that the Indians are getting rowdy around the Agencies."

"'Bout what?"

"I don't know, but I heard that the Agents won't give out the food that they have in their storehouses that's supposed to go to the Indians."

"I'd get rowdy too."

There were three sleds with six dogs harnessed to each one. Lorraine came over leading a gray horse. "You riding?" I asked.

"Well, I'm certainly not going to ride in that sled for a hundred miles. I'd freeze to death."

Rolette was running around hollering orders at the people who were bringing packs to load onto the sleds. I wasn't sure I could stand much of his loud mouth so I stayed away from him as much as I could.

"You riding with me, boy?"

"That's the plan."

"Well git on that animal and let's go."

"Go ahead on, I'll catch up."

"We ain't waitin' around so make it quick."

I walked over to Jean, "Well, guess this is goodbye."

"Don't never say goodbye, Hawk. Sounds too final. See you down the road."

"Right. See you down the road."

"Hawk?"

"Yeah?"

"Here, this is for you," he handed me a leather sack. I opened it and inside found a stack of gold coins.

"What's this?"

"Wages. You earned it."

"I didn't do anything to earn wages."

"Dammit Hawk, just take the money and go. You earned it."

I stuffed the sack inside my shirt and thanked him.

"Where's Renard?" Jean pointed to one of the sleds. "Ah."

I mounted my horse and walked him out of camp to join the sled train. It had all happened so suddenly that I didn't have time to say goodbye to the friends I'd made with these wonderful people. They all stood in a line and waved as we marched out of camp.

I rode up next to Goodhorse, "If we're going north how come we're going south?"

"We'll be crossing the river at Mendota and stopping at Fort Snelling for some goods to go to the Agency in Redwood. Then we'll take the trail on the west side of the valley and cross again to Fort Ridgely, and from there, straight north to Pembina."

"How long a ride is that gonna be for you?"

"Three, four weeks. Depends on the weather. The dogs don't have any trouble getting through the snow but the horses might. Food's going to be scarce too, that's why we have so few coming along."

When we got to the river, I saw another river running into the Mississippi. Above it was Fort Snelling on a high point between the two rivers, "What river is this, Goodhorse?"

"That is the Minnesota River. The valley you are looking for starts here."

I got a funny feeling inside me. I'm finally looking at what, before now, was just a thought in my mind. It had become a real thing and I felt like I was about to enter a dream.

There were five on horseback, including me, Lorraine, and one man for each dog team. Rolette told us to stay apart as we crossed the ice on the river. There were boards laid like a wooden road on the ice to keep anyone from going through. Traveling was slow, the dogs pulled at a trot and we on horseback had to walk so they could keep up. We were at Fort Snelling in a few hours and Rolette told us to stay mounted. He didn't seem to trust the Indians camped around the fort. He drove his dogs across the Minnesota. He was gone for about an hour and when he came back we were on the trail again.

I watched as the countryside turned from rolling plain to flat ground with hills on both sides of us. Before long I could see that we were in the Minnesota Valley by the high ridge on both sides of us. It gave me a kind of a thrill to finally be where my mind had imagined for so long. My imagination didn't do the valley justice. It was beautiful with trees and water everywhere. Sometimes we'd travel on the bottom of the valley and then climb to one of the shelves where we were high enough to see down to the bottom. It was huge—three and four miles across and hundreds of feet deep. Streams and rivers twisted their way through the entire valley. Some places you could see where the valley changed direction, some you could see down the length of it from horizon to horizon. It looked like a great river had carved this valley out sometime long ago. Or was it a huge crack on the Earth? Guess I'll never know. Some say it was a river that drained a big lake in the North. Could be, but I couldn't imagine a river as big as this ever existing.

We came to a town that was busy with people going about their business.

"What's this town?" I asked Lorraine.

"This is Shakopee."

It was as big and crowded as Saint Paul, with the large wooden frame buildings and hard packed roads. As in Saint Paul, there were wagons and horses all up and down the main street and people rushing in all directions. It sure was different than the open country of Otter Tail County where you might walk for days without seeing a single person. We stopped for the night and set up our tents in a small circle with a common fire in the middle.

"Hawk!" Rolette yelled.

"What?" I yelled back.

"I'm going to town, wanna come along?"

"Nope, don't like the crowds."

"Come on, you can get a bath."

"Anyone around here needs a bath it's you," I said. He laughed and walked away.

"A bath wouldn't do you any harm, Hawk." Lorraine said.

"It ain't a bath he's talkin' about."

"What does he mean then?"

"Never mind. You don't want to know."

"If I didn't want to know I would not have asked."

"Take my word for it, you don't want to know."

"Hawk, I'm a grown woman."

"Okay, that bathhouse is not a bathhouse. It's a place where men can have a prostitute."

"Oh." She looked at the ground and for once had nothing to say.

"Told you ye didn't want to know."

"I'll remember, when you say I don't want to know, I'll not pursue it."

"Good idea."

"Now, about learning to read…" She opened a book and slid close. The book had pictures of apples and rabbits and chickens. Each page had big red letters on it. She turned the pages to where it had a whole string of these letters that didn't make a bit of sense to me. "This is the alphabet. It contains all of the letters in the English language that we use to make words. Each letter represents a different sound. Like A represents the sound 'aye' or 'ah'. Apple starts with the sound 'aa'. B has the sound 'buh' as in bunny. Understand?"

"I think so."

"Each word starts with the sound of the first letter in the word. N has the 'nnnnn' sound to it, like night, or never. Each of those words starts with N."

"Like knife, right?"

"Oh, dear Lord. This is going to be more difficult than I had expected. Hawk, we'll work on this at another time. It's getting late."

Lorraine helped me with reading every chance we got. Sometimes I felt sorta dumb because I couldn't remember the sounds of the letters, then after a while I started to know them pretty good. I found I could sound out a word but when they were in a row to make a sentence, I was too slow to know what the sentence was trying to say. She told me to keep working on it and soon I would recognize the combinations of letters and know the word at a glance. I had my doubts about that. I remembered when Ma would read to us that I was amazed at how fast she could read the words. When she put them together they all made sense. Jake could read too, but not as fast as Ma.

When morning came, everyone crawled out of their tents shivering. It had gotten bitter cold during the night. The Indians called this "the moon of the cracking trees". I knew what they meant because during the night I could hear what sounded like shooting but it was just the sound of the trees splitting from the cold. The dogs were curled up on the snow with their noses buried in their tails. They didn't seem to notice the freezing air. The air was so cold you could see it shimmer with ice crystals. There was no wind, just terrible cold. Of course this is the time that Mother Nature begins making her demands on a man's body. Going out to the trees and dropping my drawers was not what I had planned for this morning, but as Uncle Robert used to say, "Mother Nature is the only woman I can't say no to."

The fire was built to a blazing roar and people huddled around it to warm themselves. We'd stand facing the flames for a few minutes, then turn and warm the other side—like roasting a squirrel. Each would face the fire and open his coat to let the heat in, then turn around and lift the coat to warm his backside. Rolette didn't seem to be aware of the cold. He wore a heavy wool coat and a knit stocking cap under a coyote skin hat on his head. His feet were covered with thick moccasins and he had fur-lined mittens on his hands. Around his neck he wore a wool scarf. Lorraine, too, had plenty of clothing covering her from top to bottom. I wore my wool coat and my buckskin pants that might as well have not been there at all. The flannel underwear I wore under it did little to help.

"You need to get some wool ponts to wear, Hawk. Those leather ponts are not warm enough for this kind of cold."

"Yer tellin' me," I said through chattering teeth.

The cook soon had a pot of stew for us and we all drank it boiling hot, hoping it would help to warm us. It did some, but it didn't last long.

Rolette was shouting orders, "*Alons, alons, nos gens.* Time to get going, we have a long hard trail to Pembina."

We struck our camps, loaded the sleds and, amidst the barks of the dogs, the cracking of whips, and at the commands of the drivers, we were back on the trail. I sat on The Brute with a heavy blanket wrapped around me, trying to stop shivering. The other riders were doing the same. Goodhorse rode up next to me and walked alongside.

"Ready?"

"For what?"

"Race you to that grove of trees." He pointed to a stand of poplars half a mile distant and kicked his horse. With a yell, all the riders including Lorraine whipped their mounts and we were off to the trees. I kicked The Brute and he jumped into action. He took off so suddenly I nearly rolled off his back, but I stayed on and rode as hard as I could. The horse must have known this was a race because he stretched out his legs, lowered his head, and opened up faster than I had realized he could go. The other riders were way ahead of us by the time I got going but it didn't take The Brute long to catch up and gallop past the rest. The Métis were yelling and laughing through it all, but when The Brute zipped by them things changed—they got serious. The laughing stopped and the kicking and whipping started. They were determined to win this race. But they didn't. My Brute entered the trees three lengths ahead of the rest.

"That is one crazy horse you have there, Mister Hawk," Goodhorse said as he rode up.

"Surprised the hell out of me," I said. Brute couldn't stand still. He pranced around in circles blowing and rumbling from deep in his throat. It seemed like he wanted to run some more. We cantered our horses back to the sleds. Each man who passed me reached out and slapped me on the back with a big grin. I would've liked to have taken credit for the race but I knew it was all horseflesh that won.

We traveled for three days without stopping for anything but eating and sleeping. The air stayed cold and there was no getting used to it. My hands got so cold I couldn't hold onto the reins. The skin on my legs had gone numb early in the ride and I had to get down from the horse and walk to keep them from freezing. The moisture from my breath froze so thick in my beard and mustache I could hardly open my mouth.

"Thirty-five below," Rolette said as he mushed by me.

"Nice and warm in this coat—only twenty-five below," I said.

"Next stop, Mankato."

"Is it warm there?" I asked.

"They have a few nice warm bathhouses."

"Go away."

He cracked his whip at the dogs and drove off laughing.

That night we camped outside of Mankato, a town as busy as the others.

Rolette announced, "We'll stay here a couple of nights to rest the animals. They got a feed mill here where we can get some grain for the horses and meat for the dogs."

After we got our camp set up and the horses picketed we had a meal of boiled meat and peas then crawled into our tents for a cold night of sleep. I didn't know why but Lorraine didn't set up a tent. "Ain't you staying here?" I asked.

"Yes, I thought if it's all right with you we would sleep in the same tent. It will be warmer that way."

"Fine with me but…"

"Hawk, if you will notice, everyone is sleeping with someone. You would freeze to death if you tried to sleep without the extra body heat. We will sleep under the same robes and share our body heat."

"Why don't you sleep with Goodhorse? He's your brother."

"He will be riding most of the night scouting the trail ahead. Besides, he doesn't sleep well. He takes short naps on his horse while we ride. He sleeps like an animal."

I wasn't too sure about this arrangement but Lorraine seemed comfortable with it so I agreed. I crawled into my tent and got under the robes. Lorraine came in after me, lifted the buffalo robe, and slipped in next to me. I had never had a woman's body next to me in bed and didn't know where to put my hands and arms, so I curled them up against my chest and laid on my back.

"We won't stay warm if you stay away from me. Move next to me."

I just laid there scared out of my wits. She turned away from me and slid back until our bodies were against each other. I rolled over to my side and put my back against hers. It was thirty-five below outside but I was sweating. I finally did fall asleep but was awake more than asleep. I was afraid of moving for fear of waking her. I woke up with a jump when she rolled over in her sleep and put one arm around me and slid close to my back. My eyes were wide open and I stared at the wall of the tent. That was probably the worst night I had ever experienced. I got maybe an hour of sleep. Lorraine slept well, I suspect. We did stay warm though.

The next day I couldn't get warmed up. After sweating so much during the night, my clothes were wet on the inside. The weather had warmed a little and a light snow had fallen during the night. Goodhorse came to me.

"Would you like to go to town with us and get supplies?"

"Sure, might be interesting. Who's going?"

"You, Lorraine, me, and Henri."

"Rolette ain't goin'?"

"He's already there. He left before you got up. We'll go to a restaurant and get a good hot meal."

I went to get The Brute, threw the saddle on him, and rode to where they were preparing a sled to go to town. The sled was empty when we left. I rode next to Lorraine and Goodhorse rode out front. Before long we arrived at the town and when we got there Lorraine said, "I will see you at sundown."

"Where you going?" I asked.

"To the post office and then to the library, if they have one."

"Library? Ye mean for books?"

"Unless they have a bathhouse there, I will find books," she said, showing a sense of humor that, until now, was kept well hidden.

"Good God, not you too," I said under my breath.

We rode down the main street to one of the stores where Rolette was waiting for us. We stopped to pick up meat for the dogs and oats for the horses. We also bought dried fruit, a big sack of dried beans, flour, salt pork, and some other things we'd need on the trail.

"Let's eat," Goodhorse said.

He led the way to a building with a sign that said "CAFÉ". I could read that now. We walked in and took a table in the far corner of the room. I sat with my back to the wall so I could look at the people. Everyone in the room was talking at the same time. Some were dressed in nice business clothes but most were ragged like us. Two ladies worked hard to bring out the meals and take orders back to the kitchen. One was about my age and the other one was a little older. I couldn't help but think that I had seen the younger one before, but then I didn't know anyone out here and tried to get it out of my mind. I watched her walk around the room laughing at the stupid jokes the men told her and trying hard to ignore the raggedy man who kept reaching out to touch her. There were three men at his table. All three were in very worn-out rags—old coats that were too big for them, caps that were pulled down over their ears, and their faces were as dirty as their hands. One had his back to me so I couldn't see his face but he seemed to be the leader of the three. He'd tell them to be quiet but they ignored him and kept up their foolishness.

"How do we get a waitress over here?" Rolette said, a little too loud.

"Just keep yer shirt on—I'm getting there." The younger of the two gave Rolette a dirty look and walked into the kitchen.

The older of the two ladies walked over to us and said, "What can I get you boys?"

"He's the boy," Rolette said, pointing his thumb at me.

"Rolette, I was a boy when I was your size."

"He's quick for a boy. I'll have the beef steak."

"Same for me," said Goodhorse.

"Me too, I guess," I said, on account I didn't know what else to do. If she'd handed me one of those books they gave the other people who came in, I still wouldn't know what they had.

The younger waitress walked by me humming a tune my mother used to sing while she worked, *Ah La Claire Fountaine*—Ma learned it from her grandfather who came from the East in a canoe. I smelled her as she went by. I ain't never smelled anything that sweet in my life—kinda like flowers and kinda like something good to eat all mixed into one sweet scent. Rolette saw me raise my nose and said, "Jist like a damn dog sniffing out a mate."

"How'd you like yer sniffer slapped off yer face?" I snapped at him.

He chuckled and looked at Goodhorse. "Touchy ain't he?"

Goodhorse grinned and said, "I'd be careful."

I tried to keep from looking at the lady but something about her kept my attention. She had long auburn hair that shined as it hung over her shoulders and draped down the front of her dress. Her dress was white with little pink stripes that showed her shape. Her shoulders were wide and tapered down to her waist where her apron strings pulled the material of her dress in and shaped her like the hourglass Ma used when she cooked. Her breasts pushed at the front of her dress and her hair laid on top of them. When she walked her hips moved from side to side just a little, just enough to bring my attention to them. I didn't know what it was about that part of her that I liked so well but that didn't matter, I liked looking at her. Of course Rolette and Goodhorse were watching me watch the lady. When I came out of my trance and looked at their grinning faces I was just a little embarrassed.

Rolette looked at Goodhorse, "I think it's time we find this boy a bathhouse."

"BATHHOUSE! That's it. That's where I saw that woman. That's gotta be Sophie," I said too loud.

She turned around and at the same time the dirty man at the far corner put his hand on her backside. She spun around to face him and said in a loud voice, "I told you to keep your filthy hands off me."

"Aw, come on, give old John a kiss."

With that she picked up the tin plate he was eating from and slapped him across the mouth with it so hard it rang like a church bell. Two men who were sitting close by got up, grabbed the three beggars, and threw them out the door. The lady stomped into the kitchen. I could hear shouting coming from back there but in a few minutes she came out and picked up the mess and went back to being a waitress. I watched her move around the room, not daring to make myself known. I wanted to go to her and talk to her but I was kind of uncomfortable with it so I contented myself with just looking. When she turned my way, I was careful to look down or off in another direction. I could feel that she knew I was looking by the way she made it a point to avoid my eyes. I watched her and wanted her. Suddenly my chair wasn't under me anymore—my feet were. *What the hell am I doing?* I thought. *Damn, I'm walking over to her. Where the hell did that kind of courage come from?* She was leaned over a table when I walked up. She knew I was there and she stayed busy gathering plates.

I stood behind her and said, "Sophie?" She kept on working. "Sophie, is that you?"

She turned and looked at me with the most beautiful blue eyes I'd ever seen.

"Sophie?" I said again.

"Um, no, I um…" She looked around the room like she was scared someone would jump her for talking to me.

"You don't remember me?"

"Um, no."

"Hawk," I said.

"Hawk. Hawk! Oh my God, what are you doing here?" she said in a half-whisper.

"Just passing through with a train heading to Pembina." She looked nervous and kept looking around the room. "Sophie, don't worry. I ain't gonna say nothin' about where I know you from."

"Hawk, can we talk later? I get off in about two hours."

"Sure, want me to come back here?"

"No, there's another restaurant at the end of the street. Meet me there."

Two hours can be an awfully long time when you have to spend it with the likes of Joe Rolette. He took us into a saloon and tried to get me to drink whiskey, but I knew what it did to Pa so I refused.

"Rolette," I said, "would you die if you stopped talking?"

"Don't know, boy. Only way to find out is to stop talking and I ain't got that curious about it yet."

His constant talking about nothing was getting on my nerves so I got up and walked out the door. I ended up on the street headed toward where I was to meet Sophie. It was way too cold to stand on the street so I went into the restaurant to wait.

Soon Sophie came in and looked around until she found me. She walked over to the table and said, "Let's go to another table."

I got up and followed her to the back of the room where it was a little darker.

"Hawk, how did you find me?"

"I didn't find you, I just happened to be in there at the same time you were. How did you get here? I thought you were going to wait till spring."

"Linda told me about an old German guy who was setting up a restaurant here and needed help, so I got in the wagon and here I am. I work for him now."

"Well, good for you. I'm glad you got out of that town. You look different," I said, looking deep into her eyes. "What's different?"

"Could it be I don't have that makeup on my face?"

"Oh yeah, the paint and lines. Damn Sophie, yer prettier without it."

"Well, I don't know about that."

With one finger she pushed the hair from one side of her face and looked at me with a half-smile. Her hair was brushed down over her forehead, which gave her eyes a mischievous and challenging look. My mother had blue eyes, but Sophie's were different. Hers were so blue you could almost see through them—like the blue glass marbles I got from Uncle Robert and kept in the chest at the foot of my bed. We sat and talked about nothing in particular. I let her do most of the talking. All I wanted to do was look at her. I wanted to take that pretty, impish face in my hands and kiss her on the lips like I'd seen Jean and Linda do. I wanted to touch her body and feel her hair and run my hands over her curves. I had never had these feelings before and didn't know what to do about them. I hoped she didn't see me looking at her each time she looked away. My heart was doing things I had never experienced before and my palms were sweating.

"Hawk, I really would like to stay but I have wash I have to get done."

"I don't want you to go, but I guess if you have to, I'd better let you." We got up from the table and I followed her out the door. She had a long coat on but I could still see the sway of her hips as she walked.

She turned and said, "Goodby,e Hawk. I hope to see you again someday."

I couldn't speak. I wanted to take her into my arms and hold her, but I said, "It was good to see you too, Sophie. Let's do this again."

"I hope so, Hawk. Good night." And with that she walked away and disappeared into the darkness.

Everyone had gone back to camp by the time I came out of the restaurant. I took The Brute and led him out of town. I walked—I was in no hurry to get back there. When I arrived the fire in the middle of camp was still burning and there were a few people sitting around talking.

"Well, the lost is found."

"I wasn't lost, Joe. I was talking to Sophie."

"Well, the boy has found himself a lady friend."

"She's just a friend, Joe. That's all."

"You just meet her today in town?" He looked at Goodhorse, "Boy's fast."

I almost told him where I knew her from but thought better of it and said, "Yeah, the girl in the restaurant. Nice lady."

"She the one from Linda's place?"

"Now what the hell makes you think that?"

"Hawk, I know the whole story. Don't worry, I might talk too much but I know what not to talk about. Yer right, she's a good woman. Gonna be seeing her again?"

"I don't know, depends on how far I go with you. Then there's Lorraine— I think she's sweet on me."

"Nothing to worry about there, Hawk. She ain't with us no more."

"What do ye mean she ain't with us no more?"

"She went to see the Agent in town and he is taking her right up to Redwood tomorrow."

"How the hell can she do that without saying goodbye or anything?"

"Let's see here, seems you said she was sweet on *you.*"

"Well hell, I liked her too. I thought…"

"You thought what? You and Lorraine were gonna get married? I thought

Jean told you all about that."

"Well he did, but…"

"But nothin', boy. Lorraine is gone. You knew she was going and that's the end of it. Go git some sleep and git over it."

I got up and walked to my tent and crawled under the robes. It was cold under the robes without Lorraine there. Even though we'd only spent two nights together I couldn't sleep for thinking about her. I thought to myself, *this must be what Jean meant when he said I'd have to learn for myself how a woman can hurt a man.* I felt like I was going to start crying but I made myself think of different things to get her out of my head. I thought about hunting, the battle we'd had on the Elk River, Jean, Sophie… Sophie. She was as pretty as Lorraine and a lot more fun to talk with. Now that I thought about it, Lorraine had a way of making me feel small and dumb. Sophie made me feel good about myself. I went to sleep thinking about blue marbles and devilish eyes.

In the morning, Rolette woke us before the sun was up. It was cold getting out of the robes but not as cold as it was a couple of days back.

"We got a day's ride to get to New Ulm. We'll be crossing the river there and then half a day to Fort Ridgely. We had Injuns prowling around the camp last night so you riders stay awake and keep an eye skinned for any sign of them. I don't think they're any trouble but they will steal your mounts if they get a chance—steal any damn thing they can get their hands on for that matter."

The sleds were loaded and we left. We traveled all day at a dogtrot. We saw a few Indians in the distance but as soon as we saw them they were gone. New Ulm was set on a series of shelves on the south side of the valley. A small settlement with a main street and probably a hundred buildings spread out away from them. Several farms were close to the town. We drove right past the main part of town and down a road that led to the edge of the river.

"We ain't stopping in New Ulm, Joe?"

"No reason to stop. People there don't like visitors much. They're all Germans and got no time for anyone else. Hell, the Indians even call them the Bad Talkers because they refuse to learn the English language, or the Sioux language. Sometimes an Indian will come to a man's door begging food for his family. Most times the white man is glad to share, but these Germans don't. They run 'em off with pitchforks. Injuns around here are almost completely dependent on the Whites for their survival. White men made them that way by killin' off all the game in these parts and trying to make the Indians farmers. An Injun ain't made for workin'— he is born to hunt and fish for his meals. Now the traders won't give out the food stores they have that's supposed to go to the Indians because they say the Indians have to wait for the annuities that come from Washington. Then they will distribute all of it at once."

"What's annuities?"

"Back in fifty-one the Indians sold part of their land to the Whites so the Whites could open the land for settlers. Truth is, the big land speculators are the ones who want the land opened up so they can buy it cheap from the state through some of their crooked friends then sell it for big profits to the settlers. That's part of what I was fighting in Saint Paul—trying to get some laws passed so the money men can't steal the land from the Indians then make big profits from the people who move in. The Indians were supposed to get a big chunk of money. That's the annuities. The food and blankets are too, but the white businessmen hold onto it and won't let the Indians have what's rightfully theirs."

"How much did the government give the Indians for their lands?"

"The worst of the deal was to the lower Sioux. They got ninety-six thousand dollars. That comes to thirty cents an acre for land that's worth five dollars an acre. Of course, the Indian has no concept of money so he had to take the white man's word that he was getting a fair price. On top of that, before any Indian could receive his share, any and all money owed to the traders for credit given the Indian the year before was to be paid directly out of the annuities fund. Like I said, Indians have no concept of money and they don't know how to keep records, so whatever the trader said the Indian owed him was paid to him, no questions asked. And the traders don't have no problem with jackin' up the debt because he knows the Indian has no records to check on him. Most times the Indian got nothing."

"Why doesn't the Indian do something about it? Can't they get help from someone?"

"Like who, me? I've been trying, but I can't fight the men with the money. They pay someone to pass a law that's in their favor and there ain't a damn thing I can do about it. Come to think of it, I ain't even a councilmember no more. In fifty-eight, Minnesota became a state and the new boundaries made Pembina part of the Dakota Territory so that leaves me out. Guess they pulled one over on me that time! Now the Indians are starving on their reservations, and they don't like it. Someone's going to pay for all this and I think the white man is the one. Some of the Indians have taken up farming like the white man wants him to—give up his religion, his old ways, his dress, hunting and fishing, everything. The ones who don't move to farms are mad at the farmer Indians because the white man treats him better—gives him more food, blankets, clothing, and tools while the blanket Indians, as they're called, starve. It's all a big, cruel game the white man plays to try to get dominion over something he can't control. The Indian's life is based on survival. The white man's life is driven by the need to accumulate all he can whether he needs it or not. In the Indian community, if one man has food, they all have food. In the white man's world, if one man has food, someone is there to try to cheat him out of it. The old saying that 'money is the root of all evil' is all too true. Money allows a person to own something he doesn't need or even have any use for. Some people even own land in other countries. What the hell is he gonna do with something he'll never even see? Make more money from it, money he doesn't need."

As I listened to Mister Rolette talk I realized that even though he is an overbearing bore most of the time, he is a good man.

"HA!" he said suddenly. "Damn land grabbers even tried to move the territorial Capitol from Saint Paul to Saint Peter. Land speculators spent five thousand dollars on a big white building thinking it would impress the legislators into moving the capitol. Some of the legislators were even given deeds to land by some of the speculators, hoping they'd vote for the move. The president of that bunch was none other than the governor of the territory. Well, they didn't get their Capitol moved. Someone run out with the bill before it could be voted on and stayed gone till the session was over and it was too late to vote on it. Therefore, Saint Paul is still the Capitol."

"And that someone was?"

Rolette threw out his chest and said, "Me," with a proud grin on his chubby face. "Yep, that time I pulled one over on them crooked sons-uh-bitches."

"How long did you stay gone?"

"Records say a hundred twenty-three hours."

"That's a coupl'a days. Where'd ye go?"

Joe looked at me. His thick eyebrows bounced up and down a couple of times. "Stayed at a friend's place downtown. *The Saint Paul Pioneer* and *The Democrat* newspapers say I was at the Fuller House Hotel. I was at a hotel all right, 'Linda's Home for Wayward Council Members'. Hell, the sergeant at arms they sent to look for me sat and played poker with me a couple of nights. Get it?" He looked at me, "Pok-er? Get it? Poke-her? You don't get it...never mind."

It took a few seconds for that to soak in, but when it did I laughed, "You spent two days in a whorehouse?"

"Son, a hundred twenty-three hours is damn near a week."

I guess I was supposed to be impressed. I was young and innocent. Joe continued to chatter until we had all fallen asleep. He might have talked all night long, I don't know, but he was talking when I woke up in the morning. The sun was just coming up in the east when we mounted our horses and hitched up the dogs.

"How far today, Mister Rolette?"

"Where the hell'd this Mister Rolette bullshit come from?"

"I figured you bein' a government man and all you should be..."

"I ain't no damn government man out here. They can call me Mister Rolette at the Capitol but I'll not have it here. Just go back to callin' me Rolette. Anywise," he said with a childish grin, "it's kinda fun when you git mad at me and call me Rolette like you do." He looked up at nothing, cocked his head and said, "Kinda took to it." He paused. "Ye know Hawk, Joe is a very common name. Wish people would call me Joseph." He said it bobbing his head to add strength to the word. "That sounds better than Joe—more dignified, don't ye think? Every other man you meet is called Joe. They even got a term that says 'He's just a plain ol' Joe'." He turned to me suddenly and said, "Hawk!" It made me jump. "Do I look like a plain ole Joe to you?"

"Rolette, there ain't nothin' plain about you. 'Specially your mouth."

"Hmm, you think I talk too much. Well let me tell you about this guy down in Saint Paul..." I turned away from him and climbed onto The Brute and started toward the river.

"Walk that horse over. That ice is plenty thick but ain't no point in testing it. Don't want to lose that horse—might need him when meat gets scarce later."

I climbed off The Brute and walked him to the other side. Rolette and his dogs got there ahead of me and were climbing diagonally up the bluff to a shelf that followed the river northward. About an hour into the ride we came to a place called Redwood Ferry. A sign pointed down the bluff and across the prairie but the brush was so thick I couldn't see anything down there.

"That's where they cross the river from the Lower Agency in the summertime on their way from New Ulm or Mankato—or from just about anywhere on the other side. Ain't no need for a ferry this time of the year. Couldn't float a boat on that ice anywise."

"Hawk!" he yelled at me.

"What!" I barked back.

"Ever been on a boat?"

"'Course I have. I growed up in Otter Tail County. Anyone who's been there knows about the lakes. Must be a thousand of them right around Otter Tail."

"I been to Otter Tail, nice country. Did I ever tell you about the time..."

"Rolette, you have just about covered the history of mankind. I'm sure you have touched—at least briefly—on that too." I touched my heels to The Brute and trotted him about a quarter-mile ahead of the noise. I could hear the dogs but not Rolette, and that was fine with me. Goodhorse and Henri were bringing up the rear. An hour later I realized I wasn't hearing the dogs. I stopped and turned in the saddle but couldn't see anyone back there. I stood for a few minutes waiting to see if they'd show up. They didn't, so I turned The Brute around and followed the trail back until I saw their tracks heading up the bluff. I kicked my horse and ran him until I caught up.

"Why the hell didn't you tell me you were turning?"

"You didn't want to hear anything else I had to say—didn't figure you wanted the hear that either."

"Asshole."

I stayed with Goodhorse and Henri from then on. All of a sudden a loud boom from above split the air. "What the hell was that?" I shouted at Rolette.

"Just the soldiers at the fort playing with their li'l cannon—nothing to get all excited over. That cannon is there for peace, not war. Long as they keep shootin' that thing off now and then the Injuns will stay peaceable." Then he added, "I think."

We climbed the hill for half a mile. Coming around a bend Rolette almost ran his dogs over a rider leading a packhorse. The rider had a thick red beard and wore a badgerskin hat. His horse was being troublesome and he rode by quietly. He had such a familiar look about him that I couldn't help but stare. I think he saw me looking because when he had passed he turned in the saddle and looked back.

"You know him?" I said to Goodhorse.

"Nope, never seen him before."

"He looked familiar."

"You see a lot of familiar faces, don't you Hawk?"

"Yeah, guess you're right. How would I know someone in a place I've never been?" We rode into Fort Ridgely listening to Rolette's chattering and headed for the sutler's store for some hot food.

"Damn," the man behind the counter said, "I thought the whole Sioux nation was coming in the door, but it's just Jolly Joe Rolette." Then he said softly, "I'd rather have the Indians."

"Now wait a minute here," I said. "Jolly Joe Rolette? *Jolly* Joe Rolette?"

"Let it be, Hawk," he said without smiling.

"Not on your life, Jolly Joe. Hey, Jolly Joe... funny how the name Joe takes on a whole new ring when you add 'Jolly' to it. It ain't so common no more, is it Jolly Joe?" I leaned my elbow on the counter and looked at him.

"Hawk, one of these days I'm gonna take you out behind the woodshed and show you some manners."

"One of these days, Jolly Joe? So what's wrong with today?"

"I'm busy, go away."

The two men talked while I walked around the place looking at the things on the shelves. I spotted a pistol like I had heard of but had never seen before. It was a revolver.

"How much for this pistol?"

"Twenty-five bucks, Jake. That includes..."

"What did you call me?"

The man looked closer at me and said, "Oh sorry, I thought you was someone else."

"Someone else like who?"

"Young fella over at the hospital, calls his self Jake Owen."

"Where's the hospital?" I said almost shouting.

"Go on up into the fort, through the parade grounds, and past the soldiers' barracks—fourth building you come to."

I turned and ran out the door and around the barracks. I slid to a stop at the door of the fourth building, opened it, and looked inside—a row of beds, two of them occupied. I yelled in, "Jake?"

"You lookin' for Jake Owen? He ain't here, you missed him by about an hour."

"Where'd he go?"

"Hell, I don't know. Don't think anyone around here knows where that boy hides out."

"Did he say where he comes from?"

"Otter Tail County, I think he said."

"Damn, that's my brother."

"Been a while since you seen him?"

"Last August. Wonder why he's down here? Maybe got in a fight with Pa too," I said more to myself than anyone. Then I remembered the man on the horse as we walked into camp, "Damn, that had to be Jake."

"Huh? Speak up, I can't hear ye."

"Never mind, talkin' to myself." I ran out the door and jumped up onto The Brute and whipped him into full gallop down the hill toward the river. At the bottom the road went both ways. The freshest tracks went north so that's where I went. I kept the horse at a run for more than an hour but saw no sign of Jake. It was getting dark and I was in strange country so I had to turn back to the fort.

When I got there I went straight to the hospital and talked to the man in the bed.

"What was Jake doing in the hospital? He sick?"

"Took a Sioux arrow in the back. Would'a killed anyone else but that boy's too damned ornery to die. Specially dyin' on account of some damned Injun."

"Why would any Indian want to kill Jake? He's the peaceable one in the family. I mean, why would they want to do that?"

"Way I heard it from Jake his self was, they tried to steal his horses and he didn't want them to have them. Makes sense to me."

"Jake's got horses?"

"'Course he does. That stallion he rides is the goddamnedest critter you ever saw. While Jake was in here healin' up some of the men out there thought they could ride it. Nope, they couldn't. Couldn't get a saddle on his back. Then Jake comes out and walks right up to the horse and puts a saddle on him and rides him like he was born there. And the mare follows along like a hungry puppy. Rag-lar little family they whar. Ye say he's yer brother?"

"Yeah."

"You be Hawk then?" he said, more as a statement than a question.

"Yeah," I said without knowing it.

"Hawk, I ain't the one who should tell you this, but onna conna Jake ain't here, guess I will."

"Tell me what?"

"Well, yer ma is dead and yer pa ain't been found yet."

"What the hell does that mean, ain't been found? And how did Ma die?"

"Injuns, Hawk. Injuns attacked yer place, kilt yer ma and burned the place down."

"Jake told you that?"

"Yeah he did, an there's been rumors about Injun trouble up around Crow Wing country. Chippaway chief up there named Hole-in-the-Day causing trouble. Mostly with the Sioux but it's gittin' to be a problem for the Whites too.

Might have been some of his renegades what did yer ma."

"You sure about all this? You sure you got the story right? Ma's really dead?"

"Got it from Jake his self. That's where he comes up with the horses. He tracked the killers down, scalped 'em, and took their horses."

"What about Pa?"

"He didn't say nothin' about yer pa. Kinda like he didn't want me to know."

His heart was like a stone, cold and emotionless...
He promised himself he would never again get so close
to anyone that he couldn't watch them die,
or even kill them himself if need be...

C H A P T E R   F I V E

T H E   S O U N D   O F   T H E   C A N N O N   W O K E   J A K E   from his nap. His
nurse Sisoka sat on his bed looking at him. During the past two months she had
cared for him through hard times when he was deathly ill with fever. Now he
was healed up and ready to ride.

"Where's Doc Muller?"

Sisoka didn't speak English but she knew what Jake was asking and she signed
that he had gone to Saint Paul.

"Some guy in Saint Paul got his head split open in a fight and he's para-
lyzed on one side," the man in the next bed told him. "Doc Muller went down
there to study it. Guess all the doctors are curious about it."

Doctor Muller had done all he could for Jake. Jake had taken a fever from
the arrow and the drugs Doctor Muller was giving him weren't helping. Doctor
Muller had a great respect for the Indian remedies and herb tonics so he'd asked
Sisoka to treat Jake, and before long he was on his way to full recovery. He was
up and around and anxious to get back to his horses and his cave. He'd been up
since before dawn, had dressed and prepared for his ride. Sisoka had told him
not to go out but Jake was ready and she could do nothing to stop him.

"I will go with you," she signed by sliding the edge of her index finger length-
wise along the palm of her hand.

"No," he signed back. She stood and walked out the door.

Jake put on his coat and winter moccasins and walked out the door. He
went to the barn to get his horse. He saddled up, loaded the mare with what

equipment he had, and rode through the fort and down the hill to the trail that led to his cave. Ahead of him he could hear the barking of dogs and the crack of a whip. His stallion got skittish. A dog team suddenly appeared before him with a stocky man riding on the back rails of a sled. Three riders followed. Jake was tending to the worried stallion and barely noticed the man with the red beard riding the big, black horse and looking curiously at him. He rode past them and looked back when he realized that the red-bearded man had stared at him so hard. He saw the man turn in the saddle and look back at him. There was an instant of recognition in Jake but he shook it off and rode on. Two miles down the road he turned at the sound of hooves behind him. He raised his Hawken and aimed it at the rider, then he lowered it when he saw it was Sisoka.

"Thought I told you to stay home."

She shrugged her shoulders and looked at Jake. She didn't understand him. Jake signed that she should go back.

"No, I go with you," she signed.

With his finger under his chin and a sinuous motion away from the throat he said, "I go alone."

Sisoka looked into his eyes and said nothing.

He touched the stallion to a cantor and rode through the night with Sisoka and the mare trailing behind. Halfway through the next day he came to his cave in the walls of the Minnesota Valley. He found everything in its place and was content to be away from the world. Sisoka began at once making order of the camp that Jake had made for himself. She moved the fire pit closer to the outside wall and built a fire. What little smoke there was rolled out the hole she'd made in the top of the wall rather than gathering at the ceiling of the cave. She pulled dried meat from her packs and made Jake's dinner. He sat back and watched her work. He smiled as he puffed on a pipe that he'd gotten from his friend Charley Bell in the hospital. *Jacob Owen is a rich man*, he thought to himself.

When they had eaten, Sisoka went about tidying up and busying herself with small chores around the cave. Jake sat quietly rubbing oil on his rifle that had been neglected since January. He kept the shotgun loaded while he cleaned the rifle, and the rifle was loaded when he cleaned the shotgun.

When night fell, Sisoka spread pine boughs on the floor and laid robes over them. She signed for Jacob to get in the bed. Jake pulled his moccasins off and started to slide under the robes. She said "No," and motioned for him to remove the rest of his clothes. Somewhat confused, he did as he was told. He stood before her in his long, red flannel underwear. She motioned him into the bed and slid in next to him. Sisoka slid her warm body against Jake and wrapped her arms around his neck and chest and licked his face like a puppy. Her leg was over his and she was pushing her hips against him. Jake felt the physical changes happening in his body. Sisoka guided him into her body and they made love there in the darkness.

"I think I could get used to this," he said, and they made love again and again that first night.

The next morning, Jake couldn't think of any reason to hurry out of bed so they lay in each other's arms until his back started to hurt and Mother Nature demanded his attention.

The two stayed in their camp for two weeks before Jake got the urge to roam. He saddled his horse and Sisoka saddled hers. They rode northwest, away from the fort. Jake had had enough of fort life and wanted to scout the country across the river. They crossed the river on the ice to the other side.

For the remainder of the winter Sisoka showed Jake the Minnesota Valley from one end of the Sioux reservations to the other. He became familiar with the Upper and Lower Agencies, with all of the towns and settlements in the valley, and some outside the valley as well. She showed him the springs that ran with fresh cold water all year long and the one waterfall on the Minnesota River. She showed him the falls of Minneopa Creek. There the water drops in a double-falls thirty feet into a rock-lined amphitheater with walls forty feet above the river. For a thousand years Indians had come here to experience visions and seek guidance from the spirits. He also learned about Indian spiritualism. He saw the big woods to the north of the valley. He saw the blue clay that made men dream of untold wealth in copper mines—of course, they went home disappointed for there was no copper in this valley. He saw the boiling springs and the Giant Louisville swamp. She told him the Indian legends about the Minnesota Valley being the river that drained the big lake to the North after the Great Spirit had flooded the land to purify it of evil. He thought to himself that that had to be a legend that came to the Indians through missionaries.

Sisoka also showed Jake how to use a knife and tomahawk in battle. She showed him the art of throwing a hatchet to kill an enemy when it became necessary, and to use a knife in the same way. She worked with him at shooting his bow more effectively. She taught him the Sioux language and she learned English.

"Why do I need to know these things, Sisoka?"

"There will be great trouble in the valley. You will need to be able to defend yourself and live like the Indian to survive."

"What does that mean, great trouble?"

"The white men in this valley are making themselves a road that will lead them to their death."

"More…"

"The Agent at the Lower Agency will not give out the food that belongs to the Indians. He says we must wait for the annuity payment to arrive. The young men of the villages are calling for war on the Whites to drive them from our valley. One called Little Crow is being asked to lead the warriors but he does not think it is a war the Indians can win."

"Do you think you can win?"

"I will not fight in the war. No, I do not think the Indian can win. We will be chased from this last home when the fighting is over, if we are not all killed."

One morning, Sisoka called Jake out of his cave and pointed at a red-breasted bird on the ground, "Look, that is Sisoka."

"Ah, Sisoka means robin?"

"Yes, robin. I am robin." She smiled at him.

"Robin," he said and touched her face.

"Yes, and you are Pa Hin Sa."

"And that means?"

"Red hair."

"I might have known."

"Jacob," Sisoka looked at Jake.

"What is it?"

"I must go back to my people."

"Why?"

"I have been away for all of winter and it is time to begin the spring gathering. My family will need me."

"You will come back?"

"I will see you again."

The next morning Sisoka began gathering her belongings into a deerskin sack. She loaded them onto her horse behind the saddle and mounted. Jake saddled and mounted his stallion and they rode off together toward Fort Ridgely. Jake had his Hawken rifle across his lap and a ten-inch butcher knife in a rawhide sheath at his belt. In his belt at his back he carried a tomahawk he'd gotten from the Chippewas back in Otter Tail County. Sisoka carried Jake's shotgun across her lap. They rode the trail toward Fort Ridgely without talking. Jake didn't want this woman to go back to her people but she had promised to return and that made it easier to accept. They rode silently.

Jake's horse suddenly got skittish. He tightened his grip on the Hawken rifle. Suddenly, two shots rang out almost simultaneously. Sisoka pitched sideways from her horse and dropped to the ground. A bullet ripped across the front of Jake's shirt without touching him. He raised the Hawken and aimed it toward the smoke cloud in the brush fifty yards away. He saw a man kneeling in the brush. He centered his sights on the man's chest and killed him. Instantly he jumped from his horse and ran to Sisoka, keeping the horse between himself and his attackers. Before kneeling, he loaded his rifle and looked carefully through the brush surrounding him, then at the woman on the ground. Blood poured from both sides of her chest and Jake knew she was dead. Numbness came over him. He was exploding inside.

Again he looked up toward the place where the shots came from and studied it for a moment. Suddenly, a man jumped up and ran through the brush away from him. His rifle came up and sent a ball slamming into the running man's back carrying parts of his heart out through his chest. Jake reloaded and walked slowly to the dying man keeping his eyes and ears open for any movement or sound around him. He could feel the presence of another man close by but knew that if he were going to shoot he would have done it already. He knew that a scared man would not risk his life even if he were sure of his shot. He kneeled down next to the dying man.

"Who the hell are you, and why did you have to kill the girl?"

The man looked at Jake and said, "I didn't kill no one—it was John made us do it."

"Who's John?" But he knew he would get no answer—the man was dead. He pulled out his butcher knife and took the scalps of both of his attackers. *Didn't ever think I'd pull a white man's scalp, but then I guess it don't matter what color yer skin is. Ye can be just as bad in any color,* he said to himself. Then he smashed in their faces with his clenched fist. He kneeled down in the dirt and scanned the underbrush for the man whose presence he could feel but not see. Not wanting to take chances, he backed slowly out of the thicket until he was almost to the road.

Jake walked back to the girl and carried her body into the brush. He dug a shallow grave and laid her in it. His heart was like a stone, cold and emotionless. To Jacob Owen there was not another soul in the valley who meant anything to him. He promised himself he would never again get so close to anyone that he couldn't watch them die, or even kill them himself if need be. Jacob Owen was now an emotionless animal. He gathered up the reins and led the horses down the trail toward the fort.

He rode through the fort without stopping, to the camp of Sioux on the north side. He walked up to the tepee where Sisoka's father lived. The old Indian came out and greeted Jake.

"Sisoka is dead?" the old Indian signed.

"Yes. White men killed her," Jake answered in the Sioux language. "They paid with their lives. There is one more who was there. I will find him and he will die slowly." He handed the Indian the scalps of Eddy and Arty Grenges.

"Jacob," the old man said, "there is a man looking for you. He says he is your brother."

"I got no brother in this country."

"He is your brother I think. People mistake him for you. They say he looks like you. He walks like you and he talks like you. He has a red beard and red hair like you. His name is Hawk."

"Then he *is* my brother." In a voice that showed only curiosity, he asked, "Where is he now?"

"He is in the hills looking for you."

"Wish he'd stayed here, would'a been easier to find him."

"He stayed around here for two weeks hoping you would come back but he got restless and went looking for you. You have been gone for almost two moons, Jake. Hawk has been here three times since you left. He will come back."

"Well, I ain't stayin' here. You tell him when he gets back to stay on the north side of the valley and I will find him." Jake left Sisoka's horse and her belongings with her family and rode back to his cave.

My heart was beating so loudly I could hear it.
I also realized at that moment that my hands were shaking so badly
I couldn't get my finger in the trigger guard of the pistol…

6

C H A P T E R   S I X

"WONDER IF PA'S ALIVE OR DEAD OUT THERE where Jake just couldn't find him?"

"Dunno, he didn't say."

"Well, first thing in the morning I'm heading up the valley to find him. You don't have any idea where to start looking?"

"There was a couple of Injuns killed about twenty miles north of here last fall. Folks are sayin' it was Jake what killed 'em. I figger he's holed up somewhere close to that. Chances of you findin' his place are perty slim though. Injuns been lookin' for it since the killins and ain't found it yet. He's got a horse that can go where other horses cain't onna conna it was a wild mustang before Jake got holt of it. Wild horses are more sure-footed than farm horses."

"I think I have the horse that will keep up with Jake's—he was wild too. How long you gonna be in the hospital?"

"Dunno. Had me a good fever and the Doc says when it breaks and I can take care of myself, he'll let me out. Perty soon, I figger."

"Well, I'll be comin' back and be lookin' for you. What's yer name?"

"Private Charles Bell. Call me Charlie, ever'one does."

"Good to meet ye, Charlie. Take care of yourself."

"Yeah you too, Hawk." I walked out the door and went straight to the sutler's store.

"Where'd Rolette go?"

"Hell, Rolette's been gone fer hours. He told me to give you this as payment for ridin' guard for him." He handed me a leather folder. I opened it and inside was one hundred dollars.

"Is everyone out here tryin' to get rid of their money? That's two people now who gave me money for doin' what I like doin'."

"That ain't all. He told me to give you this too." He handed me the pistol I was looking at earlier. "Said this is 'cause he likes you. I ain't s'pose to tell you that, but he said you was more fun to ride with than anyone he's ever rode with. Guess he liked it when he pissed you off and you jumped back at him. That's Jolly Joe—always pissin' people off."

"He's good at it, that's for sure. Tell me about this pistol."

"Forty-four caliber Colt's Second Model Dragoon. Shoots fifty grains of powder and uses number eleven caps, just like that Hawken you got there."

"This is fifty-four."

"I know, I meant the caps."

"Oh."

"That there's one powerful handgun—knock a small deer down jest as sure as yer rifle will. And you can shoot it six times before having to reload. Hell of a weapon you got there—only pistol that has more power is Colt's Walker. That monster'll knock down a buffler. But that's a horse pistol, too heavy to carry on your belt."

"Damn, I never figgered I'd ever own something like this."

"Here's feed for it." He handed me a bag of balls, a tin of caps, and a copper powder flask with a measuring spout on it.

"Wanna show me how to load it?"

"Oh, yeah, I suppose you should know that."

Mister Randal showed me how to load the pistol and told me to always leave the cap off the chamber under the hammer so it wouldn't go off accidentally and blow my foot into the ground.

"So how do I carry this thing?"

"That, my redheaded friend, is your problem. Personally I wouldn't carry something that big if I didn't have to. I got me a thirty-six caliber eighteen fifty-one Colt's Navy. Weighs about half what that one does and it gets heavy after a day's riding."

"Thirty-six? Would that kill a man?"

"Why the hell I wanna kill anyone? I use it for fun, that's all. Thirty-six'll make a man damn mad if you hit him with it, but it sure won't stop him. That dragoon will—drop him right quick."

HAWK'S VALLEY

"Any idea where I might start lookin' for Jake?"

"Only thing I can tell you is he's somewhere in this valley."

"Thanks a lot. How far is it to the other end?"

"About two hunnert miles."

"Might take a day or two to cover it. See ye later, Ben."

"You be careful, Hawk. And if you see Jake, tell him who you are before you walk up to him—safer that-a-way."

"Will do."

I walked out and hopped on The Brute. The first thing I had to do was to find a pack animal so I went to the stables.

"What can I do fer ya, Jake?"

"I ain't Jake."

"Oh sorry," the man said, looking up at my eyes. "Thought you was someone else."

"You got something I can use for a pack animal?"

"Yeah, got a couple of horses and a few mules. Mules is better in this hilly country, but horses are faster."

"Don't need fast, I need dependable."

"Take you a mule then. They're good workers and they're more sure-footed in the hills, too." We walked out to the yard and he showed me a couple of mules. One was brown like the ones back home so I asked how much.

"Damn good mule there. I'll let her go for a hunnert."

"Mister, I've worked mules. That critter ain't worth a hundred dollars. I'll give you fifty."

"Gotta have at least ninety."

"Sixty… that's it."

"Damn, I guess I can starve one more night. Sixty it is."

I handed him the sixty dollars and led the mule to where Rolette had left my gear and loaded it on her back. I went to the bottom of the valley and struck a trail north. I rode until dark and set up a camp in a thicket of aspen for the night. I rode north for a week before I turned back, then headed to the top of the valley walls and rode south for another two weeks, riding hard over the ground I had already covered. I passed Fort Ridgely without stopping and stayed on the south road. I found several small towns and lots of farms. I asked a few people if they knew Jake Owen but none of them did. I came to a town called Courtland and stepped into the Crow Bar Saloon. When I walked in the door the man behind the bar looked at me, then at the girl standing next to him and said softly, "Go git yer ma."

He turned to me, "What can I get you sir?"

"Just some information."

"Nothin' to drink?"

"Cup of water'd be nice."

Without taking his eyes off of me he thumbed the girl to the bucket and she brought me a cup.

"How can I help you, Mister, um…didn't catch the name."

"Owen. Harlan Owen. Lookin' for a man looks about like me, name's Jake Owen. He's my brother. Ye ain't seen him around have ye?"

"You ain't him?"

"His brother."

"Oh, we thought…um, well, he was in town last Christmas. Just passed through though—didn't talk to anyone—just rode through. Some said he was lookin' for his horse what got stole by the Injuns. Ain't seen hide nor hair of him since."

"No idea where he might be holed up?"

"The man's a ghost. Here one minute, gone the next so they say."

"How is it you know of him but you don't know him personal?"

"Jake Owen's been in the valley for five months they say, and he's killed a couple of Injuns already that I know of—some say more. Also heard he was shot in the back with an arrow and he's been in the hospital at Ridgely."

"He just left there a month ago."

"Then he'll be around somewhere. Just follow the trail of dead Injuns and you'll find him."

"Thanks for the water. I'll be on my way."

"Come on back when you can—beer's on the house."

"Thanks, will do."

I didn't think there was much point to running up and down this side of the valley so I headed back to Ridgely. I got information about the south side of the valley and took off in that direction. I was told not to stay long on the south side because it's getting warmer and the river will be rising as the snow melts. I walked The Brute to the south side and took a road that led north. I knew Redwood would be somewhere up there and was looking forward to seeing Lorraine. It wasn't long before I came to a small settlement at the top of the bluff. I stopped a man on the street and asked where I was.

"Lower Sioux Agency," he said and walked on without looking at my face.

"That's Andy Myrick. Runs a store on the road west of here," a tall, thin man said.

"Not very friendly, is he?"

"Andrew Myrick likes Andrew Myrick—no one else. Injuns around here hate the man. He treats them like animals."

"I been seein' lots of Injuns around here. How come?"

"Indian Agency. Lower Sioux Agency they call it. Some call it the Redwood Agency."

"This is Redwood?"

"Yep."

"You got an Indian school here?"

"Oh, forgive me. I'm Samuel Hinman, pastor of the Episcopal Church we will be building this spring." He stuck out his hand, "And yes, we will have a school for Indian children when it is finished. Why do you ask?"

"I had a friend who was coming here to teach Indian children. Lorraine, her name is." It was at this moment I realized that I had no idea what Lorraine's last name was.

"Oh yes, Miss Bernier. Lovely girl. I'm sorry to tell you that she has been sent to the Upper Agency. We are not ready to open our school yet and they have one running as we speak."

"How far is the Upper Agency?"

"About thirty miles. You can be there tomorrow if you ride all day."

"I won't be moving that fast. I'm looking for my brother Jake. I don't s'pose you've heard of him?"

"Jake. What's his last name?"

"Owen."

"Jake Owen... nope. Some Owens living down by New Ulm, but none around here that I know of."

"Well, nice talking with you Reverend, guess I'll be on my way."

"Good luck in your search. I didn't get your name."

"Sorry, Harlan Owen. People call me Hawk."

Reverend Hinman stuck out his hand and said, "Nice to meet you Hawk, perhaps we will meet again."

"Maybe. See ye down the road."

Reverend Hinman walked to his house on the south side of the road. I got up onto The Brute and headed west past the square, a warehouse, and a few other buildings, and then passed four trade stores to the open prairie. The road led me to the edge of the valley and I took another road down to a wide terrace and followed that until sundown. I found a small depression in the bank and made my night's camp.

The next morning I was up with the sun and took the trail to the top. About midmorning I came to an Indian village. People stood and watched as I walked my horse around the outside of the village. An Indian came out on horseback and said something in Sioux that I couldn't understand. He talked loud like he was mad at me but kept a distance between us. I raised my hand as a sign that I meant no harm. He motioned me to come with him. I declined the invite and heeled The Brute on. We started to walk away and the Indian shouted at me. I stopped and looked back. He had closed the distance between us and had a double-barreled shotgun pointed at me. Discretion told me that I should go with him. I turned The Brute around and walked toward the man, then he reached out to take my rifle and I jerked it back.

"Not hardly," I said, staring him in the eyes. He raised the shotgun and held out his hand as if to say 'give me the gun'. I looked at him and said, "No." Then he put his other hand on the shotgun and aimed it at my face. He made the mistake of getting just a little too close—he was only a couple of feet away from me. I swung my Hawken and knocked the shotgun out of his hands and pointed my rifle at him.

"Git," I said. He reached for the knife at his belt and I hit him in the face with the butt of my rifle. He went backwards off his horse. I stood for a second to see if he was finished and rode away at a cantor. Behind me I could hear shouts and hoof beats so I spurred The Brute into a gallop and rode out of the area.

No sooner had I gotten out of sight of that village than I came to another. I turned The Brute and made a wide circle around it. I didn't need anymore of what I'd had in the first village. In all, I saw four Indian camps. The whole country seemed to be filling up with Indians. The ones that saw me stopped what they were doing and watched until I was out of sight. It was a little unnerving to be watched so closely. I soon realized that I was being followed. All the while I was on the road there was a party of anywhere from two to ten Indians just out of range. They kept their pace to match mine, sometimes disappearing, only to reappear a few minutes later over the top of a ridge or down in a depression. I stayed in the open where there would be less chance of someone surprising me in an ambush. For some reason they watched every move I made. This went on for the full day and I was starting to wonder when I would be able to get some rest. It was obvious that I couldn't sleep with all of these

HAWK'S VALLEY

Indians around.

Suddenly they were gone, not an Indian or a horse in sight. Over the next rise I saw the reason—straight ahead of me was a white man's village. I rode down into a ravine and climbed up the other side to the town. There were few buildings there. When I rode into town the Indians stopped what they were doing and watched me ride in. By now it had become just an annoyance and I could ignore it.

I stopped a man and said, "What is this place?"

"Yellow Medicine Agency."

"How far to the Upper Agency?"

"This is it. You're at the Upper Agency. We call it the Yellow Medicine on account of the river you just crossed."

"Where's the school?"

"Look right between those two buildings, you can see it from here," he said as he pointed the direction.

"Thanks, Mister." I walked The Brute between the buildings to the schoolhouse and swung down, carrying my rifle with me, and knocked on the door. It opened and there she stood, just as beautiful as ever.

"Hawk! What in the world are you doing here? I didn't ever expect to see you again. How are you? It's been so lonely around here. Tell me about Jean. Is he well?"

"Well if you keep quiet for a second I'll tell you..." She came to me and put her arms around me and hugged me hard. "Wow," I said, "if I thought I'd get that kind of welcome I'd have come sooner."

"Well don't just stand there, come on in and sit down." I sat on a bench and Lorraine sat on the one facing me.

"Well, tell me, what brings you to Pajutazee?"

"What's that word?"

"Pajutazee—it means 'Yellow Medicine', the name of this place."

"I heard that my brother Jacob is in the valley and I'm looking for him. He was lying in the Fort Ridgely hospital and left the day I got there."

"Jacob Owen? I have not heard that name. Perhaps some of the Indians here have heard it. I will ask around."

"I don't think that would be a good idea. Seems Jake has a bad reputation among the Indians—had some trouble with them last fall."

"What sort of trouble?"

"I don't know. One man told me he killed two of them and maybe more."

"Why in the world would he do that?"

"Well, the way I got it figured, he's taking revenge for our mother being killed by Indians."

"Your mother was killed by Indians? Hawk, you never told me that."

"I just learned about it when I got to Ridgely. It happened after I left the farm."

"That could be the reason your brother is seeking revenge. But Hawk, it wasn't all Indians who did this. It was just the ones who were there. Jacob shouldn't take revenge on all Indians for the sins of a few."

"Hey, I know that. And it might not even be the reason he did it. And I'm not sure he killed anyone, anyway. I just heard it from someone. I won't know until I talk to Jake himself."

"You are right. We mustn't jump to conclusions." The door opened and an Indian walked in. He started to say something to Lorraine but when he saw me he turned and quickly walked back out the door.

"What the hell was that all about?"

"There is no need for profanity in here, Hawk."

"Yeah, well what made him leave so fast?"

"I don't know. He seemed to be afraid of you. Perhaps it is just that you are a strange face around here and he was being careful."

"No, I think there's more to it than that. Indians followed me all the way from Redwood to here. I had to fight one of them to keep from losing my rifle and pack mule."

"Hawk, you were in another fight? Why must you do that?"

"Lorraine, when a man tries to take my rifle and my horses I need to fight to keep them—there ain't no other choice. I can't just give them to him, can I?"

"Couldn't you have talked to him and reasoned things out like civilized men?"

"In the first place, I don't speak Sioux. Second, he didn't speak English. Third, he had a twelve-gauge shotgun pointed at my face. You tell me what I could have done but fight."

"I'm sorry, Hawk. I spoke out of turn."

"Nothing to worry about, I know how you feel about fighting. I ain't real crazy about it myself."

"Well you certainly do your share of something you say you don't like to do."

"Lorraine, it ain't me who starts the fights. I just happen to be there when it starts."

"And you are not the one to walk away from it either like a civilized man would."

"I think it's time to go."

"Where will you go from here?"

"Up the valley for a ways then, I don't know, maybe cross the river and look over there again. This is such a big place and finding someone who doesn't want to be found can be a chore."

"I will listen and watch for you. How can I reach you if I learn anything about your brother?"

"I'll be going to Ridgely ever so often. You can leave a message at the store."

"Will you be coming back through here?"

"Of course I will. How can I stay away?"

Lorraine was just as beautiful as she was when I met her but somehow the feelings I had for her were gone. She was more like a good friend than someone I wanted to marry. After I got another hug, I walked out the door and straight into a crowd of Indians. They opened a path for me and I walked through them with both hands on my rifle. I was hoping my dragoon was still in the bag strapped to the side of The Brute where I left it. When I got to the horse the first thing I checked was the sack with the gun in it. It was there. I pulled it out and held it up pretending to check the loads but my real intention was to let the Indians see what I had and hopefully give them a good reason to stay clear of me. I heard a murmur go through the crowd when they saw the pistol. I also heard the words "Pa Hin Sa" from several of the men in the crowd. Lorraine stood in the door and watched as I rode slowly out of the Agency.

I rode through the day with my Indian escort always in sight—sometimes one man, sometimes a group. It was getting close to night and I needed to get some rest, so I turned my horse down the bluff to find a good place to make a camp. About halfway down I found a flat spot that would serve as a campsite with a patch of good grass showing through the snow for the animals. I picketed them close to my camp and built a small fire to warm some dried beef and peas in water from a stream close by. Then I rolled up in my robes for the night. I had just fallen asleep when I heard The Brute whinny and rumble in his throat. I woke up and wrapped my hands around the Hawken as I tried in vain to see what was moving out there. I could hear Brute close to me and another sound moving away and figured it was the mule, but it was so dark I couldn't see the rifle I was holding onto, much less what was moving in the brush. I lay motionless and as quietly as I could. I was scared to breathe. My fire was no more than red coals and shed no light. The sound got more distant until it was gone completely. I began to relax but there would be no sleep for the rest of the night.

As soon as it was light enough to see, I pushed the robe off me and crawled to where the sound was in the night. The picket pin was still in the ground and half of the rope that held the mule. A sharp knife had cut the rope. *Indians*, I thought to myself. The Brute was still tied to his stake close to my bedroll. All of my gear was where I had put it the night before. Then, since I no longer had a pack animal, I had to decide what to take with me and what I didn't need. I took my weapons and food and my bedroll, then buried the rest in a cache in the side of the hill. I really didn't expect to find it when I came back this way but I figured I'd try to save it anyway. I mounted up and took off back to Fort Ridgely—no use staying on this side of the valley if I had to stay on the lookout for thieves and killers.

I was back at the Yellow Medicine Agency by late afternoon and went directly to the schoolhouse. Wearing my dragoon in my belt and carrying my Hawken, I knocked on the door. The door opened and instead of seeing Lorraine, I saw a burly man with a beard under his chin and ears that stood straight out from the side of his head. He looked at me with eyes that showed no sign of friendliness.

"You must be the man Lorraine told me about. Harlan Owen, am I correct?"

"Yes, is Lorraine here?"

"She is out visiting with some of the Indian children. Is there something I can do for you?"

"Well no, not really. I don't think there is anything anyone can do for me. I just lost my pack mule to Indians last night. Anything you can do about that?"

"No, but I can tell you, it is not good for you to be around this Agency."

"And why is that?"

"Mister Owen, I don't especially like your kind at all, and particularly around here stirring up trouble with my Indians. The Sissetons and Wahpetons are generally a peace-loving people, but when the likes of you comes around there is sure to be trouble."

"Mister...whatever your name is..."

"I am Doctor Williamson. I am Pastor at the Pajutazee mission two miles from here."

"Well, Mister Williamson, I don't know *who* you think I am, but I am not *what* you think I am. I have caused no trouble here. Your peaceful Indians have harassed me since I got close to this peaceful place. I have lost my mule and have been threatened by a man with a shotgun. I'm here looking for my brother who is somewhere in this valley. I want no more than to find him and settle down somewhere and to be left alone. Somehow you have come to believe I am here making trouble—I ain't."

"I have talked to the Indians and they say you are the one they call Pa Hin Sa, and looking at you, I can see why."

"I don't understand."

"Pa Hin Sa means red hair."

"And a red-haired man is bad to the Indians around here?"

"No, not as a rule, but it is when a man with red hair earns himself a reputation like yours."

"Reputation? I just got to this valley. How in hell could I have a reputation?"

"Yes, Mister Owen, you probably have a reputation there too."

"Where?"

"In hell."

"You're crazy, Doctor Williamson. Goodbye." I turned and walked out thoroughly confused by that conversation. I climbed aboard The Brute and headed south toward Fort Ridgely. There seemed to be more Indians along the road than there were when I came through earlier, but they stayed away and didn't bother me. Some came close and looked me over like I was some animal in a zoo, but said nothing. I walked by an Indian in white man's clothes sitting alongside the road smoking a pipe.

"Good day, Mister Owen." I reined The Brute to a stop in front of the man.

"You know me?"

"No, but I may know your brother."

"Jake? You know Jake?"

"Yes, I know him."

"Do you know where he is? Can you find him?"

"You are searching the wrong side of the valley. Jacob lives on the north side, upstream from Fort Ridgely about two days' ride, maybe longer, depends on your animal."

"My horse can do it if his can."

"Don't be too sure of that, Hawk."

"You know my name."

"Yes, I have heard of you for several days now. I knew sooner or later I would find you, or you would find me." There was a short silence.

"Well, can you tell me how to find Jake?"

"I can only head you in the right direction. I do not know where he lives. I have not tried to find it. He wishes to be left alone and I must respect that wish as I would expect him to if it were me."

"Well? Which way?"

"You need to go to the other side of the valley and head north. Ride for two days and stay in that area until Jacob finds you. That is the only way you will find him. There have been bad Indians looking for him up there for almost a year and they haven't found him yet. It is better for them that they don't find him because he would surely kill them on sight. He has had bad experiences with Indians and he is not one to ask questions when confronted."

"Who are you that you know my brother so well?"

"I am John Other Day. I became acquainted with Jacob at Fort Ridgely last fall. He is a good man but has fallen into bad times. It would be good for him to have you there with him."

"Will you come with me?"

"No, I must stay here. Hawk, before you go I have something to say. A while back, Jacob was hit in the back by an arrow and spent the winter in the hospital at Fort Ridgely."

"I knew that."

"A Sioux girl named Sisoka healed him with wild herbs and medicines. When he got out of the hospital he left the fort and went back to his hideout. The girl went with him. Sometime during her stay with him two white men killed her. There was a third man involved and Jacob has sworn to find him and kill him. The two men Jacob shot were Eddy and Arty Grenges. They were wanted in Saint Paul for the killing of the hostler at the stables there. The third man is called John Olson. He was in jail with the Grenges boys in Saint Paul. He has not been heard of and no one knows who he is or where he comes from. There have been reports of burglaries around New Ulm and the farms in that area. Some think it is John Olson who is doing it."

"It ain't Indians doing the stealing?"

"No, Indians will steal food and guns. This man steals things he can sell for money. Indians have no use for money. If they're going to steal they will steal the things the white man would buy with money. It is a white man doing the stealing this time."

"How do you know all of these things?"

"Hawk, the Indian knows everything that goes on in the valley. It is our home just like it is the home of the deer and elk. We need to know everything to survive."

"Thanks, Mister Other Day. I'll be on my way. Hope to see you again."

"I'm sure we will meet again," and I started down the road.

"Hawk." I turned to Mister Other Day and he was pointing to the road behind me, "...your mule." I looked, and there in the middle of the road stood my mule. I figured this was one of those times when questions were not to be asked, so I rode to the mule, took the reins, and started back to pick up my bags I had buried in the hillside. "Where are you going, Hawk?"

"To get my belongings."

"Your belongings are not there. They are payment for returning your mule." I looked at Mister Other Day. He puffed on his pipe, raised one eyebrow, and shrugged one shoulder.

"The Indian Way?" I asked.

"Yep."

I rode by him, nodded his way, and took to the road to Fort Ridgely.

The boom of the fort's cannons greeted me as I rode in. I could hear Sergeant Jones calling commands as he drilled his artillery troop. The Brute wasn't real crazy about the noise and I had a time keeping him calm. My first stop was the hospital to see if Charley Bell was still there. I walked in and found only one man in bed.

"Where's Charley?"

"He got out two days ago. Doc says he's over the fever he had."

"Where'd he go?"

"Out there drillin' with the rest of the troops. You gonna join up?"

"What do ye mean, join up?"

"Join the army—go South and fight for President Lincoln."

"Now why in the world would I do that? I got no idea what they're fightin' about and wouldn't know which side to fight for."

"Some say they're fightin' to stop the slavery in the South. Some say they're fightin' over the prices of goods from the North that the southern plantation owners pay for the things they buy from the Yankees."

"Which is it? Neither of them has anything to do with me."

"Danged if I know. The Captain says it's our duty as citizens to go and fight."

"How's this? If the war comes here I'll fight. I figure we got our own problems right where we are. Got my mule stole from me—an Injun named John

Other Day got her back for me. Hadda give up my camp to get her back though—'The Indian way', Other Day said."

"Yep, they got their own ways of doin' things. John Other Day's a good man. All Injuns should be like him. We wouldn't have to feed them, they could feed themselves."

"I'm Hawk Owen," I stuck out my hand.

"Sergeant Russ Findley, at your service." He took my hand.

"What ye in here for?" He threw the blanket back to show a wooden splint on his lower leg.

"Busted?"

"Nah. Doc says I sprained the knee. I'll be up and about in a day or two."

"Well, I'll let ye be. I got some things I gotta do yet. I wanna go up the valley and look for Jake."

"Oh say, I heard he was seen at Sacred Heart."

"Where's that?"

"Northwest about forty miles."

"South side of the valley?"

"North side. They figure it was him on account he had that Injun girl with him what kept him alive last winter. "

"When was this? Other Day told me he had a girl with him but she was killed by a couple of white men."

"Might not have been him then. This was just a few days ago I heard about him being spotted."

"How far is this Sacred Heart?"

"About a day's ride."

"See ye down the road."

"Watch that red hair of yorn. Make a damn nice wall hanger for some Sioux warrior."

"Will do," I waved and walked out the door.

I rode down out of the fort and took the road north. I crossed a couple of streams that were flowing almost too hard. The snow was melting fast now and the rivers were filling to their brims and flooding the flat places. I couldn't travel at the bottom of the valley because the water was everywhere. In some places it covered the floor of the valley from one side to the other. The streams that ran into the Minnesota were now churning rivers of mud rushing down the valley walls and muddying up the main river. *How long had these rivers been washing away the sides of the valley?* Some of the small tributary rivers had their valleys cut fifty feet and more into the earth. In some places I had to ride upstream to find a safe place to cross. The water was just too deep or too fast in the streams for The Brute to wade though. I finally settled on a spot along a stream that came in from the north, with a valley deep enough to have some overturned trees, and enough dead wood around to keep a good fire going. The water was high and the bottom and banks were covered with stones. The flowing water made a soothing whisper. Deer tracks told me that there would be plenty of food for the taking. Other Day had said to ride for two days north and settle in until Jake found me. Well, that's exactly what I intended to do—sit and wait. I set my canvas over a fallen tree, built a fire pit, then found some grass for The Brute and the mule and settled in.

That lasted for two days. I had to get out and ride. Sitting and waiting was just not going to work. I saddled up, pinned the mule to the ground, and went for a ride up the valley. I rode for a day and slept on the ground under a fallen tree. In the morning I climbed aboard The Brute and walked north. About halfway through the day as I passed a clump of willow and tall dead grass, the Brute's ears turned back. I felt his flanks tighten like he was about to break and run. Then I heard the hammer on a gun lock back. I stopped, balanced my rifle on my lap, and raised my hands.

"That you, Jake?" I said without turning around.

"Pull that pistol otta yer belt and throw it on the ground," a voice said from behind. The voice was a white man's.

"Rather not do that, Jake. It's brand new."

"I ain't Jake," the voice said. "Throw the damn gun down."

"I ain't throwin' no guns down. If you want em yer gonna have to shoot me in the back to get them. I ain't here to cause anyone trouble—I'm lookin' for my brother. Now, I'm turning around so don't get nervous."

"There's two rifles pointed at you."

"Is that all? Seems like if you wanted a battle you'da found more than that." I turned around and saw nothing. Whoever it was kept themselves well hidden. "You gonna show yer self?"

"Lay them guns on the ground." I did as the voice said.

"That's more like it. Now step forward one step."

"What the hell ye scared of? I promise I won't hurt you." The brush to the right moved and a big red-haired man walked out slowly. He kept his rifle pointed at me as he came closer.

"Who are ye?"

"Harlan Owen. People call me Hawk."

"What you doin' around these parts?"

"Got me a brother I ain't seen since last fall. Lives around here somewhere. Trying to find him."

"Too damn many people around this valley for me. I'm on my way out west where the country ain't so crowded." He lowered his rifle and motioned toward the trees. An Indian woman stepped out and walked toward us. She had a Springfield rifle pointed at me. The big red-haired man motioned to her and she lowered the rifle and stared at me like she could burn holes in my head with her eyes. "Name's Whistler—they call me Sunkist on account the sun burns my face so bad in the summer. Red Irish, ye see. This here's Posey, mu wife. Her real name's Flower in the Rock." He looked at me as if he was expecting me to ask a question. I had none to ask.

"Ye say yer lookin' fer yer brother?"

"Yeah, Jake Owen. Ye know him?"

"Owen...hmm, the name sounds familiar but I don't know no Jake." Posey touched Sunkist on the arm. He looked at her and said something in Indian. She turned back to me. Her eyes showed no emotion and never left mine. It was very discomforting.

"Got me a small camp back there. Got fresh venison too if yer hungry."

"Sounds good, let's go. Not that we ain't been fed or nothin' mind ye. It's just gonna be nice to let someone else do the cookin' for a change, huh Posey?" She looked at him with blank eyes.

I thought that was just an excuse to get fed, that they were hungry and hadn't eaten in a while—I was wrong. Posey brought out smoked venison seasoned with wild herbs and dried wild plants and roots, dried smoked fish, and tobacco. She put it all before us without lookin' at either of us. It was done slowly and very deliberately but it took no time at all. We ate like we were at a banquet, and the conversation didn't stop until way into the night. Posey stayed busy in the shadows mostly and didn't talk at all.

"She don't speak English. I wanted to learn her but she don't want nothin' to do with white man ways—not even to talk the language."

"But you speak her language, right?"

"Yup, Cherokee. She's Cherokee."

"Pardon my saying so, but she is beautiful." Sunkist turned to Posey and said something to her in Cherokee. She looked directly at me and I thought I saw a smile shine from her eyes, but I think it might have been the fire reflecting from them.

Sunkist and I went to sleep while Posey was busy doing what women do after the men go to bed. I don't know if she slept but she was still busy when I woke up in the morning. Breakfast was leftovers from the night before, warmed up and served on birch bark plates.

"Lemme see that pistol you got there, Hawk." I handed it to him.

"It's called a Colt's dragoon. The man at the store told me it's the most powerful handgun made."

"By the look of that cylinder you might pack two loads in there. Kinda wasteful if ye ask me. One load from a rifle will take out an Injun a lot farther out than this thing will."

"True enough, but this thing shoots six times before you need to reload. One shot will stop a man in his tracks. I ain't never tried it so I really don't know, but that's what Mister Randal told me. I doubt if he knows for sure either."

"Well, let's try it."

"S'pose we could. No better time than now."

"Ye ain't gonna shoot around yer camp, are ye? Ye want everyone in the valley knowing where you are?"

"Good thinking. Maybe we should hold off for a while."

"On the other hand, maybe that brother of yorn might hear it and come find you."

"The stories I've been hearing about Jake, I don't think I want him coming into my camp mad. I'd just as soon keep things peaceful with him."

"You know this valley perty good Hawk?"

"Not too good. I've only been here a few months, and it's a big place."

"Where's the best place to cross?"

"Can't answer that one. The river has come up so fast and high I doubt you can get across. Ice flows would kill a horse trying to cross, and the ferries ain't runnin' in this current, that's for sure. Ye might have to find a hole and crawl in it for a while till the water goes down."

"Maybe so. Which way to the settlements?"

"It gets crowdeder as you move south torts Saint Paul. I don't know what lies north of here. I know there's towns all up and down the valley and there ain't no such a thing as peace and quiet. Injuns are coming in by the hundreds to get their share of the money they got for the land they sold to the Whites." I felt so informed to be able to tell someone about that. I should have just kept my mouth shut.

"I know all about the Indians being cheated out of what's theirs. Saw it happen out East, down South, here, up by Pembina—everywhere the white man goes he's cheating someone out of their land. Damned embarrassing to be a white man these days."

Sunkist told me how Posey got her name and all about the trail of tears. I had to agree that the way the white man has treated the Indians is embarrassing.

"How long you figure on staying up here Hawk?"

"At least till the water goes down. Might do some wandering and learn something about this valley. I've only been here for a few months and it seems like home already. Maybe go north and see what kind of land a man can get. I hear it's free for the taking."

"Was, but not no more."

"Say, yer from Otter Tail County, Hawk?"

"Don't remember saying that, but yes I am. How'd you know?"

"Heard of a family up that way what got massacred by Injuns. Name was Owen. You one of 'em?"

"My ma was killed and my pa ain't been seen since. My brother trailed the Indians what did it and killed 'em, so they say."

"I think I know yer pa."

"You do? How?"

"Rode with a John Olson last fall for a few weeks. Small guy? Kinda skittish? Whines a lot."

"That'd be Pa. Where'd ye leave him off?"

"He was on his way to Saint Paul last I heard of him. Don't know how he fared, and don't much care. Sorry to say this to you Hawk, but yer pa ain't much of a man. Can't seem to tell the truth about nothing. He ain't to be trusted."

"No need to be sorry. I know what my pa is—that's part of why I'm here in this valley."

"You gonna go down to Saint Paul and find him?"

"What for? I left that farm and never looked back. I don't care any more than you do about that man. Far as I'm concerned he's been dead since last August."

"Awful thing for a boy to say about his own pa. But if it's the way you feel then it should be said out loud—that way you know it in yer heart to be true."

Sunkist and Posey stayed for another night then drifted away to see my valley. I went back to being alone and waiting for Jake to find me. I didn't try to stay concealed and rode the trails often, hoping Jake would spot me and come out of hiding.

As I lay in my robes one morning I heard The Brute snort and whinny. Thinking it might be Jake coming to my camp I rolled out of my robes and crawled to the opening of my canvas shelter. It was light enough for me to see three Indians coming up through the brush toward my camp. Brute whinnied loudly and the Indians rushed him. He pulled the pin from the ground and ran into the brush. I reached inside and grabbed the Hawken rifle and stepped out the door.

"Git the hell away from my horse!" I yelled.

One of the Indians saw me and shot an arrow my way. He was so surprised that the arrow went ten feet over my head.

"Pa Hin Sa!" I heard him yell.

At that, they scattered and ran in three directions. From the thick brush a distance away I heard one of the Indians yell something in Sioux and heard the words Pa Hin Sa. I figured it was a warning to me that they would be back. I went for a slow walk and found The Brute standing in some thick brush. His rope had tangled in the roots of a fallen tree and stopped him. The mule ignored the whole thing and grazed as if nothing had happened.

The rest of that day was spent watching for Indians. My heart jumped at every twig I heard snap. I had never before been afraid of a squirrel but this day one fell from his perch in a tall maple and landed twenty feet from me. It made me jump like a thunderbolt had just struck me. I had to do something to get this fear out of my system so I cleaned my guns. I pulled the old load from the Tennessee while leaving the Hawken loaded. I quickly wiped the bore, sharpened the flint, tried it, loaded the gun, and primed the pan. Then, the Hawken—I was reluctant to unload that one because it would leave me the forty-five to defend myself. I could shoot the Tennessee just as well and probably better, but I had become acquainted with Renard's Hawken and had made it my primary weapon. I liked the extra power of the larger bullet. After a quick wipe I poured the powder down and shoved a Minie ball in place. I picked the nipple and put on a fresh cap. Now I had to figure out how to clean that big dragoon. I picked it up, looked at it, and decided I'd just have to trust it to go off when I needed it.

Night fell and I was ready for some sleep. I laid down in my shelter but couldn't get to sleep for the sounds of the forest around me. Each sound was an Indian sneaking up on me. I picked up my robe and moved to a spot fifty feet from my shelter and laid down in a thick patch of hazelbrush where I would be less apt to be surprised. The night passed slowly.

When dawn finally started to lighten the eastern sky I packed my camp and headed up the valley. As the day got brighter I suddenly realized that the trees were almost fully leafed out and the valley was taking on a brilliant green. Brown water rushed everywhere. There was no way to get across the valley, even if I wanted to. I came to another stream that was running into the valley and there I set my camp, back away from the valley a little, but not so far that I couldn't see across it and marvel at the beauty of it all. My camp was down in the valley of this small stream and hidden from any eyes that might be wandering this way. On the north side of my camp was an opening where the animals could graze on the fresh grass that was shooting up on these warm days of spring. I rode The Brute up and down the valley making myself visible but staying alert for any signs of Indians who might want my horse.

I figured it must be about June and time for a ride to the fort to get any news of Jake that they might have. As I rode toward the fort I saw too many Indians. The closer I got, the more there were. None of them seemed to be troublesome but they all kept a close eye on me as I passed.

I rode into the fort and the first man I saw was Sergeant Jones.

"Come in to sign up, Hawk?"

"Sign up for what?"

"The United States Army."

"Army? No, I got no use for the Army. I already had this talk with someone else and I didn't sign up then and I ain't signin' nothin' now. Don't know what they're fighting about in the South and I don't care to get involved. Like I told the other guy, when they start fighting around here I'll do my part, but I ain't goin' chasin' trouble. Had me a bit of it up north a couple of days ago—couple of Injuns tried to steal my mount."

"Plenty of that goin' on lately. Young Injun boys out stealing horses and cattle tryin' to make a name for themselves. Better watch yer self—they ain't above killin' for a horse."

Sergeant Jones was dressed in an army uniform that I thought threatened to choke the life out of him—tight fitting and buttoned clear to the chin. He had heavy boots on his feet, wool trousers, and a thick black beard covered his face. It was getting warm this time of year and I couldn't imagine having to wear something like that on a hot summer day. My buckskin trousers were warm enough.

I walked to the store and found Mister Randal.

"Howdy, Hawk. Long time no see. Whatcha been up to?"

"Nothing much. Why are all these Indians around here?"

"Annuity payment's due."

"Oh, that. Heard anything about Jake?"

"Jake was through here a couple of weeks back. The Indian girl he had livin' with him was killed by a couple of white men. He brought the killers' scalps to the girl's father out on the prairie. He didn't stop to talk to anyone—just rode through. No one even tried to talk to him. He had death in his eyes and we all figgered we'd best leave him be. Hawk, yer brother is out for revenge and everyone is scared of him now, 'specially the Injuns."

"Who were the men who did the killin'?"

"Couple of no-goods from New Ulm—name of Arty and Eddy Grenges. The whole damned family is nothin' but a bunch of lame-brained outlaws."

"Jake know who they were?"

"I doubt it. He left before he could learn about them."

"How'd you come to know about all this?"

"Injuns been talkin about it, and the sheriff from Saint Paul was up here lookin' for the Grenges boys. Seems they were wanted for killing a hostler last winter. Now they're looking for a man named Olson they say was with them. No one seems to know anything about this Olson except that he showed up in Saint Paul with the Grenges boys last winter. Got his self and the boys throwed out of a tavern in Mankato too, I hear."

"When was that?" I asked.

"I don't know—couple of months ago, I guess."

"Damn, Ben...I think I saw the three of them. I know a girl who works in a café down there. The old one was making moves on her and she smacked him with a tin plate. Two guys threw them out."

"That's them. The two younger ones were the Grenges boys. The older one was John Olson. Damn Hawk, you might be the only one around here who knows what this Olson looks like. Sheriff might like to talk to you."

"I don't know what he looks like. He had his back to me. All I could tell anyone was he was raggedy and smelled bad."

"Yeah, well, that don't narrow it down much. It describes just about all the men out here. Oh say, Hawk, got a message for ye from Yellow Medicine. Ye had me yappin' and I dang near forgot it. Rider brought it in a couple days ago. You be Harlan Owen, I 'spect?"

"Yeah, that's me. Who's it from?"

"Don't know."

He handed me an envelope with writing on the front. I opened it and found a paper inside. I made out the words 'Dear Hawk' but then handed it to Mister Randal to read for me.

> *Dear Hawk,*
> *I hope you are doing well. I have just heard that your brother*
> *was seen in New Ulm. The Indians say he is on the warpath.*
> *I hope this helps you find Jacob. He truly needs you to be with*
> *him. I will pray for you and your brother.*
>
>

Yours truly,
Lorraine.

It was dated June second. "What day is this?" I asked.

"June seventh."

"I'm on my way to New Ulm."

"You been there before, Hawk?"

"Yeah, we rode through there to get here."

"So you know the road…" he said, more telling than asking.

"I can find it. Ben, is there a good way to pull the balls on this dragoon to clean it?"

"Nope, yer gonna have to shoot 'em out if you want 'em out. Damn dangerous to try to pull caps, too. That thing might blow up on ye and take a hand off. Best to shoot 'em out ever' couple of months and load 'er fresh. Keep 'er clean, Hawk, and she'll treat you good for the rest of yer young life."

"Well, I'm on my way first light. Talk to you when I get back, Ben."

"Good luck, Hawk. Say hey to Jake when you find him."

"Will do. See ye down the road."

I waved and walked out.

The next day I got on the road to New Ulm that I had been on with Jolly Joe Rolette. When I came to the ferry I paid the man the ten cents to ride across.

"You ain't seen a man looks like me lately have you?"

"You lookin' for the Pa Hin Sa?"

"Lookin' for Jacob Owen. You seen him?"

"He forded the river north of here a couple of weeks back. Jake Owen don't ride the ferries. I didn't see him then and I ain't seen him after."

"You know a man named Grenges?"

"I know everyone around here. They want to git to the other side they gotta ride my boat. Yes, I know Amos Grenges. Ain't seen him around in a hell of a while. Hear say he lost his boys. That weren't no great loss—someone's gonna put Amos under too afore too long."

"Why do you say that?"

"Well he ain't no damn good for nothin'. Him and those pea-brained boys of his was nothin' but a pack of thieves. Someone otta put a slug threw his head and rid this valley of a lump of trash."

"Any idea where he lives?"

"Fifteen miles southwest of town. Follow the Shakopee road till you come to a fork. Take that to the right and it'll lead you right to the place—first farm you come to. If ye come to a lake you can't get around, you went too far. That's Lake Hanska—he's just before that."

We pulled up to the bank and I led The Brute off the ferry and rode up the hill to New Ulm. Once again I felt like the entertainment for the townspeople as each one I walked by stopped and watched as I rode through. I passed a woman who was looking at me with her chin held high and a shawl pulled over her nose like she thought I smelled bad—maybe I did but then she should have stood farther back. Thinking this might be another case of mistaken identity and people thought I was Pa Hin Sa, I figured to have a bit of fun at this lady's expense. I rode close to her and leaned down from the saddle and said, "BOO!" She screamed and ran into a store. People stepped back and let me ride through. It was close to nightfall when I found the branch in the road so I found a ravine and built a small fire and settled in for the night.

Next morning, I found the farm—nothing but a pile of ashes. The barn and house were burned to the ground. A stone fireplace and chimney were all that remained. In the ashes of the barn I found the remains of the tack that had been a harness, wagon wheels, and blacksmith tools. All that was left were the iron things that wouldn't burn.

Suddenly, I heard a shot and a bullet dug into the dirt just past my feet. Then another. I dove into the ashes and found a shallow hole to hide in. I looked over the top of the hole to try to see who was shooting at me. I watched the smoke from the rifle drift away. I figured it must be Amos Grenges thinking I was the one who burned his farm down. Suddenly another bullet hit the dirt right in front of me. I saw the smoke from that shot and put my sights on the spot.

"That you, Amos?" I yelled. A head with a feather in the hair popped up. I lined up my sights on the man's head.

"Don't you shoot at me again!" I yelled. I saw a ball of smoke come from a rise to the right of the first man and heard the bullet snap over my head.

"Damn, there's more than one," I said, and squeezed off my first shot. The feather dropped out of sight. I wasn't sure if I'd hit my mark but I did cause some commotion out there. I saw two feathers moving through the grass—one to the right and the other to the left. Loading was a trick laying on my belly, but after starting an unmeasured amount of powder down the bore and slipping a Minie ball down on top of it, I was loaded. I capped the rifle and waited for my next shot. I started to think they had left when a bullet creased my back from the right. I knew I was hit but didn't have any idea how bad it was. I rolled to the left and aimed the Hawken at a man kneeled forty yards away loading his rifle. I drove a slug through his chest and he tumbled backwards dead. All of a sudden two young Indian boys jumped up from the grass.

"Pa Hin Sa!" they yelled. "Now you die."

"I don't think so," I said, and pulled the dragoon from my belt.

One of the men pulled a double-barreled shotgun to his shoulder as he ran. I saw him line up the sights and I ducked my head just as the spray of pellets went over. I raised up and leveled the dragoon at him and pulled the trigger. It went off with a crack to match the sound of my Hawken. The recoil raised the muzzle about ten inches and the Indian dropped to his knees. He looked at me and my pistol with a look of confusion and fell to the ground dead. I caught the fourth in the corner of my eye and turned just in time to bore a hole through him and stopped him from pulling the trigger on his shotgun. I quickly loaded the Hawken and stayed in the dirt for a few minutes, which seemed like hours.

My heart was beating so loudly I could hear it. I also realized at that moment that my hands were shaking so badly that I couldn't get my finger in the trigger guard of the pistol. My emotions were running so high I had a tough time not crying. I heard a moan come from one of the Indians. I couldn't tell where it came from but it kept coming. Slowly I rose up, keeping my Hawken to my shoulder, and carefully stepped out of the ash pile toward the sound. When I came to the Indian I saw that he was no more than a kid, maybe fourteen years old. His face was white from the wound in his chest and he lay still trying to breathe through the gurgling in his lungs. He looked at me with young black eyes, reached up and touched my face and said, "Pa Hin Sa." He coughed and blood shot from his mouth. He stopped breathing and died. I couldn't hold it back. I cried for this young Indian boy from whom I had taken everything he owns or ever will own. He will never laugh again or cry or enjoy the love of a woman. He will never see his mother again nor his father or brothers and sisters.

"What made you do that? Why did you try to kill me?" I said to the dead boy.

"You are Pa Hin Sa." I jumped and whirled around with my Hawken aimed right at John Other Day's chest.

"To take your scalp would bring the greatest honor to a man."

"You scared the shit out of me!" I yelled. "What the hell are you doing here? Why didn't you stop these damn fools? Goddammit, I just killed a boy. Not a man—a BOY."

"You killed a Sioux warrior. His age has nothing to do with it. If he thinks he is old enough to go to war then he is old enough to die honorably. Death to a Sioux is part of life. To die in battle is what a Sioux warrior prefers. This man died proud. He was not defeated by starvation or cold. He died in a battle with the Pa Hin Sa."

"John, I am not Pa Hin Sa. That's my brother Jacob."

"No, Hawk. Pa Hin Sa is you and your brother. There is another in the valley who is also called Pa Hin Sa but he is not *the* Pa Hin Sa. Jake and Hawk Owen are the Pa Hin Sa."

"How the hell did I get messed up in this Pa Hin Sa thing? I came here to live peaceful, maybe move out West from here. I didn't want any of this."

"You became Pa Hin Sa by killing four Sioux warriors who tried to kill you. From now on Hawk, you will have to defend yourself many times. Your scalp is worth dying to take."

"Guess I'll just find Jake and leave this damn country—head out West."

"That would be best for you and Jake."

We started to walk away and I said, "Shouldn't we bury these men?"

"They will be buried by their relatives with all of the honors due a Sioux warrior. Leave them and go."

"Tell me something, why didn't you stop these men?"

"That was my purpose for being here. I came too late. I am sorry. Go now."

"Mister Other Day?"

"Yes?"

"I've been shot. Can you look and see how bad it is?"

I turned around and John lifted my shirt and said, "We will go to Mankato and let the doctor there look at it. It is not bad but it will cause you trouble if it is not taken care of."

The wound started to hurt now. I tried to swing onto The Brute but John had to help me. I sat high in the saddle because to bend over was too painful. We were in Mankato just after dark and John led us to the hospital. The Doctor was at his dinner when we knocked on the door.

A woman answered the knock and said, "How can we help you?" I turned to John, thinking he would answer but he was gone.

"I've been shot." I turned around and the lady lifted my shirt and looked at the wound.

"Come with me," she said. She led me into a room with a bed on high legs.

"Can you sit up here?" I pushed myself up and sat on the bed with my legs hanging down. "Please lie on your stomach. I'll get the doctor."

The doctor came in and said, "What happened, son?"

"Hunting accident."

"You shot yourself in the back accidentally?"

"Yep."

"Okay, whatever you say."

"How bad is it?"

"Just plowed a furrow in yer hide. We'll sew it up and you'll be back to hunting in no time." The doctor washed the wound, then stitched it up and put some greasy stuff on my back. He wrapped a cloth around my chest and told me that I would have to stay the night. That was fine with me. Trying to sleep in the open that night would be pointless after the day's events.

"How ye feeling, son?" I woke up and looked at the doctor.

"Feelin' fine. Guess I'll just git dressed and be on my way."

"Yeah, you do that. Git up and be on yer way."

"Huh?"

"Well? You gonna git up and be on yer way?"

What the hell's he mad about now? I thought to myself. I started to get off the bed but pain shot through my back and the muscles cramped up so bad I almost hollered out. I dropped back onto the bed.

"Thought you were getting up and leaving."

"Changed my mind," I said between groans.

"You're going to be here for a few days, so just relax. I'll have some break-fast brought in. What do you like?"

"Right now I'm not real partic'lar, maybe nothin'."

"You have to eat. I'll send for something for you."

"Fine, do what you want." I was fighting another cramp in my back and was in no mood to argue.

He handed me a glass filled with liquid and said, "Here, drink this. It'll help the cramping."

"What is it?"

"The Indians make it from the roots of a wild plant called Mexican Yams. It works, try it."

I drank it. "No more cramps?"

"Not as bad."

He walked out. I tried to get up again and was hit with another cramp that knocked me down to the bed again. I found that if I lay still I didn't get the cramps.

I was awakened by a sweet voice saying, "Your breakfast is here."

I opened my eyes and at first I thought I had died and went to heaven. Blue eyes and an angel's face was looking at me.

"Hawk?"

"Sophie?"

"Oh my God, what are you doing here?"

"Just stopped in for a visit."

"You stopped a bullet so you could visit the doctor?" I started to get up but a cramp hit me and I groaned and dropped to the bed. "Lay still for heaven's sake. What happened?"

"Hunting accident."

"How bad is it?"

"Just scraped a chunk out of my back—nothing big. I won't be here long."

"Doc gave me some stuff to stop the cramps. What are you doing here? You a nurse now?"

"No, I moved here when they closed the restaurant in Shakopee and took a waitress job here. They get their meals from us and I deliver them. I brought you some hot cakes and eggs and coffee. Can you sit up and eat?" I tried to sit up but couldn't, "Here, let me feed you."

"I don't need to be fed. I can do it for myself."

"Have it your way," she said.

"How are things going for you? Anything new in your life?"

"No, everything is the way it was last winter."

We talked for an hour until Sophie had to go back to work. She brought my meals three times a day for three days. By the end of the third day I was able to get up and walk around and take care of myself.

"You can leave here when you're ready, Hawk," the doctor said. "But you won't be riding for a couple of weeks. Better get yourself a place to stay and sit it out. You'll be back to normal soon."

Sophie came in with my dinner. "Doc says I can leave."

"Where will you go?"

"He says I should find a room and stay for a week or so till I can ride."

"Hawk, you can stay with me if you like. I have an extra bed in my house in a separate room. No charge."

"No, I can't do that. I'll take a room at the hotel."

"Like hell you will. You'll stay with me."

"Such language."

"Get out of that bed and come with me."

I got up and followed Sophie out of the hospital and down the street to a house on the edge of town. She led me into a small place decorated with lots of glass figurines and pictures on the walls. She had nice furniture and carpet on the floors. We went through the kitchen, down a short hall, and to a bedroom in the back.

"This will be your room for as long as you need it. Make it your home."

"You sure about this?"

"Hawk, just relax. It won't hurt you to stay here for a while."

"I ain't worried about me. I'm thinking about you."

"This is what I want. Enough now, get into that bed. I'll get you some dinner."

I got out of my clothes and laid down on the bed. I had trouble sleeping the first two nights but after that I slept like a dead log.

Sophie and I had our meals together and went for walks at night. She read books and taught me more about reading. Soon I was reading books with her. One night while I was sleeping, I felt the blankets being pulled up and a warm body moving into the bed next to me. It felt like the nights Lorraine slept with me in the tent outside Mankato, except this time the body was naked. Sophie slid tight against me and put her arms around me. I couldn't help but wrap my arms around her and kiss her lips. Her body was pressed tight against mine. That night I found out that there was something better than hunting and being in the woods.

When I woke up in the morning Sophie was gone. I got out of the bed and slipped into my clothes and went out to the kitchen. Sophie was busy at the stove making breakfast.

"Good morning sleepy-head," she said.

"Morning," I said.

"You slept well, I assume?"

I walked to her and put my hands on her shoulders. "Sophie."

"We're having eggs and hot cakes for breakfast."

"Sophie."

"Do you drink coffee?"

"No. Sophie…"

"Here, try this. I make a great cup of coffee."

Apparently last night was not going to be discussed. I sat at the table and took a sip of the coffee. "Youch! Hot." I'd burned the tip of my tongue.

"I guess I should have told you it was hot. Coffee has to be hot to be good."

"Sophie, you know I can't stay here."

"I know, Hawk. You have to go and find your brother."

"How'd you know that?"

"People talk about you and your brother all over this valley. I work in a café where the stories are told. You should hear some of the things they say. Your brother is known as Pa Hin Sa. The Indians are afraid of him."

"Have you seen him?"

"No, but I've heard he has been in Mankato and New Ulm. How he gets around without being seen is a mystery. He shows up and disappears like a ghost. He usually leaves someone dead in his tracks."

"That's not true. I've heard of a few that he might have killed but not so many as you make it sound."

"I know that Hawk, but those are the stories. Men like to make stories like that more exciting than they really are."

"I wish they wouldn't do that. It could get Jake killed for things he hasn't done."

"Your brother has taken the warpath and the result of that can only be death. It's the way of life."

"Tomorrow I will be leaving. I need to find Jake and get him out of here."

"I know you have to go, Hawk. I'm surprised you stayed this long. Will you come back?"

"Don't know how I can stay away from this good cooking."

"Is it just the cooking that will bring you back, Hawk?"

"Yup, just the cooking."

"You can come to the restaurant for that."

"Okay, the restaurant it is. Just have a table cleared when I get there." She wrapped her arms around my neck and kissed me, her blue eyes just inches from mine.

"Maybe we should have dinner here when you get back."

"That's even better."

"I have to go to work. You stay here and rest. It's going to be a long night tonight."

The next morning I was up early. Sophie had breakfast ready and my things packed. "Your horse will be here in half an hour. Are you sure you have to go?"

"Yes. I don't really want to go but I have to."

"Come back soon, Hawk. I'll miss you." After breakfast I kissed Sophie and mounted The Brute and rode back to Fort Ridgely.

"Any word about Jake, Ben?"

"Some say he got in a battle with a bunch of braves over by New Ulm— killed 'em all."

"That so? Well it wasn't Jake who done that."

"You know that for sure, Hawk?"

"I know it for a fact."

"Some also say it was you who got in the fight."

"Can't help what people say."

"Captain Marsh wants to talk to you."

"Who's Captain Marsh?"

"Army commander of this fort."

"What's he want with me? I ain't joining no army."

"He didn't say what he wants—just wants to talk with you."

"Where can I find this Captain Marsh?"

"Down at the headquarters, south end of the parade field. Big building, ye can't miss it."

I left Randal's store and headed to the headquarters and walked in.

"It's customary to knock before entering an officer's quarters."

"Harlan Owen. Hear you want to talk."

"You are known as Hawk?"

"I am Hawk."

"Stories are going around that you and your brother are stirring up trouble with the Indians around here. Now, Mister Owen, we..."

"First off, I ain't lookin' for trouble with anyone. I came here to find a place to settle, that's all. Any trouble anyone has with me has been their own doin'."

"I would appreciate it if you would not interrupt me when I'm talking."

"You say something that ain't what someone else has told you and I'll listen. Otherwise, I'll be leaving."

"Okay, Mister Owen, let's start over. Whether or not you are causing trouble, the fact is that trouble seems to follow you and your brother. We try to keep things peaceful in this valley. When you have problems with the Indians I would appreciate it if you would come to us before pulling those guns."

"When a man has a shotgun pointed at my face or when a man is shooting at me, I'm gonna do what I have to do to stay alive. Your attempts at keeping the peace don't seem to be working—not where I'm concerned at least."

"Have you given thought to joining the U.S. Army, Hawk?"

"Yeah, I've thought about it and have decided that I don't want to be in any army. No, I'm not joining."

"If I were you, Hawk, I'd leave this valley and find another place to settle. You and your brother are in great danger from the Indians. They have it in their heads that taking your scalps would be a great honor. If you stay here you will surely die."

"I've been in this valley for five months and I like it here. I think it is a good place to die."

"You are a stubborn man and have trouble listening to good advice, but I like you. Find your brother and leave this valley. That's not an order, just good advice."

"You done with me? I got places to go."

"Yes, you may go." I started to leave.

"Hawk."

"Yeah?"

"When you come back, stop in for a cup of coffee."

"Will do. See ye down the road."

"Hawk, the Indians are in a hell of a state—some meaner'n a snake. Be careful."

"Why the hell don't they give them what they got coming? Maybe then the Indians would settle down."

"I have nothing to do with that. If I did, I'd do just like you say and give them their food. That bone-headed Galbraith up at the Redwood Agency is the one who is being tight with it. Always worried about what they'll say in Saint Paul. Damn fool's gonna have us in a war yet. You watch."

"Well, I ain't gonna be around. I'm headed up north to find Jake and git the hell out of here."

"That's good thinking, Hawk. Good luck."

"Thanks, see ye."

I walked out the door and got aboard The Brute and took the road north. Travel was quiet and peaceful most of the time. It was hot and sticky and the mosquitoes and biting flies nearly drove me and The Brute crazy. I did my best to keep the flies off him but it was useless. I had all I could do to keep my own blood in my veins. I ran The Brute as much as I could and it helped to keep the flies off, but even a horse like Brute gets tired after a while.

At night I set up my camp and lit a smoky fire that seemed to help to keep the mosquitoes away, and when it cooled down after sunset the mosquitoes were not a problem. I slept with one hand on my dragoon and the other on the Hawken. I thought about the mule I'd left at the river camp a month ago and didn't expect to ever see it again. I was sure Indians had found her and taken her by now.

Morning came and I was up and on my way north before the sun came up. I heard shots from somewhere in the valley but they were too far away for me to get too worried about it. It did cause me to sharpen my wits and keep a closer eye on my back trail though. I rode for two days before I finally found my camp. As I suspected, the mule was gone. I didn't know if she had wandered off or if she had been stolen. It really didn't matter anymore anyway, I had me a place to camp and had no more use for a mule. I settled in and rolled out my robes ready for a night's sleep. Then I realized that all of my gear was still in the camp. If Indians had found my camp they would have taken everything, but it was all there. Tomorrow, I decided, I would see about finding my mule. I had settled in for the night when I spotted something on the wall—a piece of white paper. I got up and pulled it down. I held it up to the firelight. It read:

> *hawk if you are reeding this i am jake i dont no wat day it is meet me in fort riglee in augist i will be thare i herd you was in the valee and want to see you ma is killed by indans and pa is mising i think he is in the valee to i got yer mule jake*

My heart nearly jumped out of my chest. Jake had actually been in my camp. *How long ago*, I wondered. *Where is he now? Is he looking for me now?* So many questions—*What day is it? When is August? Why August? Why not today?* I guessed he just didn't know when I'd be back. Tomorrow, I'd head back to the fort and see what day it is and wait for Jake. It was a long night. I hardly slept thinking about finding Jake soon. The sun was lighting the eastern sky when I woke up and I quickly saddled The Brute and started back to the fort.

It was cool and we had no mosquitoes to worry about. I walked the horse through the morning and into the afternoon. I was just about to stop and let Brute graze and have a bite to eat when his ears turned forward and he let out a soft rumble. He blew and threw his head back and tested the air. I felt for the dragoon at my belt and checked the lock on the Hawken. Suddenly, from below the road I heard a shot and a bullet whiz by my head. Then another that ripped through my shirtsleeve. I kicked the animal into a full run forward just as a pack of Indians came up from the brush to my right—another bunch of young boys after my scalp. Brute opened up and thundered past them before they could get a good sight on either of us. Suddenly before us were three men on horses coming right at us. I raised the Hawken and aimed at the front man and jerked the trigger. He rolled off his mount backward in the path of the others. The other two had unloaded their shotguns at me but didn't do any damage. They came hard with war clubs raised, hoping to hit me on their way by. The dragoon took one off his horse but the second shot missed and he was on me in a second. As he went by I saw the start of his swing and ducked as the stone club went over my head. Having no desire to continue this fracas I whipped The Brute and stayed on the run. I could hear hoofbeats and war whoops behind me but I had no doubt The Brute could outrun them. Not knowing how far it was to the fort I slowed to a cantor when I heard the sounds from behind fade away.

I loaded the Hawken on the run, which was no easy task. The dragoon would have to wait for another time. All got quiet and I felt safe enough to stop and load the pistol and give Brute a rest. I wiped out the bore, loaded the used chambers, and capped it. I was stepping into the saddle when the shooting started again, this time from a longer distance. The bullets hit before I heard the gunshot but it was just as frightening as if they were right next to me.

The Brute was scared and would not let me get aboard so I led him into a grove of oaks and turned him loose. He trotted a short distance and stopped to graze while I took a place behind a fallen log to look for who it was shooting at me. I saw a puff of smoke followed by a crack and the sound of heavy buckshot crackling through the trees. I shouldered the Hawken and watched the spot. Another puff of smoke appeared from a spot to the left of the first. I couldn't see any targets to shoot at. Another shot went over my head. I thought, *these guys can't hit a sitting target so I might as well make a run for it.*

Just then I saw some movement. A head covered with grass and twigs appeared. That was why I couldn't see them—they looked like the brush that surrounded them. I set the sights on the man and dropped him. The other, thinking I'd fired my gun and would need time to reload, jumped up and came running up the hill toward me. I stood up and let him see me with the dragoon in my hand hanging at my side. About twenty-five yards away he slowed and started to raise his shotgun. I leveled the big pistol at his chest and squeezed the trigger. The bullet struck him and he dropped like a wagonload of brick had fallen on him.

I stood, shaking so hard I could hardly load the Hawken. I sat on the ground for a few minutes breathing deep trying to get myself relaxed enough to fetch the horse. The Brute had moved down the slope to the other side of the dead Indian, so I had to walk by him to get to him. When I walked by, I saw a leather sack hanging from his belt with two blond scalps. A rush went through my ears when I saw the scalps. This Indian had killed white women.

"You son-of-a-bitch!" I said and crushed his face with the butt of the Hawken. I took the scalps from his belt and put them on the ground next to him. Then I pulled the leather sack from his belt and opened it. Inside was a stack of gold coins. There must have been two hundred of them.

"Stolen from whoever you murdered." I smashed his face again. I didn't think I could ever take a scalp but this made it easy for me to do. I cut around his forehead and ripped it off without ceremony. Then I went to the other man and did the same. After smashing in his face I took his scalp. I took their guns and put the barrels between the crotch of a double tree and bent them in a half circle. "Ain't no more white women gonna die from these guns."

I found The Brute and headed toward Fort Ridgely.

I walked into the Captain's office and dropped the scalps on his desk.

He looked up startled, "Where the hell'd you get these?"

"Took 'em off a couple of Injuns what tried to take mine. Captain, you and your soldier-boys ain't doin' a very good job of keepin' the peace around here. I just came out of one hell of a fight with a bunch of Injuns. I don't know what they have against me and Jake but it's gettin' old. One of these times I ain't gonna be so lucky and they're gonna be taking my scalp home."

"Hawk, dammit! That's what I tried to tell you last week. Find Jake and get the hell out of this valley. Better yet, just go. Jake will catch on sooner or later and follow you out. These Indians get it in their heads that there's a trophy growin' on yer head and they'll chase you till one of you is dead. There's a lot of Injuns out there Hawk, you can't fight 'em all."

"What day is this?"

"Friday."

"What day of the month?"

"First of August."

"Jake's coming here."

"Oh good. That should be interesting, having the both of you here at the same time. Hawk, I'm ordering you and your brother to stay in this fort unless you are planning on moving out of the valley for good. And, I'm also ordering you to shave off that beard and get your hair cut."

"You're ordering me?"

"That's an order."

"You seem to have forgotten I ain't in your army. You can't give me orders like one of your soldiers."

"I am commander of this fort and that makes me the law, too. Now will you do as you're directed or do I have to send you to the guard house?"

"You give me one good reason why I should do it and I will."

"Hawk, it's for your own good I'm telling you this. That beard shows up like a lantern in the night. It singles you out in a crowd. It's what the Indians see when they see you. They'd love to have your hair and beard hanging in their lodge. Whoever takes your hair, or your brother's, will be made a chief immediately. That's a little too strong an invite for a young brave to pass up. I hope when they take it you're already dead, but it makes no difference to them—alive or dead, they'll take it if they can. There's five thousand of 'em assembled at the Yellow Medicine Agency right now wanting their money. And besides that, Ink pa duta's bunch is in the area. That's probably who's chasing you."

"I thought he was dead."

"So did the army, but he ain't. We can't seem to get close to him. Indians all around here protect him. They think he's a hero. You gonna shave that beard?"

"Sounds like good advice. I'll do it. Where the hell did five thousand Indians come from?"

"All over the territory—even as far as the Missouri country."

"They all come here for food?"

"Most are entitled to it but there are some who just come in to try to get it. Makes it difficult to dole it out to the right people."

"Where do I find a barber?"

"Anyone in the fort can do it. You're best off going to the surgeon's wife. She does a good job."

"Oh, one more thing," I said.

"What's that?"

I dropped the sack of gold on his desk. "I took this from one of the Indians who attacked me." Captain Marsh opened the sack and looked inside.

"You took this from an Indian?"

"Yes."

"Looks like your lucky day."

"It should go back to whoever it belongs to."

"The person it belongs to is dead. They have no more use for gold. It's yours. Just don't go telling people about it. You won't have it long."

"Captain, I can't keep this money. It belongs to someone else."

"If you don't want it I'll take it."

"Never mind. I'll just hang on to it."

Off I went to get a haircut, the first since I'd left the farm. I'd kept it cut myself with my hunting knife but I don't guess it looked as good as Ma used to do it. I spent the weekend in the fort getting used to not having my beard and hair. But staying in the fort was not easy so I got The Brute and headed up to Yellow Medicine. Thought I'd pay a visit to Lorraine.

The trail up there was uneventful. I passed through hundreds of Indian camps and villages. The Indians didn't seem to pay me any attention. There were more Indians than I ever thought there could be in Minnesota. When I rode into the Agency there was a crowd of Indians assembled around the warehouse, and surrounding a company of troops who were camped a hundred yards out from the buildings.

I stepped up to a man who was standing watching the affair. "What's going on?"

"Injuns want their food and Galbraith won't give it to them."

"Why the hell not? They're hungry and it belongs to them—and there's sure as hell enough of them to take it if they want."

"The way it works is that all of the provisions are given out when the annuities arrive and Galbraith is too damned worried about doing things by the book and getting himself in trouble with the people in Saint Paul to change the routine a little. He doesn't know what a pickle he's putting us all in by not giving it to the Injuns. Damned Injuns are ready to take it whether he likes it or not."

Suddenly the leader of the Indians rode up to the door of the warehouse and stuck his tomahawk into it. Then a group of Indians ran to the door, broke it open, and started to carry out sacks of flour and barrels of pork. The Indians surrounding the soldiers and warehouse were loading, priming, and cocking their weapons. I thought this is going to be the end, with soldiers out-numbered ten to one and completely surrounded. If shooting started, every white soul in this camp would be on his way to his reward in an instant. One shot—even an accidental discharge—and all hell would break loose.

Soldiers came up and rolled a twelve-pounder Mountain Howitzer into place in the field in front of the warehouse. The commander of the soldiers pulled the canvas cover off of it and told the men at the cannon, "Load that thing up with canister and let them see what you're putting in it and aim it at the door." The Indians saw the soldiers load the canister and the big gun being trained on the door and stopped what they were doing. They opened a path from the cannon to the door, scrambling over one another trying to get out from in front of the big gun. The commander, with a squad of men, marched down the path to the door and formed a line facing the Indians. His face showed not the least sign of fear. It said, "I am in charge here and you will do as I say."

"Who's the officer?"

"That's Lieutenant Sheehan from Fort Ripley on the Mississippi. He just got here a month ago to guard the distribution of the annuities. Damn good officer—he should be in charge of the fort instead of Marsh."

"What's wrong with Marsh? He seems like a good man."

"He is a good soldier. He fought with the Wisconsin regiment in the war down South at Bull Run. He served his time there and was sent here, but he don't know nothin' about fightin' Injuns."

Lieutenant Sheehan left the soldiers and a sergeant named Trescott at the door to watch the Indians and went inside. In fifteen minutes Sheehan came out with Agent Galbraith right behind him. Galbraith was white in the face and looked every bit like he was going to throw up.

"Galbraith's scared shitless," the man said. "I wouldn't be surprised if he's half tanked-up."

The Indians surrounding the camp started moving toward the warehouse and formed into smaller groups where they were talked to by the chiefs and among themselves.

They said that the food in the warehouse was theirs and they had a right to have it. But Agent Galbraith would not budge. He wanted to wait until the annuity money arrived and distribute all of it at once. After a while of talking, Sheehan convinced Galbraith that if he didn't issue the flour and pork that the Indians were ready and able to take it. With that, Galbraith reluctantly ordered some of the flour and pork to be given out with the concession that the Indians would go back to their camps and wait quietly for the annuity arrival.

A squad of men went into the warehouse and began bringing out sacks and barrels and giving it to the Indians. They threw it onto their horses and loaded it into wagons. Some of the men carried them over their shoulders.

Some refused to leave insisting on receiving the rest of the food. Lieutenant Sheehan formed a battle line and loaded the other cannon, ready for action. I lifted my Hawken and felt for the dragoon at my belt. The Indians saw he was ready to fight and slowly moved back to their camps. The thought of the cannons loaded with canister ammunition, capable of taking out two dozen warriors with a single shot, undoubtedly convinced them it would be the wise thing to do. The men in the front of the mass moved out first because they would receive the first shot, and seeing them move caused the others to follow along.

The next day the soldier camp was moved closer to the government buildings and stood ready for an attack by the Indians. The citizens were hustled into the warehouse with all the guns they could find. Galbraith was among them—he wanted nothing to do with fighting Indians. I stayed with the soldiers. Lieutenant Sheehan stayed busy trying to get Galbraith to give out the provisions to the Indians but Galbraith stayed on the idea that to give in now would be to forever relinquish control of the Indians.

"He actually thinks he has control of these Indians?" I asked Sergeant Trescott.

"He ain't got no more control of this situation than he has of the clouds. If them Injuns want their food, ain't a damn thing we can do about it. Fer da cripes sake there's six thousand of them and a hunnert of us. Dammit, he ought to give 'em the damn food."

No attack came and life went back to somewhat normal at the Agency. The next day I saw Lieutenant Gere and Agent Galbraith's interpreter, Simon Quinn, heading out toward Ridgely.

"What's that all about?' I asked the sergeant.

"Galbraith don't trust Quinn. He thinks he tells the Injuns things what's s'pose to be secret. He's sending him to the fort to get him out of his hair. I think he's just scared of Quinn—he's half-Injun you know. Galbraith, he's skeered to death of the Injuns," Trescott laughed. It was obvious that he didn't think too highly of Agent Galbraith.

At about noon the next day, Lieutenant Gere and Captain Marsh came into camp. I walked out to meet them.

"Hey, Captain. What brings you to these parts?"

"Hawk, what the hell you doing here? I thought I told you to stay at the fort."

"Ye did? Oh yeah. You did didn't you? Guess I forgot."

"Forgot my ass. You deliberately disobeyed a direct order."

"I got my hair cut and shaved, ain't that enough?" I said, looking up at him on his mule.

"I ordered you to stay in camp and you disobeyed me."

"Captain, disobeying orders is something a soldier does. I ain't no soldier, remember? And I ain't gonna be one—remember that too."

"That's for damn sure you won't be a soldier. Yer a bone-headed Welshman. Where's that crazy mustang of yours?"

"Grazin' over in the field."

"Get him and come to the warehouse."

"What fer?"

"Hawk, just get yer damn horse and come with me." He looked at Gere and said, "I get so damn tired of explaining things to this boy."

I got The Brute and rode to the warehouse. Inside were Sheehan, Marsh, Galbraith, and Reverend Steven Riggs, whom I had met on my latest trip to the Upper Agency.

"Doctor Riggs," Galbraith said. "If there's anything between the lids of that Bible that will meet this cause, I wish you would use it."

"Major, I would suggest a council with the principle men of the different villages and resolve this peacefully. I'll go out to the Sissetons and talk with Standing Buffalo."

I tapped Marsh on the shoulder and said, "I'm here."

"Sit down and be quiet."

"Where do you want me to sit?"

He turned to me and said, "Hawk, I don't care where you sit. Sit on that cracker barrel and be quiet."

"Can I have a cracker?"

"NO! You stay out of…wait, on second thought put a handful in your mouth, you won't be able to talk that way."

"Captain, why am I here?"

"Consider it for your own protection. Those Indians figure out who you are and we've got a war on our hands. Let's say I'm keeping the weasel out of the hen house." He pointed at the cracker barrel, "Sit." I went and sat on a flour barrel looking at Marsh. Marsh shook his head and went back to counseling.

"Tomorrow we will invite all of the chiefs here and get this straightened out," Marsh said.

"Captain Marsh, I have ordered your Lieutenant Sheehan to go to the Indians and bring back what they illegally stole from my warehouse. He refused. What are you going to do about it?"

"Major, that food is gone by now. Even if it weren't, the Indians would not give it up without a fight. Lieutenant Sheehan made a good decision."

"And what of the men who stole it? They need to be punished."

"Major, the Indians who took the food are as gone as the food. The Indians are sitting quietly. Let it go. Tomorrow we will counsel with them and settle it."

The next day a group of chiefs came to the Agency. Along with Marsh and Galbraith were clerks from the different traders, and Andrew Myrick to act as spokesman for the other traders who had elected to stay home and let their clerks handle what they thought to be a minor difficulty. The chiefs agreed that taking the food from the warehouse was wrong and that the goods would be paid for out of the annuity funds when they arrived, along with the cost of repairs to the warehouse door.

"Major Galbraith, I am ordering you to distribute the goods from your warehouse immediately."

"I can't do that. The State has set down rules for stores distribution that I have to abide by."

"Major, if that food is not given out, the Indians will be back to take it. I am not suggesting that you distribute the goods—I am ordering you to. Distribute the food and I will take full responsibility."

"All right, I'll give out the food if the chiefs will promise to keep their Indians in their villages and wait for the cash to arrive." The chiefs agreed to this and the council·was over. Galbraith ordered his men to load the goods into wagons and take it to the Indians.

The second day of the distribution, Little Crow, Chief of the Lower Agency Indians, came into the fort with an escort of two of his warriors and a small following of braves behind him. He rode to the warehouse and walked in. Myrick summoned his clerks and followed him.

Marsh walked by. "Hawk, come with me. We're going to sit in on that."

"Keeping me out of trouble again, Captain?"

"Yes," and we headed to the warehouse.

When we walked in, Little Crow looked directly at me and said *"Tse tan waka wa mani."*

I turned to Marsh, "What did that mean?"

One of the Indians said to me, "The Hawk That Hunts Walking."

"What the hell's that supposed to mean?"

"It means he knows who you are. Be quiet if you want to walk out of here with your hair on your head."

"I saw him once down at Ridgely."

"Hawk, shut your mouth," he said angrily. "This is serious."

I shut my mouth.

The tension in the room was thick. Little Crow stood glaring at Galbraith. He was as tall as I was and had a look of confidence that scared Galbraith to the bone. I wasn't real calm either.

John Williamson translated Little Crow's words: "When we come here to get our money the traders are always there to take it before we get it. Many times we go home with nothing. We want your soldiers to keep the traders away from the tables and we will pay what we owe them ourselves."

Myrick said, "We cannot do that. The Indians would not pay us."

"Our women and children are starving. If we can't buy food on credit they will die. We have waited a long time. The money is ours, but we cannot get it. We have no food, but these stores are filled with food. We ask that you, the Agent, find some way that we can get food from the stores, or else we might find our own way to keep from starving. Like when they took food before, when men are hungry they help themselves."

Myrick said, "We cannot give you the food until the money arrives. No more credit will be given to the Indians unless you sign papers stating that you owe us the money and we are allowed to sit at the pay tables to collect it."

"This is our land. Is that not true?"

Galbraith said, "Yes it is your land but the goods are ours until we give them to you."

"If this is our land, then you are taking our grass to feed your horses and our trees to warm your houses and our earth to build your roads. If we cannot have the food, you cannot use our land unless you pay us for it."

"Can you eat your grass or your trees?" Myrick asked, "No, you cannot. If you have to eat grass, then go ahead and eat grass, but don't come around here asking for food." After the interpreter spoke, a murmur went though the Indians. Little Crow hushed them with a grunt and spoke to them.

Williamson said to Myrick, "They misunderstood what you just said and thought you told them to eat grass. I hope he straightened them out or we've got a war on our hands."

Then Little Crow said, "We will feed our women and children whatever way we can." And with that he left the meeting.

"Who put Myrick in charge of this meeting?" Marsh asked.

"No one. He just likes to hear himself talk. Sometimes he should listen to what he is saying," said Galbraith.

"Well, hopefully this is over. Let's get back to the fort."

"If my hair is so valuable how come I wasn't scalped in there?" I asked Captain Marsh.

"Apparently you don't worry him. He don't scare easy. Hawk, that name he called you was his grandfather's name. Calling you by that name means he respects you as a warrior."

"Ye mean he ain't after my hair?"

"Nope, it means you better watch your back. More Injuns than ever will be after you."

"Somehow that doesn't make me feel so good about being respected."

We went back to Fort Ridgely. A week later I saw Lieutenant Sheehan and his troop moving out. Edwin Cole was standing close and I asked him, "Where are they off to?"

"I guess Marsh thinks the Injun troubles are over and he's sending Sheehan back to Ripley."

"I got a feeling he'll be back."

"What makes you say that?"

"They tell me there's five thousand Indians around the Agencies. You see any around here?"

"They're all in their villages waiting for the annuity money."

"They're sitting around waiting for money they don't think is coming? I think there's some angry Indians out there stirring up trouble."

"Hell, we ain't had no serious Injun trouble around here in twenty years. They ain't gonna do nothin."

"Let's hope not."

I sat around the fort doing nothing, waiting for Jake to get there. The fort was quiet except for the troops practicing loading and firing the cannon and drilling on the parade ground. Marsh stayed in his office most of the time but came out several times a day to look around. I think he was making sure I stayed inside and out of trouble. Lieutenant Gere was in the infirmary with a case of the mumps. I figured he was too much the kid to be in charge of men anyway, and having him out of sight was to my liking.

One afternoon, I went to the sutler's store and laid down twenty-five dollars and asked Mister Randal, "You got another one of them dragoons?"

"Yep, right there on the shelf."

"I'm paying for it now and when my brother Jake comes in you give it to him and tell him it's a birthday present."

"Where you gonna be?"

"I'll probably be around but this is just in case I ain't."

"Will do, Hawk."

"Thanks."

7

C H A P T E R   S E V E N

THE EIGHTEENTH OF AUGUST dawned bright and clear. I was getting a little concerned about whether Jake was going to show up and wanted to go looking for him again, but I knew that as soon as I left the fort he would ride in, so I forced myself to stay. At about eight-thirty in the morning Captain Marsh came out of his office and walked to the edge of the fort. Coming down the road we saw a wagonload of people yelling things I couldn't hear. When they got to the fort I went over to the wagon and saw a man lying in the bed bleeding. People around the wagon were crying and wailing. Marsh hushed them and asked what happened.

A woman said through her crying, "The Indians are killing all the people at the Agency and robbing the stores!"

"What the hell are you talking about?"

"The Indians have come in and killed all of the traders and the people there and are taking everything from the stores. Help them, please!"

J.C. Dickinson spoke up and told Captain Marsh that Little Crow and his warriors were attacking the Agency, killing white people and looting the stores.

"You know it's Little Crow?"

"Yes, I saw him there. I saw him tell some of his men to shoot the stable workers. He said, 'What are you doing? Why don't you shoot these men?' It was as if he was saying, 'If you're going to do this, do it right,' and the Indians shot the men cold."

Meantime, more people came in, some in wagons and some on foot. Most of them were bleeding from wounds and some were horribly burned.

Marsh turned and hollered, "Sound long roll!" A bugle sounded and the soldiers came running out of the barracks and formed four lines on the parade grounds. Captain Marsh told a private to take the best horse in camp and catch Sheehan and bring him back.

"Take Hawk's horse."

"He won't let him ride him, Captain."

"Take mine then. I don't care what horse you take, just go. Ride like hell till you catch him and get him back here."

"Hawk, get that Hawken and your horse saddled. We're riding to the Lower Agency to see what's going on."

More people were coming into the fort at a steady stream now, mostly crying, screaming women and children. The soldiers took up their guns and the ordinance officer issued ammunition. Wagons were ordered up to carry the troops but Captain Marsh was in a hurry so the troops would walk until the wagons caught up. Marsh left the post in the charge of the sickly Lieutenant Gere and we left about nine o'clock. I was on The Brute and Marsh was on his mule. I had my Hawken, a hunting knife, and the war club that Lorraine had put the handle on last winter tucked in the back of my belt. We had a six-mule team hitched to a wagon carrying rations, extra ammunition, and blankets for any wounded we might find. A couple of miles away from the fort the train of wagons came up and the soldiers climbed onto them to ride the distance.

Along the way, we came to a log house that was burning. On the doorstep lay the body of a man with his head broken open from a tomahawk wound.

"You know him?" I asked.

"It's Doctor Humphrey from the Lower Agency."

We went into the house and found Mrs. Humphrey dead on the floor with a baby on her breast.

"What do we do about this?"

"Nothing we can do. The baby's too far gone to help."

"We gotta do something."

"Like what, Hawk? That baby ain't gonna live ten minutes," Captain Marsh took hold of my arm and pulled me out the door.

We marched on for another mile and found a wounded man on the side of the road. Marsh called for volunteers to help the man to the fort. Two people came up and carried him off. Another was found a mile further down the road. He'd been tomahawked and was near dead. Blood was still oozing from the wound and it looked like it had been done just minutes before we got there. We laid him on the side of the road and marched on.

"Captain," I said, "this is looking like more than just a few drunk Indians."

"I think you're right, Hawk. There's too many dead and wounded for that. This is big. I'm thinking the Indians have gone to war."

A man came up to Marsh and said, "Captain, I think we should go back. There's too many Injuns out there for us."

"Get back in line, Private. Can't you see these people need help? How in hell can we go back?"

We passed below a tall hill that the men were calling Faribault's Hill. They said Faribault had a log cabin at the bottom of it. There we found the dead bodies of the four people who lived there. Out from the bottom of a creek bed came about twenty-five women and children. Captain Marsh instructed them to make haste to the fort, which they did at a run.

"We going to the ferry, Captain?"

"We'll cross there and go on up to the Agency and see what can be done." We passed two more dead men before we got to the ferry crossing. One of them was the ferryman, Charlie Martel. He had been terribly mutilated.

When we got to the ferry the sun was high. The air was warm and the mosquitoes were thick as soup. The grass and hazelbrush on each side of the road was high. The bluffs on the side of the river were covered with a thick blanket of hazelbrush and small trees. The other side was covered with heavy, thick grass in front of the steep bank of the valley. When we came close to the crossing the men jumped out of the wagons and marched single-file on the road. I was in the rear of the line on The Brute along with a few other civilians on horseback and mules. The ferry was on our side of the river and Captain Marsh said that the ferryman must have just come over and left it there for us.

Marsh raised his hand signaling a halt. He was at the edge of the river looking at a lone Indian on the other side. I recognized him from seeing him at the fort several times. His name was White Dog, chief of a small band of farmer Indians near the Upper Agency. I rode up to stand next to Captain Marsh and the interpreter Quinn. I didn't want to miss any of this.

Quinn said, "Captain, I don't know this Indian. He don't belong here."

"I've seen that man around the Upper Agency, Captain—drunk and chasing white women," I said.

Marsh said to him across the river, "You are not from here. Why are you here?"

White Dog said, "I am here for few days visiting relatives. Come on over, the chiefs are up the bluff and would talk and all will be right. We had trouble with some of the traders but the Captain can make it all right. Come over, Captain."

A couple of the men had gone down to the river to get a drink. It was warm and everyone was thirsty. One of them came to the Captain and said, "Captain, there's something going on upriver. The water is stirred up and there are leaves and twigs floating on top. I think the Indians are moving around behind us."

White Dog said, "Come on over, everything is right over here. We do not want to fight anymore. Come on up to the Agency and we will hold a council."

A drunk man in the ferryhouse said to the soldiers, "You are all gone up. The Indians are all around you—that side of the hill is covered with Indians."

Where this man came from is beyond me. How he survived the massacre at the Agency I don't know.

Captain Marsh ordered the troop to close ranks and prepare to board the ferry.

"Captain," I said, "there are horses in the brush on the other side of the river. I can see their tails swishing the flies."

"White Dog," Marsh said. "If all of the Indians are up at the Agency, why are your horses down here?"

Just then, White Dog raised his rifle and fired across at the Captain.

"Look out!" yelled Quinn.

At that instant a hundred rifles went off and Quinn's body jerked this way and that and he fell dead. Twelve of our men fell dead to the ground in an instant. Captain Marsh's mule dropped out from under him. The Brute screamed and took off for different places leaving me on the ground on my back. An Indian jumped over me running to get to another victim. I suppose he thought I was dead.

"Stand steady, men," called Marsh.

The Indians were firing from all sides. The sound of their guns was terrifying. Captain Marsh ordered the men to ranks and turned them around to fire a volley to our rear. More men fell. Captain Marsh ordered the men to take cover in the ferryhouse. When they turned and ran toward it the side of the house was suddenly enveloped in gun smoke. More men fell dead. The building was full of Indians.

Indians rushed in from all sides to face the soldiers hand to hand. I took aim at the closest Indian and he fell dead at my feet. Indians came in so fast there was no time to reload. I shot three of the red devils with my dragoon as they came on and clubbed some with my rifle barrel, but they were coming too fast to keep them off me. Every time I turned there was another Indian after me. I turned and ran toward the brush on the side of the river. About halfway there, I felt a load of buckshot hit my back and legs. It must have been fired from a long distance because all it did was sting me and make me lose my footing. I fell to my knees then scrambled to my feet and continued my run. Most of the men who were able were already there. It was the only direction we could go that there weren't Indians. They came in behind us and followed us into the grass and hazel shooting without aiming. Most of their shots went over our heads or into the dirt at our feet. I was scared and just kept running. I fired the last three balls from my dragoon at the Indians behind me but don't know if I hit any. I was in too big a hurry to get out of there to stop and look.

All of a sudden an Indian appeared in front of me. I startled him as much as he did me and he fired both barrels of his shotgun into the dirt at my feet. I had no choice, I reached for the war axe in my belt and rushed him. He was desperately trying to load his shotgun when the axe split his scull. He went down with the stone axe still buried in his head. I tried to get it out but it was stuck in the bone so tight I couldn't move it. Another Indian came rushing at me from the right. He was just about to pull his gun up when I heard a shot from behind me and the Indian fell to the ground.

"Best to use the flat of the tomahawk," I heard from behind me. "It'll stop him just as quick and you don't have to try to pull it out. Mean-assed weapon, this dragoon." I turned and saw a man with a red beard standing looking at me.

"Jake?"

"Hawk?"

"Let's git the hell otta here. You take the lead, my guns are empty," I said.

We ran through the brush until we found another group of soldiers. It was Captain Marsh and about ten other men. The Indians closed in on us and surrounded our little group. They fired their guns into the thicket without doing any more than make us keep our heads down. I loaded the Hawken first, with Minie ball and an extra dribble of powder. Then I loaded the dragoon.

"Better load your empty chambers," I said to Jake.

"Ain't never had one of these things before. Seems to be a hell of a lot of work loading."

"There'll come a time you'll be glad you did."

"Men," the Captain said, "ain't no way out of here but to swim the river to the other side. All ready to come with me?"

"Ready, Captain," I said.

"You can't swim with all that iron you got, Hawk. Yer gonna have to leave one or the other here."

"I'm gonna try."

"Follow me," said the Captain and he waded into the river. We fired back at the Indians as we could see a target but the ammunition was running low. I had plenty of lead and powder and so did Jake but the rest in the group were almost out—down to about four shots each. Marsh waded out till he could no longer reach bottom and began to swim. About halfway across he yelled back, "Help me, I'm sinking!" He had gotten a cramp and couldn't swim. Two of the men jumped into the river and swam out to save him, but they were too late. The Captain went down for the last time. I'll never forget the look of terror on that brave officer's face as he went under.

Suddenly all the Indians were gone.

"I think they all went to the other side to wait for us there," Jake said.

"Could be you're right. I'm going to make my way up the hill and try to get back to the fort. You coming?"

"Right behind you." Jake and I and five others crawled up the hill to the flat ground and started for the fort. One of the men in the group had a bad wound in the leg and we took turns carrying him.

It was about five in the afternoon now and we could see no sign of Indians but we stayed in the tall grass and willow patches for cover. Progress was slow but we kept going, following the river bluff to the fort. It was early in the morning when we came to the fort. A few of the men who were in the ambush had made it back and were telling people about it. The first building we came to was the store. Ben Randal was just coming back from hearing the stories.

"Hawk, we thought you was dead. Yer horse came in yesterday with a big cut across his rump. We thought for sure you went under. I'm not sure what your horse looks like, Jake, but I think he's here too."

"Seen anything of Sunkist?" Jake said.

"Don't know no Sunkist. That the redhead you came in with?"

"Yeah, that's him. He come back?"

"You know Sunkist?" I asked Jake.

"Met up with him down by Courtland—said he knew you."

"He got the drop on me north of here one day while I was on the trail to my digs. Had a good-lookin' Indian woman with him."

"Yeah, Posey—dangerous woman there."

"She still with him?"

"Damn sure is. She won't let go of that man fer nothing. She's out there with him somewhere."

"He come to the fight with you?"

"Yeah, he was right behind me till the Injuns came up, then he and the girl disappeared. Ain't seen 'em since."

"Wanna go look for them?"

"Like to, but where the hell would we look? If he's alive he'll be in."

The fort was chaos—wounded men and women all around. Lieutenant Gere was running from one building to the other trying to figure out what to do.

He walked by us and Jake said, "Gere, those Injuns are fifteen miles from here. If they come here we're shit otta luck. How many soldiers you got here? Thirty? Best you get some barricades built for when they get here." Gere walked by without saying anything.

"Boy's got the mumps," I said.

"Best he sits down and stops wandering around if he expects to have grand-babies someday."

"Come on boys," Ben said. "You look like you could use a bite to eat." We went to the store and Ben put out biscuits and jerky for us. "Enjoy them biscuits boys, that's the last you'll have for a while. Blodget was one of 'em killed today." Then he brought out beer. "Don't tell anyone where you got this. I ain't supposed to have it on the post."

"What is it?" I asked.

"Beer. Ain't ye never had no beer before?"

"Nope, got no use for it."

"It ain't gonna hurt you, Hawk," Jake said.

"Damn, we just got back from a battle that we could have all been killed in and you guys wanna drink beer."

"So what the hell should we do—sit down and cry about it? Here, drink up." I took the cup and tipped it up.

"Hey, this ain't bad." I tipped it again and downed the rest.

"Hawk, that stuff ain't water. Drink it slow."

"Nice and cold, too."

"I keep it down in the cellar where it stays cool. More?"

"Nope, thanks. That'll do. I'm going to see about my horse."

"Wait up, I'll come with you. I got one over there too, I hope." Jake and I walked to the stables.

Lieutenant Gere had ordered all of the women and children into the soldiers' barracks in case the Indians attacked. While they were slowly moving to the barracks one of the soldiers on guard fired a shot and came running into the fort crying, "Indians!" Suddenly everyone got in a hurry to get to the barracks. The warning was a false alarm but it did get the people into the stone building a lot quicker. And the soldiers were on their battle stations, too.

When I walked into the stables The Brute whinnied loud and turned his head around to see me. I walked to him and stroked his neck and nose. "We made it through another one, handsome." Then I walked to his rump and looked at the gash across the top. It was about an inch wide and twelve inches long, side to side. I looked at the hostler and asked, "How bad is it?"

"Ain't nothin' for a horse like that one. They take worse beatings than that in the wild and do all right. I'd stay off him for a week, but he'll be fine."

Jake stood by me without talking.

"Yer horse here?"

"Nope. Musta ran off and got captured. Damn. Best horse in the valley too."

"I don't doubt that Jake. I heard about him." I said it to make him feel good but I knew my Brute was the best in the valley.

Around nine in the morning Indians were spotted out on the prairie two miles west of the fort. Some were on horseback, some on foot and in wagons. Little Crow was seen in the center of the mass talking to them. The soldiers watched through a telescope on top of the barracks and reported what they were seeing to Lieutenant Gere. Around noon they started moving off to the south.

"S'pose they're going to attack New Ulm?" I said to Jake.

"Nothing we can do about that," he said, looking at the disappearing Indians.

About that time there came a commotion at the north end of the fort. Expecting to see Indians coming up the bluffs, I ran with Jake to see what was happening. It was Lieutenant Sheehan coming back. The runner had caught up with him near Glencoe and told him about the troubles here. He'd made a forced march of forty miles through the night to get here. Immediately, due to the illness that had taken Lieutenant Gere out of service, he took command of the fort and put people to work putting up breast-works around the fort.

At about five that afternoon another column of fifty troops came into the fort. Leading them was Agent Galbraith. He called his company the Renville Rangers. They were made up of some of the employees from the Agencies and other civilian volunteers. He had made up the company to answer President Lincoln's call for more men from Minnesota to fight in the South. There were by now about two hundred-fifty people in the fort, some wounded and burnt and some unhurt. Some of the men volunteered to fight when the Indians came. Now Lieutenant Sheehan had about one hundred-eighty men who could fight.

We stayed on our weapons all day waiting for the Indians to attack. Sergeant Jones was drilling his artillerymen and positioning his guns around the fort. Sheehan sent men out to watch the roads for any sign of Indians.

Through the night we stayed awake and watched and waited. Several people who had survived the massacre at the Agency came in during the night. They scared the hell out of a couple of the pickets watching the roads. We knew the Indians would be coming but had no idea when. If Little Crow had been a better leader they would have come in and taken the fort right after Marsh died when there was only about thirty men guarding it. We were outnumbered ten to one and Little Crow could still take us if his warriors had the urge to make an all-out attack.

The next morning we were all still at our posts and wide awake. The Indians were coming sometime and we were determined to be here when they arrived. We ate our meals on post and slept only a few minutes at a time. The only activity in the fort was the men putting up barricades in selected locations. Horses and mules were brought in from the outlying stables to the parade grounds. The morning passed slowly and quietly. We could see columns of smoke all around from burning farms and settlements. Heavy, black smoke rose from the direction of New Ulm, telling us that the town had been attacked.

At about one in the afternoon, Little Crow showed up on a prancing pony just out of range of a good rifle.

"Think you could hit him from here, Jake?"

"Might have to load heavy, but I'll bet I could make him shit on his horse," he said, leveling his Hawken at the Indian. "Better not. Wouldn't want to be the one who starts this war."

Little Crow looked as if he wanted to gather a council. Sergeant Bishop, who was the sergeant of the guard at the time, motioned for him to come in closer but Little Crow refused. Suddenly, shots came from the northeast corner of the fort and the shooting began.

Sheehan ordered some of his troops to the north end of the commissary building facing east. Indians came up from the ravines and onto the level ground and were firing heavily into the fort. They took control of the outbuildings on that side. Gere and his men took a position directly in front of the attack with Sergeant Whipple and his Howitzer, which he stationed between the bakery and Sergeant Jones' log house to the north. Sergeant McGrew wheeled his Howitzer to the northwest corner of the fort beside the last building and pointed it toward the oncoming Indians. The two cannons fired canister and spherical into the attackers from two sides—one firing northeast, the other firing northwest—and quickly removed them from the buildings they had reached and had them on the run back to the safety of the ravines. The infantry around each cannon kept up a steady fire and held the Indians down while the guns were loaded.

I stayed with Sergeant Jones and Jake moved around the fort to wherever he thought he could get a good shot at an Indian. A cannon shot went off out over the valley—one of the gunners had cut his fuse too long. His next shot exploded directly over the heads of the enemy just above the grass, showering them with steel balls and sending them scrambling back to the ravine. The Indians were coming at us from all sides. The ravine to our right was close enough for short-range rifle fire from the Indians, which could have been deadly for us if not for the canister shot from Jones' gun.

"What the hell you shootin' at 'em, Sarge?"

"Spherical. A round ball filled with iron balls and a powder charge in the middle of it. It explodes over their heads and throws the balls at 'em. And canister, a tin can that breaks away when it's fired. It's filled with iron balls and it works jist like a great big shotgun. Flyin' death, they are."

"We're going to run out of ammo if we don't get to the magazine and bring it into the fort," Jones hollered to Lieutenant Sheehan.

The ammunition was stored in two log buildings two hundred yards northwest of the fort. Sheehan asked for volunteers to go after it. I said I'd go but Jones said I should stay by him. He needed the rifle support. McGrew placed his cannon so he could cover the men assigned to fetch the ammo. They all made it back with the powder and ammunition for the cannon.

A large party of Indians came out of the close ravine west of us yelling and shooting. They were determined to take our guns at all cost.

"Watch this," Jones said.

He brought the muzzle of the gun to just below level with the ground and touched it off. The canister shot tore up the grass in front of us and through the cloud of white smoke we could see Indians scrambling back to the ravines and trees. Apparently the cost was more than they had figured on. Jones laughed like a crazy man.

"Hot dammit, I love this gun," he said as he and his men quickly wheeled it behind the building.

"Having a good time, Sarge?"

"This is what all that drilling was for, Hawk."

He'd fire a round and wheel the gun behind the building to reload. The riflemen around him and I kept up a steady fire to keep the Indians from rushing us. When the gun came out and pointed at the grass in front of us, the Indians made a mad scramble back to the ravines before it could fire. Jones held his fire until they came out and then let them have another blast. Most of them who were hit by the cannon shot were hit in the back. Sergeant Jones was loading heavy and each time the gun went off I could feel the concussion on my pant legs and shirt, though I think the Indians felt it more than I did. The barrel of my Hawken was getting too hot to handle but I kept firing. A woman came to our post with water to drink and I poured some of it over the barrel to cool it down but it didn't do much good. I began to wish I had my Tennessee for backup. The dragoon was in my belt but the ranges we were shooting from were too far for it to be effective.

For five hours the Indians kept up their fire. Not a minute went by that there wasn't shooting coming from the ravines. The buildings in the fort were cut to pieces by their bullets. They had stopped their rushes but a few of them still tried to get to the horses and mules. Each time they stuck their heads up from the grass half a dozen guns went off and either killed one or sent them scurrying back to safety. Sheehan gave an order to hold our fire until we were sure of our targets. We had no trouble finding a target—the Indians were coming through the grass in groups of anywhere from one to a dozen.

Around sundown the shooting stopped. The Indians disappeared and things got quiet. We stayed at our positions through the night. Rain began to fall about midnight but we stayed in spite of it. It rained through the night and into the next day. Most of us got up and wandered around the fort. Men and women were busy putting up barricades made of anything that would hide a soldier. A detail was set to work building earth ramparts around the gun positions to protect the gunners. Jones had a twelve-pounder field gun brought into action and placed it in the middle of the parade field to be used wherever they needed it most.

I found Jake and we sat down to talk.

"Having any fun yet?" he asked me.

"The game ain't over yet. Tell me about Ma. How'd she die?"

"Figured you'd get around to that sooner or later. Remember those three Chippewas that came around beggin' food all the time?"

"Yeah."

"I figger it this way. They saw you and Pa having the fight and you leaving. Next day Pa sent me to town to get a new saw blade. The Injuns saw me leave and figgered Ma and Pa was alone and came in to take what they wanted. I don't know if Pa tried to stop them or what, but they knocked him down and went after Ma in the house."

"How'd you know they knocked him down?"

"His shotgun was layin' on the ground with a busted stock. I told him he should'a put a fresh load in that damn thing before I left but he didn't. He never was one to take care of things when they needed it. I don't know what happened after that but I do know that the Injuns was mean and Ma and Pa ran to the woods to get away. Hawk, I don't know if I can say this but Pa was a goddamned cowered. He ran into the woods and left Ma behind."

"How do you know that?"

"Hawk, yer a better tracker than I am and if you was there you would have seen it too. Ma's tracks were on top of Pa's. That means he ran ahead of her. The dirty bastard ran and left her behind."

"How'd Ma die?"

"I found her in the brush at the edge of the woods dead with two arrows in her back. Hawk, she was scalped."

I had trouble keeping my tears from running at hearing that. "You don't know where Pa is now?"

"I think he's in Saint Paul or somewhere in the valley. Sunkist told me he rode with him last winter."

"Yeah, he told me too. What makes you think he's in the valley?"

"Ma and Pa always talked about leaving that worthless farm and coming here, but you know Pa—always talking and never doing."

"Damn I wish I'd stayed there and all this wouldn't have happened."

"Hawk, it was going to happen sooner or later. Them Injuns had that planned for a long time. Sometime when you and me was out of the way they would have come in. No doubt about it."

"They say you caught up with them and did 'em in. That true?"

"Yeah, followed them for three days. Caught 'em and scalped 'em—left their hearts for the coyotes."

"How'd you meet up with Sunkist?"

"I was camped north of Courtland in a streambed when he came in with Posey. He looked like he was getting too close so I stepped out in front of him. Scared the shit otta the old boy. Posey damn near got me with that Springfield of hers but Sunkist stopped her just in time. He asked me if I was Jake. He knew me right off. Guess you and me look a lot alike."

"I know that all too well," I said. "Been called Jake more than once. Folks say you been on the warpath all summer. They say you killed a bunch of people. Any truth to that?"

"I ain't killed no one who wasn't trying to kill me."

A commotion came up at the west side of the fort. "Riders coming in, Lieutenant," someone shouted. Sheehan and a few soldiers stood at the end of the commissary watching the riders come in. Soon he turned and walked back to the fort. The riders walked their horses through the parade grounds.

"That's my horse," Jake said.

It was Sunkist and Posey. They came up to Jake and me. "Lookin fer yer horse, Jake? Howdy Hawk. You boys been having lots of fun here I see." He handed the reins to Jake. He nuzzled the horse's nose and rubbed his neck, then gave him a big kiss on the nose.

"Wish you wouldn't run off like that. I missed you," he said to the horse.

"What the hell happened to you two when the shootin' started?" Jake asked.

"Posey saw the Indians before they got up and knocked me off my mount. She knew the men on horses would be the first to go down, that's why she knocked me off. We had some fun fightin' redskins for a while. I saw you was having a little fun too and you was makin' it to the brush so we hightailed it. This woman knows how to find hiding places when we need it. I caught yer horse after the battle and brought him in."

"You missed a good party yesterday. We fought Injuns for five hours."

"We didn't miss nothing. We was on the other side pickin' 'em off from behind. I knew this woman could handle a rifle but I didn't know just how good till yesterday. Ever' time that Springfield went off an Injun fell. She had us all covered with leaves and sticks so the Injuns didn't know where we were shootin' from. Damn good woman I got."

Nothing happened that day and we stayed at our posts until the next day.

About one o'clock on Thursday, we saw a large gathering of Indians about a mile away. They left their horses there and came at a run toward the fort from all sides.

"This looks serious," I said.

The Indians were running and shooting as they came on. The soldiers in the fort opened fire. The sound was like a roar. I couldn't tell one shot from the next, they were firing so fast. It was plain that the Indians expected to make a run right through the fort and capture it but the rifle fire from our troops stopped them. They laid in the grass and hid behind low slopes and continued shooting. All we could see were heads moving through the grass covered with leaves and grass to hide them from our shooters. Most of the Indians were on the southwest side of the fort firing steadily. They took the stables and Mister Randal's store.

Jones ran his cannon behind the officers' quarters and loaded it. Then he pointed it at the door of the building and told the surgeon's wife, Eliza Muller, to open the door at his command. He looked around the corner of the building, grinning, until the stables were full of Indians. He hollered "NOW!" and Mrs. Muller swung the door open. Jones touched off the cannon and the shot went through the main hall, out the other end and exploded in the stables, sending pieces of the enemy flying through the air and setting the stables on fire. Jones laughed so hard he doubled over.

"Hot damn, I love this gun!" Sergeant Jones, normally a quiet man, was a ball of energy at this point. He seemed to be having the time of his life. He jumped into the air and clapped his hands laughing.

"I call this baby my 'piece-maker'," he laughed. "She makes pieces of whatever she hits." After each shot his squad wet-swabbed the bore and had another round loaded in a matter of seconds. It was a treat to watch such an expert run his weapon.

Our fire ripped the buildings up so badly we thought they would fall over any minute. Sergeant Jones aimed his gun at each of the buildings and blew them apart, leaving the Indians without cover. Fire arrows came in as the Indians tried to set things ablaze but the rain the night before had everything too wet to burn.

From the ravine to the northeast came a party whooping and shooting. Sergeant Whipple with his cannon and Gere's soldiers laid down such a heavy fire on the Indians, it mowed down the grass to its roots and sent the Indians scrambling back to the ravine. McGrew ran his Howitzer out of hiding and followed the Indians to the edge of the ravine and aimed it down the slope. He was loaded with canister and fired several rounds directly into the trees and brush, taking everything down like a corn broom in the granary, including a bunch of Indians.

Suddenly the Indians appeared on the southwest running to meet a party to the south. They had to make a wide sweep around the field of McGrew's gun to reach the others. They were in the open prairie and we could see what they were up to. They were planning on joining in an all-out assault from the southwest. Jones was shooting fast now. He didn't bother to roll the gun behind the building. Instead, he stayed in the open while he loaded, saving time and getting off more rounds faster.

"Lieutenant," yelled McGrew, "the Indians are going to make a charge from the southwest. Request permission to bring out the twenty-four pounder."

"How we doin' for powder?"

"I think we're okay there, Lieutenant."

"Permission granted. Be quick about it."

At a dead run McGrew and his squad went to the commissary and rolled out the big gun. He positioned it on the west side of the fort at the south end of the commissary building. We could hear Little Crow yelling at his men to get into the fight. I think the Indians were getting a little scared of the guns and rifle fire. Jones double-loaded his gun with canister and waited.

Suddenly there was a huge blast from the twenty-four pounder cannon. It shook the barricades we were standing behind and raised dust from the ground. I jumped clear off the ground.

"What the hell was that?"

"That's mu baby talkin'," Jones said. "Ain't she got the sweetest voice ye ever heard?"

"I like it," I said.

McGrew fired a round of canister at a party of Indians who had joined the reserves with the women, dogs, and ponies to the west of the main body of Indians. The round, the size of a two-pound coffee can, exploded in the middle of them killing some and sending the rest running for cover. Two bodies of warriors were coming together to the left of the big gun. McGrew turned the gun to face them. The gun went off, shaking the whole fort to its foundations. Its roar echoed up and down the valley for five seconds. At hearing this, the Indians panicked and took off across the prairie at a full run. Jones lowered his gun close to the ground and fired his double canister into the party of Indians, killing and wounding seventeen with the single shot. The Indians turned like scalded hounds and retreated to the valley and across the prairie, hastened along by shots from Jones' and McGrew's cannon. After six solid hours of incessant fighting the world got quiet. The fort was ablaze and thick smoke rolled up from the fires and from the guns.

"Guess that'll larn 'em," said Jones.

"Let's just hope they remember their lessons well," Jake said.

During the fighting the men ran low on ammunition and some of the women and men in the barracks had made bullets for the rifles from the canister ammunition. The blacksmith had cut nails into small pieces to use as shot for the rifles and shotguns.

We stayed on our positions for the rest of the day waiting for the next assault, but it never came. During the attack Doctor Muller and his dear wife Eliza were kept busy attending to the wounded. Their work didn't stop through the entire day.

Throughout the day we worked at building an earthwork barricade on the fort. The roof of the barracks was covered with sod to prevent fires from fire arrows. Friday was quiet in the fort. People were busy putting out fires and rebuilding the fortifications that had been destroyed in the fighting.

"Man coming in!" someone shouted. I recognized the man as Andrew Hunter from the Yellow Medicine Agency. I walked over to meet him when he came to Lieutenant Sheehan.

"Hello, Mister Hunter," I said.

"Hi, Hawk. Who's in charge here?"

"The Lieutenant," I said pointing to Sheehan.

"Lieutenant, we have a party of refugees with Doctor Riggs coming in from Pajutazee. We would like to have permission to come into the fort till this is over."

"We have over three hundred refugees here already. Food is short and there is really no room to house anymore people. I would suggest you go to Mankato or Henderson. The Indians have been chased out of that area and I think it would be better for you. Besides that, as you can see we have been under attack and expect more any moment. Right now this is not the best choice for you."

Andrew Hunter looked around and said, "I see what you mean. I'll talk to Riggs and advise him to keep moving south."

"Good. Good luck." Sheehan walked away to tend to the repairs.

"Mister Hunter?"

"Yeah, she's there Hawk."

"Mind if I ride out there with you?"

"Not at all. Be comforting to have someone to travel with. Got a mule staked out half a mile from here. Let's go."

"I'll get my horse and maybe my brother will ride with us." I fetched up The Brute and found Jake standing with Sunkist.

"I'm ridin' out to see the Riggs party out on the prairie, wanna come along?"

"Yep, gettin' itchy feet sittin' here."

"Count me in too, Hawk. If ye don't mind," Sunkist said.

"Let's go. Bring Posey, too. Might as well make a party of it." So the four of us got on our horses and followed Hunter to his mule and took off across the open prairie. It took us an hour to reach the party. Doctor Riggs came to the edge of the camp and greeted us.

"Good day, gentlemen. What brings you out here?"

"I'm looking for Lorraine Bernier. She with you?"

"Hello, Hawk. Yes, she's standing right over there by the wagon."

"She looks different."

"I think we all look a little different these days. We've been traveling for a week trying to find a safe place to be." I walked over to Lorraine. Doctor Riggs followed me and sat down on the ground in front of us.

"Lorraine?"

"Yes?" She looked at me for a second before recognizing me. "Hawk! What in the world are you doing here? I hardly recognized you without your beard. When did you shave it off?"

"Captain Marsh made me shave it off so the Indians wouldn't recognize me so easy. It seems to have worked."

"Did you ever find your brother?"

"Sure did. He's standing right over there." I yelled at Jake to come over.

"This is Lorraine. Lorraine, this is my brother Jake. Jacob."

"Ah, so this is the lady I've been hearing about. She's jist as perty as people say."

"I don't remember saying anything about her to you, Jake."

"Didn't have to. People been tellin' me about you chasin' her around."

"I haven't been chasing her around. She's just a friend I traveled with last winter."

"Okay, whatever you say. Nice to meet you, Lorraine. I'll leave you two alone," and he walked back to Sunkist and Posey.

"So, where are you going?" I asked.

"Oh, Hawk. This has been so terrible—all the killing and fighting. The whole valley will be destroyed if this keeps up. The Agency is ruined, the school is burned to the ground, and all the people have left."

"Did anyone get hurt up there?"

"I think most of them got out before the Agency was attacked. John Other Day saved most of the people who worked at the Agency. He hid them in the warehouse until the early morning and led them across the river to safety. Oh, I pray they are all right."

"If John Other Day was leading them, they got away. No doubt about that."

"He is such a good man. I wish all men could be like him. Indians and white men."

"I can't stay long. We have to get back to the fort in case the Indians come back."

"Have you talked to Jacob about the stories about him?"

"We talked."

"And?"

"He's had a bad time of it. He never killed anyone who wasn't trying to kill him. Same as Sunkist and a few others I could mention."

"Including you, Hawk?"

"It's a rough country, Lorraine. Sometimes a man has to take strong measures to stay alive."

"One could leave this country if things are that bad for him."

"If every man who had a tough time of it left there wouldn't be anyone in the whole country."

Someone was carrying a picture-taking machine and took a picture of the group of people on the ground.

"Do you carry that gun everywhere you go?" She looked at the rifle I was leaning on.

"Look at it this way. If an enemy saw me without it he would surely come after me. Then I'd have to get rough. Someone would get hurt. As long as a man has a weapon close the bad men will think twice before trying to steal from him or kill him. Look at my carrying this gun as a way of saving lives rather than taking them."

Lorraine thought about that and said, "I suppose you have a point, but I still don't like seeing everyone carrying guns."

I think I won that one, but I'm not too sure. "I have to go, they're waiting for me." I made a move to give her a hug but she moved back so I stopped and took a step back and said, "Have a good life, Lorraine. Maybe our paths will cross again someday."

"Goodbye, Hawk. I will never forget you."

I turned and walked away from Lorraine forever.

The ride back to the fort was a quiet one. I couldn't think about anything but Lorraine, and the others knew I was hurting inside. Again that woman has hurt me, just as Jean had predicted. I remembered his words when I asked, "How's a girl gonna hurt me? Tell me that." He said, "I have a feeling yer gonna find the answer to that one all by yourself." I rode behind the rest so they couldn't see the tears.

When we got back to the fort people were busy repairing the buildings and reinforcing the barricades. The only thing we could do while we were there was to help the people with their tasks. Four days went by without the slightest sign of Indians.

On the twenty-seventh a company of soldiers rode into the fort. It was Colonel McPhail with an advance troop from Saint Peter.

Lieutenant Sheehan asked, "Where's Sibley?"

"Who's Sibley?" I asked Sergeant Jones.

"You don't know who Sibley is?"

"No, should I?"

"Well, I should hope so. He was the first governor of our wonderful state. Ramsey appointed him to command the forces that are supposed to come and wipe out the Injuns."

"And Ramsey is...?"

"Where the hell you been, boy? He's the governor of the state."

"I thought you just said Sibley was."

"No, Sibley *was* the governor. He ain't no more—Ramsey is."

I just looked at Jones for a minute before saying, "So he's coming here to fight Injuns?"

"Yes."

"Kinda late ain't he? Fightin's over."

"It ain't over yet. There's Injuns killin' people all up and down the valley. They attacked New Ulm twice while we was fightin' them here. People whipped 'em good. Lost a lot of men and citizens but the Injuns got run off."

"New Ulm? How'd you know that?"

"I get to sit in on the officers' meetings—you don't. Hey, I trained these so-called officers. They better let me sit in."

"Think they'll attack Shakopee?"

"I imagine they plan on attacking every town in the valley before they get to Saint Paul. Little Crow is determined to wipe out the whole white population in Minnesota. He just might do it if Sibley don't get here soon. He's sittin' in Saint Peter right now with about fourteen hundred men waiting for supplies and guns. You know people in Shakopee?"

"Yeah, a girl who works at the café there."

"You got girls all over this country, huh Hawk?"

"He's got fourteen hundred men and we just fought off a thousand with two hundred men? If he'da been here the Indians would never have attacked in the first place."

"Well, that's the same thing they're saying in the office. People are kinda pissed about it. Guess Sibley ain't too anxious to fight Indians. Lincoln's got the same problem with one of his generals. Sits on his ass whining for more men and supplies instead of fighting. Sibley's supposed to be here tomorrow—we'll see."

Sibley did finally show up on Thursday, the twenty-eighth. He set up a big camp on the west side of the fort. First thing he did was walk into the officers' quarters and choose a room for himself. Then he ordered all of the refugees that were in the barracks to load up in wagons and move to Saint Peter. Most of them went but some stayed to find out about their relatives who were in the Agencies when they were attacked. They insisted that Sibley send out a party to locate any survivors and to bury the dead.

The dead had been laying out in the hot August sun for ten days and they wanted them buried as soon as possible. Sibley called roll and appointed Captain Anderson and Captain Hiram Grant to lead the troops. He said that anyone who wanted to ride along was welcome so Jake, Sunkist and I volunteered. Of course Posey wasn't going to miss out on this so she would be coming along too.

We left the fort about nine-thirty in the morning. In all, there were about one hundred-fifty men and one woman. The soldiers were issued forty rounds of ammunition and two days' rations. The soldiers were carrying fifty-six caliber Harpers Ferry rifles. Jake and I had fifty-four caliber Hawkens and plenty of ammunition for them. Sunkist had a fifty-six Springfield and all the bullets he could carry. We moved out of the fort along the road to the ferry below the Lower Agency, the same route we took on our way to the battle where Captain Marsh was killed. Captain Grant had told us that we would be riding in wagons so we left our horses at the fort and walked. It was scary walking down that road knowing what we had gone through at the ferry crossing.

"Spooky, ain't it?" said Jake.

"I ain't gonna like this," I said.

Along the way to the ferry we buried too many bodies. Most of them had been shot or tomahawked. Mostly men and boys but some women too—and even babies. The man we had left on the road when we were going to the ferry was still there. We buried him where we found him. We saw a young boy's body hanging in a tree alongside the road. One of the men jumped from the wagon and ran to the body. "My God, my God!" he cried. "My brother!" He wrapped his arms around the lifeless body and cried. We helped him take the boy's body down and laid it across his horse and sent him back to the fort.

I was trembling when we came to the road that led down to the river. I expected to see Indians pop up from the grass at any moment. The first few bodies we found turned my stomach and I threw up at the sight. Jake didn't have any trouble with it. I couldn't bring myself to even touch the bodies. They had been lying in the hot August sun for ten days and they were black and bloated. Flies buzzed around them and maggots squirmed in the wounds. The smell was unbearable. I did the digging while the other soldiers put the bodies in the ground.

The company was silent as we approached the river. There in front of us strewn all around were the bodies of Marsh's men. The biggest share of them were still in two ranks as they had been when the first volley took them down. Some of them had been terribly mutilated and chopped to pieces. We had to find the arms or legs of some of the men to bury with them. I would guess that some were buried with the limbs of someone else, but we had no idea whose was whose so we buried them where we found them. We found the body of interpreter Quinn. He'd been shot with about fifteen bullets. Captain Marsh's mule lay where he had fallen. We continued to bury the men as we found them then went into the brush to look for more. Captain Grant sent a squad across the river with Captain Anderson to the Lower Agency to bury the dead there.

When that job was finished at the ferry we moved up the east side of the river and went into camp where Captain Anderson joined us. Guards were put out around the camp and everyone crawled into their tents for the night. In the morning we had breakfast and Grant split our company into two groups. Major Brown went across the river to search the west side. We went up the east side burying dead bodies as we went. Entire families were murdered in their homes and the houses burned to the ground. We found a woman half-burned away on a pile of mattresses that had been set ablaze. The travelers' house on Beaver Creek was burned to the ground and we found a half-dozen bodies lying around the ashes.

We were walking through tall grass when Captain Grant raised his hand to stop the troop. He'd seen someone in the grass ahead. "I want twenty men to go up there and see what that is. If it's a white man—bring him in. If it's an Indian— kill him." The four of us joined the twenty men and rode forward. We surrounded the spot with rifles raised. Suddenly a woman's head popped up from the grass. She was dirty and covered with blood. She had been hit in the back with a load of buckshot. Her clothes had been ripped off of her and she had a long gash across the front of her belly.

"Dear God, you're white men. I am saved?" she cried.

"Who are you?"

She was so badly wounded and tired from wandering up and down Beaver Creek that she could hardly talk.

"I am Justina Krieger. My family has been murdered and I have been wandering around for thirteen days," she said through her tears and sobs. Then she passed out. Posey wrapped her in blankets and laid her in a wagon on a bed of fresh grass and tried to make her as comfortable as she could.

We found even more dead bodies to bury. We found so many that it was too late to get back to the fort when we were supposed to, so Grant went ahead to find a spot to camp for the night. The only place close to us where we could find water was in the meadow near Birch Coulee. There we set up camp. We set the wagons in a circle around the campsite and stretched ropes between them to tie the horses to. I set up my tent close to Captain Grant about fifty yards from the coulee. To the north the prairie stretched to the horizon. West of the camp was a prairie with some small rises covered with tall prairie grass. Thick woods lined the coulee to the south and east. Captain Anderson came in about sundown and set his camp on the south side of the enclosure. He had been all the way to Yellow Medicine and crossed the river seven miles up. Major Brown was with Captain Anderson who said that from what he could tell there wasn't an Indian within twenty miles of us.

Major Brown was an expert on the Indians. Having been around them for so many years he knew their habits, their religion, and their language better than anyone in the valley. He could read Indian sign and it was said that he could smell an Indian five miles away. Guards were set outside the camp with three men on each post. We were not regular army so we were not asked to stand guard, which was all right with me. Posey stayed close to the wagon with Mrs. Krieger.

Grant talked with Major Anderson about what he found on the east side of the river. He reported that the entire Lower Agency was destroyed. Most of the traders' stores were burned to the ground. Andrew Myrick was found halfway between his store and the woods. His mouth was stuffed with grass.

"Sounds like Little Crow didn't explain Myrick's comment about them eating grass," I said.

"You heard that comment, Hawk?" asked Grant.

"Yeah, he told the Indians that they can't eat grass, but they thought he said they *can* eat grass when they get hungry. Little Crow tried to straighten it out but apparently didn't do a very good job."

"Myrick has been a pain in the ass for the Indians from the start."

"Yeah, well, Galbraith could have been a little more understanding too."

"True enough."

"Well, maybe the Indians have moved off and this war can come to an end. We showed them it ain't gonna be easy to whip the white men around here." We had our supper and everyone went into their tents for a night's rest. Some slept under the wagons.

"I don't think I'm going to get much sleep tonight," I said to Jake and Sunkist.

"We've seen some terrible things today—more coming tomorrow. Better buck up to it."

"Does a man ever get used to this stuff?"

Sunkist said, "I seen lots of this sort of thing and let me tell you, it don't get any easier."

The sun was setting and we crawled into our tents for the night. The night went without anything happening. I laid awake for most of it. I could hear the movements of the sentries as they changed shifts. Each sound they made woke me from my occasional sleep.

In the morning we were up before the sun. It looked like it was going to be a beautiful Minnesota day. I was about to get a fire started to make breakfast when a shot went off. One of the sentries thought he'd seen a wolf and took a shot at it. All of a sudden Indians appeared all around us. They came out of the ravines and from the woods and over the low rises to the west and north. They gave their war whoops and ran through the grass until they were fifty yards from the camp and began firing. Men fell around me just like they did at Redwood Ferry. I hit the ground instantly.

"You hit?" Jake yelled.

"Not yet!" I hollered back.

Most of the horses went down at the first volley. I crawled on my belly behind one of them and laid my Hawken over its thrashing body. The echo from their guns coming from the woods around us made it sound like one continuous roar. Men fell one after the other. I heard a thump next to me and saw one of the men standing there dead with the top of his head gone. He fell across my legs. I panicked and scrambled to get out from under him. Men were crying and screaming from the wounds.

"Good God," Jake said. "They're all around us."

"Where did they come from? Brown said there ain't an Indian within twenty miles of here."

"Guess he was wrong."

"I guess." I laid my sights on an Indian running toward the camp. He fell with a hole in his chest.

The troops came out of their tents and started to form a battle line. Captain Grant yelled, "Get down!" He ordered his men to break right and left and get behind the wagons and to commence firing.

Lieutenant Gillian called out, "Follow, boys!" Thirty of his men rose and followed him to the east side of the camp and opened fire in that direction. Grant and his men took the west and north sides. All but two of the horses were dead or dying. One of them was Grant's. He ran to him and pulled the halter off him and slapped his rump to send him out of the battle zone. The horse only ran a short distance and stopped to graze on the prairie. Grant was obviously worried about him and wanted to go to the horse. The bond between man and horse is strong and Grant would have given his life to save his animal. The horse wandered around the field for the day unconcerned about the battle that was raging around him. All day the Indians kept up their shooting. We had put ourselves down behind dead horses and dead men to stay hidden from the Indians' guns. We began digging into the hard ground to make holes to hide in. We had nothing to dig with but a couple of shovels which were broken in the process so we were obliged to use bayonets and tin pans to dig with.

The shooting from the grass and woods slowed as the Indians waited for someone to show their head. We watched for targets. All day the enemy kept us down. We were running very short on ammunition. Some of the men were down to their last round. Grant had three thousand rounds in one of the wagons and ordered some of the men to try to retrieve them. Jake and Sunkist jumped to their feet and went along. They distributed the ammo to the men.

"Captain," some of the men yelled, "this ammo don't fit our guns. It's too damn big." The ordinance officer had issued fifty-eight caliber ammunition to men carrying fifty-six caliber guns. Grant put them to work whittling the bullets down to fit their guns.

Grant got up thinking the Indians had left and went to his horse. He put the halter on him and was about to lead him in. Someone shouted, "Down, Captain!" At the same moment a volley came from the grass and Captain Grant and his horse fell at the same time. Grant got up and ran back to the camp but the horse stayed where he fell thrashing from seven wounds in his body. Grant cried.

The Indians retreated to the ravines and the shooting stopped. We were issued crackers and raw cabbage to live on. Jake offered me his share of the cabbage saying he really didn't like the stuff anyway.

I rubbed my stomach and said, "No thanks, I'm full." Some of the others had taken a comical attitude about the whole affair and were making silly remarks about the feast.

About four in the afternoon the Indians began moving around in the ravines. We thought they were forming to make a direct attack on the camp.

"Looks like the thing to do would be to make a run for the trees and get the hell out of here," I said to Jake.

"We'd never make it. There's Injuns behind every tree and blade of grass out there." He pointed to the east, "Look at that." I looked and saw a large group of Indians moving on horseback. Two miles east we saw a command of troops coming our way. Some of the men jumped up and yelled at the sight—we thought we were finally saved. McPhail's company was coming. Grant ordered a few shots fired to let the company know we were still alive. The Indians fired a few wasted shots toward the troops, doing no damage but to make McPhail think there were too many Indians for his small command. He encamped to the east of the coulee and sent runners back to the fort to get reinforcement. About then the Indians looked as if they were forming to take our camp with one swift attack. We opened fire on them and they retired to the coulees. We stayed at our posts as the sun went down and spent a long night listening for anything that might be an Indian.

The next day we saw Indians circling and moving closer to our camp. An Indian approached carrying a white flag—some said he was Little Crow's brother. He came within a few yards of our camp. Our interpreter talked with him for a few minutes and reported to Grant that he had offered all of the half-breeds and anyone with Indian blood to leave. During the night they had brought in reinforcements and now numbered as the leaves on the trees and we could no longer keep them down. They were ready to rush the camp and kill all the white men. Eight or ten half-breeds gathered around the interpreter.

"What will you do?" Grant asked them.

"We will stay with you, Captain," they said.

Grant said to the interpreter, "Tell them that they don't have enough Indians to take our camp. We still had two hundred men and each of them had two rifles. Tell that Indian to get out of the way. We cannot respect a white flag with such an offer." The Indian turned to return to his party. Grant ordered, "Fire!" We opened fire and killed his horse but he got away.

At that time we were down to about sixty-five men—but the Indians didn't know that. All the while the parley was going on the Indians circled the camp getting closer and closer. They got excited when they heard the message the Captain sent and it appeared that they were forming for an all-out attack. We stopped shooting and waited for the Indians to get close enough for a sure shot. Grant assured the troops that the Indians couldn't take the camp, that we were enough men to keep them out if we make every shot count. Suddenly an Indian came out of the woods yelling at the top of his lungs. The Indians in the grass turned around to see what the commotion was. When they did we opened fire.

The interpreter said, "There are three miles of soldiers coming from the fort."

The soldiers shouted with joy knowing that someone besides McPhail was coming to the rescue. The Indians moved off to the woods and prairie and abandoned the attack. They started across the coulee away from the rescuers and fired a few ineffective shots as they left. They didn't seem to be in much of a hurry and some of them stayed behind taking potshots at the soldiers. The force came into sight where we had seen McPhail's company the day before. They halted for a few minutes and resumed their march across the coulee and into our camp. There they found eighty-seven dead horses and twenty-two dead men and sixty more wounded.

All of the wagons had been turned over but the one that contained the wounded Justina Krieger. Mrs. Krieger had been hit in the arm but it was not a bad wound. Her blankets, someone said, had two hundred new holes where bullets had penetrated the wagon and hit her. Posey tended to her new wound and wrapped her in more blankets.

The wounded were cared for and loaded into wagons and the whole command left for Fort Ridgely. We arrived there at about eight in the evening. We had been gone from the fort for four days. Two of those days were spent in unceasing battle with hoards of painted Indians.

"I'm down to ten bullets," I said to Jake.

"Never count your bullets, Hawk. You should always fight like you're down to your last one."

Sergeant Jones came to me. "Hawk, the Colonel wants to talk to you."

"What Colonel?"

"Colonel Henry Sibley. He's in the officers' quarters."

"What the hell does he want with me?"

"How the hell do I know? I'm just a runner around here."

I told the others to wait here and I walked to the officers' quarters.

"You wanted to talk to me?"

"Yes. There are reports of people pillaging the damaged homes and stores, stealing things left behind. I have been told that you and your brother know this valley better than most of the troops. I want you to take a small troop and search these people out and bring them in. You'll be supplied with ammunition and rations for a week and you'll be paid by the state for your services."

"Why don't you assign some of your troops to the job?"

"We need all of the men we have to fight the Indians. We intend to find them and destroy them before they can do anymore damage. You and your friends come highly recommended—that's why I have chosen you."

"We ain't regular army, you know. We ain't gonna have to join up are we, Henry?"

"No, this is a civil problem and you will be working for the army as civilians. And it is military courtesy to call me Colonel Sibley."

"Well, I ain't military, Henry."

"I've heard that you are not one to follow orders very well."

"We'll talk about it."

"Very well. Let me know as soon as you have decided."

"Will do, Henry."

He shook his head and saluted as we left. I saluted back. When I got to the rest of the boys I told them what Sibley had offered.

"Sounds like the Colonel thinks mighty highly of us, Hawk."

"No, Colonel Henry thinks we are expendable. What do you think? Should we take the job?"

"It's up to you, Hawk," Jake said.

"Sounds like the best fight goin' right now. I think we should do it."

"I'm in," Jake said.

"Count me in, too. I don't much care for this fort life anyway," said Sunkist. "Too many rules."

I went back to the Colonel and said we'd do it. "Good. Go see the quarter master and get your supplies. He's been ordered to furnish all you will need. Hawk, when you find these fiends it will be up to you to make sure they are brought to me and not killed. You will be in charge of the expedition, and you will be responsible for their actions."

"Ain't gonna be any one person in charge of this expedition. Each of these men knows what needs to be done and I know they will do what it takes to get it done."

"I understand, but I will be holding you responsible if anything goes wrong.

Don't forget you have five military men going, too. They are green and you will need to watch them."

"Understood, Henry. Where do we start?"

"The town of New Ulm has been evacuated and there are lots of stores and homes left unguarded. I think that would be a good place to start. That seems to be the most likely place for these types of people to target."

"And then?"

"Go wherever you think you will find these men and stop them."

I saluted the Colonel, stood straight and tall, and said, "Very good, Colonel."

"That's more like it, Hawk. We might make a soldier of you yet."

"Don't count on it, Henry." I went out to gather my troops. We went to the commissary and talked to the sergeant there.

"The Colonel has authorized me to issue each of you forty rounds of ammunition and a week's rations. That gonna be enough?"

Sunkist, seeing an opportunity to increase his wealth, said, "Better make it a hundred rounds. I used up a lot of ammo at the battle."

"Be reasonable. I can't do that. I'll make it fifty rounds."

"Guess that'll do for now."

I said, "I need fifty-four caliber. You got any of that?"

"Fifty-four? No, all we got is military ammo, and it's fifty-six and fifty-eight."

"I'll bet you have more fifty-six than fifty-eight."

"I heard all about it and there ain't no need to rub salt in the wounds."

"You got lead bars? I can pour my own balls."

"All the lead you can carry."

We took our supplies and left the next day. The skyline had columns of smoke at all corners from the burning haystacks, wheat fields, and farms. We went to a few of the farms and found them either burned to the ground or completely ransacked. We also found and buried a few bodies on our way to New Ulm. The town was a complete ruin—buildings burned down and everything destroyed. A few of the townspeople were wandering around like they were lost.

I stopped a man, "Have there been any people here that don't belong here rummaging through the houses?"

"Goddamn thieves! Yes, they've been here. Stole everything I had that was worth stealing. If I ever find out who it was I'll kill them on the spot."

"That's what we're doing, looking for the people who are doing this."

"Amos Grenges is one of them. Him and that bunch of no-goods he rides with are the ones. Best thing to happen to this valley when them boys of his got killed." I looked at Jake. He didn't even twitch at the comment.

"Any idea where this Grenges is now?"

"Could be anywhere. Might be at his place for all I know."

Jake said, "He ain't got no place."

"Injuns get that, too?"

"Nope," Jake said looking at the man.

We walked off leaving the man to his misery.

"You know about Amos Grenges, Jake?"

"Yep, I'm the one who rid this valley of them two boys of his, then went after their partner, John Olson. Found Grenges' house and burned it to the ground. He ain't got nowhere to go. Them boys ambushed me up the valley and killed my woman."

"I heard you had an Indian woman who was killed. Don't blame you for goin' after them. Did you ever find Olson?"

"No, but I think we just might when we find Grenges."

"Well, let's get moving."

"Where do we go from here?"

"I know someone in Mankato who might be able to help us. Lady who works at the restaurant there."

"Sophie?"

"Damn, man. Do you know every move I made?"

"Pert'neer, you got a reputation with the ladies around these parts."

We rode into Mankato and went into the restaurant. Sophie was working tables and didn't notice us when we walked in. We took a table next to the wall and sat down. "How does a man get any service in here?" I said loudly.

Sophie turned to me and said, "Decided to take your dinner here, Hawk?"

"Much rather take it at your house, but considerin' all this company I'll have to take it here."

"Come with me," she said. She led me to the back room, put her arms around my neck, and kissed me hard on the mouth. "You ain't going nowhere without me again."

"Sophie, I can't…"

"No back talk. I'm going with you."

"Sophie, we're riding hard. We sleep on the ground and eat what we can find. You wouldn't like where we're going."

"I can ride and I've slept in some awful places. I'm going with you."

"I'm going back to the table."

"I'll get your food. Everyone gets beef steaks."

"Looks like you got a friend there, Hawk," Sunkist said.

"She wants to come with us."

"Bring her along."

"She can't ride with us. She's a woman."

Sunkist pointed his thumb at Posey and raised his eyebrow.

 "All right, she comes along."

"Sophie, have you heard about the robbing going on around the territory?"

"Yes, people are losing things all around the towns."

"Ever heard of Amos Grenges?"

"He's one of them but there's more. Lots of people are looting the towns. They take advantage of the poor victims of the Indian war."

We rode for days around the valley looking for the thieves but found nothing to follow. Lots of farms and small villages were in shambles and some of them had been ransacked. We couldn't get a grip on where or when these people were doing their stealing.

"Hawk," Sophie said, "maybe they're doing it at night. That would be the safest for them."

"Damn, why didn't I think of that? Good thinking, Sophie."

"Ain't ye glad I came along, Hawk?"

"Wouldn't know what to do without you, Soph."

By this time we had covered the area south of the valley almost to Yellow Medicine. It was clear that the robbers had been there and we couldn't be far from them. Late in the evening when we were about to go into camp, one of the soldiers pointed out a large barn just over the next hill. We went to investigate. The barn had been spared in the attack on the farm. In a room in the back we found piles of goods—cloth, furniture, jewelry, clothes, guns, knives—things that would have been destroyed or taken had it been Indians.

"This has got to be the place they hide things. We'll stay close and wait for them to come in."

We set up a camp in the trees south of the barn. A small fire was built to cook our supper and then put out. We stayed here for three days without any sign of the thieves. During that time we made trips around the area to see how many homes had been robbed. There were plenty of deserted farms and homes—most of them burned. On the fourth day, just before sunrise, a wagon pulled by oxen and four riders showed up on the horizon. We were a quarter-mile away and watched as they pulled up to the barn and began unloading freight.

"Saddle up," I said. We sat our horses until everyone was ready. "Let's go."

We whipped our horses to a run and made for the barn. The men saw us coming and ran to the wagon for their guns. They all fired at the same time but their bullets went way over our heads. Their horses had not been tied and scattered when we rode up. There was no time for them to reload and we came into their group as they scattered and ran for the woods. Sunkist took off after the one farthest away and overtook him quickly. He reached down from his horse and clubbed the man with the butt of his rifle. Posey was right with him and when the man hit the ground she was on top of him with a butcher knife at his throat. She jerked him to his feet and led the frightened man to Sunkist who stayed on his horse. He was put in front of them and brought back to the barn.

When the others saw that they had no chance of getting away they ran into the barn and closed the door.

We surrounded the barn and I yelled to them, "You ain't got no way out so you might as well show yourselves!" A shotgun poked through the window of the barn and a blast of shot hit Posey on her side. She fell from the saddle and jumped to her feet the instant she hit the ground. She ran toward the barn and stood with her back to it. Then she motioned to Sunkist that she was all right. Sunkist signed for her to get down on the ground. There were no targets for us to shoot at so our guns were of no use to us.

"That was a stupid thing to do," Sunkist yelled. "Now you will all die."

He jumped to the ground and gathered up prairie grass and lit it with his flint and steel. A window opened and a gun barrel appeared from it. Jake's Hawken roared and a small hole appeared below the window and the gun barrel disappeared inside the barn. Sunkist took his small blaze and ran to the barn and threw it through the window. We opened fire at the side of the barn where the fire was. Sophie had my Tennessee rifle and was shooting right along with us. I don't know if she was hitting what she was aiming at but she seemed to know how to handle the gun. None of us had any particular target, we were just keeping the men inside away from the fire so it could get a start.

"Hold your fire, we're coming out," someone yelled from inside. We were loaded and had our guns pointed at the door when they came out.

"Which one of you is Amos Grenges?" Jake asked.

"Amos ain't here. He's up the valley."

"Where'd you get all of this stuff?"

"It's ours. We been puttin' it here so's the Injuns don't get it."

"Why in this barn? It ain't yours."

"This is my farm," one of them said.

"Like hell it is. I know the man this farm belongs to, and it ain't you."

"What you gonna do with us? This stuff ain't no good to the people who had it. They're all dead."

"You're going to see Colonel Sibley at the fort," I said to him. "What he does with you is up to him. Personally, I'd just as soon rid this valley of your kind, but he wants that pleasure himself." I assigned the five army men to take them in. "If any one of them gives you any trouble—shoot him. That's an order."

"Yessir," they saluted.

"And stop that damn saluting. I ain't an officer and I ain't in the army."

"Um, yes sir." The men were tied together and marched in the direction of the fort on foot.

"Well we don't have them tenderfoot soldiers to worry about anymore."

"You know who owns this farm, Hawk?"

"I got no idea who owns this place but I knew it wasn't his and he fell for it."

"Well, what now?" Jake asked.

"Don't know. Head up the valley and look for Grenges, I guess."

"Sophie, you've done some shooting before, haven't you?"

"Hawk, there's a lot of things you don't know about me and I like it that way."

Sunkist looked at Posey's wounds and found them to be just a few small bruises on her arms and legs. We spent that night in our little camp in the woods. The fire from the burning barn kept our camp well-lit until midnight. A large burst of light told us that the barn had collapsed, then the light went away. We made a cookfire and had a warm meal, which Posey furnished. Everyone slept through the night—except for Sophie and me. Sleep for us was in one-hour intervals.

We were up and moving at sunrise heading northwest up the valley. The beauty of the Minnesota Valley is breathtaking in late September. The fall colors blanketed the valley like one of Ma's patchwork quilts. We had to stop every time we found a place that overlooked the scenery. We passed lots of farms and towns on our trail. In this part of the country the Indians hadn't done as much damage as they had further south, so we turned back toward the fort.

On the way, we saw in front of us a large company of soldiers.

"That's got to be Sibley," I said.

We whipped our horses and galloped to the front of the column. "Mornin'

Captain," I said.

"I am a Colonel, Hawk...what are you doing here? I thought I sent you after thieves."

"We sent a bunch of them back to you. Didn't they get there?"

"When did you send them?"

"Couple of days ago. They should have been there."

"We left the fort before that."

"Where we going now?"

"*We* are not going anywhere. *You* are going back to finding thieves."

"Think maybe we'll just tag along with you for a while. Things are more exciting around soldiers."

"Yes, and you don't help that situation at all."

"Thanks, Captain—I mean, Colonel."

"Fall in at the rear of the formation."

"Thanks, Henry."

We stayed where we were until the company had gone by us and fell in the rear, as we were told.

"Colonel Sibley doesn't like the way you talk to him, Hawk," Sophie said. "He likes to be military and get his recognition as an officer."

"I know. That's why I do it. It ruffles his feathers knowing he can't order me around like one of his soldiers."

"You're bad, Hawk."

"I try."

The morning of September twenty-third was another one of those beautiful autumn days in Minnesota when we left our camp. We traveled for a short distance when some of the men decided that it would be a good idea to go raid some of the Indians' gardens for potatoes and corn. Sibley wasn't aware that they were going or he would have stopped them. Sunkist and I went along.

The men we were riding with were from the Third Minnesota Infantry who had been fighting in the South and had been captured at Murfreesborough after their commander surrendered. They were released from the prison camp and sent to Minnesota to fight Indians until they could prove their worth in battle. These men were not your regular army men. They didn't take orders very well and pretty much did as they pleased—kinda like some of the people I knew.

We took a couple of wagons and crossed a small creek to a high spot about a half-mile from the command. Suddenly twenty-five warriors jumped up from the grass and started shooting at us. The first shots were aimed at the soldiers in the wagon and Degrove Kimbal was hit hard. The men in the other wagons jumped out and formed a line and returned fire. From our rear we saw two hundred men running to our aid. They were coming in two groups—one group ahead to dive directly into the battle and one behind for backup. The foragers joined with the main body of men and formed a battle line and moved forward. The Indians now moved in. They came over hills and out of low spots. There were about eight hundred of them. Now the fighting became intense—men fell, Indians fell, and guns were going off with an incessant clatter. We moved forward. The men from the Third Minnesota Infantry fought like real soldiers—not one of them hesitated to walk forward. We had Indians on three sides of us but they lacked the discipline of trained soldiers and fell back as we moved forward. The Indians formed a semi-circle around our front all the while moving, making it hard for us to pick out a target. They'd form into small parties and suddenly jump up from the grass to fire a volley of shots our way. We could only see the grass moving out there and when they popped up they caught us by surprise. Their quick movements made it look as if there were more than we had figured on. We moved forward now with a steady walk and the Indians began moving back as we came on.

Suddenly an officer from Sibley's camp came riding in yelling for Major Welch. When he found him he yelled, "Sibley has ordered the whole command back to the camp the best way you can!"

"What the hell's wrong with that man? We got the enemy on the run and he wants us to retreat? Not likely. What the hell's wrong with him?"

The bugle sounded, which caused some confusion, but the men kept up the fight. We could hear Sergeant Bowler's booming voice yelling to his men, "Remember Murfreesborough!" This seemed to excite the men of the Third to fight even harder to win their respect back as men worthy of being called soldiers. Sergeants Bowler and McDonald kept the line of fighting men in control but the battle was now unorganized because of the bugle. The soldiers were moving back without any direction, each man doing what he had to in order to stay alive. Indians started to move between us and the main camp and we concentrated our fire on them to drive them back. Our line of retreat was down a slope lined with low rolling hills on each side to the creek we had crossed. We had Indians on both sides of us and to our front. It was complete chaos. We made it across the creek and made a stand on a high piece of ground between the creek and the camp. The Renville Rangers joined us and the fight went on for an hour from this spot.

We put grass and sticks in our hatbands as the Indians did and fought them their way. We fired on them while hiding in the grass and their small parties of warriors were kept in slow retreat. Bunches of them were kept very busy carrying their dead and wounded out of the fight. A detachment of the Sixth Minnesota stopped a charge from around the lake that was supposed to catch us off guard.

Major Welch fell when a ball hit his thigh and broke his leg. "I'm hit," he yelled, "Take me in!" Captain Ezra Champlin and I picked him up and carried him to the camp, about a quarter-mile back.

As we ran carrying the Major two men ran past us away from the fight. He yelled at them, "Go back and fight, you white-livered cowards, or I'll shoot you myself." On reaching the camp we were about to set him behind a wagon for protection but he said, "No, not here…over there on that hill. I want to watch the battle." We carried him and sat him next to a tree and went back to the fight.

While we were in the midst of this battle Lieutenant Olin and about fifty men from the Third had been crawling through the grass to get close to the Indians. Suddenly they all jumped up and made a head-on charge into the middle of the Indians scattering them across the prairie at a full run. Fifteen Indians were killed or wounded and left by their comrades who were in too big a hurry to leave to pick them up. At the same time that Olin made his charge some of the companies from the Sixth charged the Indians on our right, driving them from the grass and hollows, sending them over the hills and out of the fight. We sent a few shots their way but they didn't stop running until they were two miles from our camp. We reorganized and moved back to the main camp.

Posey and Sophie had become friends and were busy tending to the wounded. Even though they couldn't speak each other's language they seemed to be able to communicate.

Captain Champlin walked up to Sibley and yelled at him, "Just what the hell was that order about retreating for? We had the Indians on the run then you send some spineless asshole up there to tell us to retreat. What the hell's wrong with you? You damn near got the whole army killed with that stupid bugle of yours. And why in hell aren't we chasing them back to their camps? We could wipe out Little Crow's whole army. We got two thousand men itchin' for a fight and we got Little Crow runnin' scared."

"Captain, you are addressing a Colonel. You will hold your tongue while you talk to me!"

"BULL-SHIT! You ain't no Colonel or any other kind of military man. You should be back in Saint Paul hiding behind your wife's skirt. This is men's work and you don't qualify." He walked away from Sibley, "Where's that gad-damned bugle? I'm gonna shove it up someone's ass." From somewhere in the camp we heard a bugle clatter down a ravine.

"Hawk!" Sibley yelled.

"What!" I yelled back.

"You take your party and get back to hunting thieves. We don't need civilians out here getting in the way."

"If anyone is in the way, Sibley, it's you. We'll just stay here and help out where we can. You might consider running back to the fort where it ain't so dangerous."

Sibley went into his tent and stayed there the rest of the day.

"Well, where we goin' from here?" I asked.

"Don't much care, but if it's all right with you I'd like to go looking for Olson," Jake said.

"How you doing, Sophie?"

"Nothing to worry about here. I thought it was all quite exciting."

"Such a woman."

"I thought you wanted to stay with the army," Jake said.

"I just said that to let Sibley know he ain't in charge like he thinks. Let's get out of here. I think the Injuns are finished here."

We got our horses and walked away from the camp. We rode past the Yellow Medicine Agency. Knowing there would be no one there doing anything that would interest us, we rode on down the valley. We traveled for three days and crossed the river at Redwood. From there, we headed south toward Courtland. Jake took us to his camp hidden in the valley of a small stream where we settled in for some rest.

"Anyone care to go to town and see the bartender?" Jake asked.

"We have to do something, and that seems like a good place to do it," Sophie replied.

We rode into the town and walked into the Crow Bar Saloon. Sunkist and Posey went in first.

"We don't allow Injuns in here," the bartender yelled when he saw Posey.

Sunkist stopped and said, "This here is my wife and she goes where I go."

"We had our share of Indians around here and we don't want no more."

Just then Jake walked in. "What's the trouble here?"

"We don't let no Injuns in here even if it is his squaw."

Sunkist reached over the bar, grabbed the bartender by the shirt, and hauled him over the bar. "This here's my wife. You call her a squaw agin and I'll knock you on your ass and let her have you."

Jake stepped up to the bar and took Sunkist's arm and said, "Put him down. He's a little upset over the people who was killed here a month ago. Tom, this is a friend of mine. He's on our side and so is the woman."

"Jake! I didn't see you walk in. If you say she can stay, then she stays. This is your brother I guess?" he said.

Three men at a table stood up and said, "We don't drink with Injuns."

"You boys ever heard of the Pa Hin Sa?" Tom asked.

"Yeah, we heard of 'em—so what?"

"Well, I'd sit down and be quiet. This is them."

They looked at us for a second and sat down. "Sorry boys, we didn't know."

Jake turned to the bartender and asked, "You heard of any thieving going on around here?"

"Hell yeah. There's a bunch of guys stealing all they can get their hands on. They work at night and don't seem to follow any sort of path so no one can catch them. You boys lookin' for 'em?"

"Colonel Sibley sent us out to find them—told us to bring them in alive. We'll see about that."

"I'd say your best bet is to stay on this side of the valley. That's where most of the stealing has been goin' on lately. You boys thirsty?"

"Yeah, give us all a beer." He poured five glasses and put them on the bar. Posey turned hers down.

Sophie grabbed hers and held it up for a toast. "Here's to the Pa Hin Sa." We clanked glasses and drank it down.

"Thanks, Tom. Guess we'll be on our way."

"One more?"

"Maybe another time. We got work needs doin'."

"Uh, Jake. Bonnie's in town. Might be she'd like to see you."

"Tell her I'll be back soon."

"Will do, Jake."

"Bonnie? Someone we should know about?"

"I get around too, Hawk. You don't get all the good-lookin' ones."

Back at Jake's camp we sat down together and talked about the best way to handle the situation.

"I think we should scour the country and see where they hide the goods, then wait for them to show up like the last bunch we found," Sunkist said.

"That would work but it could take all winter to find it."

"Got a better plan?"

"Nope. How about we split up and meet back here in a week. We could cover more ground that way."

"Sounds good. We'll leave in the morning."

At daybreak we split up and went four different directions. Sophie and I went north. We traveled all week and found nothing.

Back at camp at the end of the week we found the whole gang waiting for us. "Sunkist found a burned-out warehouse east of here that just might be the place."

"Lots of jewelry and expensive white man's junk piled up all over the place. Looks like a bunch of pigs been rootin' around in there."

"Unless anyone thinks we should be in a hurry, I think we could use a couple of nights' sleep."

"Sounds good to me," Jake said. We stayed in the camp for another day and headed out the morning of the third day. We rode east across the flat prairie for two more days.

Sunkist led us down into a shallow valley and said, "It's just around the bend on top of a hill."

When we got to the warehouse we saw several more buildings around it but no one in sight. We set our camp about a quarter-mile from it and set up a watch. Two days went by with only a couple of buggies and a wagon on the road.

Early on the morning of the third day Jake woke me up. He sat down and lit his pipe. "Wagon just pulled up to the warehouse—six men on horseback and one driver." I got out of my blankets waking Sophie and took my Hawken. Sunkist and Posey were up in an instant.

"Let the sun come up a little before we move in. We better be sure these are the thieves and not just some farmer coming home from town."

We watched as the men unloaded bags and boxes from the wagon into the warehouse. Suddenly Posey got excited. She shook Sunkist's shirtsleeve and pointed at one of the men. She said something to him and he squinted his eyes and stretched his neck forward.

"Them's scalps," he said.

"That's our guys," I said. "Let's go."

We quietly saddled our horses and walked out of the ravine. The men didn't see us at first, but when they did they all went to their horses and pulled out their guns. They ran into the warehouse and stuck their guns out the windows.

"Split up," I said. And the five of us spread out to about ten yards apart. Suddenly a shot came from the window.

"Who's out there?" a voice shouted from inside.

"We come to see what you're doing in my barn," I yelled back.

"This ain't yer barn. Git the hell away from here."

"You boys come on out and there won't be no trouble."

Suddenly, every gun in the warehouse went off.

"Rush 'em!" I yelled.

We all whipped our horses and ran full-gallop to the building, which was about fifty yards away, and went around both sides. I jumped off The Brute and told Sophie to keep riding and get out of there. She ran her horse out a short distance and turned back. I was against the building where they couldn't see me. When Sophie ran by a rifle barrel came out of the building. I grabbed it and pulled. The gun came out and landed on the ground. I stood up and stuck the barrel of my dragoon in and shot the man standing there in the chest.

"Ain't ye glad you brought me along, Hawk?" Sophie yelled from her horse.

"Git away! Yer gonna get yerself killed!" Sophie ran her horse around the building drawing shots from inside. Each time she passed one of the men showed himself and got hurt for it. There were six men in the building and I only knew of one that was dead. Smoke came out the window I was under. I figured Sunkist had set the warehouse on fire. The men inside stayed and fired at us when we gave them a chance but soon they were coughing from the smoke and tried to make a break. Three ran out the front and three ran out the back. I was standing near the door when they came out.

"STOP!" I yelled. One turned to shoot at me but was too slow. I heard shooting from the other side of the building. The other men who came out in front of me kept running and dropped down in the grass. Sophie had left her horse and was on the ground in the grass about ten feet from where the men laid. I stepped into the doorway and aimed the Hawken at the spot where I saw the men drop.

"You ain't got a chance. Give it up and you might live through this." One of the men rose up to shoot but I shot first. Then the other one stood up thinking I had emptied my gun. He raised his rifle and suddenly a shot came from where Sophie was laying. He fell dead. The three men on my side of the building were dead so I ran to the other side. One of the men had ducked back into the building.

"You sons-a-bitches. I could'a been a rich man! Why does everything happen to me?" His voice was a high-pitched whine that reminded me of Pa.

Jake reached out and pushed my pistol down. "That voice can only come from one man," he said. I looked at the broken-down man hunched over at the shoulders, glaring at us from under his shaggy eyebrows. His hair hung in greasy strings alongside his shaggy beard and his arms hung down at his sides. He held a small Navy Colt in his right hand.

"Goddamn you all. This here stuff ain't no good to them people. They're all dead. What the hell business is it of yours what happens to it anyway?"

"Pa?" Jake said.

The old man turned his head to the side and peered at us, "Jacob? Is that you?"

"Yeah, Pa—it's me and Hawk."

"I thought you was dead."

"No, Pa. I ain't dead—you're the one who should be dead. You ran off and left Ma to the Indians and now she's dead."

"It wasn't that way, Jacob. I tried to fight them. I really did!"

"Yer a lying coward. You ran into the woods and left Ma behind. She was shot and scalped, you goddamned bastard!"

John raised the pistol and fired a round that hit me just above the knee of my right leg. Jake and I pulled up and fired our dragoons, both hitting Pa in the chest and knocking him backward into the barn. We looked at each other for a few seconds before going into the barn. The man lying on the straw was nothing like the man we knew from back home. Pa was always clean and freshly shaven and dressed in good clothes. This man was a picture of evil—dirty, unshaven, and he had a foul odor about him that made me gag.

"We killed our own pa," Jake finally said.

Sunkist stepped up and said, "I gotta tell you boys something."

"What's that?"

"That ain't yer pa."

"What do you mean by that?"

"Did you ever wonder why an old mountain man like me would come to Minnesota?"

"No," I said. "Guess I figured it wasn't none of my business."

"Well, back in the old days I trapped with a man from Minnesota. When I decided to retire from it he told me about Minnesota and asked me to come here and settle down. He said it's good country and a man can live in peace—

HAWK'S VALLEY

guess he had that figured wrong—so I came here looking for him. His name was Robert Owen. Yer Uncle."

"You knew Uncle Robert?"

"Yeah, I knew Robert. We called him Curly Jack onna conna he had this head of curly red hair, just like yourn."

"How come Jack?"

"'Cause he always rode a jack mule. He figured it was better in the mountains than a horse."

"So you knew Uncle Robert. What's that got to do with this not being our pa?"

"I never figured I'd have to tell you boys this but John wasn't yer pa—Robert was."

You could have cut the silence with a knife.

Then Sunkist said, "Ye see boys, yer ma and Robert were meant to be together. Your grandmother saw to it that they would never be. She didn't cotton to the likes of Robert and me and was determined that her daughter would be hitched up with John, so she arranged for them to be married.

"Now don't be thinking bad on yer ma. John here wasn't worth a good goddamn and she knew it, and he couldn't make babies like she wanted. She was in love with Robert and it just happened kinda natural-like that they would be together. You knew all along that yer ma got on better with Robert than she did with John, didn't ye?"

"Well, yeah but…"

"But nothing—yer ma and Robert were in love. What they did wasn't something bad. Yer ma having to marry John was what was bad."

Jake turned to me and said, "Ye know, Hawk, I have always thought of Robert as being my pa. It figures that we turned out more like him than Pa. It all makes sense to me."

"Guess you're right. Robert did spend a lot more time with us than … *he* did. I only wish I'd known this when he was still around—things might have been a lot different."

"Where you boys going from here?" Sunkist asked. "Sibley's gonna keep chasing them Indians up and out of the valley. Are you gonna tag along?"

I looked at Sophie then at Sunkist. "Nope. Got me one hell of woman here and me and her are going up to Hawk Creek and make us a home."

"You mean that, Hawk? You really want to settle down to a farm?"

"Sure, why not?"

ARVID LLOYD WILLIAMS   277

"I'll tell you why not, 'cause you ain't ready to take up farming. You wouldn't last a year scratching in the ground trying to make corn grow."

"Well, I ain't goin' after Little Crow. We'll find something to do to make a living."

"Jake, what's your plans?"

"Me, I got me a good woman waiting in Courtland. Guess I'll go back there and see what happens. How about you, Sunkist—you going back to the mountains?"

Sunkist walked over to the rim of the Minnesota Valley and looked across the wide, deep gorge. The bottom was filled with the bright reds, yellows, and greens of autumn. The river at the bottom lay like a silver snake in its twisted channel and shimmered in the sunlight. Ducks and geese flew over in flocks of millions. Now and then, one would fold its wings and drop from the sky and, just before he hit the water, would open his wings and he'd glide in gracefully to set peacefully on the marsh.

"Nope," he finally said. "I ain't goin' back to nothing. Me and Posey found us a nice little place north of here that we figure on callin' home. I'll just stick around here till they call me. I kinda like this valley—it's a good place to die."

TO BE CONTINUED...

Hawk's Valley: A Good Place to Die is a work of historical fiction.

· · ·

The stories about the Sioux Conflict have been told by countless voices. As to be expected, with each telling the stories are embellished by the narrator to add excitement or drama. This inevitably discredits the original accounts and changes the story from fact to partial or complete fiction. This book is part fact and part fiction.

While the story follows the historical record, it must not be used as a source for historical research. Many of the names used in this work are those of actual persons alive at the time of the Sioux Conflict and their stories are told here with modifications, in some cases, to complement my story. I have included facts about the history of Minnesota and have kept them as accurate as my abilities and resources will allow.

· · ·

The names of the personnel at the forts and other locations are taken from historical accounts and all of the names can be found in the records. Some imagination was employed in the creation of the personalities of each of these characters.

Many of the main characters in the story are fictional; Hawk, Jake, and John Owen, Sophie, Sunkist, Posey, Smith (The Swede), Eddy and Arty Grenges and their father, Lorraine, Bon Cheval, and the Renard. All of the Métis, as well as Linda and her dance studio, are also fictional.

The personalities of the people in this story, both real and fictional, are of my own creation. Care should be taken to avoid forming opinions of these individuals based on my writing. Please feel free to like or dislike any of these characters.

The story of Justina Kreiger's rescue by Hiram Grant's troops and her miraculous survival at the battle of Birch Coulee is true. The story of her capture by the Sioux, her escape and survival, is in itself an exhilarating tale of courage, stamina, and the will to live.

Henry Hastings Sibley, the first Governor of the state of Minnesota, was an intelligent man who spoke several languages fluently, including the Dakota language. He was familiar with the Dakota and was friends with Little Crow and other important men of the Indian nation. It was because of this acquaintance that he was appointed by then Governor Alexander Ramsey to lead the army against the Dakota. His actions, though criticized by newspapers and the general public, were calculated and cautious because he knew he needed men and supplies to win that conflict. He is a man to be honored and held in high esteem by the people of Minnesota, and the opinions of the characters in this book echo the feelings of frightened and angry citizens.

Joseph Rolette was an actual character in Minnesota history. Mr. Rolette was the son of Joseph Rolette Sr., a man instrumental in building the ox cart trade routes from Pembina on Minnesota's northwestern border to Saint Paul. The story about him saving Saint Paul from losing the capitol city status to Saint Peter is true. History has it that Joseph Rolette Jr. spent that one hundred twenty-three hours at the Fuller House Hotel in Saint Paul which, in fact, he did. He did not spend it at 'Linda's House for Wayward Council Members'. Private dance academies did exist but they were just that—dance academies—not the establishments as depicted in my story. A portrait of Joseph Rolette Jr. hangs in the Minnesota Historical Society inscribed with the words, "Joseph Rolette, who saved the capitol to Saint Paul by running away with the bill to remove it to Saint Peter, 1857."

. . .

The battles at Fort Ridgely, Redwood Ferry, Birch Coulee, and Wood Lake are historical fact. The battle on the Elk River is a work of fiction.

Several battles fought in and around the Minnesota Valley that were not detailed in this book are: the attack on the Lower Sioux Agency, two attacks on New Ulm, the battle at Acton, raids on Forest City and Hutchinson, the attack on Fort Abercrombie in Dakota Territory, the attack on the Yellow Medicine Agency, the battle of Slaughter Slough, and many more assaults on farms and villages and scattered strikes on unwary travelers.

Descriptions of the battles were taken from military records and accounts given by individuals, both White and Dakota, who witnessed the war. I visited all of the sites and drew my geographic descriptions from those visits.

. . .

The Sioux Conflict in the Minnesota Valley—the bloodiest of all of the Indian wars—is historical fact. It began on August 17, 1862, at Acton, Minnesota when five settlers were murdered by four young braves. It continued until September 19, 1862, when the Sioux were defeated by Henry Sibley's army at the battle of Wood Lake. An estimated four to five hundred people died in the six week-long conflict.

The Mdewakanton band of Sioux, under leadership of Chief Little Crow, left the Minnesota Valley and moved to Devil's Lake in Dakota Territory. From there the wars moved west onto the plains and beyond. It was the beginning of the plains wars on which writers and moviemakers have focused so heavily.

. . .

The sites of the Sioux Conflict are maintained by the Minnesota Historical Society and are open to viewing by the public through the summer months. Interpreters are on hand to answer your questions.

Walk on the ground where it all happened and experience the reality of history. Walk the interpretive trail around the site of the Birch Coulee Battlefield and imagine the fear in the young soldiers as they came under attack from all four sides.

Tour the grounds of old Fort Ridgely and walk on the earth that Henry Sibley, Sergeant Jones, Lieutenant Sheehan, Little Crow, John Other Day, and so many others walked.

Visit the cemetery and see the graves of Captain Marsh and his men, and the grave of Eliza Muller, the wife of Doctor Muller, who worked so hard during the battles at Fort Ridgely bandaging wounds and helping Sergeant Jones with his cannon. The story of Sergeant Jones firing his cannon through the hallway of the officers' quarters is true. The foundation of the building is still there.

Walk down the hill into the valley below Fort Ridgely and visualize the Indians lurking there during the attack. Look for the rock on which Little Crow hit his head when he ducked a cannonball and gave himself a headache that lasted for a week. We don't know which rock it was but use your imagination—you might find the one. It's still there.

. . .

For those who would like to find more information on this exciting and important chapter of Minnesota history, I would recommend reading:

A History of Minnesota, Volume II
William Watts Folwell
Minnesota Historical Society Press

Soldier, Settler, Sioux: Fort Ridgely and the Minnesota River Valley, 1853-1867
Paul N. Beck
Pine Hill Press

Little Crow: Spokesman for the Sioux
Gary Clayton Anderson
Minnesota Historical Society Press

Through Dakota Eyes: Narrative Accounts of the Minnesota Indian War of 1862
Gary Clayton Anderson and Alan R. Woolworth
Minnesota Historical Society Press

. . .

I do hope you enjoyed this book and I encourage you to read on as the adventures of the *Pa Hin Sa* continue.

— ARVID LLOYD WILLIAMS